# Frontier Defiant

# Leonie Rogers

FRONTIER DEFIANT
Book 3 of the FRONTIER series

The moral rights of Leonie Rogers to be identified as the author of this work have been asserted.



Hague Publishing
PO Box 451
Bassendean Western Australia 6934
*Email:* contact@haguepublishing.com
*Web:* www.haguepublishing.com

ISBN 978-0-9925437-6-1

Cover Art: *Frontier Defiant* by Jade Zivanovic
Typography cover design by Ross MacLennan of Book Covers Australia

Typeset Garamond 11/12

# Dedication

ONCE again, I need to say thank you to my family. To Mal, who puts up with all kinds of speculative fiction stuff – much love. To Briana, my plot hole finder, and always honest critic, thank you again – you always make sure the continuity works, and that starcats do not change sex four times in one paragraph. And to Lachlan, fellow enjoyer of much good spec fic stuff, who helps me by finding interesting things to watch, which helps me to refuel my creative batteries.

I'd also like to mention the lovely people who send me messages telling me how much they've enjoyed these stories, and who ask me when the next one's coming out – thank you so much! Your encouragement has helped me write with enthusiasm.

To the Brook and Beyond Writers Group, who put up with my speculative fiction weirdness each month, and who love words and stories as much as I do – thank you too! It's so nice to laugh and chat and discuss the significance of the apostrophe (and the abuses inflicted upon it by unthinking Philistines) with like minded people.

And once again, many thanks to Andrew Harvey from Hague Publishing, who took a chance on a book full of glow in the dark cats and a complete unknown, and published these stories.

# Chapter 1

SHANNA felt slow tears slide down her cheeks as she stood with her friends and their starcats in a circle on the small hill, a short distance from the Starlyne habitation.

A soft breeze stirred the trees, and the early morning shadows danced and flickered as Spiron's sombre voice echoed in her ears, its tones heavy with sorrow. A small pile of Challon's possessions sat forlornly at Spiron's feet. A half-finished starcat harness topped the pile, its leather carved with Dipper's name. Shanna felt a sob tear its way free of her throat.

"Let us take a moment to remember Challon and Dipper." As Spiron spoke, his eyes wandered around the assembled group, pausing one by one on the six cadets. He bent and placed a wreath formed of pungo leaves and plybrush flowers on the pack. The entwined scents spoke eloquently of a Scout's days. Haven and risk, braided together in life and now part of his memory.

"He was our friend, and a fine Scout," Spiron said, straightening back up, "and his actions in opening those doors on the spacecraft saved us all. Who would like to speak first?"

There was a brief silence as the pungo scent washed over them, comforting, then Amma took a step forwards, lifting her face to address them. "Challon was a Scout of amazing skill. But more importantly he was kind and helpful. He was so patient with me when I was learning how to move in the bush." She smiled sadly in remembrance. "I will miss both him and Dipper." Spider's tidemarks dimmed slightly as Amma's voice cracked on the last word and as she stepped back into the circle, her hand touched her starcat's head for comfort.

Karri took her place. "When I met my first slider swarm it was Challon who kept me calm. He saved my life. Without him I wouldn't be here." Shanna's throat tightened, aching until she felt as if she almost couldn't breathe. Two more spoke. Finally, she swallowed convulsively, and with her hands on her starcats, buffered by their love, she stepped forwards herself.

"Wounded, Challon still managed to open the door of the Garsal spacecraft to save us. And Dipper …" she paused, remembering their escape, Dipper's form shimmering past her in a blur, the cat a spitting, shrieking fury of destruction heedless of his own safety. "Dipper …" she tried again, then shook her head, unable to continue. "I miss them both." Tears fell furiously then, and around her she could hear muffled sounds of grief echoed by sad starcat hums. Their tidemarks dimmed in sorrow.

One by one the other Scouts and cadets spoke of Challon and Dipper, memories and thoughts shared in joined sadness. As the stories rolled over her, Shanna felt the grief recede slightly, become a little more bearable, and then diminish slowly to a background ache. She knew, deep in her bones, that Challon's death was only one of the first in the war against the alien invaders. For the moment though it was close and immediate, and there was time, however brief, to express the grief and cherish the memories.

"Because of the Garsal we live in uncertain times," Spiron said finally, as Shanna brushed the last tears from her face. The Patrol First was sombre. "The hope that our ancestors had, that eventually we would be found and rescued by the Federation has turned out to be fruitless, as we now know that the Federation has been destroyed by the Garsal. Yet in Challon's death we see a different hope. He died helping to protect our people, and we must honour his death by our future actions. I remind you that Keeper died believing the same things, protecting our shared people because he saw a hope for the future if we could learn to work together. None of us know what might lie ahead, but we have always been a people of hope, always a people who strive to make things better, and we have a great purpose ahead of us. We," and he gestured around the circle, "will be the spearhead that frees our people from the threat that now faces us. Today we remember Challon and Dipper, thankful for the time we had with them, but in their memory, I ask all of you to pledge to fight on, no matter how hard it becomes."

Bending, Spiron pulled a pungo leaf from the wreath, and crushing it, smeared it across his chest. Its pungent scent filled the air. "Use the scent of pungo to remind you of our purpose, and of Challon's sacrifice." He placed his hand on Allad's shoulder beside him, allowing the crushed leaf to drop to join the forest litter beneath his feet. A heartbeat later, Barron, on the other side of the circle, mirrored him, and then the rest followed suit.

There was a lump in Shanna's throat as she smeared the crushed pungo leaf across her chest. The scent, that so often meant safety Below filled her nostrils, and she knew she'd never smell it again without remembering this moment. They remained like that for a moment then, one by one, they turned and returned to the habitation, but now Shanna knew that their resolve was stronger than ever.

***

The Matriarch inclined her head graciously as one of her seniors placed the list of initiates on the polished desktop in front of her. It was shorter than she had hoped for, but they were all well schooled, and among the most skilled in the next generation of females on the colony ship. A small frisson of fear rippled through her as she contemplated the task ahead. The secret had always weighed on her, but the full weight of the actions she must take to fulfil her duty now felt like a mountain upon her.

Laretai returned with a plate of sliced fruits, and the Matriarch took one with a manipulator arm, savouring the exotic tastes of this new world. Her faceted eyes met those of her closest confidant. "We will need to inform the seniors as soon as possible. Set up a secure room for the meeting and notify them in secret. Set the meeting for this evening."

Laretai inclined her head in assent.

"I have rechecked the pattern again, and set a watching tap on the Overlord's communications with Trooper Hoth. There is no doubt that it matches our records of the Great Enemy. I will be alerted immediately if anything further is detected. Do you require anything more Matriarch?"

The Matriarch pondered her response, faceted eyes distant, as memories of her own initiation played through her thoughts. "One more thing," she said finally. "You are to prepare a list of those who are suitable, but not yet initiated."

"Are you sure Matriarch? Is it wise at this time?"

"I am certain. There are many tasks to perform, and although the risks are very high, this may well be our crowning achievement. We must ensure that all who can be, are with us." There were other considerations as well, but this was not the time to air them with Laretai, newly cut off from the rest of the galaxy as they were by the human raid on their ship. For a moment she thought that her assistant might argue, but the habits of long years overcame Laretai's hesitation, and she bowed her head in acquiescence before departing in a flutter of filmy robes.

Alone, the Matriarch stared at the windowless walls sightlessly as the mountain leaned more heavily upon her, and the list was forgotten again at the enormity of her task. If she failed, she wondered if anyone would ever know.

***

Shanna scrubbed at the tear marks on her face as she entered the communal room in the Starlyne habitation, the pungent scent of the crushed pungo still surrounding them. The trip back to the plateau after destroying the Garsal communications systems had been remarkably smooth, and much faster than their trek south. There had been no pursuit and they'd arrived at the habitation well after midnight last night. For a moment, the memory of the destruction she and the others had visited upon their pursuers tapped a torrent of guilt, but she pushed it away as she'd learned to during the long trek back. It was war, and the future of her people was at stake. Guilt could wait until her people were safe.

A few moments later, as they sat, plates on laps and cats eating from bowls on the perimeter, Spiron spoke again. "I thought we'd be returning to the plateau after this mission, but it appears that a number of things have changed in our absence. The Garsal have attacked Watchtower."

There was a flurry of voices, all asking questions at once, and Spiron was forced to raise his voice. "I have few details yet," the hubbub quieted, "but some of those aircraft that were searching for us, have apparently damaged a substantial portion of Watchtower. The population has dispersed to the old storm shelters, but Scout HQ was largely unharmed, and our command structure is intact." He looked briefly around the group and continued. "Our Starlyne hosts tell me that Master Peron is on his way with one of the older Scouts, and I'll be suggesting that we continue as one larger Patrol rather than detaching the cadets."

Shanna sighed with relief, exchanging quick glances with her fellow cadets. Despite the strength of her longing to see her family, one of her major fears was the possibility of being sidelined as 'just a cadet' again. "Do you think we'll hear anything about our families?" she whispered to Amma beside her.

"I hope so. I just hope they weren't at Watchtower when it was attacked."

Cold struck suddenly deep into Shanna's bones and her hand holding the plate trembled. The possibility of injury or death of any of her family members hadn't crossed her mind. Now, almost numbed by fear, she remembered Kaidan's last farewell as he headed back to the plateau, and wondered if he'd left Watchtower for the safety of Hillview before the aircraft had struck. He'd have been back on the plateau for several months by now, by her calculations, but she'd lost track of just how long it had been since the battle with the Garsal vehicles. Dimly, she realised that Spiron was still speaking.

"I can't give you details of dead and injured yet. Our communications are relayed through the Starlyne network, and there are higher priorities." There was a slightly angry murmur. "I know, I know, and I don't like not knowing either. But personal fears aside, we must remember that there *are* more essential communications that must take priority. We'll find out soon enough." His face was grim, and Shanna noticed that there were more lines etched into his brow than she remembered from their first meeting. "In the meantime empty your packs, wash your clothes, and take it easy today. We'll be working hard tomorrow as it's now imperative that we figure out what you lot did when you dropped that cliff on the Garsal." He frowned in mock exasperation at the cadets.

They resumed eating in a very subdued mood, and again the cadets grouped themselves together, starcats sprawled about them. "And now we'll be wondering about our families," Verren said. His tone was resigned, and his face was solemn. There were nods, and a few sighs.

"It's going to be a long few days" said Taya, "until Master Peron brings us information. Surely he will."

Zandany nodded. "I certainly hope so." They sat there together in silence, for a few more moments, and then Ragar pushed himself to his feet.

"I'm going to take our esteemed leader's advice and spend today cleaning my pack. And then, if I finish that before midnight, I'm going to sleep." He held out a hand to Taya and she nodded and he pulled her to her feet. "Coming?" The group placed their empty plates on the table and together headed to their sleeping room. Shanna was glad of the distraction. There were too many thoughts buzzing around in her head for her to want to sit quietly, but she did sigh when she thought about what might be in her pack. Storm hummed as he paced next to her, and she fancied that he sounded amused. Twister simply swiped her leg so vigorously that she was momentarily off balanced, and had to grab at him to stay upright.

"All right you two," she grumbled, "you can help." As she spoke, a gentle feeling of violet and blue tinged amusement trickled into her mind, and she looked at her two cats, slightly surprised, but there was nothing further. Pondering on the communication that seemed to deepen with every day, she followed the other cadets into their room.

She sniffed at her clothes with disgust as Storm and Twister flowed into the room with pleased hums.

"Guys, look!" Taya's voice was almost reverent as she pointed to the pile of clean clothing that had been placed on the foot of each bed. It was obvious that each pile had been freshly made up during the memorial service. "I can't remember when I last wore clean clothes!"

"And I'm not touching them until I've had a bath. I should have had one last night but I was too exhausted," Ragar's voice came from the bathing room. There was a splash, and Amma made a disgusted noise.

"You're a selfish monster Ragar!" The curly haired girl upended her pack onto the floor and stared down at its contents, her hands on her hips.

"Well, *you* might think so," replied Verren with a grin, "But *I* think he's got the right idea." He scooped some clean clothes off his bed with an easy motion, and vanished after Ragar. Taya shrugged helplessly as Zandany grinned and followed.

"Anyone need a hand detangling hair while we wait?" Taya asked.

"Now that's a good idea," replied Shanna, running her hand over the wisps of greasy hair sticking out of her braids. None of the girls had felt up to washing their hair last night. "Although I'm not entirely sure that mine will ever detangle again. Are you sure you want to touch it though? There could be anything in there."

Taya laughed, and Shanna was again struck by the change in the other girl. Her confession, which now seemed so long ago, and her sure skills with mechanical equipment, seemed to have worked an amazing change within her, and the six cadets were now truly a united group. "I'm game, but only if you agree to do mine."

Shanna's hair was so filthy she was almost itching. And now, with the prospect of hot, clean water and clean clothes so close, she could hardly wait for her own soak. The three girls perched themselves cross legged on the floor in a triangle and began the long task of removing the tangles and debris from each others' hair. Their cats sprawled in utter relaxation on the spongy flooring, although when there was a particularly large splash from the bathing room, all four sets of ears would prick, and the flickering and glowing of tidemarks could only be described as anticipatory.

"I wonder how our families are?" asked Amma again as she began to pick pieces of twigs out of Taya's hair. Shanna felt Taya's hands pause for a moment, before she resumed the slow unpicking of her braids in the suddenly uncomfortable silence.

"It seems ages since I've seen Mum, Dad and Kaidan," Shanna said eventually. "Do you reckon we'll get to see them now we're back? Or will we just have to stay Below, until we figure out how we did what we did?" She worried a stick out of Amma's hair.

"I hope they're all right," replied Amma, and her voice was filled with all the sadness that Shanna felt in her own heart, and her throat was suddenly so tight that she had to force the words out.

"Me too."

"I'm not sure if Dad will want to see me." Taya's hands were steady on Shanna's hair, but Shanna could feel her tension. She kept her head still as Taya undid the last of her braids and ran her hands carefully through the greasy strands to separate them.

"Tay, who knows if our families were even in Watchtower when the aircraft attacked?" replied Amma carefully. "And by now our families must know a fair amount of what we've been doing. Maybe your Dad will be proud of you instead." Taya's hands stopped again as the last strands separated with a slight pull.

"Sorry Shan," she ran her hands through Shanna's hair again, and a small shower of fine twigs fell out of it, "That's just revolting." She turned around to look at Amma. "I hope so, but I'm not so sure." With a small shake, she pushed herself upright and walked over to the door and banged on it loudly, while Amma and Shanna exchanged uncomfortable glances. "Hurry up you lot!" There were muffled noises from the other side of the door, and Taya banged on it again. "Maybe they'll get a move on now. I'm so filthy I can smell myself."

Neither of the other girls were fooled by the sudden change of subject, but Shanna didn't know what to say. She missed her family so much it was an almost physical pain, but she knew, surely and completely, that there was no chance that they'd have disowned her, no matter what she might have done. As she and Amma sat there in awkward silence, Spinner rose gracefully to his feet and thrust his large head under Taya's hand, humming gently. She looked down at him, and one tear slid its way down her cheek and she bent and hugged the cat strongly to her chest. He leaned into the hug, and his purring was deafening. Standing up, Taya wiped the tear from her face with the back of her hand, inadvertently smearing the grime even more. "*I'm* proud of me, anyway," she said defiantly.

And then suddenly the three of them and their four cats were together. When they finally separated Shanna looked Taya in the eye. "I'm proud of you as well," Shanna told her. "Without you, we wouldn't have killed their communications, or got through the ring of sentinels." Amma nodded in agreement.

"But without you, they'd have found us before we got in," said Taya, "And without Amma we wouldn't have found them at all."

There was a giggle from Amma, and the other two looked at her, surprised.

"And not that long ago the two of you wouldn't have exchanged the time of day." She snorted slightly. "And *I* would have been stuck in the middle."

Shanna looked at her curly headed friend and then back to Taya. Taya's expression was startled, but then softened to a smile. "True. But now you know all of my secrets, and you *could* say that we're all freaks really ..." She broke off again and smiled, and the three of them shared another hug, and then broke apart, laughing, as the door to the bathing room opened and the others bounced into the room.

"Wow! You three stink! I'm sure *we* weren't that gross!" exclaimed Ragar. "Mind you, I think I left half my skin in the pool, I scrubbed so hard."

"I hope the water's had time to clear then, I don't fancy bathing in skin soup!" The other two girls joined her and the three of them shed their clothes as fast as possible. Shanna was almost quivering with the desire to be clean, and had to restrain herself from diving headfirst into the clear water.

Her two cats had no such inhibitions however, and launched themselves gleefully into the hot water, creating two huge splashes and a wave that lurched over the edge of the pool. Shanna grabbed her clean clothes just before the wave reached them. "Storm, Twister!" she called, "No more jumping!" There were happy, but slightly disappointed hums, and then there were four cats paddling around in the water, rolling and revelling as they soaked themselves. No more tidal waves eventuated, but the water lapped over the edge, spilling small puddles onto the floor with some regularity. With a thankful sigh, Shanna slid into the water and dropped under the surface, feeling her filthy hair float around her. The water was hot and relaxing and she held her breath for a minute or so, enjoying the feel of its softness on her limbs and then pushed herself to the surface.

Taya handed her a handful of soapleaves and she began to lather her hair, grimacing as the normally white froth clouded with dirt as she scrubbed. "I think I'm even dirtier than I first thought," she groaned.

"Who cares?" replied Amma. "All I can think of is being clean, smelling nice, and putting on a clean set of clothes. Can't you just imagine it? Clean socks!" The three laughed again and resumed scrubbing, and the clouds of dirty water were sucked into the filtration system to return clean and clear and hot, from jets on the floor of the pool.

Two hours later, exhausted but clean, and with her backpack and its contents washed and hanging up to dry, Shanna toppled tiredly back into bed, Storm and Twister draping their weights around her. The relief of being back near her people was tempered by the fear that her family had been injured or killed by the Garsal.

# Chapter 2

SHANNA felt a shock run through her body as she saw who had arrived at the Starlyne habitat. The three days since they'd returned had been spent recovering. None of them had realised how tired they were, and all of them had found themselves feeling slow and fatigued when they trained. Spiron halted the Patrol with a hand signal as Master Cerren hurried forwards, accompanied by Socks.

Cerren looked tired and drawn, and was flanked by Master Perron and an old Scout who Shanna didn't know, but who, judging from the nods around her, was well known to the Scouts of Patrol Ten. Shanna's eyes hunted behind them, hoping desperately that she might catch a glimpse of her family, despite the rational part of her mind telling her that it would be ridiculous to expect them. "Welcome home, Patrol Ten. We have much to discuss." Cerren turned on his heel as the old Scout gestured peremptorily to them to follow. The Scout's starcat cast her gaze over them with an unmistakable command, and Shanna felt mild surprise from her two. She shrugged, exchanged a quizzical glance with Verren next to her, and followed the others as they filed silently through the entrance and back into the Starlyne habitat.

Shanna fretted at the possibility of bad news from home. She wasn't the only one. Close knit as they'd become, Shanna easily read the emotion of her friends in the way they stood, and the tightening of their mouths. She held onto the hope of evacuation, despite the fear that gnawed at her insides. Surely Kaidan was all right, and her parents, and Amma's family, and Verren's, and ..." She tried to stop the train of thought that said that none of her loved ones lived, crushing it ruthlessly as she tried to concentrate on Master Cerren's words.

"I'm sure you have many questions for me," said Master Cerren. "I will be speaking with each of you individually over the next day or so, but firstly I need to thank you all for the task you have just undertaken. You've given us a breathing space to prepare. We can only hope that the Garsal did not send a message requesting reinforcements before you disabled their offworld communications. Our Starlyne friends are of the opinion that we'd already be under attack if they had requested help, so it appears that for the moment at least, the only invaders we must battle are the ones already here."

He paused for a moment, and ran both hands over what was left of his greying hair. Shanna had never seen him look so old. No, not old, tired. So tired that deep lines curved around his mouth, and there was no sign of his normally buoyant nature. Socks brushed him gently with her head and he went on, taking a deep breath. "For now, the important points are simple. The Garsal have killed a significant number of our people." Shanna felt her heart pause in her chest at the abrupt tone. "Tamazine is dead, along with a large portion of the Starfall Council and several of Watchtower' s councillors, and there were significant casualties among those who remained in Watchtower. Fortunately most of the children were already gone, and we were able to evacuate most of our key personnel. As it currently stands, I am Tamazine's successor."

There was a quiet buzz, and Master Cerren raised one hand. "In the interim, it has been decided that I will direct our people in their campaign against the Garsal, with the assistance of the newly elected Council. For now, Cally has the list of the dead and injured, as I am sure that you must wish to know about your families and your friends. Please see Peron or myself if you need some privacy, and when you have had time to eat and drink and look at Cally's list, we will talk again. Spiron, if I could see you for a moment." He looked even more fatigued than ever, and Shanna felt a stab of compassion for him as she joined the queue in front of Cally. It momentarily overcame her anxiety about her own family. She watched as he spoke quietly to the Patrol leader, one hand unconsciously stroking Socks' head as he did. The grey starcat's blue tidemarks flowed in soft waves of love and Cerren paused to stare down at her violet eyes.

"Shanna," Master Peron's quiet voice cut through her thoughts, and she turned towards her mentor, who was standing off to one side with his part grown starcat cub.

"Yes, Master Peron?" He beckoned, and she cast one more look at the line in front of her. Anxiety was evident in every face, and already she could see that at the head of the queue, Kalli's shoulders had suddenly slumped. Resignedly she left the line and joined Peron.

"There's no need for you to line up, Shanna, I was talking to your father only yesterday." A flood of relief hit Shanna like a tidal wave, and she almost crumbled at the knees.

"You did? And Mum? And Kaidan?" It was almost too difficult to get the words out through the relief.

"They're all fine. Your parents have returned to Hillview with the breeding cats and Josen and his family." His mouth quirked briefly, but Shanna was too distracted to wonder why, "and your brother and Anjo are currently acting as messengers for us. Their base is with your parents, but they move around frequently."

"When can I see them?" the words burst from her.

Master Peron looked slightly uncomfortable. "That's a question I really can't answer, Shanna. It will depend on our decisions of the next few days. Unfortunately the fifteen of you here are absolutely essential to our defence and we can't have you haring off on family business in all directions." Shanna nodded in resigned understanding. At least her family were alive.

"They're well? No-one's injured? And the cats?"

"There are a few bumps and scratches among them, but nothing serious, and the cats are fine. And Anjo has a starcat – one of Josen's actually. Ember."

"He does?" Shanna was intrigued. She was about to ask another question, when she heard a muffled sob and spun on the spot.

"Taya?" The dark haired girl was standing a short distance away, face stricken, and tears once again tracking down her face. Spinner had wrapped himself around her, tidemarks pulsing in ruby tones. Shanna took three steps to Taya's side and her cats joined Spinner, bright tidemarks muted for once.

"He's gone, Shan. I'll never see him again. Never be able to tell him I still love him …" her shoulders shook, and Shanna awkwardly put an arm around her and drew her to a chair.

"Your Dad?"

The other girl nodded, tears dripping off her chin. "And Mum as well."

Shanna's throat closed tightly with a painful ache, her relief of the moment before subsumed in shared grief as the other girl shook in her arms, and once again, tears welled in her own eyes. She felt suddenly selfish, as the pain that Taya was experiencing dropped her abruptly from her cloud of relief into the harsh wasteland of reality. She felt horribly inadequate as she hugged Taya's shaking form to her. Storm and Twister flanked Spinner, and then Ragar was there as well on Taya's other side, joined shortly after by the other cadets. There were traces of tears on Verren's cheeks, and a stunned look in Zandany's eyes.

"One of my brothers," said Verren, rubbing at his cheeks. "He was pulling people from the rubble, and an aircraft blew it apart. Everyone else is all right, but Jamber's gone. And Zandany's Aunt and Uncle were working in one of the destroyed buildings." He gestured helplessly.

The six cadets stood together again, cats around them, sharing each other's sadness. Words were so inadequate, thought Shanna sadly. A few moments ago she'd been overjoyed at her family's survival. Now, she was devastated at the losses suffered by her friends, and as she looked around, she could see that there were tears on more than just the cadets' faces. The Garsal invaders had struck deeply into all of their lives. Challon had indeed been the first of them, but his death was not the only one. Their shared promise seemed even more important now. Amongst the grief, Shanna began to feel the hot spark of anger deep in her heart and mind. She remembered her fear of becoming a monster, after they had dropped a cliff face on the pursuing aliens, but now she felt as if that was the least of what she could have done, had they been nearby right then.

There was a hum from Storm, and she saw that his tidemarks had begun to cycle in brighter tones as he picked up her emotion. Twister growled, almost inaudibly, but the vibration of his anger where he pressed against her side, hardened her determination to do her utmost to remove the Garsal from her planet. An image of the Garsal slaves, long suppressed, rose to the surface of her mind as well, and she clenched her jaw, firming her arm around Taya. "It's not OK Taya, none of this is OK, but you know we're with you, and you too, Verren, Zandany. We're together, and together we're strong."

"Yes!" Ragar's voice echoed her determination, and she could see glints of anger in his eyes. Taya's sobs continued, but she lifted her head, and Shanna could see the defiance rising inside her. Verren's face was set, despite the tears on his face. Amma's normally serene face mirrored the anger Shanna could feel fanning to a flame inside herself, and Zandany's face had hardened to determination.

"We *are* together," said Taya, voice unsteady, and eyes red. "And the Garsal have no idea what we're capable of." A small snort, slightly incongruous under the circumstances, came from Amma's direction, and they all turned towards her, surprised despite their grief.

"And neither do we," she said. "Not really, anyway. But, you know? I'm pretty keen to find out now." Her expression turned grim. "And I never thought I'd say that." She closed her eyes briefly, and then looked up at the others. "That's our priority now isn't it?"

"It is," replied Ragar.

"It is," echoed Allad and the cadets turned towards him. "For all of us. There is no time to waste. The seven of us need to figure out how we did what we did, and then we need to find out what else we can do. And whether others can too." Beside him, Satin hummed quietly. Her emerald tidemarks brightened to an intensity Shanna had never seen before, and there was an answering hum from all of the cats in the room. Spiron stepped up from behind Allad.

"Well, Master Cerren," he said, "As Allad has said, there is no time to waste. There is grief now, and there will be more grief to come, but we're ready to do what needs to be done."

Master Cerren nodded slowly, looking around at the cadets and Patrol Ten. He still looked tired, Shanna noted, but something had changed. For a moment she wondered what it was, and then she realised, their determination seemed to have re-energised him. Socks' tidemarks were as intense as Satin's, glowing jewel bright and pulsing in steadfast tones, tones that were overshadowed with the brightness of renewed hope.

***

The Overlord sent an eating utensil flying off the table with an enraged snarl. Zoash stepped to one side to avoid its path, and spread his manipulator arms in a posture of apology. Apology that did not include subservience, the

Overlord noted with displeasure. He regretted his momentary lack of control briefly, but decided to maintain his own posture of overt anger. "How many have we lost now?"

"Last night's missing sentry brings the total to seven," he replied. The Overlord deliberately folded his manipulator arms and tucked them into his thorax.

"Seven." His tone was flat.

"This time there is no trace of a body."

"The sentries are in pairs every night?"

"They are."

"Then how can one be 'missing' without the other knowing?"

"We are unable to explain it other than to say that I believe it to be the feline. The one we saw briefly when the humans exited the ship."

"Then we need to find it and kill it."

"But it appears to be invisible, Overlord. We've spent every night scanning with our equipment, and with extra sentries on patrol. Some nights nothing happens, but every now and then, another guard goes missing. It's likely we'll find this body sometime in the next few days."

"It doesn't matter whether it's invisible or not – I want it dead and gone! Morale is plummeting. The humans have penetrated to the most secure areas of our ship, leaving destruction in their wake – and now this. We need to catch and kill it. Soon." His tone moved to cruel amusement. "It is your task alone. And I will be informing the Matriarch so this afternoon." He saw a momentary blanching of his hatching sib's carapace before he managed to control his emotions. Good. Let the threat of no offspring spur him to greater efforts. He cursed the chance that had landed him on this planet. Recently he had begun to feel small stings of doubt prick away at the shell of arrogance he'd encased himself in. With a brisk motion he dismissed Zoash and then he deliberately pushed the doubts aside. He was Garsal, he reminded himself, and recited the mantra to himself. "We hold, we stay, we breed." It *would* be all right. There *would* be offspring. He reminded himself again of the news that he would take to the Matriarch that very afternoon. The female quarters were nearing completion in the new hive. Very soon, she and her females would be ensconced in all of the comfort and luxury that he could muster. This world was his, and he would hold it, and from here he would launch his own empire. There was nothing else. He knew that it was right, and good, and his due.

***

Several hours later, with a sigh of pure relief, Shanna sat down and began to unlace her boots. She was a bit like her boots now, she mused. Slightly scuffed, a bit the worse for wear, but well broken in and very much fitting the task at hand. There was a feeling of amusement from her cats, and Storm hummed gently at her, great violet eyes soft, as the blue of his ear tip tide-marks twinkled in what she liked to think of as a starcat smile. She ran her hands over his head and scratched his cheek, and he leaned into her hand, purring. With her left foot she gently rubbed her toes up and down Twister's belly. He was warm, and his purring rumbled through her foot as his eyelids lowered to half-mast and he relaxed into her touch. *Just as well I have feet as well as hands,* she thought with an inward smile. For a moment she allowed herself to treasure the knowledge that her family was safe, and then pushed the thought away firmly and sat thinking about what might happen next.

She expected that it would still be some time until she saw her parents and Kaidan again. Master Cerren had sympathetically but firmly explained that the population was now being relocated to the old storm shelters and various Starlyne habitations. Each storm shelter was under the command of one or two of the retired Scouts, now recalled to duty, and Watchtower's militia had small squads stationed at each of the habitations. Many of the shelters had Starlynes stationed in them, allowing instantaneous communication in the case of enemy attack. Apparently both Starfall and Northaven were reorganising into similar structures. The farmers would continue to farm, but they were heavily guarded, and roving Scout Patrols worked overlapping patterns around the settlements. Shanna had been amazed at the amount of reorganisation that had occurred since she and the others had left the plateau. But then remembering the description of devastation visited on Watchtower by just three enemy aircraft, she knew that the incentive for change had come at a high cost.

And fortunately three of the Garsal's aircraft had been pursuing her and her friends at the time of the attack on Watchtower. She shuddered to think of what might have happened if all six had attacked Watchtower at once. Her throat tightened in remembered sorrow as she contemplated her friends' grief. She wondered how her old school friends had fared – friends that now seemed as far away as the once distant stars. Always ahead of her peers, her friends from school had dropped away one by one after she entered Scout training. They'd shared little enough at school, and the little they'd had in common had disappeared once she'd chosen her career. The intensity of cadetship had left little time for socialising, and Shanna realised with a shock that she knew nothing of her former friends' lives. Her world seemed to have shrunk and expanded at the same time. Shrunk to the life of a cadet Scout and her training, but expanding to encompass Below, and indeed the whole galaxy.

She finished with her boots and pushed them wearily away, absently looking at her socked feet, both now cushioned on Twister. There was a small hole in one toe, and she pulled them off and decided that she needed a bath before bed. With a sigh, she pushed herself to her feet and began to investigate her belongings. "Want another bath boys?" she queried as she pulled clean underwear out. Twister rolled over and cocked his head, and Storm glanced at his brother. He stretched luxuriously, and pointedly made his way over to the bed and climbed onto it, one paw at a time, and then lay down comfortably, tucking his tail around so that it cushioned his nose. He looked up at Shanna, and closed one eye, watching to see what she did. She snorted slightly, gathered a clean towel to add to the underwear, and left the two cats to their sleep.

# Chapter 3

THE Overlord pondered the information scrolling across the screen. He tapped it to pause the flow briefly, studying the estimates from the engineering section. No matter how he fiddled with the figures, they remained the same. The five aircraft would be all he had for some months. Despite the raw materials now available, some of the smaller components would take time to manufacture, time in fact, to manufacture the equipment needed to begin constructing the specialised parts. He was frustrated at his inability to take the fight immediately to the humans. The primitive weaponry that they'd used to bring down the aircraft had been ridiculously effective, whatever it was. At every turn they'd surprised him. Accustomed to easy victory, the Overlord now quietly admitted to himself that he'd underestimated his opponents. If he had access to more aircraft it would be easy to overwhelm the technologically primitive humans – but he didn't, and it was a source of major frustration to him. He jabbed at the screen with a manipulator arm again, and it resumed its scrolling. The Communications Chief had not changed his time estimates – another source of frustration. He closed the messages, and sat back, tapping the desktop irritably. He brooded over the lack of progress, and the devastation that the humans had wreaked upon his ship.

Most of all, he brooded on the slowly rising death toll from the feline still prowling within the defensive perimeter around the ship. Eight troopers were now dead or missing. He assumed that they were dead. The feline was a silent and deadly killer, leaving no trace of its presence. He leaned forwards again and tapped the screen several times. The images of the human beings in the comms room replayed themselves in an endless loop. An empty lift, followed by sudden chaos, then the abrupt appearance of several human beings and the huge felines who accompanied them. Again he pulled up the sensor readings for the felines. Nothing. None of them registered at all, or at least, not in a pattern that any of his experts had been able to determine.

He switched files as his annoyance grew, and in frustration reviewed the images captured from both the interior and exterior of the ship as the humans effected their escape. The feline now harassing his troopers *must* be wounded. He watched again as it erupted into a snarling spitting rage, tackling two of his troopers at once, but then blurring away, demonstrating an astonishing turn of speed despite its obvious injuries. Perhaps it might die of its wounds, he thought, but it had already been many days since the humans had escaped, and the hope was probably futile. He wondered why it remained in the area. It was only a beast, with no capacity for revenge. Perhaps it liked the taste of Garsal flesh. The thought chilled him to his vitals. *Nothing* preyed on the Garsal, they were the ultimate top order predator as they had proved time after time. Anger replaced the chill, and he tapped the console again. A frontal assault was out of the question right now, but he still had Trooper Hoth on the plateau, and raiding had always been a favourite pastime of the Garsal.

His mind turned the idea over. Fast hit and run attacks might well demoralise the humans. Prolonged attacks might be more satisfying but they carried higher risks, which in his previous arrogance he had neglected to consider. He tapped decisively at his screen again. "Zoash! I will meet with the senior commanders tonight." His hatching sib sent an acknowledgment.

"I will set the meeting for after your tour of the new hive with the Matriarch, Overlord."

The Overlord folded his manipulator arms, satisfied. There were ways to hurt the humans still, hurt them until he was ready to enslave them completely. It was time they began to understand who their new masters would be.

***

The Matriarch left the female section of the ship without a backwards glance. Her regal bearing was carefully calculated, and she kept her stately progress to a deliberate cadence. In her wake, her senior attendants maintained the same measured pace. They were well versed in the formalities, and she knew that there would be no hint of compromise in their postures.

Not so the four juniors included in her entourage for the first time. The four had been suggested as the most suitable for initiation by Laretai, and she had decided to include them in today's procession so that she could observe them herself. They were trying hard to maintain the composure of the seniors, but their inexperience showed itself in small ways; the slightly awkward drape of their robes, and the uneven spacing as they struggled to maintain the measured pace. By her side, the Overlord gestured towards the entrance to the new hive. The archway was well-formed, she noted, and the sentries on either side of it moved promptly to positions of respect, shouldering their weapons in a display of devotion as she passed.

The hive was well lit, and she inclined her head to the Overlord as she passed one of the inset lighting units. The slight reddish cast to the light was easy to the multifaceted Garsal eye, and enhanced the colour of the female contingent's robes. The clever paving smoothed the way underfoot, and the Matriarch's group moved easily down the gentle incline.

"Please, the left hand entrance, Matriarch." The Overlord's obsequious voice grated in the Matriarch's ears, but she quelled her irritation. He knew no better, being only a product of his upbringing and culture. She took the indicated entrance, graciously nodding at the door attendants as she passed. Their slave garb was clean but colourless, their flat human faces downcast. She wanted to stop, to query them about their origins, to try and better understand the invaders who had been so close to her quarters when they made their way through the ship.

There were few humans in the female section of the ship, and most were too cowed to reply to any queries from a Garsal. She wished she could question the young female with the green eyes and the feline companions, a human who was not a slave – a rarity she'd never encountered. She turned her attention back to the job at hand, and entered the antechamber of what was clearly the female section of the hive. There was a small flurry of hastily suppressed surprise from behind her. Laretai would describe the potential initiates in detail for her later, but she motioned for them to step forwards with her as she paused to appreciate the details now pointed out by the Overlord.

Presentation trays sat on decorative pillars of native stone at the front of the antechamber, and neatly curtained alcoves lined each sidewall. An impressive doorway hinted at more luxuries deeper inside the hive. With the four juniors now in clear view of herself, the Matriarch decided that the Overlord had earned a few words from Laretai. She gave her attendant a coded arm motion.

"The Matriarch wishes me to indicate her satisfaction with the antechamber. It is tastefully done."

The Matriarch watched the four juniors. Two of them stood impassively, but the other two had the air of a lesson learned. She was pleased to see them grasp the careful nature of her compliment. Voiced by Laretai, it only hinted of offspring. The same words voiced by herself would have been close to a declaration. It was not lost on either the Overlord, or the two juniors. The other two? She decided to watch and wait.

"You have more to show?" she asked the Overlord, careful to keep her voice imperious.

"Please," he motioned to the doorway at the far end. The door slaves rushed to open the heavy metal doors. Engraved and embossed decorative panels were cleverly recessed into its heavy metal. The Matriarch was impressed, despite her irritation with the Overlord. Passing through the heavy doors, the Overlord directed them through a well-planned series of tastefully decorated rooms. Themes from many different worlds featured in the furnishings, and not for the first time, the Matriarch wondered at the many contradictions of her people. A capacity for beauty that was almost as unsurpassed as their capacity for destruction. The female quarters were everything any Matriarch could have hoped for. Individual accommodation spaces were interspersed with shared accommodations for the junior females. Technology was discreetly built into each room, always present but never jarringly so.

As the tour drew to an end, the Overlord stood to one side of an irised doorway. He gestured, and the Matriarch stepped through. It was a hatching suite. Her mood darkened abruptly. As beautiful as the female quarters were, the Overlord's presumption angered her beyond belief.

"You overstep your rights, Overlord." Her voice was cold and calculating. "Offspring approval has not yet been given to any male." She felt and saw the startled reactions of the juniors. Her seniors knew better; at her first words they had closed ranks behind her, and they now faced him with her, displeasure in their bearing. She heard the shuffle as the juniors followed suit. She waited until the last one had ceased moving.

"We return to the ship now. You will remove this – immediately! No hatching suite is to be constructed until the first approval has been ratified." She stalked from the room, her entourage moving in lockstep behind her. Laretai's familiar step just behind her sounded outraged, and she knew that her attendant was mirroring her thoughts. The arrogance of the Overlord was insupportable, and stiffened her resolve.

As they walked, she mused on the four juniors. The tour and its aftermath would prove instructive for them. She looked forwards to interviewing them one by one; their reactions would be revealing, and help her to ensure that if any of them was unready for initiation it would be easy to weed them out. Yes, today's indignity would be put to good use.

***

The Overlord fumed as he paced. The Matriarch had left in a fury, followed by her attendants. Her departure had been precipitous, and any who had encountered her party as they stalked back to the female quarters would know that the hive tour had not gone well. The slaves would say nothing, because they knew that their lives depended on their silence, but some of his underlings were not as reliable. Some would hope that his disgrace would lead to their elevation and the chance of their own offspring. Others might hope that the Matriarch might demand a change of commander. The hatching suite had been a monumental miscalculation on his part.

He paused and allowed his manipulator arms to tuck themselves back around his thorax. The nonfunctional communication equipment might yet be a blessing in disguise. There was no way that the Matriarch could communicate offworld to demand his demotion. He relaxed slightly, and the speed of his pacing slowed as he began to plan again. Rationality reasserted itself as he changed direction and strode towards the elevator to the equipment hangar. As he walked, he thought. Before he entered the elevator, he gestured to one of the slaves labouring away at a cleaning task. "Send word to the Architect. I will consult with him in the hangar." The slave dropped his eyes and bowed, and then hurried off.

The Overlord pondered as the elevator descended to the hangar level. The hatching suite must be made unrecognisable, but what to turn it into? Perhaps the Architect would have an appropriate suggestion for him. In the meantime, he needed to take stock of the resources at his command.

The elevator doors opened and he stalked out into the hangar. One of his technicians hurried towards him, head bowed in respect. Obviously word of the Matriarch's displeasure had not yet reached this level. He put the dilemma behind him as they walked down the neat rows of vehicles. He paused at the aircraft and surveyed them. The five of them sat there, sleek and shining, with their pilots arrayed in ranks before them. He had plenty of pilots. The thought left a sour taste in his mind.

"How long until we are able to manufacture more aircraft?" The technician consulted his tablet, manipulator arms flashing across its surface. The pause was probably unnecessary, he thought; the technician was most likely arranging his words carefully.

"The frames are easily constructed, Sir," he said, "but some of the internal control components will take significantly longer. We have some spares in storage, but as this was a colony ship bound for an uninhabited world … the manifest was not designed with conquest in mind, consequently – "

"I know all of that!" hissed the Overlord. He was tired of platitudes, and underlings who bowed and scraped but were not forthcoming with the information he needed. "I need real figures, and real time estimates! You will provide them now, unless you wish demotion to follow very rapidly." He watched the import of his words strike home in the underling, watched the internal struggle, mirrored by his posture, and waited.

"It will be moon cycles, Overlord, many cycles, at least more than five for the aircraft." He shuffled uncomfortably, hesitated slightly, and then went on. "There are enough spares for two aircraft, but if we use them and something happens to our five remaining craft, then there will be no repairs." He waited in silence as the Overlord quelled his rising frustration again.

"And the land vehicles? The climbers and crawlers?"

"We have more latitude there, Overlord. A colony world is expected to use their land vehicles hard, but again, early losses have us well over the estimated damage rate. The loss of four crawlers so soon after landing has set us back, and then the issues with the cliff face collapse have left us shorter of spares than we would like at this stage. We have more manufacturing capacity, but it will be at least two cycles until we are at full production." He stopped speaking again and allowed his arms to flicker across the tablet. There was hesitation in his voice again as he spoke. "If we turn our resources to manufacturing land craft, we will have to divert some of our hive construction workers. We will be well behind schedule there within two cycles."

The Overlord was tempted to break the wretched technician's neck then and there, but at least the fool had been courageous enough to speak the truth, so he arrested the impulse before it translated to action. The technician looked at him, fear obvious in his stance, but still standing his ground. "Your name, technician?"

"I am Hath, Overlord." The name piqued the Overlord's interest.

"You were hatching sibs with Trooper Hoth?"

"Yes, Overlord." The connection between hatching sibs was often strong, but it was unusual to have two in one colony ship.

"Are there more of your hatching on this planet?"

"No, Overlord. Many of our hatching have perished in the wars of conquest."

The Overlord was oddly disappointed. Both Hoth and Hath had demonstrated more fortitude than most of his underlings. "You will advance a grade to Senior Tech and oversee the manufacturing process. You will have the hive construction workers within one cycle. There is construction work that must be completed first." If he was to ever have any chance of offspring. "Your tablet?" Senior Technician Hath proffered the tablet with reverence, and the Overlord tapped rapidly, authorising the grade rise. Hath was his now. He could see it in the other's posture. "You will continue to speak the truth to me when I ask."

"I will, Overlord."

"You will commence this task immediately. You will find that your orders have you reporting directly to Zoash, who will report to me. I will expect a report every five days."

"Yes, Overlord." Hath bowed himself with proper respect and departed on his new task, evidence of pride in every step.

The Overlord surveyed the aircraft and beckoned to the Senior Pilot.

"You will plan a raid. Three craft, in seven days time. The plan is to be lodged before sunset today." The pilot bowed in acquiescence and returned to the ranks. The Overlord stood for a few more moments and then began to inspect the ranks of ground vehicles. For the moment, he dismissed the crawlers. Until there was easier access to the plateau, they were effectively useless for assaulting the humans.

The climbers, however … He beckoned to the Climber Squadron Commander.

"You have Hoth's updates?"

"Yes Overlord."

"You will plan a variety of assault scenarios for the plateau. Do not include aerial support in your estimates. I will see the early simulations in one moon cycle, and we will finalise the planning within two. Include casualty estimates and the likelihood of damage to machinery. You will also contact Hoth. He should bring us at least one human specimen to study. Tell him to obtain it as soon as possible." He turned away from the squadron commander and stalked towards the elevator again.

'Where was the Architect?' he wondered. 'Surely the slave had summoned him promptly.' The elevator doors hissed open and the Architect, as if reading his thoughts, hurried out. His posture was deferential, but there was a hint of arrogance underlying it. The creature had advised against the hatching suite, and was no doubt wishing to capitalise upon the Overlord's discomfort. The knowledge of his fall from grace with the Matriarch was likely to be common knowledge by now. He would have to be on guard against the ambitions of those, like the Architect, who had enough rank to have their own schemes for offspring and advancement. He went on the offensive immediately.

"The hive has flaws that displease the Matriarch. You will rectify them. The hatching suite design is not up to her standards, so you will restructure it into something more pleasing that bears no resemblance to what it was. She wishes no reminders of its poor workmanship." There, the blame was laid firmly upon the Architect, and the Overlord could see several technicians listening avidly while pretending to be diligently assessing the machinery nearby. "She will notify us of her requirements in time. At that point, and only at that point, will a suite be constructed."

There was a glint of enmity in the Architect's eyes as he bowed, and there was still a hint of arrogance in his posture as he departed without speaking. He hadn't been fooled by the Overlord's prevarications. The Overlord watched him dispassionately. Trooper Hoth's martial skills might well become useful on his return, should the Architect overstep his bounds. He knew he deserved offspring – they were his right.

# Chapter 4

SHANNA eyed Cally with some trepidation. The old Scout looked her up and down, then took her time inspecting Storm and Twister. Old Mirror prowled around them in a fashion that reminded Shanna of their first encounter with Satin, except that this time, Satin had been subject to precisely the same inspection. She'd been hard pressed to avoid giggling at the emerald toned cat's slightly indignant expression. Mirror's ruby tidemarks had flickered in patterns that Shanna had never seen before as she paced around Satin. Then the two starcats had spent some time staring at each other. Satin had finally ducked her head briefly, before fixing Mirror with her unblinking stare once more. The old starcat had returned her stare levelly, then with an amused hum brushed herself up against Satin in a greeting of equals. The green tidemarked cat had hummed in reply, then watched with narrowed eyes as Mirror began her inspection of the other starcats.

Cally and Mirror finished their respective inspections, then as Shanna stood there trying to ignore the feeling that she was in trouble again, the two turned their attention to the other cadets and Allad. Allad was only the Scout with them at the moment as the others were at a strategy meeting with Peron and Cerren. Apparently Cally had co-opted the Starlyne training facilities for herself and was there to help find out how they'd done what they did.

"You've done some good things with your cats, I hear," Cally drawled, "so let's see if you're as good as I've been told. Follow me." The group stood bemused for a moment, until Mirror hummed impatiently, and followed her partner. Storm and Twister both flicked anxious eyes towards Shanna, and with a slightly nervous snicker she took a step forwards.

"Coming?" she asked the others. There was a general shuffle – even Allad had been caught slightly off balance by Cally – and they all followed Shanna down the tunnel out of the habitation.

Two hours later, Shanna collapsed on the ground, dirtier and sweatier than she'd been since returning from Below. The Starlyne obstacle course had been revamped in their absence and it had been a revealing test of partnership between starcat and human. Cally and Mirror had insisted they work together in a group, and not as individual pairings. Skills developed Below had helped, but Shanna knew that Cally had revealed some previously undiscovered cracks in their teamwork, particularly when they had to work with someone else's cat. Storm plonked himself on the ground next to her with a sigh, and she groaned slightly as Twister laid his head on her chest and the weight of it interfered with her puffing.

"You're heavy, cat!"

There was a slightly plaintive grumble from Twister, but he moved his head slightly, and Shanna took a deeper breath, starting to relax.

"Up you get," came Cally's imperative voice. "Go and get clean, and we'll talk." With that, she turned and vanished down the hallway to the common room, Mirror pacing by her side.

"I don't think I *can* get up," Zandany sighed. "And I thought I was fit."

"I thought I was too," replied Taya, "but apparently I was wrong."

"I ache," said Ragar.

"And me," Amma's voice was an exhausted sigh, and Shanna opened her mouth to add her own comment, when Allad's voice interrupted them.

"And if we want to eat, I'd suggest we get moving. Cally's well known for her unusual approaches to teaching. If we're not back there shortly, clean, neat and tidy, it's entirely possible she'll cancel dinner." Even Allad sounded tired, mused Shanna. She was tempted to stay lying on the soft ground, but her stomach rumbled, and the thought of missing her meal spurred her to movement. It was hard to roll over, and even harder to push herself upright, but she did, sighing as her joints creaked.

A bath and food later, and the seven of them were clustered around Cally's small table in her private quarters. 'And just how had the old Scout managed that?' wondered Shanna. The six of them were still sharing the one room, and Patrol Ten's arrangement was still the same. Cally pushed a small bowl of nuts across the table, and then sat back in her chair, propping her feet on the edge of the table. "Your cats are quite well trained, but I think we can improve upon your teamwork. And Master Cerren's briefing has told me that there are other things you're able to do as well."

"You know about the spark of course?" Allad said.

Cally nodded, and for a moment, there was a ball of light floating just above her palm. It was smaller than Spiron's, but well-formed and bright.

Allad nodded back at the aged Scout. "Shanna, show Cally, please, and then the rest of you one by one."

Shanna concentrated, and faded. She felt the others fade one by one. She dropped the fade, explained briefly about seeing through her cats' eyes, and then watched as Taya made the walls mirror her hair, and Ragar and Zandany balanced flames on their fingertips and described their fireballs. (She was rather glad that they had decided description was better than demonstration.) Allad picked up the table rather casually, so that the bowl of nuts nearly fell off one edge, and then Cally turned her eyes on Amma and Verren.

"And what do the two of you do?"

"I fly, and always know what the weather's doing," said Amma quietly.

"And I always know where I am," said Verren. His voice wobbled slightly, and then he went on. "And apparently I can sense sliders."

Cally's eyebrows disappeared into her hairline and Allad took the opportunity to explain the multiple talents of a few of them. He finished by describing the assault on the Garsal ship and the subsequent dropping of the cliff face on top of their pursuers.

Finally, Cally turned her eyes on Shanna. "And that picture in the Starlyne images – the one of you and your cats? What's that about?"

Shanna shrugged uncomfortably, and dropped her eyes briefly before replying.

"I'm not sure, really. I can do most of the things the others can, but some of my skills aren't as good as theirs – take Taya's ability to stop stuff, for example. I can do it, and I'm better when the boys are helping, but I don't have her finesse. And I can sort of sense the sliders, but not like Verren can. I can fly, though, and I'm fairly good at knowing where I am." She stopped.

"Hmmph." Cally's tone was thoughtful. "Well, while you're here, I'll think on it. Tomorrow you can all show me what you can do. There's somewhere near here you can fly from?" She dropped her feet off the table as Allad nodded, and pushed her chair back. "In the meantime, I'd suggest you get to bed early. We'll be busy tomorrow, and I have much to discuss with Spiron and Barron." With that, she left the room, limping for the first few steps before her gait smoothed out into the gliding walk of the experienced Scout.

"Well, you heard her," said Allad. "I'm tired now, and it's a sure thing that we'll be even more tired after tomorrow." His mobile eyebrows wriggled expressively, and Satin added a hum that sounded suspiciously amused.

Lying in her soft bed a little later, Shanna ran a hand idly down Twister's soft flank. Storm had laid his head on her middle, and the weight of it was comfortingly warm.

"So, what do you think the Garsal are going to do next?" asked Amma.

"I'd like to know what *we're* going to do next," replied Taya. "Look, I know we'll learn heaps from Cally, but really, aren't we meant to be the planet's first line of defence?" She sounded frustrated, and Shanna lifted her head in surprise and looked across the room. Taya had her chin propped on one hand, and was staring into space, her face fixed in unhappy lines. Shanna reminded herself that the other girl had just lost the majority of her family, and had more right to be angry than any of them.

"I know, Tay," said Amma, "but if we're still uncertain about how we do what we do, then how can we be the first line of defence? What if it doesn't work again?"

Shanna rolled onto her side, eliciting a slightly annoyed hum from Storm, to watch the other two girls.

"I know, Amma, but if we were out there *doing* the defence, I'm sure we'd figure it out." Taya let out a frustrated sigh. Shanna sympathised with Taya; she wanted more than anything to be doing something. Something that seemed more productive than training, even if it was training with one of the legends of the Scout Corps. It seemed stupidly anticlimactic.

"Maybe we'll learn more from Cally than we think," she said, hoping that was true. "I'm sure we'll be out there soon, doing more. There has to be some reason that Master Cerren wants us to work here with Cally."

"I know," replied Taya with a sigh, "it's just … you know." She broke off, and Shanna knew. She'd heard the other girl crying quietly at night. They'd all tried their best to help, but what did you say to someone who'd lost so much so suddenly, except to be there? Taya dimmed the lights and lay back on her bed, and as the light faded, Shanna deliberately closed her eyes.

She wondered when she'd see the three Starlynes who'd travelled with them again. She missed their friendly presence and was curious what they were doing. She hadn't realised how used she'd become to their silent conversation and insightful comments. And she wondered when she'd finally meet Fractus' daughter, the young Starlyne of the vision.

Thoughts and images danced in her mind as she lay there in the dark, and once more, she felt that the weight of the world rested on her shoulders. What was it about her and her cats that the Starlynes felt was so important? There was no doubt that her ability to fade was unsurpassed, and her multiple skills with 'the spark' were in a greater quantity than anyone else's. But she'd spent hours thinking about whether that made her, Storm and Twister more powerful, or clever, or prepared than anyone else, and she couldn't see how. In fact, she could imagine being stuck trying to decide what she'd do with so many skills at her fingertips. She could see it clearly in her imagination. Hundreds of Garsal pouring towards the plateau as she stood on the edge trying to figure out what to do. It wasn't as if she could fade the whole plateau, or make the Garsal vanish in one enormous fireball. There were limits to her abilities. She might have many, but her skills were surest when she faded, or when she flew, but even then, Amma was a better flyer.

Shanna rolled over restlessly and punched her pillow into a better shape. She could see the muted tidemarks of the cats in the darkness. Close by, Storm and Twister were a puddle of blue and violet on her bed, with Spider not far away, and Spinner glowed faintly, like a partially banked fire. The boys' cats' marks reflected faintly on the far wall.

Shanna wriggled, trying to get comfortable. Her pillow seemed to be developing lumps, or maybe it was just that she'd slept for so long without a pillow that she was struggling with it. No, it hadn't bothered her at all the first few nights. She was forced to realise that despite her fatigue, she was in for a restless night. There was a quiet hum from the bed, and Storm's tidemarks brightened slightly. "Sorry boys," she whispered, and the tidemarks dimmed again. What was it that was so special about the three of them? Shanna ran the images through her mind again. Her, her two starcats, and then a myriad of others in the background. Her memory refused to show them clearly, no matter how much she reran the image. Finally, she heaved a frustrated sigh, deliberately closed her eyes and began to count her breaths. It was rare that she had a restless night, but when she did, counting her breaths usually helped.

The next morning, Shanna felt scratchy eyed, tired, and unaccustomedly grumpy. Cally had dragged them out of bed unconscionably early, even by Scout standards, pointed them at the breakfast table and then herded them out to the bluff where they'd had their initial flights. She'd had Verren show her precisely where they were on the map every kilometre or so. Then, when they'd struck a bare patch of rock, she'd asked Ragar and Zandany to toss a fireball or two, before requesting Allad pick up the largest rock he could. Shanna had been rather impressed at the size of it — almost as big as a horgal wagon. As the echoes of the rock hitting the ground died away, Shanna had wondered if perhaps the Starlynes had made an error about her. She could imagine Allad mowing down hundreds of Garsal with a rock that size if he managed to toss it far enough. And then she remembered how tired everyone became if they use their abilities for any length of time; even Allad wasn't exempt. The Starlynes had replenished the energy patches, but they'd cautioned them all against overusing them. It appeared that they were difficult to manufacture, and required a number of specialised ingredients that were hard to find.

By the time they'd climbed the small spire, some of the cobwebs had cleared from her mind. There was a light breeze, and the flying conditions looked perfect. As she, Amma and Allad removed their wingsuits from their packs, Cally and Mirror watched intently. Verren, Ragar, Taya and Zandany assisted with the final checks and the three flyers prepared themselves to launch.

"We may as well use the flight for a recon," Allad said. "We'll sweep in three directions — Amma, you take due south, Shanna you'll head southeast, and I'll take the southwest. Look for anything unusual. For Cally's benefit, we'll fly in formation for a few minutes, normal arrowhead, Amma in front, and then we'll separate on Amma's signal. Half an hour out, and half back." Shanna and Amma nodded. Shanna readied herself as Amma leaped into the air, dropping carefully into that odd vision that allowed her to 'see' the air currents.

She leaped in turn, allowing the cool air rushing past her face to blow out the last of the grumpiness. She dropped neatly in behind Amma, admiring as ever, the effortless way the other girl flew. Allad flew much as he moved — gracefully, but purposefully — and as he joined Shanna behind Amma, the three of them flew in careful formation in a rising spiral. Amma took them past the top of the spire several times at various altitudes, and then directly over the top of it and arrowed south. At Amma's wing waggle, the three separated, and Shanna headed southeast.

It was hard to concentrate on the task at hand as the sheer joy of flying overtook her. It had been weeks since she'd been in the air, and Shanna was pleased to note that none of her hard won skill seemed to have left her. She scanned the ground conscientiously, noting the varicoloured vegetation of Below in all its deadly, beautiful majesty. She 'felt' carefully for Twister and Storm, waiting on the spire with the others, making sure she knew precisely where they were in relation to her position. Her direction sense, although not as good as Verren's, told her that she would be shortly nearing the site of the battle with the four Garsal vehicles. She estimated how long she'd been flying, and figured she had another ten minutes or so before she needed to turn around.

She soared contentedly, enjoying the sensation of flight, watching Below unroll before her. She could see the miniature plateau where they'd first made contact with the Garsal and her stomach roiled momentarily as she recalled the astounded amazement at encountering aliens, here, on her home world. Below was a place that repeatedly called her to explore, and she longed for a return to the peaceful days she'd envisaged when she first joined the Scouts. Days spiced with the adventure of exploration and study. She'd seen Below from the edge of the plateau all those months ago when they'd found the Garsal ship, but now, from high above it, she was struck all over again by its deadly mystery. The deep green of the vegetation touched a buried longing that she was almost unable to explain, and she repressed an urge to keep on flying just to see what she might find.

In her head, the time ticked by. She flew southeast steadily, trying to estimate exactly how far over Below she was. She could 'feel' Storm and Twister like anchors behind her, steadfast in their waiting, and decided to gain a little more height before turning back towards them. She was halfway through her turn when she was buffeted suddenly by an air current she hadn't 'seen,' and a thundering boom. It tumbled her over in the air, and she was completely disoriented, not knowing whether she was up or down, her arms and legs quivering with the strain of a tumbling, turbulent patch of air. Her head spun, and she blinked her eyes furiously, trying to figure out what was happening, when she realised that she was dropping rapidly towards Below. Panicked, she forced her arms and legs into position, shaking with the strain, and slowly began to level out, checking the downward plummet. Her sense of her two cats was the only thing that kept her mind to even a semblance of rational thought.

Finally, she gained control, feeling one of her shoulders aching fiercely, and looked around to estimate her height. The ground was way too close, and she searched the air currents frantically for one that would take her higher, and with a thankful sigh, angled sideways into a rising thermal. It sucked her high into the air, and she looked around to see what might have caused the boom and her tumble. Perhaps there were air currents invisible even to her enhanced vision. She spiralled higher, scanning, and to the northeast of her, spied a glint of metal, flying high in the sky. Her heart sank. At least one Garsal aircraft was in the vicinity.

Shanna was torn. Should she chase the aircraft? Should she head straight back to the spire? What was the best plan of action? She had no idea what the best choice would be, and worst of all, she could feel her shoulder beginning to throb more intensely second by second. It was thirty minutes flying time back to the bluff where Storm and Twister waited, and in that time, who knew where the aircraft might end up? At the speed it had passed her, it would probably be near the plateau in a few minutes. She took a deep breath, and began to consider her options. The aircraft would be at its destination before she could arrive. Her arrival would make no difference to the outcome, except to separate her from her cats and her team. She could 'feel' Storm and Twister in her mind, now drawing her back to the spire and she deliberately turned in the air towards them and began to speed as fast as possible towards them. She imagined she could hear sounds on the wind, awful sounds of destruction, but she kept her eyes towards her starcats.

Fifteen minutes later, she could see the spire and a speck that was either Allad or Amma mirroring her path. She concentrated on flying as well as she could for the next ten minutes and carefully gauged the wind direction as she headed in for a landing. As her feet touched the rock, she gasped her news even before she'd lowered her arms.

Cally's seamed face hardened "Verren, go straight back to the Starlyne habitation and pass the message. We'll wait here in case Amma and Allad have further information."

Shanna's shoulder throbbed dully, and she realised that Ragar was busily unsealing the wingsuit, and she began to shrug out of it, automatically telescoping the extensions as she folded it into her pack. There was a crunch, and Amma landed neatly, having apparently dropped vertically the last half metre. She was undoing her wingsuit almost before she landed.

"Garsal ship!"

"The message is on its way," replied Cally. Taya and Ragar helped Amma stow her suit as fast as possible, and then they began the wait for Allad. Remembering her own tumble, and near fall, Shanna shivered slightly, and looked at Satin. The green toned cat sat completely composed on the edge of the spire. She wasn't the least bit worried as far as Shanna could see, so she decided that Allad must be all right.

"Did you have any trouble, Amma?" she asked.

"It nearly scared the living daylights out of me," replied Amma, "It came so close it knocked me all over the sky. Took me quite a while to sort myself out, and for a moment I thought I was about to die." She shook her head.

"Me too. I think I've wrenched my shoulder as well." Shanna wriggled her shoulder. It was uncomfortable no matter where she put it, but not nastily so.

Just enough to be annoying. There was a shout from Zandany, who was perched on a rock.

"I can see Allad. Looks like he's in a hurry!" Allad's form neared the spire at full speed, turned into the wind, and landed with a thud. Sweat covered his face, and he dropped his arms with a sigh of relief.

"Garsal!"

"The message is sent," said Cally. "but I need the three of you to tell me where you were when you saw the ship, and what direction it was going in." They crouched over the map, and Shanna put her finger on her estimated position.

"It was heading towards Watchtower as far as I can tell."

Allad's face blanched. "I must have seen a different one in that case. Mine was heading northwest – in a pretty direct line towards the coastal settlements if it overflies the plateau." Amma's finger shook slightly.

"The one I saw was moving due north."

"So," Allad said, "We have three aircraft going in three different directions. And no idea where they're going, except for a compass heading."

"Well, they're certainly not on a sightseeing tour," replied Cally, her voice dry, and her expression hard. "I'd say they've embarked on a guerilla campaign. I suspect it'll be a hit and run type raid – the maximum amount of destruction in the shortest amount of time. Ideal for spreading fear and damage. They hope to panic us."

There was silence as they all contemplated the implications. Shanna's mind imagined the destruction that just one of those ships could be visiting upon some of the small settlements on the plateau right then.

"Come on," Cally said. "We need to be back at the habitation. The Starlynes will send a representative immediately I'd guess, and there'll be planning to do. Dependent on what happens, our tasks may change, so we've little time to work on the things we need to." She nodded grimly at their surprised expressions. "Cerren knows the value of the things I can teach you. He'll leave you here if he can, but our time will be short." She stomped off down the spire, and the three flyers and other cadets followed in her wake.

Shanna's mind began to worry about her family again. They had been safe. Surely they still were. They had to be. And then she felt guilty, why should her family be safe when so many others probably weren't? It was selfish, but she still clung to the thought. Kaidan would be somewhere carrying messages – he'd be all right. She pushed the worry about her parents down, and followed Cally. She wondered what the rest of Patrol Ten might have been doing. It seemed odd that Spiron wasn't demonstrating his flying skills along with the rest of them.

# Chapter 5

MASTER Cerren surveyed the damage at Thunderfall Cascades from the top of a small rise. The once picturesque town that nestled beside the spectacular waterfall that gave the town its name, had borne the brunt of the attack and now lay in smouldering ruins. He'd known that the Garsal would strike again, but the reality was worse than he'd imagined. The market square had been completely destroyed, its town hall now only a pile of rubble, recognisable only from its position at the top of the square. No building had escaped without damage, and the streets were filled with the tumbled piles of masonry from destroyed buildings. His eyes focused on the shrouded bodies lying in their neat rows outside the village storm shelter, remembering the scene he had observed inside the shelter where medics still struggled to care for the wounded and dying.

The strong smell of antiseptic had pervaded the air as Cerren had forced himself to stop by each bed, steeling himself to speak his empty words of comfort. Missing limbs were disguised with neat dressings, and while the worst of the physical damage was being assessed by Starlyne physicians and their human counterparts, the fear and desolation had no easy succour.

"It's worse than we feared," Peron said quietly from beside him, bringing him back to the present.

"And so little we could do to stop it," Cerren said. Socks growled an echo of her partner's emotions. "And so little we can do to prevent it happening again."

"The Starlynes said that the warning came from the flyers," Peron said.

"It was chance, and it was too late for this town."

"But it wasn't too late for the fishing villages and Starfall," Peron pointed out. "We may have lost buildings and boats, but we didn't lose people in either of those places." Thunder hummed in agreement.

"But we only have four flyers, and we can't keep them in the air everywhere, all of the time." Cerren sighed in exasperation. "They can do only so much, and it's imperative that they keep working on whatever it was they did to drop that cliff face." He shook his head in frustration, and began to descend the rise. "We need more of them, but we don't have them. I've got Scouts training with our allies all over the place, but there are no more flyers at this stage apparently."

"We don't necessarily need flyers. If we negotiate with the Starlynes, we could have watchers linked by Starlynes all over the plateau – it would just be an extension of the storm shelter system, and they can't help but see the need. We may have to evacuate the villages too close to the plateau edge, but the inland villages should have *some* warning time at least. That way we can continue to maintain our food production, but still keep our populace as safe as possible."

Cerren nodded slowly. "We have so little manpower left, though. And what you're suggesting needs trained personnel, which means Scouts. Again. Our people are too thin on the ground as it is. We've got patrols guarding the land approaches to the plateau, patrolling the plateau, and in training with the Starlynes."

"Just make it an additional duty for the oldsters at the storm shelters," Peron suggested. "And the militia with them."

Ceren shook his head – the never ending list of tasks suitable only for Scouts seemed to have expanded again. "It's the best we can do at this point. Talk to the Starlynes Peron, and see if there's anything else they can offer. Surely some of their technology will have the answers we need." He rubbed his hand down Socks' soft coat, and his starcat butted his leg comfortingly with her head.

***

"Run it again," came Cally's voice, "you were too slow. Up your speed, and make better use of those skills." Shanna sighed and called Storm and Twister to her. Cally had worked them hard in the days since the hit and run attack by the aliens. She pushed and pushed, and every day they'd learned a new facet to their skills. Shanna had thought that their teamwork was tight, but Cally's demands had pushed them to a new level, a level not even the Starlynes had managed to wring from them.

"Again?" sighed Ragar. "We were at least two minutes faster that time." He pushed himself reluctantly to his feet and called Sparks.

"Apparently two minutes faster isn't faster enough," replied Allad. Even the tall Scout was looking a bit ragged around the edges, and Satin's normally imperturbable nature had frayed slightly. Shanna was privately amused at the way she and Mirror continued to dance around each other. Allad still looked slightly surprised every time the two cats interacted.

They began the walk back to the beginning of the course. Cally's inventiveness seemed never ending. The obstacle course had been 'enhanced' with additional traps while they'd been away on their mission, the Starlynes also taking the opportunity to plant the area with some of Frontier's most annoying, and irritating vegetation. But now each day seemed to add another construction that had to be climbed, crawled through, or negotiated. It wasn't dangerous as such, but the potential for itching, burning, and being spiked was high. Stepping in the wrong place released missiles and nets, and each time the cadets had been through the course they'd 'discovered' another pit-fall, sometimes literally.

Shanna had faded them, Verren had guided, Ragar and Zandany had cleared some traps with fireballs, and Allad had managed to learn how to stop a falling net, but apparently Cally still expected more of them.

"What can we do differently?" asked Amma, frustration evident in her normally even toned voice. "I mean, what does Cally actually *want* from us?"

"I have no idea," replied Zandany, "we've run as hard as we can, and our cats are flawless. We've been faster every time, yet apparently we're still not fast enough." Punch nudged him gently with his head.

"Who knows?" replied Verren. "I think I know where most of the traps are now, though."

"*I* can't believe we're still stuck here with the Garsal out there," grumbled Taya. "Surely they need us elsewhere. We've *proved* ourselves, *and* we know the Garsal." There was a general chorus of agreement and Shanna was surprised to realise that even Allad was looking frustrated. They were about half way back to the start line when Satin flicked her tidemarks at the other cats. The starcats came to a complete halt and left their partners to sit in a circle with Satin.

"What do you think you're doing, Satin?" asked Allad. His cat ignored him completely, and then flickered her tidemarks in a complex pattern, almost too fast for human eyes to follow, and then the other cats rejoined their human companions.

"What was that about?" asked Verren.

There was a feeling of smugness tinged in tones of blue and violet in Shanna's mind. She narrowed her eyes slightly. "They've decided something," she said, "and they're pretty happy about it."

"They've what?" Ragar's voice was startled. "What do you mean, Shanna?"

"I meant what I said," she replied, suddenly feeling slightly awkward. "They've decided something."

"And how would you know that?"

"It's like … I can 'feel' them … inside my head." She realised she must have sounded ridiculous and flushed. "It's not words, but feelings really, sort of like the Starlynes, but not quite the same." Silence followed her last sentence. "And they have colours," she finished lamely.

"And just how long have you been 'feeling' your cats inside your head?" Allad asked exasperated. "And why didn't you mention it?"

Embarrassed by Allad's reaction she flushed again. "Since we were Be-low," she admitted, "when we were escaping from the Garsal after the ship sabotage. I didn't think it was important …" her voice trailed off, "I thought everyone could feel their cats. I suppose it probably started a bit before then though, when I began seeing through their eyes."

"You know Shan, sometimes you really are an idiot," sighed Ragar. "This could be really important. Do they actually speak?"

"No, it's just feelings and colours, but I know what they mean. It's like before we dropped the cliff."

Cally's voice came clearly through the trees. Shockingly loud in the more usual silence of Below. "Where are you? Move it along!" The group jerked into motion again.

"I'll second the idiot comment," said Allad, "but right now we need to get this right. Ragar, you're in charge this time. Maybe that's what Cally wants. She never was one to explain everything, and perhaps she's looking for you lot to organise yourselves. And speaking of Cally, we'd better move faster." He broke into a jog.

Ragar planned as they jogged. "Verren, you and Shanna lead. Shan, I want you to look through your cats' eyes but fade us as well. Can you do that?"

"Maybe ..."

"Maybe'll do for now. Zan, you and I will be just behind them with Amma. Amma, I want you spotting air currents – both to detect traps early and to help us aim our fireballs. Allad, you'll back us up. This time though, I want you to lift any of *us* if you see something coming for us. Yes, I know you haven't tried it, but none of us weigh more than those boulders you heave around so easily. Taya, you'll be attempting to detect the mechanical bits and disarm them if you can. Cats are on the circle except for Storm and Twister – they'll be up front. Allad, get Satin to direct, and get her to guard our rear."

Ragar's plan was completely different to anything they'd tried so far, but his concise instructions were clever and used their new skills in ways Shanna would never have thought of. He was without doubt, Patrol First material. His insight into individual character and skill sets sometimes astounded her.

As they lined up at the beginning of the course, Cally glowered at them. "Took your time, didn't you? When I say move, I mean it. If you perform poorly this time, you can be sure Cerren will hear from me." Her old eyes glared down at them again from her viewing platform. It was connected by a series of walkways in the trees that allowed her to observe them as they toiled their way through the course. It was also new, and Shanna wondered how the Starlynes had constructed it, or why they'd even thought to do so. Maybe Master Cerren was even more forward thinking than she'd realised. It was ideally placed for viewing the course, and allowed great visibility of the students toiling through it, or it would have, had they planned to be visible. Shanna stifled a grin and prepared herself to fade. Then she remembered that she had to look through her cats' eyes – while they moved. The grin vanished completely, and she swallowed convulsively at the thought of the nausea that was likely to follow.

"I'm apologising in advance if I vomit on you, Verren," she muttered.

"You do, and you die, Shan."

"Begin," came Cally's voice, cutting off their conversation.

Shanna faded them all, and then connected with Twister and Storm. She blinked slightly, and allowed herself to 'feel' the others around her, before trying to separate the three fields of view in her mind. It was an effort, but so far she wasn't nauseous.

"Ready?" Ragar's voice was barely audible.

"Yes."

"Then, let's move. Verren, direct us. Shan, be on the watch with your cats. I want Twister in the trees." Shanna gulped and then used her whistle to direct her cats and they moved off slowly. She almost fell over when Twister went up the tree, and she felt the fade flicker, steadied it, swallowed convulsively, and put a hand on Verren's arm to steady herself. She was abruptly aware of him. Aware of him in a way that she'd never experienced before. She could feel Cirrus as well. Her tone was less electric and more aqua than Storm's and her touch was like the feel of effervescing fluid in her mind. She almost fell over again as she felt the sudden tensing of Verren's arm muscles and the surprise in his mind. *Verren's mind?* her own mind whispered, but she pushed it away. There wasn't enough time.

A blue tinged sense of amusement came from Storm, and all of a sudden the nausea vanished and her cats' vision was neatly packaged inside her head, and she could flick from one to the other easily. Almost unaware of what she was doing, she reached blindly behind her with her other hand until she felt Ragar's arm. With a jolt, he and Sparks joined the link. There was a muffled exclamation. "What are you doing?"

"I'm not sure ... but can you reach the others?" Shanna and Verren stopped moving.

"What do you mean? Cally'll skin us alive if we don't get a move on!"

"Cally can't see us, Ragar, and I'm sure we need to do this. It'll help." There was a sense of confirmation from the cats, and she felt Ragar tremble slightly and then Zandany and Punch were there as well, Punch's red tones warm and reliable in her mind. Spinner and Taya slid into the group, radiating heat and a spikiness that meshed in an oddly fitting way, as Amma and Spider frothed coolly into the link. Then Allad and Satin joined, and Satin's touch was unmistakable. Cool, richly green in a way that reminded Shanna of Below, yet strangely tranquil.

The feeling of them all together was exhilarating, and they *were* together in a way they hadn't been since they'd dropped the cliff face on the Garsal. This time though there was no destruction and no need to funnel all that they were into one person. This time they moved as one unit. They all saw as Shanna and her cats did. The fade sheltered them all as they moved, easily evading the obvious traps and moving surely towards each obstacle. Shanna's mind marvelled as she saw the air currents as clearly as Amma, and the warmth that Ragar and Zandany generated when they rolled a fireball ahead of them. She 'felt' Allad's strength as a bastion of security, trusting easily as he lifted them one by one over obstacles that they'd previously had to labour through. Once again she saw Taya disarm the traps set for them, just as she'd disarmed the Garsal globe, but this time, her friends saw and 'felt' and watched with her.

Verren guided them unerringly, his gift of direction now shared, and over all of them, were the colours of their starcats, touches of violet and blue, ruby and emerald. The group moved completely as one, gliding through the vegetation soundlessly. The animal life had stilled to silence, but joined as they were, they were unaware.

***

Above, high on her platform, Cally knew something had happened. The vanishing was not unexpected, but the utter silence that now surrounded them was. She lifted an eyebrow at her old companion, and Mirror's tidemarks glowed and flicked in patterns that signified pleasure. "Well, whatever they're doing, it's not bothering you. Wish I could see it though," she sniffed. "I guess we'd better get a move along ourselves. I think they'll be quicker this time." She limped a few steps, and then her gait smoothed itself into her normal flow.

***

The cadets and Allad completed the course still joined. It was a strange feeling, Shanna thought, oddly detached. Part of her was completely enmeshed in the experience, while another part of her stood aside and watched. That part knew when they'd finished, realised that Cally was probably waiting for them to appear again, and heard the lack of sound around them. She 'felt' rather than heard, Ragar's request for her to drop the fade, and did so slowly and smoothly. She gently pulled her vision back from her cats, and then, slowly, and reluctantly, let the joining go.

She almost collapsed when it was gone, looking around into the slightly startled eyes about her. Amma and Zandany both stumbled as the joining went, and Verren and Ragar both steadied themselves on Shanna, one on either shoulder. Allad slowly dropped his hand from Taya's shoulder, and the dark haired girl let out a deep breath and sat down with a thud on the ground. In her mind, Shanna could 'feel' the smugness of her two cats, and Satin was frankly purring. The sound was almost thundering in its loudness.

Wonderingly, Shanna put a hand on each of her cats. The smugness intensified, and she snickered slightly in reaction. "I think we've figured out what they'd decided to do."

"*That* is an understatement." Allad bent his gaze on Satin. Her purring continued unabated, and she blinked lazily at her partner and intensified the glow of her tidemarks until the glow from them reflected off the undersides of the leaves above.

"And just what *did* they decide to do?" Cally's voice was unmistakably curious. "You were certainly doing something. Something I couldn't see at all, but whatever it was, you nearly halved your previous time. You can explain it back at the habitation. In detail." And then she smiled. "Well done."

# **Chapter 6**

KAIDAN handed the message to the Starlyne at the entrance to the habitat. No matter how often he'd seen and interacted with Starlynes, he never ceased to feel a sense of awe when he had to meet one. Their sheer size was intimidating, let alone the knowledge that they were sentient creatures. This one, Singer of Songs, known more simply as 'Singer,' thanked Kaidan and Anjo gravely with a voice that left the impression of an arpeggio echoing softly in their minds. There was an offer of refreshment, which Anjo refused politely, citing the need to continue with their message delivery, and then they were off again, gliding quietly through the bush. "You navigate this time, Anjo. You need the practice more than I do," said Kaidan.

Anjo gave him a friendly shove on the shoulder. "Yeah, right." He made a face at Kaidan, but pulled out his compass and map anyway. "And this time, no looking over my shoulder. Trust me."

"Trust you? When you're likely to drop us off a cliff, or send us to the wrong end of the plateau?"

"Yes, trust me," replied Anjo. "At some point, I have to get it right."

Kaidan shrugged his shoulders. "All right then, lead on, Anjo!" He called Tempest to his side, and gestured with one hand for Anjo to precede him. The offworlder grinned at him and hand signalled Ember.

"We'll be at The Sentinel before you know it Kaidan. Watch and learn." The two strode off again, Ember leading the way, with the growing Tempest flanking Kaidan, as they began to trek towards what had been Cally's storm shelter – that was, before she'd been tasked somewhere else.

Several hours later, Kaidan snickered quietly to himself as he watched Anjo check his bearings once more. He'd carefully taken three bearings on obvious landmarks, and was resecting his position. He took them again, and then again. Then he looked around, puzzled. Kaidan stood quietly just behind him, trying not to giggle out loud. Finally Anjo dropped his hands to his hips and turned around to look at Kaidan. "All right, there's something you're not telling me, Kaidan. Why is it when I do a resection, it puts me somewhere I know I'm not?"

Kaidan debated with himself briefly, and then allowed a small smile to trickle its way across his face.

"Come on, Kaidan!" Anjo demanded.

"Well, there is a small magnetic anomaly, just about here," Kaidan grinned, "so when you take your bearings …" he trailed off and grinned at Anjo.

Anjo sighed. "You could have told me! How many degrees is it?"

"Um, about thirty?"

"Thirty?"

"Yes, thirty." Kaidan finally allowed himself to laugh. "Sorry."

"You're sorry? I've just wasted twenty minutes trying to figure out where I'd gone wrong, and you knew that the whole time? And I suppose you know exactly where we are?"

"Well, now that you mention it …"

"Sometimes you drive me nuts!" Ember hummed quietly, but he was obviously amused at the interplay between Anjo and Kaidan.

"Want me to show you where we are?"

"No, give me a moment or two to redo these calculations. East or West?"

"West."

A few moments later, Anjo looked around, nodded, and gave a satisfied grunt, then moved off decisively. Ember gave a pleased hum, and at Anjo's hand signal, began to sweep ahead of him. Kaidan smiled again and followed in his wake. The offworlder's skills had come a long way since his first few awkward forays into the vegetation of Frontier. Anjo had proved himself a quick learner, and since beginning his partnership with Ember, he'd become even more dedicated to learning the new way of life he needed to survive on this hostile planet.

The kilometres melted away as the young man and the boy worked their way carefully through the bush towards The Sentinel. They moved mostly in silence. Despite the fact that the plateau was relatively safe compared to Below, there were always surprises, and only a few days previously, the two had almost stumbled into a small family group of weldens. It had taken a fast retreat to get them out of what might have been a real disaster. Despite his relative youth, Ember had headed off the adults while Anjo and Kaidan had made their scrambling escape.

As the sun turned to late afternoon, the ridge near the familiar sight of The Sentinel came into view. "Hope they've got something decent for dinner tonight," said Kaidan as they neared the entrance, "I'm starving!"

"You're always starving, Kaidan."

"Well, I'm growing. Anyway, you're hungry too, I heard your stomach rumbling a minute ago."

"Now that you mention it, I probably am – and I'd really like to get clean," replied Anjo with a smile. "Not far now!" They sped up as the approach came into view, and the two cats mirrored them. The militia guard on duty at the entrance hailed them quietly.

"Manda's in her office, Anjo, Kaidan, and dinner's at the normal time."

"Thanks Dana." The two dropped down the steps and into the entrance of the old shelter.

"Looks like they've made a few improvements, Kaidan," said Anjo, looking around as they passed through the vestibule. New racks lined the walls, holding a variety of bows, arrows and long knives. There were a variety of the powerful lights supplied by the Starlynes, and a few odd looking pieces of equipment placed near the entrance. A rack of the new explosive arrows stood close to the door, each arrow sitting in its individual compartment. Kaidan ran a professional eye over the rack.

"I think I detect Master Dinian's hand." He was itching to pull one of the arrows out and examine it, but restrained himself and followed Anjo into the main part of the storm shelter. There were quite a few people now living at The Sentinel, judging by the number of chairs set around the tables, which was a significant change from when Kaidan had last been there to visit Cally. Another elderly Scout hurried forwards to greet them.

"Boys, welcome! You'll be staying overnight?"

"Yes Manda," replied Anjo, "if that's all right?" He eased his pack off slowly as the old woman beckoned them towards one of the rooms behind the eating area.

"Thanks, Manda. How long to dinner?" Kaidan asked as he dropped his pack on a vacant bunk with a sigh of relief and bent to remove Manda's messages.

The old Scout frowned slightly, "It's roast marmal apparently, so I'd say another half hour or so." She smiled suddenly. "You should have time for a bath if that's what you're asking!"

Kaidan laughed at her expression. "You're right, how did you guess?"

"Well, the two of you look like you've been rolling in the dirt, not walking through it, dear, so I think you'd be wise to get clean. Y'know what Neli in the kitchen's like!" She waggled a brown finger at them. "And when you're done, there'll be a cool drink for you, and some fresh bread to keep the grumbles at bay until dinner." She left the room smiling, her walk still that of the wilderness Scout despite her age. She was missing only a starcat.

"Want a bath Tempest?" asked Kaidan. The young cat hummed eagerly, and he made haste to locate some clean clothing and then headed for the bathing room with Anjo. Tempest bounced and purred as they walked.

Thirty minutes later they were clean, and seated at one of the long tables in the living area. A number of the artificers were arguing over a blueprint, emphatically demonstrating their points with fingertips tapping on the paper diagram. "What we need is a different alloy," Kaidan heard from the far table.

"No, no, we don't. What we really need is a different approach altogether." The discussion grew more technical, and Kaidan shook his head at Anjo and offered him the plate of bread rolls on the table.

"I don't know what they're working on, and right now I don't care," Anjo said as he took a roll for himself and buttered it, sighing contentedly as he bit into it. He chased it down with a swig of the fruit juice in his cup and sat back more comfortably in his chair. Tempest lay at his feet, and Ember was reclining against Anjo's legs, eyes closing as he relaxed into Anjo's scratching hand.

The offworlder finished the bite he'd taken before replying. "No, I don't care right now at all, in fact, just about the only thing I care about is the food I can smell in the kitchen, and my bunk." He made a face at Kaidan. "Ever since I was rescued from the Garsal, all I've seemed to do is walk. Walk to the plateau. Walk through the wilderness. Walk carrying messages. How come you've never developed a riding animal? Or a faster vehicle?"

"What would we ride, Anjo?" snorted Kaidan. "The only things big enough are stauregs, jasaurs and graypods. And perhaps some of the larger weldens. But they'd be spending most of their time trying to eat you while you rode them. Can you really imagine trying to domesticate them?"

"What about horgals?" asked Anjo. "You use them to pull carts."

"We do. But they don't move very fast. And if you've ever tried to sit on one, you'd know why we don't ride them any distance at all. They have a backbone like a knife! Our legs are just as fast, and they're much better at pulling carts when we need to move more than just ourselves. And as for anything mechanical, well, we're probably getting close to that stage, but it takes time, Anjo, and more equipment and people than we have spare, what with the storm season and everything else."

"So the Garsal have really come along at just the wrong moment then?"

"Yes. From what I learned at school, Starfall has some artificers working on stuff like that, but really, as far as technology goes, there are more important things to make first."

The offworlder nodded, looking thoughtful. "I suppose that medical equipment, and weather forecasting stuff might be more practical?"

"Yes, and building materials, sturdy lighting, and strong fencing gear. It's more important to survive than to travel fast."

The conversation became even more lively, as Kaidan and Anjo discussed the relative needs of a colony world versus Anjo's memories of an inner galaxy world. It was an eye opener for both of them.

***

Trooper Hoth turned away from the message he'd just received, deep in thought. Catching one of the humans without giving his position away would be a challenge. He knew they travelled in small groups and pairs quite frequently, but their signals were often distorted and unclear. More importantly he was still without the confirmation that the Overlord desired so much.

Hoth flicked his manipulator arms over the sensor controls, trying to push the electronics beyond their limits. He needed absolute confirmation that the creature proving so elusive to his sensors was their old Enemy. A veteran of many Garsal conquests, Hoth was uncharacteristically unsure how this one might play out. He and his crew had now been hidden for many weeks on the plateau. Moving the vehicle closer to the habitations had been fraught with danger. In the end he'd had to content himself with trying to locate the climber far enough away from any chance of accidental discovery, but still within sensor range. It had proved extraordinarily difficult.

Accustomed to the Garsal method of overwhelming force, technological superiority and immediate conquest, this planet had required him to completely rethink his tactics. Despite the experience he'd gained in conquests that spanned decades in military service he had still not been chosen to breed. This assignment had been his own choice, prompted by the realisation that his last chance of offspring lay in choosing to be a settler on a colony world.

He fiddled with the controls again, and requested his crewman to increase their sensitivity at his own console. There was a confusion of patterns and life signs flickering and merging on the screen. This planet was teeming with life, but something kept interfering with the signal, causing the display to be almost unreadable at times. It had taken them a long time to be able to recognise some of the larger life forms and discount them, while they continued their search for the elusive Starlyne signature.

More signals cluttered the screen, and then, the one thing he'd been looking for separated itself briefly. The crewman's manipulator arms flickered urgently across his controls, tapping, refining and recording.

"You have it?" Hoth queried.

"Yes, finally." The crewman's tone was very flat as he ran the comparison against that first signal.

"Do you have a direction? Can you determine where it came from?"

"I have the general direction. We need one more plot, and then we'll have an approximate position."

"Good." Hoth drummed his manipulator arms against the control panel in satisfaction. His chances of offspring were climbing higher and higher. If he could be part of eliminating this threat once and for all, there would be no doubts about his value as a possible sire. He knew his crewmen harboured similar hopes, but his was the mission, and as the commander, he would either rise or fall on his own merits. It was the Garsal way.

"We will move tonight. Have you deployed the sensor bugs?"

"They will be deployed momentarily," said the trooper, limbs flashing across the board. A small click, and then a whir, and then the plot showed the tagged notations of twenty of the flying sensors spread out in a search pattern and head off on their predetermined paths.

"You have direct camera feed?"

"Of course."

"Have it sent directly to my personal screen as well as the console and the files." A few more clicks.

*****

Anjo and Kaidan marched resolutely towards Watchtower after finalising their message run. Anjo carried packets of messages from The Sentinel, including one bulky one from Manda. Surprisingly, Kaidan was now minus one starcat youngster.

Tempest had flatly refused to leave The Sentinel, firmly parking her rear end on Manda's foot. Apparently the catless older Scout was no longer catless. She'd sent Kaidan on his way with a note for Janna and Aldan, asking about purchase costs. No-one quibbled with a starcat's choice, but it seemed that the human beings involved had less and less say in the matter. Kaidan snickered quietly as he remembered the scene. He was sure that his parents would approve, as Manda was an old friend of both of them. Anyway, Ember was plenty of protection from anything between the Sentinel and Watchtower. There was the better part of a whole day's walk ahead of them, but it was a relatively straightforward navigation task, and Anjo was again navigating. This time he'd queried Kaidan about any anomalies along the way before they left. Kaidan hitched his pack slightly higher and followed Anjo and Ember. He was moving with the grace he'd once envied in his sister and Allad, but he was completely unconscious of it.

***

Hoth's alarms went off with a clamour, and he jerked upright in his chair, attention riveted to the screen at his side. He magnified the screen with a few swipes of his manipulator arms, and watched the image flicker into life at the centre of it. Two humans were paused in a grove of the pungent trees that seemed to abound on this planet. They were accompanied by one of the huge felines that seemed to be everywhere. For the first time, he had clear vision of them. Unlike the perimeter sensors, this was direct image feed, albeit from several hundred metres in the air, and there was no wavering of the signal. He watched, fascinated, as the two sat on a convenient rock and began to eat. They seemed uncaring of the possibility of being attacked by the plant or wildlife that so dangerously surrounded them.

He debated with himself for a few minutes. It wasn't really necessary to hear what they were saying. The Overlord would be pleased enough with the images, and the risk involved in directing the flyer closer, where it might well be detected was too high. They might simply be discussing the day's travel, and nothing more. He watched, fascinated. One of them was very tall – taller than any humans he'd seen on other planets. The other, shorter human, seemed slightly out of place, but was apparently the owner of the red toned feline that prowled around them with deadly grace.

The alarm sounded again, and finally, Hoth saw what he both dreaded and wished for – the image of a living Starlyne. The creature was gliding easily between the trees, oblivious to the flying sensor above it. The patterns on its sides glowed, much as those of the felines did, and unease crept into Hoth's mind on tiny feet. He pushed his concerns aside and turned to the two troopers in the cockpit. "We have the images we require, and there are two humans available close by. We will take the tall one, and leave the short one with the feline. Kill the feline and the short one if necessary, but take the tall one at all costs. We will need to move the vehicle, and at some point we will have to leave it to secure our specimen. I will remain in the climber, ready to leave, as soon as you have captured the specimen."

A few moments later, the climber lurched into movement, leaving its camouflaged, rocky niche. All its systems were functioning well, and Hoth sat back, deftly manipulating the controls as the two troopers armed themselves. The sound of the climber would no doubt alert their quarry, but the climber was fast, much faster than a walking human.

***

Kaidan offered a handful of nuts to Anjo, who took them with thanks. They were halfway to Watchtower, and making good time, so they'd decided to give themselves a good break where there was a small spring to refill their water bottles. Their packs sat leaning up against the rock they were perched on, and both young men had made an enthusiastic lunch. "Want me to fill your bottle Anjo?"

"Thanks." The offworlder unhooked his bottle from his belt and handed it to Kaidan who hopped off the rock and squatted to fill it at the spring. It was a nice little spot, he reflected. He wondered, as always, what Shanna was doing with the Starlynes Below. He hoped she was all right. He wished that Masters Cerren or Peron would be more forthcoming with information. Every time he asked after his sister, the reply was the same. "She's fine, still training with the Starlynes. We'll let you know if things change." He capped Anjo's bottle and propped it on a rock near the spring and then leaned forwards to fill his own.

"Kaidan!" Anjo's voice was urgent, and Kaidan turned to see that Ember had ranged himself in front of his partner, tidemarks flashing in patterns of alarm. He started forwards, just as a crashing sound impinged on his ears. He had barely enough time to take two steps before an alien machine, walking – walking? – on jointed limbs, thrashed into view. Ember snarled and crouched, and Kaidan ran to join Anjo, reaching out frantically for the bow in its case on the back of his pack.

The machine stopped, and two armed Garsal burst from it, moving rapidly. Ember blurred towards them, leaping at the closest one, as a red beam sliced from the second alien towards him. He ducked with starcat reflexes, and the bolt of red light left a sizzling hole in the vegetation that ringed the spring. Anjo was fumbling frantically at his knife as Ember slammed into the leading Garsal trooper, knocking its weapon from its hand, but the second one took aim at the cat with its weapon again.

"Ember!" Anjo's voice was anguished, and Ember leaped off the Garal he'd downed and blurred back towards Anjo. A more experienced cat might have taken down the second Garsal, but Ember was young, and his partner still inexperienced and unsure of a starcat's capabilities in combat. The machine swung in place as Kaidan finally reached his pack, and a small turret popped from its roof. He pulled the bow from its case, just as the first Garsal regained its feet and lurched forwards. The second one again swung its weapon towards Anjo and Ember, and they ducked behind the rock they'd just lunched upon.

Kaidan bent the bow, but as the Garsal trooper loomed closer, was forced to swing its smooth length unstrung at the alien's insectoid legs. It jumped his swing and slammed its weapon into his shoulder, and a gasp of pain erupted from his mouth. His arm felt numb, and hung by his side as he staggered sideways. "Kaidan! Duck!" He didn't let thought spoil his actions, just reacted as fast as possible to Anjo's warning. He wasn't fast enough, and the trooper's weapon slammed into the side of his head and he stumbled, dazed, and hit the ground full length. Vaguely, he was aware of the sizzling sounds of the Garsal weapons. He heard a sudden snarl of pain from Ember, and another cry from Anjo, and then his head was bumping hard across the ground. There was a confusion of metallic noises, and another searing pain, and he knew no more.

∗∗∗

Anjo slumped backwards against the rock. His left leg was a mass of pain, and he was frantic for his starcat. "Ember ..." the sound came out as a croak, and he tried again, "Ember!" There was a sliding sound, and a ragged hum, and Ember limped into view, singe marks marring his sleek hide. His left ear had the tip missing, but he was still in better shape than Anjo felt. The starcat was favouring his right front leg, and there was a long bleeding laceration on his shoulder. Anjo pushed himself upright with one hand, and reached the other towards his starcat, and ran his hand thankfully over the Ember's head.

Ember hummed softly, voice filled with fatigue and pain, and Anjo felt tears prick his eyes. His last image of Kaidan was seared into his memory — the boy's bleeding body being hauled across the ground into the climber by the Garsal troopers. He'd appeared to be unconscious. Pinned behind his rock by the rapidly firing turret of the climber, Anjo had asked Ember to make one last attempt to stop the Garsal leaving, which was when both of them had been injured. They'd sprinted out from behind the rock just in time to see the Garsal drag Kaidan across the remains of his beloved bow. As they'd emerged, the other trooper, now leaking the milky Garsal equivalent of blood, lifted his weapon and fired it shakily towards them.

Anjo was eternally grateful that Ember had damaged the Garsal enough to spoil his aim. The red beam had lanced through a confusion of hurtling bodies, striking a glancing burn to Anjo's leg. Ember was singed, but there were none of the burned holes Anjo remembered so clearly from the invasion of his own planet. He hoped that his own leg was less injured than it felt.

For a moment, he just hugged his cat's head to his chest, but then sense reasserted itself. Kaidan had been taken, and he and Ember were the only ones who knew. "We need to get to where we can sound the alarm, Ember." The words came out as almost a groan as he tried to move his injured leg. The pain was excruciating, and finally, he chanced a look at it.

His trouser leg was blackened and blood covered, and the top of his leather boot was scorched. He tried to wiggle his ankle, and the pain screamed up and down his leg. He stopped with a gasp, as Ember nudged his hand gently. "I'm in trouble, cat." He looked around, wondering where his pack might be. There were two first-aid kits in it – a human one, and a cat kit that Kaidan had given him as a gift. His pack was only a metre away, but that metre could have been ten, and just as impossible to bridge. He levered himself up again, hissing with pain as his foot bumped over the ground. He leaned sideways, trying to reach the pack strap, but the rotation caused a fresh surge of pain to roll its way up his leg and he slumped back, sweating. Ember nudged him again, and then looked quizzically at the pack. He limped over to it, and dragged it to within Anjo's reach, and then nudged his partner gently again.

"Thank you, big boy," said Anjo, blessing the day that Ember had decided he wanted him. Trying to keep his leg as still as possible, he rummaged in the pockets where he'd stored the kits. With a sigh of relief, he pulled the cat kit out and hand signalled Ember to lie beside him. The starcat hummed thankfully as Anjo slathered the antiseptic numbing cream over the laceration and singed areas of his coat. His tidemarks had darkened with pain, and now brightened slightly as his injuries were soothed. Anjo looked over the injured leg, but it was beyond his skills. A large swelling marred the normally sleek limb, and it was acutely sensitive when he probed it with his fingertips.

Finally, he turned to his own wounds. Apart from the leg, he could feel a number of bruises making themselves known, and his left arm had stinging grazes down the outside of it. Gingerly, he pulled at the blackened trouser leg. Some of the bloodied material stuck, and a shiver of pain made its way across the outside of his leg and spiralled down it. Anjo sucked in a breath and pulled the fabric more firmly to expose the scorched, bloody flesh. The beam weapon had glanced down the outside of his leg, burning into the tissue and then slicing into his boot. Fortunately the boot had protected the thin skin around his ankle and foot, but the side of it was a blackened ruin.

He attempted to move his foot again. Pulling his toes up hurt, but was doable. Pushing them down, the same, but any attempt at sideways movement caused intense pain. Anjo sat back trembling, and took several deep breaths, and then resolutely pulled supplies from his first-aid kit. He poked through the medications and tins of cream. He needed something to dull the pain before he could cover the wound and attempt to stand on it. He hesitated over the small tub of blue tinged salve. Master Peron had given it to him when he and Kaidan had begun their job as messengers. He'd cautioned both of them to use it only in a dire emergency, and then sparingly. Decisively he pulled off the lid and used the enclosed spatula to scoop a small portion of the salve onto his leg, and then gritted his teeth and spread it out over the seared flesh.

The pain was unbelievable, and Anjo shook with its intensity and then, suddenly, it began to subside, finally ebbing to a dull background throb. He sighed with relief and began to wrap one of the bandages from his kit around it, firming it up to try and reduce the bleeding. He rested back against the rock, exhausted, when he was finished, and Ember laid his head in his lap with a small sigh. After a few minutes rest, Anjo gathered himself together enough to try and stand. He dragged himself up the rock, not willing to weight bear on his injured leg lest he fall. He steadied himself for a moment, panting, and hesitantly placed his foot on the ground. And then nearly fell as the pain reasserted itself searingly. He made himself stay there, slowly increasing his weight on the injured leg until the pain slowly backed off to a pounding, burning throb. Supporting himself on the rock, he attempted to move, and found that he could manage a pained hobble if he leaned himself on the rock. Ember hummed encouragingly at him and limped over so that Anjo could lay a hand on his back if required. The limping cat nearly broke his heart.

Obviously he couldn't take the rock with him, so he cast around for a good looking stick, and realised that more time had passed than he'd realised. He wondered where Kaidan was, and how he was, and if he was even still alive. He *must* be alive, Anjo reasoned, the Garsal had no use for corpses. He fumbled at his thigh pocket for his map and spread it out on the rock, hands trembling. At least he knew where he was. He pulled his compass from the neck of his shirt and plotted the shortest route he could find to the nearest settlement. It was a Starlyne habitation, about an hour's walk at normal pace. Normal pace. He grimaced. He'd be lucky to be able to hobble the distance before night fell, and the idea of roaming the plateau alone, at night, sent shivers up his spine.

He looked at his pack, lying on the ground near his feet, and tried to decide if he wanted to pick it up and attempt to carry it. Regretfully he decided he'd have to abandon both packs, so he bent and heaved his pack upright, trying not to jolt his leg with the movement and began to pull out the most basic necessities. The packet of messages went into one of his left thigh pockets, and both first-aid kits were tucked away in the right hand ones. His firemaking kit went into the back one, and then he tucked as much dried fruit into his other pockets as possible. Dry mouthed, he reached for his water bottle, only to realise that it was sitting by the spring, several metres away.

He couldn't leave without it, so he decided that it would be his first objective. He tried a hesitant step away from the rock and nearly fell but for Ember's sudden weight propping up his failing leg. Desperately he cast around for something to use as a walking stick. A small sturdy branch lay on the ground near his water bottle, so screwing up his courage he leaned guiltily on Ember, and made a slow painful progress to the spring. He was shaking again by the time he got there and had to prop himself up on the rocks around it. A few moments later he was sipping cool water from his bottle. He drank his fill, refilled it and then put it back on his belt and picked up the stick.

Leaning heavily on the stick, he sent Ember ahead with a silent apology, took one last bearing, cast a hasty eye at the sun and hobbled slowly off. Ember ranged ahead, still limping, but Anjo knew that the starcat's superior senses were their best chance of making it to the Starlyne habitation safely so that he could raise the alarm.

# Chapter 7

SHANNA woke and stretched luxuriously. For some reason she felt more rested from the night's sleep than she had for some time. It hadn't been that she'd been sleeping poorly exactly, but since the Garsal invasion, there had always been a small level of stress murmuring away in the background. For a moment she couldn't figure out why this morning should be any different; then she remembered. They'd finally repeated the joining they'd experienced when they dropped the cliff face on the Garsal. She stretched again, and reached out a hand as a sleepy chirp sounded from the cat resting its head on her belly.

"Morning boys," she whispered. A head nudged her hand, and she scratched the offered cheek, knowing with the new sense she seemed to have developed, that it was Twister. Another head pushed the first one aside, and Storm leaned in for his share of the rub. Resignedly, she pushed herself upright and extended two hands so that the pushing match wouldn't erupt into a full blown brawl on the bed that might awaken her sleeping friends. A drowsy eye from Spider regarded her as she wriggled a bit more and then put her feet on the floor. If she hurried, she might be able to score the bathing room alone.

Half an hour later, she was breakfasting quietly by herself, sitting on the top of the hill above the Starlyne habitation. It was still cool, and the sun was not quite up, and Shanna and the two cats sat quietly for a time, just enjoying the early light. There was a rustle further down the slope, and as Twister hummed a query, she flicked a fingertip in assent, and the violet toned cat vanished in a blur of speed. Both her cats enjoyed hunting for themselves. Shanna inhaled the aroma from the warm fruit bun in her own hand with pleasure. She'd enjoyed the fresh food, cooked by someone who could actually cook for the last few weeks. Although she did wonder whether bread was something that the Starlynes ate themselves, or had just decided to provide for their human guests. Not that most of the Scouts weren't reasonably competent with the available resources, but everyone took turns at all of the duties while on the march, which meant she'd eaten more of Verren's meals than anyone should have to. She smiled at the thought. They were now edible, just, but he still had a tendency to 'improve' on recipes when he thought no-one was looking.

He was a good friend, though, and finally seemed to have recovered from discovering his ability to hear sliders. She shuddered slightly at the thought.

She'd noticed them too, but not like Verren had. He was one of the most compassionate human beings she'd ever met, and for a while, she'd been concerned that the encounter with the sliders had affected him more deeply than he'd admitted.

Shanna smiled again, as she thought of him the previous night, face flushed from the excitement of repeating their bonding. The evening had left a warm glow, even though Cally had worked them hard as they tried to figure out precisely what they'd managed the previous day. She'd had them experiment in her office, but it didn't seem to work the same way it had when they were on the obstacle course.

They had been able to establish that they could support each other in pairs or small groups quite easily, but actually 'joining' like they had, eluded them. Still, Shanna mused, it was a beginning, and it was quite obvious that the cooperation of their starcats was essential. For whatever reason, when she'd encouraged her two to help they'd suddenly become 'just cats' again. They'd felt amused, she decided as she pondered and turned to look at Storm, waiting patiently for his brother to return with breakfast, the picture of purring innocence.

A soft breeze wafted across her face, and she turned to look into the wind. It came from the north-west, and as Shanna felt the mildness of it, and the promise of dampness, she realised that the storm season was almost upon them again. That meant it was now over a year since she'd joined the Scout Corps. A year in which so much had happened, but which now meant that she and the others were probably officially in their second year of cadetship. Normally there would have been a graduation ceremony for the third years, and she felt regret that the six third years, who were now full Scouts, probably hadn't experienced their ceremony. There was little time for such things nowadays. Even the new second and third years would normally have had a brief moment with their mentors to mark the move into the next year. She wondered how they were sourcing new cadets to replace the graduating students, with so many people displaced. She pushed the thoughts from her mind. No doubt the Masters had already figured it all out, and given the things she'd learned in the last year, it was likely that they already knew who the new cadets might be.

The wind strengthened slightly, and she reorganised her vision to view the air currents. It was much easier now, and she allowed it to heighten her weather sense. There was nothing big as far as she could tell, but there was a certain 'feeling' that suggested to her that the storm season might be closer than she'd originally thought. She made a mental note to discuss it with Amma. Storm and Twister looked up from the remains of the marmal Twister had brought back, and both licked their lips lazily. "Time to head in boys. Have you finished?" Storm flicked his tidemarks at her, and dragged what was left towards a patch of carnivorous plants, and the three of them left the hilltop.

Inside the habitat, the others were helping themselves to breakfast. Shanna filled her mug again and took a seat on the cushions next to Amma. "Amma, what do you know about this year's storm season?" Amma looked at her in surprise, and Shanna continued. "I had an odd feeling this morning when I was watching the air currents. I know I sound a little vague, and I don't think there's a storm coming now, or anything, but when I looked, and listened to my weather sense, it felt … odd."

"I haven't really looked, I suppose," said Amma. "It's hard to describe, but I usually only *know* about individual weather events, and even then, I just 'know.' Tell me what you did, and I'll see whether I can replicate it." Shanna described what she'd done, the curly haired girl nodding in understanding. "In that case, I think I need to be outside." She pushed to her feet and held out a hand to Shanna. "Coming?"

Telling Spiron where they were going, the two girls returned to the hilltop overlooking the valley, and perched themselves on the granite rocks at the top. They sat in silence as Shanna waited for Amma to tell her what she thought. Finally the dark haired girl started, blinked her eyes a couple of times, and then turned to Shanna in surprise.

"OK, I think I just did the same thing you did. That felt *really* weird for a moment there! You're right about nothing in the immediate future, but I'd guess, no, I think I can say I *know* that this season's likely to be pretty violent, with more frequent cyclones than the last few years. I can't tell precisely when they'll start, but I think it'll be early."

She stared off into space for a while and then spoke again. "I think it has something to do with being able to see the air currents and differentiate what's going on with the moisture levels." She frowned. "And maybe something to do with temperature? But temperature of what?" She shook her head in frustration. "Sometimes I wish I knew more about climate and how storms actually start. Maybe I'll have to chat to Mum and Dad, or one of the Starlynes perhaps, to understand it more clearly."

"All I could tell was that it didn't feel right," said Shanna. "Maybe you should have another go."

"Let's try together, and perhaps it'll give me a bit of a boost. And Cally will be happy that we've practiced!"

Again, Shanna 'saw' the air currents with the clarity that only Amma could, but there was an added dimension, or perhaps an added range. Like her experience with Taya, the clarity and complexity of Amma's enhanced sight was astounding. Her mind worked in ways that left Shanna almost breathless. She was the passive observer, watching a master at work as Amma's mind soared and sorted. There were complex emotions overlying it all, exhilaration, excitement and joy, all mixed with foreboding. She had a sense of not just a storm system building, but the storm season, and then it was there inside her head, a complete, detailed, long range forecast. Not completely accurate, Shanna reminded herself, but certainly an indication of length, and the factors that might combine to set a cyclone building.

Abruptly Shanna was back inside her own head, and was looking into Amma's startled eyes. "That was amazing," said Amma. "It's like my range expanded or something, or everything enhanced, maybe." She wrinkled her brow in thought for a few moments. "I think you boost me," she said, "although I'm not sure how. Shall we tell the others?" She jumped off her rock and whistled for Spider, and the two girls headed back towards the habitat.

They descended rapidly, starcats beside them, chatting idly about the exercise the day before, when a silent alarm sounded. They both staggered as a flood of Starlyne emotions assaulted them. There was such an urgency in the emotion, and such a vigorous call, that both girls broke into a run, hurtling down the hill and straight into the habitation. They burst into their living quarters, driven by the intensity of the summons, to find Fractus coiled in a corner of the room, with the others grouped around him. The Starlyne turned his head unerringly towards Shanna as she entered, and the alarm cut off abruptly.

"Shanna." There was a feeling of suppressed emotion in the silent sound of her name, and Shanna stopped in her tracks, feeling the blood drain from her face as Fractus sent a series of images. There was Anjo, face bloodied and limping heavily, collapsing over the threshold of a Starlyne habitation, supported by his injured starcat. From Anjo's mind, she was sure, came a scrambled blurry image of her brother. He was falling, landing heavily on the ground, struck by a Garsal weapon butt. The next image was of Kaidan's body being dragged into one of the climbing vehicles. Kaidan's head bumped across the ground before the images decayed into a morass of emotion – Anjo's Shanna thought dimly – fear, pain and despair. Then the images ceased, and Shanna stood numbly, almost disbelieving the import of what she'd seen. Very faintly around her, she could feel hands on her arms, and people urging her to sit down.

There were kind hands leading her to a cushion, and the soft heads of her cats nudging her gently. Then the fog cleared, and the hands on her shoulders belonged to Amma and Taya, and Verren was crouched in front of her, peering intently into her eyes. "I'm so sorry, Shan."

She fumbled for something to say, words crashing and staggering around her mind, but all she could come up with was, "How?" There was silence, and then Fractus' voice came clearly.

"We don't know for certain, but it appears that the Garsal deliberately set out to take him. Anjo's memories clearly show they targeted Kaidan, while merely pinning Anjo and Ember down. They were lucky to escape alive."

The Starlyne's voice was sorrowful and Shanna could feel the depths of his emotion. She struggled to speak, struggled to arrange her thoughts into a coherent pattern. "Do Mum and Dad know?" she forced out.

"They are being told at this very moment," came Fractus' voice. "And the Council knows. Master Cerren meets with them now." He sat very still amidst his coiled length, and Shanna could feel the care and compassion emanating from him. "The question is why, rather than how. There's a Patrol and several of our people moving to the site right now, and they'll back-track the vehicle. It seems obvious that they've been on the plateau for some time, possibly monitoring and searching. There's no doubt they know about us now, and we are more grateful than ever that you managed to disable the communications systems on that ship. But why take one of your people – now?"

Shanna finally managed to bring her thoughts together. In the back of her mind, the rational part kept stacking the facts together in neat ranks, but at the forefront was a maelstrom of emotions, and that part of her spoke without thought. "We have to save him! What if he's already dead?" The words burst from her, and to her horror she dissolved into tears. The hands on her shoulders tightened, and her cats leaned firmly against her, and then two hands took hers, and through her tears she saw Verren's face looking earnestly at her.

"They wouldn't have taken him if he was dead, Shan. He's alive, I'm sure."

"Your thoughts are also ours, Verren." Fractus voice cut through her emotion.

"I suspect we're not what they expected," said Spiron, and through a blur of tears, Shanna could see that the Patrol First was pacing as he talked. "My guess, on the limited information available, is that they wish to find out what it is that makes us different. For that, they need a live captive, not simply a deceased one." His voice was sorrowful, and in that moment, Shanna realised that it was very likely that Challon's body had not been buried by the Garsal, but rather taken and examined. Much as they'd examined the Garsal pilot's body so many months ago. She shuddered slightly at the thought, and it heightened her need to be out there, looking for Kaidan.

"Fractus, what do the Garsal know about your biological expertise?" Spiron was once again the Patrol First, calm, in control. There was silence, and Shanna hurriedly scrubbed at her face with one hand. Verren retained the other, the firm pressure of his hand allowing her to slowly regain control. There was a sense of waiting in the air.

"They know some of what we could do so long ago, but there are things we have developed here, on Sanctuary, that they will not know. They may suspect that we have modified you, and that this planet may have changed you, but they will not know precisely what you are capable of. I am sure that they have images of you all though, from both the communications centre, and also your exit from the ship." For the first time, Shanna felt uncertainty from the Starlyne. "We are also certain that they will be actively seeking us now. They will know that we have allied with you. We can expect their activities to escalate." The room was full of foreboding, and even Shanna's urgent desire to hurtle after the Garsal kidnappers was overshadowed by the wider implications.

"Then we must plan," said Spiron. He turned and looked at Shanna, compassion evident in his eyes, but also resolution. "We cannot hare off into Below without a plan, Shanna. I need to know that you can stay, taking my orders, knowing that your brother has been taken? Can you do this? Can you remain a useful part of this Patrol?"

His eyes were intent, boring into Shanna, and for the first time, she realised that she might not be able to ride to the rescue of her brother. The hands on her shoulders tightened, as her imagination ran riot. Thoughts of torture, pain and of her brother's fear shook her to her core as she imagined herself standing idly by – allowing it! Her mind shouted at her and she wanted to scream back at Spiron. To shout *'No I can't!'* at the top of her lungs, and then to leave the habitat and pursue the Garsal for as long as it took to retrieve Kaidan. Her muscles contracted, as if she was about to jump up and do so, but then the rational part of her mind shoved the emotion back.

Dispassionately, the cool intellect that had been watching at the back of her brain reviewed the facts it had assembled, and with sudden deflation, she knew that haring off Below alone would not help anyone – especially Kaidan. That his best chance lay in planned response. *But what if the planned response doesn't include him?* said a small voice inside her. *But how would I know where he is, or even how he is?* replied the coherent part of her. *But it just has to!* Her mind quivered and threatened to dissolve into a swamp of emotion, and then the rational part took over again. *His best chance lies with planning. With whatever Spiron and Cerren have in mind, and whatever our Starlyne allies can do. You running off alone will do nothing. And you are not the only one to suffer loss – remember that!* Images of Taya's face swam into focus in her mind and her resolve strengthened.

Shanna raised her head and looked directly at the Patrol First, green eyes now dry of tears. "I will do my best, Spiron. I am not the first to lose a family member to the Garsal, and I will not be the last, but at least it's likely that he's alive." Verren's hand tightened on hers, and she remembered that *his* brother was gone.

"In turn, I give you my word that we will do our best to rescue him Shanna, should the opportunity arise." Spiron's tones were measured. "But I can give you no assurances that it *will* arise." His eyes searched hers. "You are necessary to the defence of our people. Integral to it perhaps, so I will ask you clearly, one more time. In fact, I will ask this of all of you." He looked around at the assembled Scouts. "Can you set aside your family ties? Can you focus yourself only on what we do, knowing that if we fail it is likely that our world will fall to the Garsal?"

Despite all of their earlier pledges, the import of Spiron's words fell heavily into the room, and Shanna looked around at her friends and their cats. There was an intensity to every face that she'd never seen before, and sadness. The implications of her pledge were very clear. She might very well never see her brother again, or her parents, or Boots, Sabre and Moshi. She swallowed her grief deliberately and then allowed the anger at the Garsal to firm her voice.

"I can. At least, at this moment, I think I can." Her throat closed up then, and she was unable to speak clearly any more, and once again, she felt the tears of grief well up in her eyes and spill from her bottom lids. They were hot, and her heart was breaking, but there was really no choice. No choice at all.

There was a murmur of sadness and agreement from around the room. Without looking, Shanna knew, in a way that seemed reminiscent of her contact with the Starlynes, that those there were re-pledging themselves to do what needed to be done, despite the personal cost.

"In that case," said Spiron, "we will put our affairs in order, write letters to our loved ones, and then we will do what is required of us." It was a very final statement. Shanna felt the hands on her shoulders squeeze briefly and Verren's nearly crushed the one he was holding. Then her cats sent a wash of love through her that was so intense that it brought the tears pouring from her eyes again, cascading unheeded down her face.

Spiron turned to Fractus. "We will meet with you again in two hours. Can you arrange to communicate directly with Master Cerren?"

"Yes, we will arrange it," replied Fractus, "We will be in the command centre when you are ready. Your dedication is more than we could ever have asked. As you have, we will also pledge to do everything required to rid this world of the invaders." He uncoiled himself silently, and glided from the room. As he exited, Shanna felt him brush her thoughts gently. As he did she remembered that he had already lost his own mate, not to the Garsal, but to her own people, and yet he still loved, and still hoped. Faintly, as if in the distance, Shanna heard Amma's voice.

"Spiron, the storm season …" She should probably go and help her friend explain, but thoughts of Kaidan began to intrude on her mind. She hoped desperately that he was still alive, and wished she could communicate as the Starlynes could. Perhaps then she could have reached across the kilometres separating them to reassure him, or tell him how much she loved him, despite all of their good natured ribbing.

"Shan?" Verren's voice was insistent and she dropped out of her reverie, and used her free hand to dry her eyes, realising that the room had emptied while she was thinking.

"Yes?"

"Are you OK?"

"No," she replied. "But I don't think any of us are, really."

"No, we're not," he responded. "I can't believe that I'll never see Jamber again, and I can't imagine what you're feeling now."

"*I* don't know what I'm feeling now. Except that it feels like I've abandoned Kaidan."

"You haven't abandoned him." Verren's tone was firm. "We don't have any idea where he is, but we do know where he'll end up."

"We do?"

"The ship."

"The ship." There was another moment when Shanna thought her heart might stop beating, and she remembered the slaves sequestered in its depths, and the bracelets worn by Anjo and Semba, and almost despaired again. "No!"

"Shan, think about it!"

"Think about what?"

"*I* think that we'll be back there at some point. I can't imagine that the Council or the Starlynes will sit idly by while other sentient beings are incarcerated in that ship and mistreated as slaves. If it's not us, then I'm sure that someone will be tasked to attempt a rescue."

A spark of hope lit Shanna as she pondered Verren's words. Whether he was just trying to make her feel better, it did make sense, and she allowed the spark to grow, before tucking it away to keep her warm. It was as if a small portion of Kaidan was back with her again, a little like one of his all encompassing blushes.

"Thank you Verren." She impulsively hugged her fellow cadet. He always seemed to be there when she was at her lowest. She was beginning to wonder if he liked being cried on. His arms tightened around her and for the first time in months, she felt comforted. She allowed herself to rest like that for several minutes, dimly noticing that he had tucked her in under his chin before gently disentangling herself, feeling slightly awkward again. She remembered the last time he'd hugged her like this. Well, perhaps not *quite* like this, because they'd been sitting, she corrected herself, and then wondered why her mind was running away with itself in such a stupid fashion.

She looked up at Verren, green eyes looking directly into his bright blue ones, and felt even more confused at the expression in them. There was his normal compassion, his normal friendship, and … something else. Something that made her take a small step backwards and look down again, blushing slightly. The rational part of her mind yammered at her. This was already a day of too much emotion and she almost panicked, and then, yet again, Verren saved her. Saved her from saying or doing something stupid.

"We'd better go and write our notes and 'put our affairs in order'. Not that we've really got anything to put in order – or at least *I* haven't," he said with a wry smile. Despite the smile, there was still something in his eyes, but the intensity of the moment had turned to something else.

"No, nothing for me either," Shanna managed, and then attempted a small smile in return. It was wobbly and uncertain, and she almost burst into tears again, but she kept the sides of her mouth wide while her chest ached, and eventually the smile became genuine, if slightly sad. "Just letters to write. And then plans to make."

They turned and headed together for the cadet room, and Shanna noticed that Verren was walking just slightly closer than normal. She tried to avoid whacking him with her arms which were suddenly much longer and more flappy than they had been, but she almost cannoned off the door frame and into him as they entered the room. Excusing herself with a degree of embarrassment, she walked to her bed and turned her attention to searching through her pack for her writing things. She kept her eyes firmly on her belongings, and tried not to sneak looks at Verren. Consequently, she failed to see the slight smirk Amma and Taya exchanged, or the small poke that Ragar gave Zandany. She did notice Storm and Twister flick their tidemarks at Cirrus. She flicked hers back. It was a pattern she didn't recognise.

And then she was sitting, staring at the blank paper in front of her, wondering how she would say everything she needed to say. Wondering how she could possibly justify her actions to her parents. She clung to the hope of returning to the ship with a rescue mission and wrote the first words.

# Chapter 8

KAIDAN groaned. Everything hurt, and his head was pounding. He tried to lift it, and a wave of nausea struck him and he fell back. The surface he was lying on was hard and unyielding, and his body protested loudly, jammed as it was into a small space. He groaned again, completely disoriented. The hard surface underneath him seemed to be in motion. It escalated his nausea, and he dry retched, which made the headache sharpen almost unbearably. For some time, all he could do was to lie as still as possible, bracing himself on the sides of the space against the lurching and rolling of the floor.

Bit by bit, memory returned, and as he attempted to move his left arm, pain sliced into him again and he remembered what had happened. Cautiously, against the pounding in his head, he opened and closed his hands. They worked, as did his elbows, although he could feel the sting of grazes on his knuckles and his left shoulder seemed to be stuck. The right one moved, but every time he tried to move the left one, the pain returned, and he finally lay still and began to explore his lower limbs. Both legs seemed bruised, and one ankle was uncomfortably swollen, but they were both functional. There were bruises everywhere on his body though, and dried blood seemed to have caked itself down the side of his head. He wondered dazedly if his shoulder was dislocated. It seemed likely, and he had no idea how to fix it if it was.

Slowly the pounding and dizziness subsided and he began to explore the space he was in. It was dark, and the movement seemed to be more rhythmic than it had been. He felt around with his good arm and both feet. There was space above him, but the space around him was barely longer than his body and just wide enough for him to fit into it. As he sat cautiously, his throbbing head brushed something hanging above him. He jerked reflexively back and had to wait for the pain in his head to subside slightly before he ventured upwards again, carefully cradling his injured arm. Whatever it was seemed like some kind of fabric. He felt around, but was none the wiser, and finally propped himself up against the cold metal wall behind him. The coolness was soothing to his bruises, and seemed to give some support to his injured shoulder. In front of him, he could faintly see a small crack of light. He pushed tentatively at it with his feet, but it didn't budge, and so he pushed harder. Still nothing. His shoulder began to throb in time with the headache, so he rested his head back against the coolness of the metal and tried to calm the thudding so that he could think.

Finally he drifted off again, and when he awoke, the headache had dulled to a background murmur, and he finally had enough brain space to think. He came to the conclusion that he was inside the Garsal vehicle. For some reason he was still alive, and he hated to think what that reason might be. His time tutoring Anjo had given him more knowledge about the Garsal than most, and Anjo had talked about his time as a slave quite frankly. He tried to still a shudder of fear, and put his mind to trying to escape. The first step would be to escape this box, which on reflection was likely to be some kind of cupboard.

He sat quietly, thinking. Until he had some idea of what the vehicle was like, or how he might get out, or even where he was, there was no point planning anything. All he knew was that if an opportunity presented itself, he needed to take it. Although with a dislocated shoulder he wasn't certain he'd be able to escape, or in fact do anything at all – every time he tried to move, he was almost incapacitated by the pain.

It seemed like hours he'd sat there before the vehicle finally stopped moving. For a while he just sat, panting, trying to gather enough will to stand. He was just gathering the scattered threads of his courage when there was a small noise from the crack and it widened abruptly, silhouetting a dark Garsal form against the light. The creature gestured, and barked a command which was recognisable, though strongly accented. Kaidan stayed where he was, fearful of what might happen next, and terrified of what the creatures might do to him.

Without warning, the creature stepped forwards, grabbed Kaidan by the left arm and dragged him out of the box. The pain was sickening, and Kaidan nearly passed out. A sudden crunching sensation sent the pain skyrocketing, and then his shoulder popped back in, and he dropped face down onto the floor with a scream. He gasped with relief, but it was short lived, as a booted Garsal foot slammed into his side, igniting the bruises and rolling him onto his back.

"Up!"

Kaidan coughed and pushed himself half upright with his right hand, unwilling to trust the still faintly throbbing left arm and eased himself to his knees.

"Up!" The foot prodded him again, and with a groan, Kaidan pushed himself to his feet, desperately trying to balance against the spinning in his head. "What do you want with me?"

"You will answer all questions immediately, and do precisely as you are told."

"Where are you taking me?"

The Garsal soldier spun Kaidan about and shoved him towards a narrow doorway. The touch of the chill chitin of the creature's appendage sent goosebumps drifting across Kaidan's skin, but he judged that resisting while inside the vehicle was futile. He just had to hope that somehow the situation would change and he would be able to escape. As he limped through the door, and saw the windows he realised that it was already night, and that the illumination was completely artificial. Two other Garsal reclined in the seating around what appeared to be a small living area flanked by covered pods. He wondered if that was what the Garsal slept in. He couldn't imagine what else they were for. He staggered to a halt as one of the creatures lifted an appendage.

Its faceted eyes were inscrutable as it looked Kaidan up and down. He tried not to tremble, or faint from the pain in his head. He felt dizzy, and very tired. "You are fortunate. The Overlord wishes a specimen for examination, so you will be fed and watered." He motioned to his companion. The other Garsal produced a pair of orange bands, and with a quick movement locked them around Kaidan's ankles. The boy's heart sank — he remembered what Anjo had said about the bands. He knew how his sister and Allad had removed them, but he'd never seen a flotter, and he had no idea if he was on the plateau or Below. "These will allow us to locate you, no matter where you are, so any attempt to run will result only in your apprehension." The Garsal motioned to a bowl of something mushy. "You will eat now. We will resume travelling in the morning. You will attend me as we travel and indicate dangerous plants and animals."

Kaidan took the bowl. Whatever the food was, it had minimal taste, but it was food and he needed to make sure he was prepared for any eventuality should the opportunity arise. His stomach was still unsettled, but he forced himself to begin to eat, scooping it out of the bowl with his fingertips. He was kept standing to eat, and when he'd finished, he was shoved back into the dark closet. Alone and frightened, he lay on his back in the dark, cradling his arm, hoping against hope that Anjo and Ember had survived, and someone knew that the Garsal had taken him.

If no-one knew he'd been taken, then there would be no rescue, and he would most likely live a slave of the Garsal until he died. Exhausted, his head and shoulder throbbing, he finally admitted to himself that the dampness on his cheeks was tears, and not perspiration. It was a long time until he finally slept.

***

Hoth lounged in his command chair and completed his meal. The living quarters of the climber were quite cramped, and he enjoyed the solitude of the command area when he was on his watch. He pondered on the human they'd taken. He was very young, as far as Hoth could tell. Nearly all humans looked the same to him. There were minor differences in skin and eye colour, but they all had the same appendage arrangements, and the strangeness of a creature with only four limbs had never left him.

He tapped the screen in front of him, replaying the image of the Starlyne. Their old Enemy was legendary, not only because of their size, but because of their tenacity. Only the Garsal's overwhelming numbers had allowed them to prevail. The sight of the glowing creature unsettled him, but he tapped again, and began to compose an update on the human captive for the Overlord.

*** 

Anjo woke with Ember draped across him. The black cat's red tidemarks were still dimmed with sleep, but he opened one eye a crack to observe his partner. Seeing Anjo awake Ember rolled slightly so that his front paws were waving kitten-like in the air, and his belly was exposed. Anjo extended a hand and rubbed his cat's belly, and Ember's purr rumbled through his body.

He wriggled slightly to move out from under the cat, and realised that his leg was no longer screaming at him. "Move over Ember." He pushed the starcat gently, and Ember rolled over slightly so that Anjo could move. He looked around at the smooth walls of a Starlyne habitat curving next to him, and he remembered. Remembered that Kaidan had been taken by the Garsal. Remembered that he'd have to explain it to Janna and Adlan. And hoped desperately that Kaidan was still alive. His last memory was of falling over the habitation's threshold, utterly spent, unable to do more than blurt out the sentences he'd memorised as he and Ember had made their slow, painful way from the ambush site.

Hastily he rolled back to his starcat and looked him over. The swelling and lacerations were gone from the sleek hide, but one ear tip was missing still, although the skin looked well healed. Relieved, he checked his own leg. It was covered in some kind of spongy dressing, but all of his other injuries appeared to have healed. The noise of his stirring must have alerted someone, because the door opened and a Starlyne glided in, accompanied, to his horror, by Kaidan's parents. Their cats followed them in, and then they were at his bedside, and all he could do was stammer. "I'm sorry, I couldn't stop them!" Tears of shame slid down his cheeks, as he struggled to a sitting position, and he dropped his face into his hands.

An arm slid its way around his shoulders, and to his surprise, Janna's voice came, rough with emotion. "We know you did everything you could, Anjo. Singer here has told us of your injuries, and that you arrived after travelling by yourself at night, worried only about Kaidan." Her voice broke, and Anjo looked up to see her red-rimmed eyes mirroring his own grief. "Master Cerren broke the news to us himself. A Scout Patrol has found the ambush site, and are following the tracks of the vehicle, but it looks as if it may have already left the plateau." Adlan put an arm around his wife's shoulders as she dissolved into tears again.

"Will they follow them?" Anjo asked.

"We don't know," Adlan replied. "We would go, we have starcats aplenty, but we've never been Below, and we don't have the skills to survive there.

The Scout Corps is stretched very thin already ..." He broke off abruptly, and sat heavily in a chair to Anjo's left, pulling Janna down with him. "We hope that Shanna's group might be sent after them if they can locate them, but," he shook his head slowly, "at this stage we don't even know where to begin looking."

"Yes we do!" replied Janna. "They'll be taking him to their ship – nothing else makes sense."

"It does seem most likely, but we can't send the whole of our planet's defences after just one person," said Adlan patiently. He didn't look happy, Anjo thought, just resigned and exhausted. "We've talked about this, Janna. You understand Master Cerren's reasoning."

"I understand his reasoning, but it isn't *his* son!" replied Janna hotly. "If I could, I'd be off Below with every cat we own, hunting them down!"

"And I'd be with you, but the fact is, we can't."

"Surely someone will go after them?" asked Anjo.

"Anjo, we're at the limit of our resources already, just trying to protect the plateau," replied Adlan. His eyes were desolate, and he had the look of a man who'd already argued the point with himself. "Kaidan's our son, and we love him desperately, but we can't risk the lives of everyone else by chasing after him." Adlan's voice trembled on the last word, and Anjo's heart almost broke. He didn't think he could have coped, had he been the one sacrificing his own child for the greater good.

"I could go," he said, steeling himself. "I've been Below."

Adlan placed a hand on Anjo's shoulder, eyes glittering with unshed tears, and shook his head. "And you're not equipped to survive Below either, although I thank you for the offer."

The Starlyne, Singer, silent up until then, glided closer. "Our fellows Below are on watch for the Garsal. They will tell us if they locate the vehicle. For now, I must remove the dressing on your leg, and then you are to leave with Adlan and Janna. There is a horgal cart outside to take you." Singer removed the dressing with delicate hands, and despite his surprise at the Starlyne's last statement, Anjo leaned forwards with some trepidation to look at his leg.

Where the blackened skin had been, was now a red and shiny scar. He moved his ankle experimentally. It felt tight and the skin pulled firmly against the movement.

"You will need to stretch the new skin and exercise the ankle before you are able to return to your duties," Singer said. "Adlan and Janna have offered their house to you for this time."

Anjo looked silently at Kaidan's parents, overcome with gratitude, and astounded at their generosity. Janna spoke slowly. "You're Kaidan's friend. He would not have wished for you to be alone, among strangers, at a time like this."

"Thank you." The words were almost impossible to articulate.

"Then we'll be on our way," said Adlan. "You'll keep us informed, Singer?" His voice was an entreaty full of emotion.

"We will."

***

Kaidan groaned as he rolled over on the hard flooring beneath him. His bruises seemed no better, and his shoulder continued to throb, despite its relocation. He'd tried moving it gently, and it was stiff and very painful. He'd finally learned to wedge himself into a corner of the closet when the vehicle was under way. It was much less painful like that. He thought it was probably now three or four days since his capture. He was allowed to stand and move out of the closet several times a day, for eating, and using the in vehicle waste facilities. Each time, he'd been closely guarded. He'd attempted to look around to try and gauge whether there was an easy escape route, but his captors insisted that he keep his eyes down. Several heavy blows had reinforced the lesson. He pulled and rubbed at the bands on his ankles, and searched his pockets once again for anything he might be able to use to cut them away. But the Garsal had removed everything: his knife, compass, map, and the other tools he carried – leaving him nothing.

He lay on his back, wondering how Anjo was, how his parents were, and how Shanna was. By now, his parents would know that something had happened. He and Anjo were well overdue. Surely someone would have investigated. The vehicle must have left tracks behind it. He'd wondered how the Garsal had scaled the plateau until the previous day.

Halfway through the day, the vehicle had halted its motion for a brief period. There had been a series of clunks, and the sounds of machinery adjusting itself, then it had lurched back into motion. This time the vehicle had tilted upwards and then vertically, and Kaidan had been hard pressed in the darkness of the closet to orient himself. He'd finally had to wedge himself between the narrow sides, only to have to reorganise himself a short time later when the orientation changed drastically again. The vehicle was a climber, which explained its odd configuration.

The time locked away in the dark had worn thin very quickly, and the hours of travel without being able to see what was happening, became boring in a terrifying kind of way. Kaidan fluctuated between fear, boredom and despair. He had no idea where he was, and no idea what would happen to him when he arrived at the ship. All he knew was that he hurt, and that he was more alone than he'd ever been in his life. He wriggled again, closed his eyes, and tried to imagine that he was somewhere else. It was very difficult, because every time he managed to create the requisite mental image, the vehicle would lurch and he'd lose the picture. Eventually, he settled on attempting to calculate how far he thought they'd travelled based on the glimpses he'd had through the windows on his brief forays with the guards.

For hour after hour, Kaidan lay there, bracing himself against the motion of the climber, wincing as his bruises contacted the hard surfaces, and trying to cushion his aching shoulder. Finally the vehicle stopped moving and he could hear a flurry of the harsh sounds of the Garsal communicating in their own language. He strained his ears, but it remained gibberish to him.

There were hurried footsteps outside the box, then as the door opened a Garsal trooper yanked him out. He stumbled slightly as he was shoved towards the living area. He blinked as his eyes adjusted to the light.

"What do you know of the Starlyne?" The question came without warning, and Kaidan didn't know what to say. "What do you know of the Starlyne?" The question was rapped out again, and Kaidan stood dumbstruck, as he struggled to decide what to say, or whether to say anything at all.

Something heavy struck him in the back and he toppled to the ground, frantically trying to protect his injured shoulder. "What do you know of the Starlyne?"

"Nothing!" He made a snap decision to deny any knowledge.

"Tell me everything you know of the Starlyne!" The phrase was emphasised with a kick, and Kaidan felt the air explode from his lungs. He spent the next few moments struggling for breath. The question was repeated, time after time, after time. Each time it was punctuated with a blow or a kick, and Kaidan was soon sobbing with pain. His nose was bleeding heavily, and he was curled around his shoulder, trying to make sure none of the blows landed on it and dislocated it again. Each time another blow landed, he gritted his teeth and refused to speak.

Finally, the blows and the questions stopped. Kaidan lay sobbing on the floor, faintly aware of the throbbing roars of some of Frontier's nastier predators reverberating through the thick steel of the vehicle's walls. There were several spates of Garsal conversation, and then one of the troopers hauled him to his feet. "You *will* tell us – eventually." The senior trooper flicked an appendage and Kaidan was dragged away and thrown roughly into his closet.

He ached, badly, and rolled slowly onto his uninjured side, shivering and shaking. His stomach rumbled, and he resigned himself to a long night of pain and hunger.

# Chapter 9

SHANNA was frustrated. Frustrated and angry. She was angry with everyone and angry with herself. Nothing seemed to be going right. Her nights were haunted with dreams of her brother being tortured and killed by the Garsal, leaving her exhausted and grumpy each morning. Her days were filled with practice. But all the practice seemed to be doing was to make her worse. Nothing seemed to be working. The more she pushed, the more everything seemed to go wrong. They hadn't managed to reproduce their meshing again and she'd even managed to lose her vision of the air currents half way through a flight the previous day. Fortunately she'd regained it in time to land safely, if not gracefully, on the bluff.

She was back on her favourite perch outside the Starlyne habitat, seated on the rocks overlooking the valley as the sun lowered itself towards the horizon. She was still sweaty from the last exercise, but she was so frustrated she felt as if she might explode. Twister and Storm sat to either side of her, heavy heads resting on her legs. "Sorry boys." She ran a hand over each silky head, and then allowed her fingers to pull gently at their ears. The breeze was warm and laden with moisture. The storm season was almost upon them. Shanna's anxiety climbed another notch. How would they rescue Kaidan if the storm season began? She wanted to swear, to let some of her frustration out, but the habits of long travel Below kept her quiet. Still, she felt as if she was about to burst.

"Want some company?" Verren's voice was unexpected, and Shanna's eyes narrowed as she realised that her cats had chosen not to warn her of his approach. She gritted her teeth and deliberately turned her head towards him.

"I'm not very good company, I'm afraid."

"I know." Verren took the rock next to her, Cirrus by his side as ever. The blue toned cat had reached her full growth, just as her two had. The three cats flickered their tidemarks rapidly in an exchange of greetings as Shanna turned her head back towards the valley.

"I'm sorry." She was repentant, but it didn't help her frustration.

"You need to give yourself a break, Shan."

"I *need* to find out how my brother is!" The words came out more hotly than she'd intended, and she shoved the boiling anger back down inside her. Verren sat silently beside her for some time while she battled with her inner voices. The rational one was driving her nuts. She'd always had that part of her – the rational voice that cut through emotional highs and lows and calmly pointed out the facts. It had been useful at times, but now it just annoyed her. For once, she just wanted to shriek, scream, and run desperately after her brother. Without a doubt, he was now at the ship. She hoped desperately that he was still alive.

"Shan, you need to slow down and not try so hard. We all know you're not sleeping properly, and you're pushing yourself too hard during the day. Spiron says you're to have a day off tomorrow."

Her anger escalated again. "Because he thinks I'm not coping?" she asked hotly.

"Because he knows you're not sleeping, so you can't concentrate properly. You could have died today – in a training accident, doing something you're really good at. We can't afford to lose you to something silly, Shan."

"It's not something silly, it's training so that we can hurt the Garsal – hurt them like they've hurt us!" she hissed. "And if I don't keep working at it, I'll let you all down, just when it matters most!" Both her cats hummed sharply, and she lowered her voice and went on. "And I can't let you all down!"

"Shan, you're too tired," said Verren patiently. "You need the day off so that you won't let us down. If you keep pushing like this there'll be a disaster and you won't be able to help us at all."

"But there's so little time!"

"There'll be less time if you get hurt!"

"But I'll be wasting time!"

"You'll be using it as it should be," he retorted. "You're no use at all like this!"

Shanna turned her head, shocked, and looked at Verren. He looked embarrassed. "I didn't mean it like that."

"Mean what? That I'm useless?" Hot tears pricked her eyes yet again, and she swallowed convulsively against the sudden lump in her throat. There was a sigh from Verren and he shook his head.

"I simply meant that you're so tired that you don't know what you're doing half the time."

The tears fell again, and Shanna felt something like a dam break inside her. Once again, Verren moved closer and wrapped an arm around her shoulders. "It's OK, Shan. We all know what it's like, although I'd go a little further and say that it's easier when your family member is dead, and not a captive." His voice, normally so steady, cracked slightly. Shocked to stillness by the sound, Shanna remembered once again that Verren had already lost one brother.

"I'm sorry Verren." She rubbed her face with one hand and wrapped her left arm around Verren, deliberately pulling him towards her to offer what comfort she could. In her anger and frustration she'd pushed the losses her friends had already experienced to the back of her mind. She felt very selfish, and very small all of a sudden. Once again, she was crying all over Verren. "I am sorry," she repeated.

"You have nothing to be sorry about," he replied eventually. "Nothing can change what's already happened, but we might be able to stop the Garsal enslaving our entire population, or at least, that's what I keep telling myself." He was silent for a time, and the two of them sat quietly watching the sun set. The darkness would fall quickly once the sun finally dropped below the horizon, but for a while, Shanna was content just to sit, in the companionship of another warm human being. She sat there, arm wrapped around Verren, feeling a lot of the stress and irritation slowly ebb from her body. The urgency to rescue Kaidan hadn't left her, but she felt as if the fire inside her mind had banked itself to a manageable level.

"So I'm to have a day off tomorrow?"

"Yes."

"And what am I meant to be doing on my day off?"

"The same thing the rest of us are meant to be doing," replied Verren, slightly sheepishly.

"The rest of you?"

"I didn't quite get to that part before."

Shanna sat taller, and looked up at him, slightly surprised. "So what are we *all* meant to be doing tomorrow?" His blue eyes twinkled slightly.

"Apparently we're just going to go for a walk. Nothing more, and nothing less."

"Right. A walk. When the fate of our world hangs in the balance?"

"Yep. That's it, apparently. Fractus says there's a spot close by with a warm spring. He said we all need to unwind and have a brief break. It's an important place to them apparently. We'll be leaving at dawn, so we'd better get back and get clean so that we can get to bed early." He paused slightly, still looking down at her.

"And how did you draw the short straw to come and tell me all of this?" asked Shanna suddenly.

"Oh, I volunteered," replied Verren, smiling slightly. "The others were too frightened."

"And you weren't?"

"I'd never be frightened of you, Shan."

"Never?"

"Never." There was the hint of a smile in his eyes, and Shanna was suddenly aware of how close they were again. And, yes, she'd been crying on him again. There was even a damp patch on his shirt where she'd dried her face. She blushed, and Verren's mouth widened to match the expression in his eyes. "You know, you're not really that scary when you look like that."

Shanna was confused. Look like what? Hot, smelly with sweat, reddened nose and eyes, and probably with her hair in a mess. She didn't know what to say, but Verren kept on relentlessly. "That blush of yours is rather fetching you know."

"Fetching?"

"Yes, fetching, in a kind of befuddled way." His teasing was gentle, and Shanna blushed again, more hotly this time.

"Well I'm glad I'm amusing you," she managed to say. He hadn't let go of her and she was slightly confused. She moved, but his arm tightened around her and then was joined by his other one gripping her gently just above her right elbow as he shifted to stare into her eyes.

"You do know that you can talk to me any time, Shan?" The blueness of his eyes was somewhat disconcerting, so close to hers.

"Yes. Thank you," she said, and his arms relaxed slightly.

"And perhaps if you talk more, you'll be easier to get along with," Verren smiled mischievously at her.

"Perhaps I will," she replied. He gave her one last squeeze and then released her and held out a hand to help her up. As he pulled her to her feet, she noticed that the three cats were watching them intently. For some reason she felt slightly embarrassed.

"Come on then." Without relinquishing her hand, Verren began to walk back down the slope behind the rocks. Slightly awkwardly, she followed his tug, and then walked beside him, strangely warmed by the feel of her hand in his.

***

The morning dawned cloudy. Not thick clouds, but enough to raise a quiver of storm sense in Shanna. She looked a query at Amma as they dressed.

"Yes, two days, a large cyclone, intense winds and heavy rain," said the other cadet as she pulled her bed together.

"So we'll have time for our 'walk' today?"

"Yes. Fractus said we'll be back by evening."

In the end, it was only two hours' walk. The warm pools were nestled in a small valley just to the north of the habitat. They sat like a string of glow-stones, linked by chains of stepped falls, their pristine water bubbling over their downstream lips towards the next pool. In the early morning air, steam rose in lazy spirals. Shanna felt her spirits lift at the beauty in front of her.

"This is our memorial grove." Fractus' voice was solemn. "This is where we remember all of our people who have gone to eternity before us, and where we make our most solemn promises. Here you will find a memorial to Keeper, and here, I will pledge on behalf of all of my people to resist to the last Starlyne." His tone was firm and full of steadfastness, and oddly, peace. Shanna turned wondering eyes towards him. He gestured with his arms and glided before them into the valley. "After you have visited the memorials, and I have pledged, we will bathe in the warm waters as is our custom." They followed in single file, cats humming in pleased tones.

Shanna let the sound of trickling water soothe her. She had woken slightly confused after the first deep sleep she'd had in days. Verren's face had wandered in and out of her dreams, but they'd been restful dreams instead of the nightmares she'd known since hearing of her brother's capture. The worry was still there, but the anger was slowly being replaced by something more controlled and useful. She was still trying to process the previous day's events, and every time she thought about Verren, she became bemusedly aware that something more than a simple conversation had passed between them. She wasn't completely sure she knew what it was, but somehow it had allowed her to subsume her anger into something more useful. The planned rest day seemed to be completing the process.

Fractus paused in front of several pillars. Trees had been planted closely around them so that they wrapped each pillar in greenery and branches. They were carved intricately, with patterns and figures that Shanna recognised as Starlyne in origin. "This is our memorial grove. Please remove your footwear and follow me." Shanna felt odd. She'd never walked on the ground Below without footwear between her and the earth. As if noticing her discomfort, Fractus went on. "There is nothing harmful in this valley. We have made sure of it."

Leaving her boots, socks and pack near the pillars, Shanna followed the line of Scouts into the grove and took up a position facing a cliff face that had thousands of plaques set into it. "Here are our memories of Keeper and all those who have gone before us on this world. Here we marry and here we dedicate our younglings." Fractus paused and then his mind spoke again. "And here now, in our most sacred space, I pledge on behalf of our people, that we are allied with you for all time. That we will fight to the last of our people to protect this world from the Garsal threat, and that our peoples will forever be one people. So do I pledge." There was complete silence and Shanna felt the import of the Starlyne's words with her whole body.

Spiron walked to stand beside the Starlyne, dwarfed by the creature's large body. "And I am authorised to accept your pledge and to give ours, on behalf of the human population of Frontier. We will be one people now, to stand against the Garsal, united together, each striving to assist the other until this conflict is settled. We stand together, joined as one." He inclined his head to the Starlyne.

"It is our custom when pledging something that will change our lives, to spend a few moments in solo, silent contemplation. The contemplation gives us time to throw off any ties that bind us to our old habits. Then we bathe in the warm pools. Not for any particular reason, but to take a moment's pleasure in living to remind us of what is important when times are difficult. There has been little pleasure for any of us lately, so I would urge you to enjoy yourselves, and spend the time with each other." He coiled himself more comfortably and gestured with his hands before tucking them away. "You may leave your outer clothing by the side of the pools, and retain your underwear for the sake of personal modesty. This is acceptable practice."

Shanna felt a quick blush start to rise. For a moment she'd thought that the Starlyne was going to insist that the humans bathe naked. Then she placed her attention back where it should be, as he continued to speak. With his ability to project his thoughts into the minds of his human companions, it was likely the Starlyne had anticipated the reaction and sought to defuse it before it became a problem. "You will be safe anywhere in this small valley. Do not fear to be Below without your equipment or as much clothing as you customarily wear. Pick a spot that seems good to you. I will join you as you bathe." He sat back on his coiled body and closed his eyes in contemplation, and Shanna felt calmness bathe the surface of her mind.

She looked around hastily, and slightly awkwardly, and then decided to take a position just near one of the pillars. The pungo tree wafted its familiar scent towards her as she sat, still checking around her by force of habit, on the soft ground. There were soft tussocks of grass and her cats made pleased humming noises as they arranged themselves around her. She still felt awkward, but she obediently closed her eyes and began to think. It was harder than she'd anticipated, because her mind kept buzzing off by itself and thinking things she didn't think she should be thinking.

Finally she managed to concentrate, by dint of listening to the small noises around her. There were birds everywhere, and a soft humid breeze was tickling the leaves above her, and beyond all of that, was the sound of the trickling, bouncing water. It silenced her too-active mind until she felt as if she too, was swept up in the gentle current. The rational part of her listed the issues she needed to let go of. Fear of failure, fear of letting everyone down, fear of loss, fear of pain, and more than anything, fear of losing those she loved most: Storm and Twister, Kaidan, her parents, her fellow Scouts, and Verren. *Verren?* she thought, almost startled out of her contemplative state. *Verren?*

And then she was honest with herself. She was more than fond of her fellow cadet, and it appeared that perhaps he was a little more than fond of her. She replayed their last few encounters in her mind. Yes, she was definitely more than just fond of Verren. And yes the idea frightened her, this idea of seeing Verren in a different light than that of friendship. She was frightened of what might happen if he died during this time of danger, or what might happen if she was misinterpreting his care for something deeper. It was hard, harder than she'd thought, to try and let any of it go. In the end, she wasn't sure she'd succeeded, but it seemed that the rational Shanna had melded with the emotional one, and finally, she let out a large sigh and opened her eyes.

She'd been crying again, she realised, and hoped she hadn't been sobbing aloud. She felt strangely composed though; perhaps just the act of wrestling with her fears had allowed her to recognise them for what they were – normal, human, emotions. She wouldn't be any the less for having acknowledged them, or any more for denying them. She was human, she was flawed, and she had a job to do. Doing her best would be all she could do. In her heart she'd fare-welled her family and friends one by one, allowing the sound of the water to wash away the grief. Grief she'd allowed to surface in advance, so that she could treasure every moment that still remained. Her cats were watching, she noticed, tidemarks flickering slowly, in pleased patterns. She rose from her spot on the ground, left the glade through the pillars, and moved towards a pool she'd spied on her entry to the valley. It was towards the top end, and was currently empty of human or Starlyne.

She shed her outwear and walked slowly into the water, Storm and Twister flanking her gravely on either side, sensitive to her mood of contemplation, and then slid under the warm water. Holding her breath she allowed the current to wash around her for a minute or two, before pushing to the surface again. She felt reborn. Not free from her fears, but readier to face them now. It was relaxing in the warm water, and the breeze kept her from overheating. Storm and Twister paddled happily about, occasionally whacking her with a tail as they spiralled around her, playing some kind of starcat water game. She remained alone for some time, until a huge splash announced someone else's presence.

It was Amma and Spider, followed quickly by the rest of the cadets. Soon the pool was awash with splashing, jumping, swimming cadets and their cats. Eventually, everyone paddled to the side of the pool, panting with the exertion of nothing but fun. Propping their arms on the rocky surrounds, or sitting on the warm rocks, they watched their cats continuing to swim and roll in the water. Their tidemarks glowed in the depths as one and then another of them dove below the surface.

"Feeling better, Shan?" asked Taya.

"I am," Shanna replied, "today was a good plan. I don't know about the rest of you, but I did need the head space, despite what I first thought about this being a waste of time."

"If you think about it, the last time we slowed down and stopped, even briefly, was last storm season," said Ragar thoughtfully. "It's been almost a year."

"And what a year." Amma's voice shook slightly.

"And who knows how much longer until we have another day of peace?" sighed Zandany. "I mean, I know that we've just got to keep on going – keep on fighting and hoping until the Garsal are gone, but I didn't realise just how exhausted my mind was until today." The others nodded thoughtfully, and Shanna realised that she wasn't the only one who'd struggled recently. As she thought back over the last week or two, she could see that nearly all of her friends had failed at least once while doing a normally easy task. She'd been so self-absorbed that she'd failed to recognise it at the time.

"I'm sorry about my behaviour," she finally said. "I had no right to behave as I did."

"You've had good reason though," replied Ragar firmly. "I'd be going just about mad if it was me."

"I think I was."

"Well, let's hope we'll be sent back to the ship again," replied Amma. "I can't get the sound of those prisoners out of my mind. It's been preying on me ever since we got back. I feel as if we abandoned them." There were nods of agreement, and there was a thoughtful silence as they rested there together.

"You know, I think I can do this now," said Shanna. "Not guarantee that we'll beat the Garsal or anything, but commit to do my best."

"I agree," said Taya. "Today has been about perspective for me. I've lost nearly all my family already, and I was just about running on automatic, but I agree with Shanna. I can go on now. Where that takes me, I don't know, but I have a score to settle with the Garsal." There were tears in her eyes, but her mouth was set firmly as she spoke. There were nods of agreement.

"Well then, you'll be glad to know that we will be heading to the ship very shortly then," said Spiron as he joined them. "Our orders have come from Master Cerren. We'll be attempting to free at least some of the slaves, and do as much damage as we can to buy the plateau more time. We leave this place in an hour to head back to the habitat. Be ready." He vanished behind a screen of trees.

"Well," said Ragar. "That's that then. Are we ready?" There were six determined nods and then the solemn mood was ended as Zandany gave Amma a shove and she toppled back into the water with a shriek. Shanna used the distraction to grab Taya by the shoulders and pull her under. Immediately the pool became a swirling maelstrom of froth and bubbles as they all tried to duck someone else or pull them in. Starcats swam and splashed as enthusiastically as their partners, and Twister even plummeted from the top of one of the surrounding trees, landing in the water with a monumental splash that fountained water everywhere.

An hour later as she dressed herself, Shanna realised that Verren hadn't spoken a word the whole time. She sneaked a look over at him. He was dressed, and he was sitting on a rock, gently stroking Cirrus as he stared into the distance. As if he sensed her regard, he turned his head and met her eyes. There was more loss in that one gaze than Shanna had ever seen and she dropped her eyes, confused.

# Chapter 10

THE Matriarch nodded, as Laretai tapped the display in front of her. "So, the Overlord has a captive on the way, and it is confirmed that there are living Starlynes on this planet." She leaned back in her chair and pushed her personal tablet towards her Senior Attendant. "These are my final thoughts on the potential initiates."

Laretai took the tablet and perused it thoughtfully. "The hive tour was very revealing. These two," she enlarged their images, "are most definitely ready. The others – I agree with your summation Matriarch. Stantai will most likely be one of us within the annual, however, Terrisei will not join our ranks. Shall I make the arrangements?"

"Please. The sooner the better. Our time is now limited. We must effect the plan as soon as possible." She stood and paced, filmy robes flaring gracefully behind her in their layers of colour. "Your tap on the communications is secure?"

"It is."

"Show me the image of the human captive."

The Matriarch leaned forward as Laretai tapped the main screen again, secure in the knowledge they would be undisturbed. A young male, judged the Matriarch. He was very tall for one so young, and much more robust than the human slaves she was familiar with. He appeared defiant, despite the blood smeared across his face, and matting his hair. She had repeatedly studied the images Laretai had downloaded from the ship's computer on the attack, and the young man's face seemed vaguely familiar. Unlike most of her race the Matriarch was something of an expert on humans but the familiarity refused to make itself known and she flicked her manipulator arms irritably. "How long until Hoth returns, Laretai?"

"He will be here within the day, Matriarch."

"I would be present for the arrival. Arrange something convenient that allows us to be present without it being obvious. Some plausible pretext."

"Another hive inspection? To confirm the removal of the hatching suite?"

"That will be ideal. Make sure that the timing is precise, so that I may observe the human myself. You will also make sure that Estei and Hirtoi are in my retinue. They will learn much from this encounter."

"Yes Matriarch." Laretai hesitated slightly, and the Matriarch looked at her sharply.

"There is something else?"

"Everything hangs in the balance Matriarch. If we succeed or fail, our sisters may still never know, and there is much that we do not yet know about either the humans or the Starlyne."

"That is a matter of some delicacy Laretai. We must proceed slowly and carefully. Too many of us have perished over the years for us to proceed too hastily. We must cover our tracks carefully." She paced again, absently adjusting the drape of her robes. "But you are correct, we must begin. We will meet after the initiation ceremony and disclosure, and plan our operations. You will arrange for all of our seniors to be present. Make sure that the room is completely secure."

Laretai bowed deeply to her and departed the room as the Matriarch transferred the image of the human captive to her tablet for later study. She carefully closed down the files she and Laretai had shared and then began her measured pacing again. She was soon deep in thought.

***

Kaidan felt the vehicle slow and then come to a complete halt. The trip had been harrowing. He'd spent most of it locked in the darkness of the closet, accumulating more bruises. His brief forays into the world of light were only for eating, drinking and questioning. He'd managed to keep his silence on the subject of the Starlynes, repeatedly denying any knowledge of them, despite the abuse from his Garsal captors. Now he lay despondently in his box, waiting to be released for the next round of questioning. As the door rattled, he braced himself, but the expected blow didn't come, just a command to get out of the closet. He quickly struggled to his feet, having already learned the consequences of any delay. As he stepped out into light he was ushered briskly towards the vehicle ramp and, for the first time, allowed himself to hope that he finally might have a chance to escape. Perhaps he'd be able to locate a flotter and remove the bracelets. Surely he could survive Below, even without a starcat, or perhaps it would be better for him to die trying than remain a Garsal captive. He braced himself to run as soon as he had a chance, and as the trooper prodded him, began to descend the ramp.

His hopes died as he emerged from the vehicle. He was in a clearing dominated by the black bulk of what must be the Garsal colony ship. Garsal trotted backwards and forwards everywhere he looked. A large vehicle ground its way across the clearing and in the distance, a group of human slaves laboured around an ornate archway. He blinked in the sudden brightness, and nearly stumbled as the Garsal trooper behind him pushed him forwards towards a group clearly assembled for the arrival. One of them was very obviously the leader.

There was a flurry of conversation, harsh to his ears, and he took the opportunity to look around, familiarising himself with his new prison. He was

Below, that was obvious. The vegetation had the subtle differences he'd noted during the battle with the Garsal, now so many months ago. He was prodded forwards again, just as a company of different Garsal appeared from the ship. These Garsal looked different. They were clothed in layers of multicoloured, filmy material. The conversation stopped as they appeared, and every Garsal in view made some kind of obeisance towards them. They changed direction and approached. The lead Garsal hurried towards the other group, his posture evidencing obvious confusion.

Another spate of harsh conversation ensued, while Kaidan stood dumbfounded. Finally, the leader of the first group bowed in acquiescence and the robed group approached. They circled around him, and Kaidan felt the faceted eyes of the elaborately garbed Garsal travel over him. He pushed his bruised body taller, trying to find in himself some sense of defiance. It was very hard. Part of him wanted to resist whatever the Garsal might have in store, while the other part simply wanted to curl up and cry. He kept his eyes on the ground, ignoring all of them. It was easier that way. There was another flurry of Garsal speech, and the robed creatures stopped their circling and stood in a stepped formation to one side. Curious now, Kaidan watched them out of the corner of his eyes. The most elaborately dressed Garsal held up its manipulator arm, and another, scarcely less dressed, hurried to its side. The two heads leaned together, and then the second one stepped forwards and made what was obviously a proclamation.

There was silence, and then the leader made a curt series of gestures and replied. There was reluctance in every line of its body, but at another imperious gesture from the robed one, bowed deeply and acquiesced. The robed one returned to its fellows, and the group swept off without any further conversation.

The leader took a step towards Kaidan, and he had to stop himself cringing away from it. "You will attend the Matriarch. It is her command that you join her household slaves when you are fully trained to our ways."

The Matriarch? Those had been female Garsal? Anjo had told him that they were rarely seen outside their sequestered dwelling areas. His moment of surprise was cut short.

"In the meantime, we have some days in which to question you, and attend to your training. You *will* tell me everything you know. Bring him." The menacing tone iced Kaidan to his core. His guards prodded him towards the open maw of the colony ship, and he took one, last, despairing look around him. Just before he entered the darkness, he thought he saw a twinkle of blue on his periphery. For a moment, hope sparked, but then he shook his head and left his world behind.

***

"You risk much, Matriarch," said Laretai. Her voice held no censure, but there were hints of fear for the attentive ear to hear. She sat quietly with the Matriarch, waiting for the initiates to present themselves. The ritual candles glowed in the four corners of the room and on the table at one end. The Matriarch, Laretai, and the three oldest seniors reclined around it. The Matriarch inclined her head in agreement.

"I do what must be done, so that the plan will prosper."

"But to force the Overlord to hand over his new acquisition? Was that wise?" The foremost Senior's voice cracked out across the room.

"It was necessary, sister. Would you see him condemned to die on the dissection table? He is but a child."

"I would do whatever is necessary for our people to prosper," came the retort. "But certainly it is abhorrent to kill children, no matter their species." The Senior settled back in her chair.

"It was clear from his stance, that although this human is young, that he is as yet unbowed. There is strength in him, and knowledge. Knowledge that may well serve our purpose."

"Will he still be unbowed once the Overlord has done with him?"

"If he is not, then he will at least live. As you have said, it is abhorrent to kill children. And we may yet learn more of this world's humans. He is of greater stature than we are accustomed to seeing. Who knows what we might learn of them by simple observation? He will be our new initiates' project, overseen by yourself, Laretai. They will win his trust."

There was a murmur of surprise, but all of the Seniors subsided, and the Matriarch sat back, pleased with their reactions.

"It is time. Bring in the initiates. You will provide the disclosure, Laretai. You have the injector, Answoi?" The Senior placed it on the table in full view. "Then if needs be, you will use it."

***

The Overlord was furious. So furious that he dared not express it. His hard won specimen was now to be plucked from his grasp and he had little time to extract what knowledge the human might have. Hoth had told him of the boy's refusal to speak on the subject of the Starlyne race, and his stubborn defiance when challenged, and his fury rose again. He would see to this slave's breaking personally. It might bring him some satisfaction.

***

Kaidan fell flat onto his face again, cradling his injured shoulder. He was somewhere deep in the bowels of the ship, in some sort of small pen. There were bars on the front of the cell but the remaining walls were completely featureless. The pen itself seemed to contain nothing but a basin and some kind of waste disposal area, judging by the smell. He pushed himself upright as the Garsal who'd captured him stood looking down at him.

"The Overlord will be breaking you himself. It is a great honour for you, but he is known to be harsh. I suggest you tell him everything he asks, immediately, should you wish to retain all of your faculties." The voice was dispassionate. It sent shivers down Kaidan's spine, but he remained standing defiantly until the Garsal turned away and left. Then he sat, huddling into himself in a corner of the cell. Around him, he could hear sounds of misery.

His time alone was short, however. Without warning, he was removed from his cell and hustled rapidly through the ship and into yet another small room. It contained nothing but a metal post and some equipment in one corner. The Overlord was waiting there with two other Garsal. Without warning, metallic bands were clamped around his wrists and ankles, and he was fastened to the post. He struggled frantically, and the bands cut cruelly into his limbs. The Garsal began attaching parts of the equipment to his head and body as he twisted away from them futilely, Finally, he just stood there, while the Overlord watched him impassively.

"Trooper Hoth tells me you know nothing of the Starlyne people. Or of the plans your own people have made. He tells me that you know nothing of the vicious felines that infest this planet, not even the one that you were travelling with." Kaidan said nothing. "I think that Hoth has been too gentle with you. As a slave, you will obey immediately and promptly. You have nothing left but service to the Garsal. As a slave, your mind and your thoughts belong to us." He paced an ominous circle about the post while Kaidan looked grimly into its reflective surface. "It has been a long time since I participated in the breaking of a slave. Unfortunately the Matriarch has reserved your service for herself, or I would have had no hesitation in maiming you, should you have resisted my questions. As it stands, I must provide her with a functioning body. But the mind? *That* is another matter. You will be obedient by the time I have finished with you, and willing to serve. How much pain this requires is up to you." Kaidan was unable to stop his limbs from trembling, but as his reflection shook, he gritted his teeth, and vowed to resist as long as he was able.

"I see you have spirit. The spirited ones always break first." The Overlord resumed his pacing. "I will begin with simple questions. I will ask and you will reply." There was another long silence, a drawing out of the inevitable, and then the first question. "You have a name. What is it?"

For a moment Kaidan was tempted to answer, tempted to avoid the inevitable. His conversations with Anjo replayed themselves, and then he braced himself and shook his head. And then the pain began.

***

The Overlord reached his quarters and set the door to refuse entry. He was incensed. The young human had reached collapse without breaking. He had expected the boy's youth to work in his favour, to cow him with threats and brief prods of pain, yet two days on, and he still didn't even know the slave's name. He wanted to break things, but he contented himself with thinking of the pain he'd visit on the boy the next day.

***

Kaidan woke blearily in his cell. Everything throbbed, and his throat was raw from screaming. Had he talked? He didn't think he had, but it was very hard to remember. He crawled to the basin and gulped at the water furiously before collapsing against the cell wall. It was dark. Perhaps it was night outside, he had no idea. There was a scratching sound, and then a whisper in the darkness. "Who are you? Where did you come from?" Kaidan held himself completely still. "Please, who are you?" It had been weeks since Kaidan had talked to a fellow human, and this voice was human.

"Who are you?" His voice was hoarse, and rusty from abuse.

"Just a slave. My name's Edon." Kaidan lay there in the darkness, belly empty, and body aching.

"I'm Kaidan. This planet is my home world. I'm from here." He wasn't making much sense, not even to himself, but there was a hushed murmur that ran all the way up the banks of cells on either side of him, and he realised that the inhabitants of the nearby cells were clearly listening, and passing the information on. With a stab of fear, he remembered Anjo's comments about informers, and his heart sank. He shouldn't have replied.

"You're from here?" There was surprise in the other voice. "But there are no free human worlds, and you're human." The damage was done, Kaidan supposed, but it was only his name that the Garsal didn't know. They definitely knew where he came from.

"We are free." Kaidan let his voice rise slightly. Not everyone was an informer, and these slaves needed to know that there were still free humans. Still humans fighting to retain their freedom. "Or at least everyone else is, as obviously I'm not."

Another voice joined the first one. "But how?"

Kaidan shook his head in the darkness. "That's all I will say. You know my name, and you know that there are free humans. That's enough." He lay down on the hard floor again. The Overlord would interrogate him again, he was sure. How long could he hold out? Not long without sleep. Not for the first time, he wondered if he should just give in. What he knew was actually very little, surely it couldn't hurt his people too much?

Another whisper reached him. "Kaidan." It was barely audible. He ignored it, but it came again.

"Kaidan." It was coming from his other side. He crawled as silently as possible to the other side of his cell.

"What do you want?"

"Edon's an informer. She will sell your name to the guards for more food and less labour."

"And how do I know you won't do the same?"

"You don't. But you're new here, and I know what the Garsal do to new slaves. A word of advice for you. Tell them things that don't matter. Pretend obedience. It's the only thing that will allow you to keep your mind."

"Why are you telling me this?"

"Because you're the first hope I've seen for twenty years. You give me hope that perhaps I won't die a slave." The voice stayed almost inaudible, carefully controlled in volume so that the conversation wasn't able to be heard from adjacent cells. "And if you want to have a chance of escape or survival yourself, you need to pretend to obey. Otherwise you'll simply be killed."

"Apparently I won't be killed. The Matriarch has requested my service." There was a long silence from the other cell.

"In that case, it is good fortune that has placed you next to me. This is essential information. Kaidan, you *must* do as I've told you. You *must* retain your mind. I'll ..." The voice broke off as the lights in the cell bay switched on blindingly, and Kaidan heard muffled scuttling from the other cell. A troop of Garsal marched to the front of his cell and he was dragged out without ceremony and marched away. He was able to get a glimpse of the inhabitant next to his cell. It was old, old and ragged, and female, as far as he could tell. It raised a fingertip to its lips in the universal gesture of silence. Wondering at himself, Kaidan deliberately dropped his head in a brief nod, hoping that anyone else watching would think he was fearful of what was ahead. He stumbled and let the Garsal drag him off without too much struggling, because he was fearful, and he was still hurting from the last session.

It was all he'd dreaded. The Overlord was merciless, and his underlings alternated between shocking him with the equipment attached to his body and striking him with a variety of weapons. Kaidan could feel the warmth of sticky blood tracking its way down his back. "What do you know of the Starlynes, Kaidan?" The shock of hearing his name from a Garsal mouth jerked Kaidan's head up. Sweat, or blood, trickled between his shoulder blades. "Your name is Kaidan. You told me at our last meeting." For a moment Kaidan was confused, had he or hadn't he told the Overlord his name? The memories were hazy, perhaps blocked out by his mind in case they threatened to overwhelm him. And then Anjo's quiet voice mixed with that of the old woman next door, and he decided that he hadn't told the Overlord, and that Edon was definitely an informer.

A lash hit the back of his head, and his forehead struck the post, leaving a smear of blood. Kaidan's mind raced as he tried to think above the pain. The Overlord shouted his name, and sprayed questions at him in a froth of words and fury. It formed a kind of rhythmic cadence in time with the blows from his torturers. He let the pain reach a pinnacle, and then he gasped out one short sentence. "Starlynes are our allies." The beating stopped as the Overlord raised a hand, and Kaidan stood trembling. He dropped his head and tried to look beaten. It wasn't hard, because he almost had been.

"You will tell me more."

Pain knifed through him. "I don't know anything else! I'm too young. I just run messages."

"Perhaps you *are* telling the truth, and perhaps not. We shall see." The Overlord walked behind Kaidan, and a hot pain burned through all of the others. "Are you certain?"

Kaidan sobbed his answer. "Yes! I'll tell you anything else, but I don't know anything more about the Starlyncs! I've only ever seen one!" He allowed himself to collapse against the cold steel post, welcoming its coolness against his pain.

"Then we will discuss your people, their locations and their plans and talk of those feline creatures you all seem to hold so dear."

Kaidan took a sobbing breath, and slowly and carefully began to talk. He was clever, he reminded himself, clever enough to solve mathematical problems that challenged others years his senior. This was just a game. A strategy game like the ones he'd played with Balto. He had to seem to tell the truth, while concealing anything of importance. As he was struck again, for being too slow to answer, he reminded himself, 'just a game,' but in his world, games didn't hurt.

***

The Overlord sat back with a sigh of accomplishment. The informant had done well. Supplying Kaidan's name had been the key. His stubborn resistance had faded in the face of his apparent failure and the night's session had been fruitful. It was just a pity that the boy had so little knowledge. He was too young, and too uninformed, and apparently just what he'd said he was – a simple messenger. The Overlord had seen many slaves break, and this one was no different. His youth had provided the initial stamina, but the abuse had done its work as it had so many times in the past. It was disappointing that his body would not be available for proper examination, but there had been ample opportunity to gain tissue samples and brain scans from the captive.

There were distinct differences, his scientists had told him. They'd been all abuzz as they'd begun to analyse the scans of this young human. What those differences meant, they were unsure, but they had pointed excitedly to comparisons of Kaidan's brain and the human norm. The Overlord had pressed them on the point, but they had made haste to point out that these were only preliminary results, and that they required further information.

He would continue to interrogate the boy tomorrow. He'd let him sleep and then contemplate the enormity of having betrayed his people's trust, and then begin the process of turning him into an exemplary slave for the Matriarch. For once on this planet, something had gone as planned.

# Chapter 11

THE wind howled as it slammed itself against the building, humming around the outside of the structure. Even though the Starlyne habitation was mostly below ground, the intensity of the storm was such that the sound of it penetrated almost everywhere. Sadly, Shanna imagined her parents at home in Hillview, sitting safely by the fire, lonely in their childless solitude. No, she reminded herself, not alone, most of the starcat breeders were there too. She was thankful that they had company. She couldn't have imagined coping without the support of her friends.

For the first time in days, everything had gone well, and Shanna was beginning to regain her confidence. As the day wore on, and the wind howled more violently, Fractus called a halt to the exercises. "Time to plan, I think."

Shanna relaxed and allowed the doubled vision from Storm and Twister to fade. For the first time since the news of Kaidan's capture, she hadn't been nauseous. At least the storm allowed them a few days grace to plan their trek southwards. Given it was unlikely the Garsal could travel in this weather either, the plateau was probably safe for at least the duration of the high winds. Once they were back in their common room, planning for the trip began.

"Amma, how much longer will this cyclone last?" asked Fractus.

Amma cocked her head in thought. "The eye is close. We'll have another twelve hours of dangerous winds, followed by torrential rain for at least two days. This system is large, and very wet. Why?"

"We need to try and coordinate our travel plans. We'll have several additions to our numbers for this trip," replied Spiron. "We're hoping that the heavy rain will prevent those climbing vehicles from manoeuvring easily. Although foot travel is slow in comparison, we won't be stopped by much except flooded river crossings – and they should be manageable. The one bottleneck will be the gorge through the southern range, but hopefully it'll be passable by the time we arrive. We can always go up and over if we really have to, although I'd prefer not to if we can avoid it."

"So what's our objective then?" asked Ragar.

"We have two, actually," said Barron. "We'll be establishing supply caches at suitable sites on the way down, and then we'll be attempting to assess whether it will be possible to attempt a rescue of the slaves from the ship – and how many we can safely take with us. Anjo has told us as much as he knew, but his duties had him removed from the centres of power. We need more information – ideally from slaves with access to places he couldn't go.

Semba's original duties placed her closer, and she's finally managed to give us several names. Ideally, you'll bring at least one or two of them back with you. Obviously we can't try anything without knowing how many we need to rescue, or without good support lines. Any camps we establish can then become forward posts." Ragar was nodding as Barron ticked off the points one by one.

"The Council, in conjunction with the Starlyne people, have a variety of strategies in place to protect all of our people," Fractus said. "For the moment, our task is to discover if we can go on the offensive. Your role is pivotal to this, as are our communication skills. This trip will involve quite a number of our people as well as yours. Our role will be to develop and maintain a secure communication network between the area of the ship and the plateau, and also to transport supplies and equipment. Our size will be helpful." His tone was tinged with amusement. "The relay still won't be instantaneous, but it will be fast, and we plan to build in redundancies in case the Garsal detect any part of the network. Our people will be supported by small groups of yours. That means that several other Scout patrols will follow shortly. They, and we, will establish way posts in locations that you specify. Then they'll follow on as escorts for any rescues."

Shanna sat listening as Fractus, Spiron and Barron outlined the requirements of the mission. It carried a high degree of risk, yet when she thought about it, the options open to them were limited. They could hole up on the plateau, a place where the Garsal knew they were, and try to outlast the their superior technology and manufacturing ability, or they could go on the offensive and attempt to wear the Garsal down.

"I sometimes wish we'd retained more of our technological capacity," sighed Radiant, his thoughts regretful.

"Our people have discussed this much lately," replied Teacher, "but there is no turning back. Our ancestors, and original survivors of the Garsal massacre, chose to hide, hoping that the Garsal might pass us by, retaining only our biological expertise in order to make this world our new home. We can wish all we like for lost weaponry and lost manufacturing capacity, but our choices have shaped our culture and our society, and longing after those things will not help us now."

Shanna felt as if she was eavesdropping on a private conversation, and dropped her eyes, embarrassed. There was a sense of amusement from the three Starlynes, and then Teacher spoke again. "Don't be embarrassed – if we'd wanted to keep the conversation private it would have been impossible for you to overhear. And you do need to know that we're not hiding things from you. Many of your people have speculated on this – if we can provide such medical aid, why can't we simply wipe the Garsal from the face of the planet?" Her tone was self deprecating. "If only we could."

The planning continued. Shanna, Allad, and Verren were tasked with devising the route, co-opting all of the maps from their last trip, and combining them with the knowledge the Starlynes had of Below. Steadily they plotted a path southwards, and as they did the map became dotted with notations that signified areas where they hoped to establish communication outposts. It was nerve racking, trying to think of everything. And it was made all the more difficult by the awareness that one day they might need to escort groups of not only humans, but other Federation members through the dangers of Below. Even with the assistance of several other Scout Patrols, Shanna wondered if it would be possible. Her initial impulse to rush after her brother seemed even more hair-brained in the face of the detailed planning she was now helping with. There seemed to be so many things to consider, but slowly Shanna began to see a coherent plan take shape.

Two days later, the planning was complete, and once again, she was packing her gear carefully into her back pack. Communication from the plateau had indicated a routine, post storm clean up operation in progress, and no sign of the Garsal. Shanna hoped that they stayed holed up in their ship for days. She ran her hands over each strap on her pack, checking for wear, and making sure it was all well adjusted. She had a fair supply of the energy patches, carefully stowed in a weatherproof pocket, and she checked to see what space she had left as she stowed treats for her cats.

Both of them had spent the last two days watching the preparations avidly, and seemed to know precisely what was being planned. After hefting her pack to check the weight, Shanna decided that she'd see if the rain had finally stopped, so that she, Storm and Twister could spend a little time alone outside.

Being inside for long periods chafed on her now. Perhaps it was all the travelling she'd done in the past year. She called her cats with a quick hand signal, and they wound their way through the habitation and out through the flight hangar. It was late afternoon, and the rain had reduced to a slight mistiness that was more dampness than actual rain. Shanna decided she didn't mind the dampness if she could sit on a rock and look into the distance for a little while. Both cats flicked their tidemarks at her somewhat reproachfully, but followed without much protest as she walked out into the coolness. A soft breeze touched her face with tiny, glistening, beads of water, and her cats' tidemarks glowed against the overcast sky as she climbed the rise to the granite boulders. As she took the last few strides to the top, she realised that she wasn't alone. Verren was already seated on her favourite rock.

He'd been there for some time, judging by his soaking clothes. Neither of her cats had seen fit to warn her that he was there either, but they must have known. For a moment she hesitated, uncertain of whether to stay or go, and then Storm hummed loudly and deliberately at her, and Twister bounced up the slope to rub against Verren. He nearly fell off his rock. "Twister!" was followed immediately by "Cirrus!" in exasperated tones, and then Storm was herding her up the hill to the rock next to Verren. He was looking smug. Cirrus nose touched first Storm, and then Twister, and then all three cats sat themselves on rocks about their partners and relaxed.

"Sorry to startle you, Verren," apologised Shanna. She perched awkwardly on the rock next to her fellow cadet drawing one knee into her chest, and leaving the other leg dangling down. "Thought we'd just a get a little air."

"No, no, that's OK. I was just sitting here thinking." He turned back to look out over the valley again. Shanna sat there awkwardly, wishing she'd turned around and gone back to the habitat once she'd realised that Verren was there. After a few moments, she felt a little more relaxed, and eased her hanging leg up onto the rock and sat there cross legged in the dampness.

She was completely unprepared when Storm leaped from his rock to hers, and knocked her into Verren's lap. He overbalanced as well, and they landed heavily in a wet heap on the muddy ground. All the wind was knocked out of Shanna, and she lay there, convulsively trying to draw in that first vital breath.

Water soaked through the back of her shirt as she struggled for breath, even as Verren scrambled awkwardly off her middle so that she could breathe.

"Are you all right, Shan?" Verren asked frantically as he lifted her head out of the mud. Behind him three cats were watching them avidly.

Shanna coughed and finally drew in a wheezing breath. "I'm fine, just winded," she managed to gasp out, waving a hand weakly.

"Just lie there for a moment while you get your breath."

Shanna nodded again, drawing in deep gasping breaths. "Sorry!" she finally managed to say, "I have no idea what got into Storm!" She managed to turn her head enough to eyeball the blue toned cat. His tidemarks were brightly blue, and he seemed amused. "That was not funny cat!" Cirrus chirruped at Twister, and the starcat flashed his tidemarks at her, and then the three cats returned to their rock perches, very deliberately setting themselves to watch over Verren and Shanna.

There was another awkward silence, and then Shanna regained her breath enough to struggle to a sitting position. Her ribs ached. She looked up at Verren, and was surprised to see him looking at her with that same expression of loss in his eyes. She held his gaze, uncomfortably aware of her own feelings for the other cadet.

"What's wrong?" she asked.

He dropped his eyes and breathed out heavily, and then his eyes sought hers.

"It's you, Shan." Shanna's heart sank. She *had* misinterpreted his feelings. She closed her eyes as her stomach plummeted.

"What's wrong with me, Verren?" she finally managed to ask.

"Nothing. That's the problem."

She frowned. "I'm confused then."

Verren dropped his eyes again, then sighed. "I like you, Shan. I like you a lot."

Shanna opened her mouth to speak, but he held up a hand.

"In fact, I like you more than is appropriate right now." It seemed that now Verren was speaking, he couldn't stop. "A few days ago I decided that I'd see if you might like me too, and I think you did. But then I realised that I'd capitalised on your brother's capture and caught you at a vulnerable time. It was completely unfair of me. And then we had that time of contemplation, and I realised that whatever I was thinking or feeling, this wasn't the time to pursue it, not if we're going to put all of our energy into ridding our planet of the Garsal, so I had to let you go. And then I tried – tried so hard to force those feelings back down, and I couldn't. And now all I can think of is what might happen if something happens to you." Shanna was startled to see that Verren's face was red, and that his hands were trembling. She took them, holding them firmly as he tried to pull them back. There was an approving hum from the three cats, and Shanna glared at them all. Hers had the grace to look slightly abashed. Her thoughts crystallised, and she took a deep breath and looked very deliberately into Verren's eyes.

"Verren, you were right, and I do like you. Probably more than is wise, too. But I was thinking about things yesterday, and I realised that while I might never see Kaidan again, or I might lose my parents, or they might lose me – my family know how I feel about them, and I know how they feel about me. But I also realised how much I like you. The difference is that you and I haven't talked, not properly. If I lost you, not knowing whether my feelings were shared, I'd have regrets that we never talked, and never knew. I'd have to grieve for you as only a friend, and never having known if there could have been anything else. Really, I think I'd rather know, and deal with it properly."

"But this isn't the time!" groaned Verren.

"It's not like we planned this," replied Shanna, exasperated. "And we're not talking about 'having' a relationship, just admitting to ourselves and to each other that we have feelings that are more than friendship for each other."

Verren sat silently, holding Shanna's eyes, and then finally relaxed, and the anguish faded from his eyes. His hands stopped trying to pull away and tightened around Shanna's properly, and then he squeezed them. "In that case, know that I find you fascinating. That I daydream about your eyes," Shanna blushed, "and that I desperately want to hug you right now."

"In that case," Shanna said, and pulled Verren towards her. His arms tightened around her, tentatively at first, then firmly. She tightened her arms around him in reply, desperate to show him the depth of her feelings by the tightness of her grip, until he laughed and they broke apart.

"So what do we do now?"

"We talk," said Verren, "and we work together, just as we've always done, and we make sure that our public behaviour is impeccable."

"But we need to spend a little time alone," said Shanna. "Some of the things we need to say, need to be said in private."

"Well, such is the life of a Scout," replied Verren. "Our privacy when on patrol is limited, so today may have to do us for some time."

"In that case, I'd like to get out of the mud," said Shanna practically. "I'm soaked through at the back and I'm getting cold."

They stood, and perched themselves on the rocks again, but this time, Shanna had no hesitation in leaning into Verren's strong warmth. "You *are* wet," he said, "but so am I," and she noticed that he didn't push her away. In fact, he pulled her closer and tucked her firmly into his chest.

"How about we begin with the behaviour recently exhibited by our cats?" asked Shanna, turning a firm gaze on her two. Both of them looked ridiculously smug, and as she turned her head to look at Cirrus, she realised that the female cat was just as pleased with the outcome of their machinations as her two were.

# Chapter 12

SOCKS padded across the floor and laid her long length at Cerren's feet. He absently rubbed her belly with his socked toes, staring blankly into the glowing red embers of the fire in the communal hall. The pounding rain had ceased, and for just a few moments, he and his cat were alone. Breaking the news of their son's kidnapping to Janna and Adlan had been one of the most difficult things he'd ever done. His mind wandered back to the day he'd told them that both of their children had been involved in a battle with the Garsal. It seemed so long ago, and so minor in comparison to their current grief. He hoped desperately that Kaidan was alive, but at the same time he worried what the Garsal might have discovered if they had interrogated the boy.

He cursed himself for his practicality, but the facts were simple. Kaidan knew more about their plans than Cerren would have liked. It was partly because of Cerren's decision to include him in the archery group, partly because he'd been a messenger to many of the Starlyne habitats, and partly because his sister and her abilities were apparently crucial to their survival.

He closed his eyes and leaned his head against the chair back. Somewhat guiltily, he visited the idea that Kaidan's death might have been better than his capture. As he examined his feelings, he was relieved to discover that he didn't really want that, no matter how much simpler it might have been in the long term. He continued staring into the fire, deliberately trying to avoid thinking about the horrors that Kaidan might be enduring at the hands of the Garsal. He was only partially successful, but some of the guilt subsided. What was done, was done, and there was no changing it.

Socks rolled onto her back, tucking her paws cub-like under her chin, and blinked her violet eyes endearingly at him. She never ceased to cheer him up when he was almost overcome by the weight of the decisions he was now having to make daily. The cyclone had been a kind of blessing, he reflected. Like the human beings on the plateau, the Garsal would have had no option but to wait the storm out. They would have at least a day or two more respite, time to take a breath and prepare themselves more thoroughly, given the distance to the ship and the slow moving nature of the storms. He doubted that the Garsal would be in a hurry to risk any of their craft in the unpredictable winds again. He rubbed Socks' belly, and she purred, the purring rumbling through his socked feet in a very comforting fashion. Socks was a wonderful companion. He'd never thought that another starcat could take Prince's place, but Socks had completely disarmed him with her engaging personality. Janna and Adlan bred the most amazing starcats.

"Cerren?" A soft voice intruded on his moment of peace, and he opened his eyes wearily. Peron and Payne had taken chairs next to him. Peron proffered a mug of tea and then leaned back in his own chair. Payne sat forwards hesitantly. "Any word from Below?" Cerren knew what he meant.

"No, so it seems likely that Kaidan is either dead, or at the ship by now. All we can do is to hope that he's still alive, and that one day we'll be able to free them all." He sighed heavily, and the three of them sat, staring into the fire for some time. How could the weight of one boy's life weigh so heavily upon him, he wondered? But he knew the answer. He knew Kaidan. Knew him well by now, and despite his maturity, he was still only a boy, and no child should ever have to bear Garsal captivity. The thought of the boy in alien hands steeled his resolve once again, and he glanced down to see Socks' eyes regarding him steadily, as her tidemarks flickered in tones and patterns of approval. Once again, Cerren wondered how much their feline companions really understood. More than they'd ever suspected, he thought.

"So Patrol Ten and the first years are off again?" asked Payne.

"Second years now," replied Peron, "And yes, they are. We've tasked Patrols Four and Eight to follow them up and establish secure supply caches, and the Starlynes are sending a number of their people as well." He leaned down and rubbed Thunder's cheek. The gangling youngster leaned heavily into the caress. "If we can organise secure hideaways between the ship and the plateau, then we have a beginning. Those small bases could be the difference between defeating the Garsal or not."

"And at Northaven?" Payne's voice was grave.

"Northaven is working with our allies on last ditch survival plans – hidden, secure enclaves of both Starlyne and human Below, that will form our last hope. Let's hope it doesn't come to that."

Payne sighed heavily and proffered a folder. "This is my list of evacuees as requested – those I'd recommend we hide away in the event of disaster."

Cerren closed his eyes. Making last ditch plans seemed an admission that the task ahead was too great. Socks butted him with her head, and he looked down at her in surprise. Her tidemarks were brilliant blue, and flickering almost faster than his eyes could follow. Apparently she didn't agree with his summation, and his spirits lifted slightly as Peron took the folder from Payne and began to leaf through it. His eyebrows lifted slightly as he reached the last page. "You'd send a full Patrol of Scouts?"

"Peron, despite your notions of defending to the last Scout, we need your genes." Payne's tone was flat. Peron flicked back through the folder again, nodding, although his expression was guarded, and then handed it over to Cerren. Cerren ran his eyes down the lists. Gradually he realised that there was a pattern.

There was only one Patrol listed. There was no number, they were identified just as 'Scout Patrol,' and there were no names in the listing. But as Cerren looked back and forth over the pages, he realised that nearly all of the names of the evacuees were familiar. All were worthy of survival in their own right, but a large percentage of the names had a family member who was a Scout. Initially it looked like nepotism on a large scale, but then reason prevailed, and Cerren leaned back with in his chair and fixed Payne with a penetrating stare.

The dark skinned man looked back imperturbably, and eased his recovering leg out towards the fire, grimacing as he extended the knee. "Don't look at me like that, Cerren. I didn't make the list. I left the individual selections to the guild heads, and none of them are stupid. We know what it takes to survive here, and what might be required to breed a new population despite Garsal occupation. These people have the skills, *and* they have the genes."

"It doesn't make me like it anymore," replied Cerren. He handed the list back to Peron and looked directly at Payne. "Let's be clear about this. This list is not to be used except in the most dire of situations. In fact, no-one is to know about this list at all, unless they're intimately involved in carrying out the escape."

"And the Patrol," prompted Peron, "Why no names, if you're so intent on preserving our gene pool?" For a moment Payne looked uncomfortable, stirring uneasily on his seat.

"Ideally, we'd like to have your second years," he said, looking deliberately at the ground, and then held a hand up as Cerren opened his mouth. "But we know that the chances of that are unlikely." He looked saddened for a moment, and Cerren suddenly knew that the man was also wracked by the guilt of using every tool at hand to resist the Garsal. "The choice is yours to make, yours and your Council of Masters. The only proviso is that they must be relatively young." *Young and able to bear offspring,* whispered Cerren's conscience. And yes, the second years represented the best of the gene pool, but if the worst came to the worst, they were needed on the front lines ensuring the escape of the others. *That is,* said his conscience, *unless they're already dead by then. They're already on the front lines.*

He closed his eyes tiredly, the peace of a few moments ago completely disrupted by the choices before him. He was so tired. There was a nudge at his hand, and he looked down at Socks. Her huge violet eyes held Cerren's, trust so evident in them that he was almost overwhelmed, and for the first time in years, felt tears almost start from his eyes. He covered his embarrassment by clearing his throat loudly.

"You know you're not alone Cerren," said Peron. "And Erilla sent a message for you."

"She did?"

"She did," replied Peron. "She said to remind you that there are often no good choices when the fate of the world hangs in the balance. That all you can do is to try and make the best choices from those you have available."

"I wish I *was* making the best choices," said Cerren softly, "but sometimes I don't really know if I am."

"And how could you?" asked Payne briskly. "None of us know the future, and we're not omniscient. We can only make choices based on what we know."

"And none of us are coerced by your choices, Cerren," Peron went on. "We could choose differently if we wished, but we haven't. We have confidence in you, and rest assured, if we think you're making poor choices, we *will* tell you, and expect you to listen." He sat back in his chair, and a hint of his normal humour returned to his eyes. "Even if we have to sit on you."

"Hah!" replied Cerren, slightly buoyed by their comfort, "that is, if you could." And then he smiled, because Peron was looking at him with one eyebrow lifted sceptically, and he remembered that no-one had ever outscored Peron in wrestling. "You'd have to get past Socks first." The starcat twinkled her tidemarks and again Cerren's spirits lifted slightly. "Thank you. Both of you," he said, "And if you see Erilla before I do, tell her I said thank you."

"As Senior Councillor, you bear a heavy burden," replied Payne, "but you're never alone in it. We're there too. Make sure you let us lift some of the load." Cerren nodded his thanks soberly as the three men sat back to watch the fire for a while.

"How are the preparations at Starfall going?" Payne asked after a while. "Do you have an arrival time for the Patrols and Militia squads you've requested?"

"They've been dispatched," Peron replied, "and they should be here within the week, which is why we have patrols to send Below on this current mission. We're stretched very thin, though." Cerren tapped the arm of his chair as Payne raised a querying eyebrow.

"We've always only just had enough Scouts to cover our normal duties, and now with everything else we need to do, we're running without almost any down time. It's less than ideal, but there's no other options. We've accelerated the cadet training programs in all of our centres, and Northaven and Starfall have doubled their intakes. But the qualities that make a good Scout can't be found everywhere, and many of the skills we need take time to develop."

"And the Starlyne training program?" prompted Payne.

"We're working on it as fast as possible, but it's dependent on the time available away from all of the other tasks." Cerren spread his hands helplessly. "You see the dilemma?"

Payne nodded. "Are others suitable for the program?"

"Some," said Peron, "but not a lot. We've concentrated on families we know have Scouts with 'the spark' among their ranks, and those who have starcats. We've found a few, but it appears that we've picked up the majority of them, and without Allad and his ability to detect that spark we're limited in targeting who might be suitable. Toman does her best, but her ability is not nearly as well developed as Allad's is, and we've yet to find any more here in Watchtower."

"So again, we're very dependent on Patrol Ten and those cadets?"

"We are. There will be more with time, but time is the one thing we don't have right now."

"How I wish that the Starlynes had contacted us earlier," sighed Cerren. "But they didn't, and there's nothing to be done about it. I have a meeting with Speaker tomorrow, though, and I'll ask him whether he has any other solutions to detecting the gifted." He leaned back again and watched the embers glow. There was a fresh spatter of raindrops across the storm shutters guarding the windows, and the wind rattled them again, a reminder of the weather that had stopped even the Garsal in its tracks. Strangely, it was a comforting thought.

"So when do those Below leave?" asked Payne.

"Today," said Cerren. "Patrol Ten, the second years and quite a number of Starlynes apparently. "We're sending Patrols Four and Eight after them in two days, when the clean up's finished. They should catch the others within a few days. Hopefully within a couple of weeks we'll have the communications stations set-up, and we can begin fortifying them as refuges." Socks leaned on his legs companionably. "Patrol Ten and the cadets will continue on to the ship. The Garsal will probably have tightened their defences significantly by the time they arrive, so they'll need some time to reconnoitre the area and to decide whether a rescue is feasible at this point. We're hopeful that we can establish hidden camps within a reasonable distance though."

"That remains to be seen, Cerren," said Peron, thoughtfully. "Who knows what they've done since we knocked out their off world communications?"

"Yes, yes, I know," replied Master Cerren. He ran a tired hand over the smooth skin of his head. "But I, for one, am sure they'll be able to find another way in. Cally had no doubts either. She said she'd never seen anything like it."

"What you actually mean, is that she didn't see anything at all," replied Peron drily. Socks purred, and flickered her tidemarks brightly at Thunder, who responded in type. "And that's enough from you two, as well!"

Cerren smiled. "No, she didn't see a thing, except a complete course of ineffective traps, until the whole group of them arrived at the finish line. She designed that course, and she was almost spitting chips when she told me."

"In that case, I have a little more hope," replied Payne. For the first time in the conversation, his eyes had regained some of their twinkle. "Cally has always struck me as formidable, so if her obstacle course couldn't trip them up, then there's some hope for the success of their mission."

"And they'll work with the other Scouts they're travelling with to share their expertise as much as they're able on the journey," added Peron. "So at least we'll have the benefit of that." His unspoken words hung heavily in the room. *If the worst happens and they all die …*

Cerren shook his head, refusing to accept the thought, though it remained at the back of his mind, gnawing at him. He got to his feet decisively. "Well, this isn't getting any of the things done that we need to do. Peron, can you deal with the storm issues?" The big Scout nodded and climbed wearily to his feet. "Payne, I'd like to meet with the guild heads and also the rest of the Council after I've met with Speaker tomorrow." Payne levered himself out of his chair, and groped momentarily for the stick he'd been using since his leg injury. He nodded absently as he located it, and as he limped the first few steps, patted Cerren on the shoulder as he passed.

"Remember what Erilla said, Cerren," Payne told him.

Cerren nodded. "I will, and I'll hold you to that promise of keeping me honest." He heard Peron's soft snort of amusement, and then they were gone.

Cerren's eyes strayed to Socks. She was sitting not far away, looking at him while her tidemarks cycled gently. "And what do you think, young lady? Will I make the right choices? Will I listen to the right people?" She purred, butted him with her head, and then rubbed her long length down his hip. "In that case, let's get back to work."

***

Anjo listened to the slowly dying wind as he helped Janna take the two horgals to their paddock in the aftermath of the storm. Spot nudged him with her nose as they walked and he stumbled slightly. Ember cycled his tidemarks in amused tones. The starcat was never far away and Anjo looked at him fondly. Not only had the cat saved his life, but he'd provided a warm, loving link to the real world that Anjo had needed more desperately than he'd known. His life on Delicata now seemed very long ago. His life on Frontier was threatened, but full of so much more than he'd ever dreamed of.

"What are you thinking about, Anjo?" Janna asked, her sad eyes watching him. Despite her grief she still greeted each day with a determination that Anjo couldn't help but admire.

"What life was like before the Garsal, actually," he replied. "It seems so long ago. Almost like it was a dream."

"The Garsal have taken so much from you." Janna said, but this time the sadness in her eyes was for Anjo.

"And you," he replied, "and I'm so sorry I couldn't stop them." He seemed to need to say the words often, although it didn't make any difference to the guilt. He remembered the stories he'd told the curious boy about his captivity with the invaders, and shuddered at the thought of his young friend in their hands. Spot snuffled his hair as they reached the open gate to the paddock. He walked through with the horgal, and Janna pulled the gate shut behind them. The fence line had been disguised with vegetation and debris to look as if it was only empty land.

"We know you are, Anjo. You did all that you could." She checked the water trough, now concealed by a collection of large rocks, for leaks. Sabre circled around them, staying close to her human companion as she had since they'd arrived back at Hillview, and Ember ran a wider circle at the periphery of the paddock. He'd learned a lot from the experienced trainers in the few weeks since Kaidan's capture, and Anjo was still astounded by the generosity shown by Kaidan's parents in taking him in.

"I only wish that there was some way of helping him," replied Anjo.

"Well, there's nothing that we can do, so we just have to make sure that we're doing everything that we can to stop the Garsal instead. And if that means breeding cats and being ready to help at a moment's notice then that's what we'll do." She motioned for him to pass out of the paddock before her, and then rechecked the gate. "Frustrating though it is."

They walked up to the house, and Anjo again admired how difficult it was to see that it was a dwelling. The front entrance, and the windows built into the side of the hill, had been camouflaged with fabricated moss and vegetation, and the well worn pathways had been covered in gravel and fallen trees. The outbuildings had been removed and most of the fence lines taken down. Those that were left had been deliberately changed, their neat geometric shapes now meandering lines that would hopefully look like tree-lined creeks from the air.

Hillview was full. Josen and his family were in two of the guest rooms, and two other breeders and their families had taken over four more. Anjo was in Kaidan's room. He wondered how Janna and Adlan had been able to put him there. It spoke of not only generosity, but a practical realisation that he might not come back. Anjo felt their loss every time he walked through the door. A high shelf contained a number of books, and there was a collection of wood carvings depicting many of Frontier's fiercest predators. The smooth stone walls held a number of drawings, and the wardrobe held a collection of Kaidan's boots. There were still clothes neatly folded on the shelves inside.

The whole room was reminiscent of his young friend. On the bedside table was a collection of feathers and a pot of glue, and an old hollow tree stump held wooden arrow shafts waiting for their fletchings. Several notebooks had been with the books. One was covered in mathematical formulas, their definitions written in Kaidan's neat hand, and another had notes on navigation. Anjo had felt like a spy, but the books spoke so clearly of Kaidan that he hadn't been able to resist sitting there each evening, reading something the boy had read, or looking at the neat figures he'd loved so much.

Only Shanna's room remained empty, but it was often used as accommodation for overnight visitors, so Anjo supposed it probably didn't count as empty. Hillview was close to the main access road to a number of the smaller settlements, so visitors passed frequently.

The whole place was full of starcats. There were now ten house cats, including Ember, and the individual cat caves were full. The cavern adjacent to the living areas had been partitioned off for the females with cubs, so that each of them had a small haven of privacy. They needed it, reflected Anjo, as he arrived at the doorway, and half-a-dozen two month old cubs galloped out to greet them.

There seemed to be starcat cubs everywhere. They were constantly underfoot, wrestling with each other, chasing each other and performing as trip hazards for any human unwary enough not to watch where they were going. But they were happy blots on a gloomy landscape. There was nothing more endearing than a starcat cub, Anjo reflected, except perhaps ten of them at once, all fluffy ears, huge eyes and pouncing paws. And there were too many of them to keep them all in the cavern all day. He felt a small regret that he'd not seen Ember at the same age, a regret quickly discarded. His starcat was endearing just as he was, although Anjo was still getting used to his propensity for sharing the pillow.

"Cup of tea Anjo?" asked Janna, carefully avoiding another couple of cubs as she moved through the door.

"Yes please." Anjo skirted two cubs wrestling on the floor near the kitchen bench and perched himself on one of the stools sitting around it.

Janna busied herself at the bench as Anjo sat. "We'd like you to consider yourself part of our family, Anjo," she said, pouring hot water over the leaves in the pot. Anjo felt his jaw drop, and didn't know what to say. "Adlan and I talked about it last night. Shanna's Below, doing who knows what, and Kaidan …" she broke off, her voice rough and then cleared her throat and went on. "You have no family left, and we have no idea when we'll see our children again." He heard the unspoken 'if' in her sentence. She turned away to pour the tea into two mugs, and Anjo had the feeling that she was composing herself again. He struggled to come up with a reply.

Finally, he cleared his own throat and spoke. "I don't know what to say, Janna, except that your children, and you and Adlan, have given me more than I can ever repay. Shanna rescued me, Kaidan taught me and befriended me, and now you've offered me the chance of having a family again." He took the cup that Janna held out to him, with slightly trembling hands, and sipped to allow himself time to regain his own self-control. Ember nudged him gently, and he ran a hand down the cat's soft coat, and the tight feeling in his chest eased.

He raised his eyes, and looked into Janna's vibrantly blue ones. "Thank you, Janna. You have no idea how much this means to me. I'm honoured to be a part of your family." Tears pricked his eyes, and as he rounded the bench for the first time in years he felt the arms of family close around him.

# Chapter 13

SHANNA worked her way steadily closer towards the edge of the crater. The four weeks they'd taken to travel to the ship seemed to have stretched out forever, but the task of identifying and marking secure forward posts was not something that could be rushed. It had been more frustrating than she could ever have believed, knowing that with each step she was closer to her brother. But each step seemed to have been taken so slowly, so carefully. That it would become a trial of patience, she'd never expected. Several times, the sounds and sights of aircraft had redoubled the urgency she'd felt as they streaked overhead, off to wreak who knew what kind of destruction on her people. Below was still Below, a place of danger and beauty, but the danger seemed almost removed from the urgency she'd found coursing through her thoughts as they'd travelled. That urgency had been mixed with the wonder of her new found relationship with Verren. The two had combined, sometimes dangerously, to interrupt her concentration.

Slowly, she'd been able to place the thoughts of Verren back into their proper slot for a Scout Below. It had been hard to compartmentalise her feelings like that, but necessary. Urgency had driven her onwards, but it was an urgency she had constantly had to rein in as the rational part of her mind pointed out the problems associated with rash action. Now, as she peered from behind a rock towards the edge of the bowl they'd dropped on the pursuing Garsal almost four months before, Shanna shoved those thoughts back down again and got on with her designated task.

Deliberately, she dropped her vision into her cats' eyes. She was momentarily disoriented, and then her vision reorganised itself and she saw more clearly. Twister slowly panned his head from his treetop perch and she saw with some dismay that there were mechanical sentinels now set at regular intervals on the shattered rim. Since their escape, the Garsal had extended their defences.

Storm was on the ground, and much closer to the nearest sentinel. In fact so close to it, that a thrill of fear pebbled her skin to goosebumps. His eyes saw the mechanical device clearly, and as close as he was, Shanna could see the small flying machines clustered in slots on its rounded top. If the starcat had been even slightly less stealthy, he would have become an instant target. She regretted not telling him to fade.

A blue tinged sense of amusement washed across her mind and she blinked slightly, withdrew her vision, and then hand signalled behind her. Allad joined her within seconds, Satin gliding smoothly by his side. "More sentinels, Allad, and more of those flying things. They've extended the perimeter enormously."

The big Scout nodded, moustache twitching. She had no need to explain the finer implications to him.

"Wait here." He vanished, and she flipped her silent whistle into her mouth and recalled her cats. Within moments, both were by her side, and she sent them out in half arcs in front of the Patrol, far enough to guard, but close enough that the sentinels wouldn't be attracted by their movement.

Allad returned with Spiron and Fury, and to Shanna's surprise, Fractus. "Send your cats out again," Spiron directed her, "and relay the images directly to Fractus. He'll share them with the rest of us."

Shanna nodded. Of course, they'd done a similar thing on their original trip southwards. A few whistles later, and she was looking through her cats' eyes again. This time, she could feel Fractus observing.

"It appears we've stopped just far enough away for the sensors to avoid detecting me," came the relieved thought from the Starlyne. Shanna recalled her cats again, and followed Spiron's signals to withdraw. They congregated in the hideaway Ragar had found after their previous escape from the ship.

"That ring of sentinels is going to slow us down," sighed Spiron. Barron nodded and pulled his map from his pocket.

"This is where they were the last time we were here." He pointed to his neat annotations on the paper. "The question is, have they simply used the same sentinels, or is this now a primary ring with a secondary one still set within it? Or are there more of them in concentric circles around the encampment? Or worse, staggered throughout the bush?" He sat back on his heels in the dim light of the grove.

"It's a problem," replied the Patrol First with an expression of frustration on his face. "Fractus, are you certain you and Teacher were out of range when we located them?"

The Starlyne's voice was firm, with just a hint of uncertainty underlying it. "By our best estimates, yes. I'm inclined to think we're still undetected because the flying sensors were not activated, even if the Garsal have made further strides in developing this technology."

"We'll have to assume that we're undetected then, but it means that we're going to be spread thin, once again, while we survey this ring. And then we've got to figure out what to do once we get past it. It's unlikely that they'll think a failing sensor is simply a mechanical issue. We won't be lucky that way more than once."

The thought of concentric rings of the sensors and their attendant mechanicals horrified Shanna. How on earth were they supposed to break through rings and rings of the things? Her train of thought was broken by Fractus again. "This is a colony ship, so we'll have to hope that they have limited amounts of the sentinels as well as limited amounts of aircraft." His tone was resigned, however, and Shanna knew that the Starlyne was as worried as she was. "In the meantime, we'll need to work on a strategy to pass them. Obviously Taya can disarm them, and by now, hopefully Kalli and Karri are proficient as well. If there is more than the one ring, though, they're likely to be exhausted by the time we reach the ship. And I'm certain there'll be roving sentries, and other traps as well. Let alone the issue of alerting them to our presence by disarming them." His tone was as frustrated as Spiron's. "Let me think on this. In fact, let all of us think on this. First of all we need to establish the extent of this deployment." He curled himself more neatly, and his tidemarks began to swirl gently.

"Fractus is right," said Allad, "first things first, and one step at a time. We can't make plans until we know the extent of the issue."

Spiron nodded. "In that case, rest up tonight, and tomorrow we'll split into groups and begin the survey. Amma, what do you think the chances are of an aerial location of these things?"

Shanna looked at her friend, as Amma considered the question.

"I don't know, Spiron. They're not large, and the canopy is quite dense." She turned her head to the Starlyne. "Fractus, how high would I need to fly to avoid detection?" Shanna started slightly. Sometimes she felt stupid when her peers considered things that had never crossed her mind.

"Good question," came the thought. "Once we establish exactly how far apart they've placed them, we'll have a better idea. The detection field is hemispherical in shape. We can extrapolate height from their placement. We'll have to calculate some overlap, not simply halve the distance ..." His thoughts faded as Spiron nodded.

"So flying won't be our initial strategy then, but we'll try it at some point — so Amma, I still want you to give it some more thought."

The planning continued on well after dusk, before Spiron had Teacher relay the information to Radiant at the nearest forward post they'd established. The information would be on the plateau within a few hours. It wasn't really reassuring, reflected Shanna, but at least this time they weren't simply disappearing Below, never to be heard of again should they fail. Anyone coming after them would have some idea what they'd encountered, and Patrols Four and Eight were relatively close, finalising the setup of the last few waystations. It didn't make it any easier for them, though. She wondered how her brother was, or if he was even alive. The pain of his loss was still there, driving the urgency, but it had dulled somewhat, simply becoming part of her background thoughts.

If he was still alive, she wondered if he'd be the same brother she remembered when she found him again. Twister and Storm hummed gently at her, and she hugged the two huge heads to her for comfort.

***

Kaidan sat exhausted in his cell again. He was so tired of the pain, so tired of the fear, and so tired of the complex web of half truths he'd 'confessed' to the Overlord. He'd tried desperately to make sure that they were accurate enough to be realistic, yet gave nothing important away, and still, he wasn't sure if he'd succeeded. He'd begun to lose track of time, which disoriented him further. The one thing that kept him sane was the old woman in the cell next to his. Sometimes she was there when he returned from his sessions with the Overlord, and sometimes not. The whispered words of encouragement were the things he'd begun to hold onto when things became unbearable.

Lately, the sessions had changed. Instead of trying to extract information, the Overlord had concentrated on the behaviours expected of a slave. "Bend slowly," had been the council from the old woman. "If you break too fast, the Overlord will be suspicious, but if you bend too slowly you risk your mind. It is a balancing act, perhaps the most difficult you will ever face, but you must pretend, play the role – because your life and mind depend upon it."

There was a rustle from next door and Kaidan scooted over to the adjoining wall as silently as his battered body would allow him to do so. He was ever mindful of the presence of Edon on the other wall, listening with all of her might. On the woman's advice, he had fed Edon tiny pieces of information that collaborated what he'd told the Overlord, trying to develop a sham relationship with her to keep her from suspicion about his motives.

"Kaidan." The whisper was almost inaudible.

"Yes, Lacey?"

"The time is approaching when I won't be able to guide you further. When you're released to the Matriarch, you'll be separate to the rest of us, and held in a different part of the ship."

"But what will I do?" Kaidan didn't need to feign the panic in his whisper. His mind was walking very close to the edge, and he wondered if he'd drop over it if he was deprived of Lacey's help.

"You'll do as you've done, and then you'll begin to understand why." The statement was cryptic, and full of overtones that Kaidan was unable to unravel. "You will remember a name. That name is Laretai. When you have the opportunity, you will say my name. Nothing more, nothing less, and in no-one else's presence." For the first time, urgency gripped the old woman's voice. "You must say nothing about this to anyone else, or in anyone else's presence. If you do, you'll most likely be responsible for more death and despair than you can possibly imagine."

"But who is Laretai? And how will I recognise them when the time comes?" Kaidan was desperate. He couldn't imagine how it would be possible to meet privately with one slave anywhere in the ship without suspicion. The suspicion of a cackle coloured Lacey's voice.

"You'll know, there is no doubt of that. Just do as I've said. If all else fails though, this is one name you must never divulge to the Overlord. Never."

She coughed slightly, and then went on. "Now, off with you. Go and talk to Edon, and then sleep. Your time in this region of the ship is very limited now. Every day here might be your last, so just in case, know that you go with my hope, Kaidan, and my farewells."

There was another rustle, and Kaidan knew that the old woman was no longer on his side of her cell, and would talk no more for the night. He crawled silently over to the basin in his cell. The water was cold and abundant, the one thing in his cell that gave him any pleasure. Slowly, he washed his face and hands, and then began the delicate task of peeling his shirt from his back. Most times when he was returned to the darkness of the slave quarters, his back was bleeding. Today had been no exception. The dried blood made removing the shirt a slow and painful task, and often his back bled again in the process. Personal hygiene had become an obsession with him since his captivity had begun. It was part of his remaining dignity and sense of self worth, and he held onto it with all his might.

This time, it wasn't as bad as it could have been, but there was still enough pain to make him gasp. Finally, he managed to slide his right arm out of the sleeve and began to pull the shirt off his back. When it was off, he explored the dried blood on the shirt by touch before dunking it into the basin, swishing it back and forth to rinse it as best he could without light. He wondered how many scars he now bore. His shoulder was still sore from its dislocation, but slowly he had begun to trust its ability to move and hold him again.

"Kaidan?" It was Edon's voice. He removed his trousers and underwear and rinsed them as well, not troubling to keep his voice down too much as he replied.

"Yes, Edon?"

"Why do you wash your clothes so much?" For a moment he debated with himself, and then decided on a version of the truth.

"Because the dried blood makes it painful to lie down." That was true enough. But everything made it painful for him to lie down, not just the dried blood. He spread the clothes across his cell bars and began to sluice water down himself. It was hard to tell whether he was doing an effective job in the dark, but something was always better than nothing, he thought, and preventing infection came with cleanliness. The cool water was soothing on his bruised back and limbs. There was silence from the other cell briefly.

"Tell me again about Frontier."

Kaidan began the fiction he'd crafted, sticking strictly to the flora and fauna, and avoiding political structure and geography. He said nothing about the Scout Corps or governing bodies, but concentrated on schooling, friendships and family, while avoiding starcats and special skills. He said nothing he'd not said before, but he did his best to dress it all up in rolling language to make it seem fresh and new. It was another exhausting recitation, as he sidestepped carefully around so many topics he needed to avoid. An hour later he finished.

"I need to sleep, Edon." He felt around in the dark. His clothes were damp, but he pulled them on anyway. There was no need for him to be marched naked through the ship if his captors came in the dark for him. As he laid himself down, carefully wriggling so that as few as possible of his bruises contacted the floor of his cell, he pondered on the name that Lacey had given him. 'Laretai.' It wasn't a name he'd ever heard, but he rolled it around in his mind, committing it to his memory along with others he treasured. Lacey's name was there now, and Shanna's and his parents, along with all their cats. And Anjo, the offworlder who'd fought so hard for him when the Garsal came. He closed his eyes and prayed that for this night at least, he might sleep the full night.

***

"Zoash, the human is well broken. Send him to the Matriarch tomorrow." The Overlord's tones were redolent with satisfaction. "It's a pity he had so little information, but the scientists tell me that his physiology is an exciting find in itself."

"As you wish, Overlord," replied Zoash. "Are there further instructions?"

"You will oversee the transfer yourself, and report anything unusual. I believe it is only a whim on the part of the Matriarch, a curiosity if you wish, but it is rare that the females take new slaves."

Zoash bowed his head and left the room as the Overlord dismissed him. The hit and run air raids on the plateau had progressed well. The live feeds from the aircraft had shown significant damage to infrastructure, and slowly, very slowly, knowing the Great Enemy was here, they had begun to note their presence on sensor sweeps. Each aircraft dropped sensor drones as they attacked, drones programmed in predetermined flight paths, and their information had been most informative. It was likely that the Overlord would rise to greatness after destroying this last bastion of the Starlyne people. Zoash savoured the sensation – those who rose with the Overlord would be assured of offspring.

***

The lights went on, and Kaidan dragged himself painfully out of a deep sleep. He rolled over, pushed himself up on his hands and knees, and felt his shirt unstick painfully from his back. Apparently he'd still been bleeding when he went to sleep. In the light, he could see that his washing attempts had been painfully inadequate. Rusty stains marked his mottled trousers and the front of his shirt. There were still several missing buttons from his capture, and the fabric was torn in places. He supposed that there was fresh blood seeping through the back of his shirt as well, judging by the warm trickle between his shoulder blades. Marching Garsal feet sounded in the slave quarters as Kaidan bent over the basin for a drink, and splashed the water on his face, futilely trying to smooth his unruly hair. His stomach rumbled vigorously.

He stiffened as the sound of marching ceased outside his cell, but remained with his back to the bars. "Out, slave." The bars slid smoothly to one side, and Kaidan docilely took his place in the midst of the marching feet. He reminded himself that his best hope of survival was now in feigned obedience. Up and down the serried ranks of cells, slaves were taken to their daily tasks by individual Garsal soldiers. Kaidan wondered at the use of troopers to do so, it seemed a waste of resources, but, he reminded himself, the system obviously worked. Apart from Lacey's whispered instructions, he'd seen no other hint of rebellion among the slaves. Any form of tardiness or task failure was met with immediate consequences and casual violence. Even a task well performed sometimes met with punishment. The slaves were in a perpetual state of fear and anxiety as a result.

He marched off with his escort, the only slave with more than one trooper, but, he noticed with a shiver, this time there were only two. As he passed Lacey's cell, he chanced a glance sideways. The old woman was out of her cell as well, and her head dipped as he passed. It was her only farewell. He knew, now. The change of escort was significant. It might be the last time he saw her.

He pretended to stumble, caught himself on her arm and whispered. "Thank you." A blow from the Garsal trooper behind him caused one of his bruises to erupt in a fountain of pain, but it had been worth it. He rolled the name around his mind once more. 'Laretai.'

Ten minutes later, his guards approached an elaborately decorated door in the ship. It was unlike any other he'd seen. Waiting outside it was a Garsal he'd never seen before. The creature was taller than the troopers with him, and intimated a sensation of coiled danger. "You will follow, and be silent."

Kaidan bowed his head as he'd been taught and followed as the door slid open.

The room beyond was large, and filled with decorative hangings. He'd never seen anything like it. He waited with the Garsal until the far door irised open. Two Garsal, dressed in filmy robes, entered. The Garsal with him bowed his head towards them. One spoke clearly in the standard tongue. "This is our new slave, Zoash?"

The Garsal with him replied in the harsh sounding tones of the insectoid race's language. Kaidan understood nothing but his name. The smaller of the two chided him, again in standard. "Zoash, he does not yet understand the true tones. You would be well to speak as we do, so that the slave clearly understands his position."

Zoash began again. "My ladies, Estei, Hirtoi, this is your new slave as requested by the Matriarch. His name is Kaidan. He has been trained to obedience by the Overlord himself. This slave knows that there is nothing beyond obedience to your wishes." He turned his head towards Kaidan, "the Overlord wishes to remind him that pain and death are the only things that await him, should he displease the Matriarch." Kaidan attempted to look fearful and properly cowed, but the differences between male and female Garsal behaviour were fascinating. He brought his attention back as Zoash continued to speak. "I will leave him to you now. Slave, floor!" Kaidan dropped to the floor as he'd been taught, hands flat on the ship's deck, and forehead beside them. He hated prostrating himself like that, but he reminded himself of Lacey's wise words and focused on survival, and the name. He wondered who the slave, Laretai, might be, and how soon he might encounter him or her. He wondered how harsh the female Garsal might be in comparison to their male counterparts. Zoash was obviously unafraid of leaving him unattended with them, and he shivered slightly with fear.

Zoash left with another bow, and then the smaller female flicked her robes to one side lightly with one of the smaller limbs at the top of her thorax. The one below tapped a baton across its mate. "Well, Hirtoi, shall we see just what this slave has learned?"

# Chapter 14

FRUSTRATION had piled on top of frustration as Patrol Ten and the cadets completed their initial survey of the ring of mechanical sentinels. The sentinels had indeed been expanded in a circle that now ringed the entire bowl. Unfortunately, the thick vegetation inside the depression had obscured the view from the rim, and they had been unable to estimate if or where, more sentinels had been placed inside the bowl. They had located the egress points used by the Garsal, and it had become increasingly clear that the larger predators had finally become wary of approaching the mechanical guards and their attendant flying machines.

"Well, it was bound to happen," said Barron. "They've been here for at least a year now, and although they're still not venturing far from their ship in anything except vehicles, even a staureg learns to leave something dangerous alone given enough time."

A year, Shanna thought, a whole year. The days had continued to march past relentlessly as they'd surveyed the area, and although rationally she knew it was important, it didn't stop her wanting to do something, anything. Their plans were stalled by the lack of information though.

"In that case, I think it's time to attempt a flight," said Spiron. "We've calculated what we hope is the range of the sentinel's detection fields, and we'll stay well above it. Hopefully we'll still be able to do a decent check of the ground."

"But what if they see us?" Amma asked.

"I don't see what other options we have, Amma," replied Spiron. "Hopefully they'll think we don't have the technology to fly, and won't look up. And if they do, maybe they'll just think we're some kind of bird."

It sounded like a fairly flimsy hope to Shanna, but what else could they do? They'd searched, mapped and planned, and without being able to see what might be beyond the outer ring, their best plans all started with getting past the initial ring of sentinels followed by – "if we find this, then we'll do that, but if we find that, we'll do this." And all of their plans had too many unknowns. Although Scouts were renowned for their ability to adapt and invent, they all knew that as soon as they breached the outer ring of sentinels, the Garsal would most likely know that they were on their way.

Several times they'd watched as animal life had set off the sentinels and their attendant clouds of flyers. It had been a fast annihilation of the animal followed by the appearance of either a crawler or climber. A sentinel that powered down would be quickly investigated, had been the consensus.

"Are we all flying?" Shanna asked.

"No," Spiron replied. "Just Amma and Allad. You and I will suit up, Shanna, but I'm not willing to risk us all for a survey flight. We'll back the others up, but only if something goes wrong."

It took them two hours to walk to a high point not covered by the sentinels, with Shanna and her cats spearheading their trek. Accustomed now to taking the forward position in the Patrol, she and her cats moved smoothly and silently through the thick greenness. They crested the top of the rock spire as the early morning light began to strengthen towards full daylight. They were all quiet as the four flyers shed their packs and began to don their flight suits.

"Thanks, Amma," Shanna said as the other girl stepped back from checking her suit, She ran her own eyes over the fasteners of Amma's suit, and tested each of them with a quick tug. "You're good." Amma nodded and took a deep breath.

"I'm ready then," she said. "Allad?"

The big Scout nodded, flicked a hand signal to Satin, who perched herself on a rock at the edge, and then walked himself to the edge of the spire. "Let's go then." Amma launched herself as Spider joined Satin, and Shanna and Spiron watched as the two of them caught the first thermal and soared quickly upward. It was hard to stand waiting on the rock, not knowing what was going on, as Allad and Amma's shapes quickly dwindled to small specks. She hoped fervently that they'd be all right.

Fractus' head appeared over the lip of the spire, and Shanna looked curiously over the edge to see what the Starlyne had done with the rest of his large body. He'd carefully wound it around the rocky face, tucking bits of himself carefully behind outcroppings as he'd ascended. She wondered how he'd get down. "I'm receiving images from Amma and Allad," came his voice. They're just about to move out over the rim. "Allad will stay high, while Amma skims as low as is safe. I'm relaying back to Radiant in the nearest shelter." Images flickered across Shanna's mind, and she put one hand on a nearby rock as the speed of the image share nearly upended her. It was akin to looking through her cats' eyes, but at the speed that Amma and Allad were flying, it was quite disorienting. Fortunately, her practice with her cats allowed her to settle herself quite quickly, but she heard the sound of gagging from behind her and she realised that Fractus was probably broadcasting the images to all of them. "Sorry, I'll slow it down," Fractus apologised, and Shanna heard Spiron's gasp of relief.

Her images remained the same, and as she opened her mouth to speak, she heard Fractus' wry voice. "I'll leave them as they are for you Shanna, if you're fine?" And she realised that she *was* fine, and then wondered how Fractus could possibly manage to do that. And apparently speak to two people at the same time, saying different things.

"And that's what makes us different to you humans, Shanna," Fractus said dryly. "Unfortunately our adaptation is too specialised, and our generations too slow — we cannot manage the scope of your abilities, but what we have is very refined. Perhaps in time we'll develop a wider scope, but for us it will take many centuries. Your individual life spans are much shorter compared to ours, but it means that genetic change can occur much faster in you. But enough. We must concentrate now." His voice cut off and the images sparked to a sharp clarity.

It was almost as if Shanna was flying as well, and as Amma swooped over the edge of the rim, carefully keeping to the altitude they'd calculated as safe, she felt her stomach wobble in sympathy. She ignored it, just as if she'd been the one flying, and concentrated on what Amma was seeing. The ring of sentinels was now behind her, and she was scanning from side to side, trying to pierce the vegetation with her eyes, seeking for the least hint of metallic shine among the multiple shades of green. The oddly doubled vision included Allad's circling watch above Amma — he was concentrating on the horizon as he circled, making sure that there were none of the alien aircraft visible. Every now and then he dipped his vision towards Amma, who was flying a grid search pattern.

Shanna was caught up in the intensity of Amma's concentration. She could 'feel' the part of Amma that watched the air currents, carefully gauging her height and her speed, calculating the next leg of her search, and simultaneously seeing what Amma saw. Most of the time, it was just an unbroken sea of varicoloured green, but then, a glimpse of one of the huge crawlers came through the trees. It looked even more menacing from the air, a squat contraption driving its huge weight into the ground beneath it, and leaving deep, muddy, devastation in its wake. Shanna shivered, despite the warmth of her position on the spire. She turned her attention to Allad's view, and with a sudden burst of alarm, realised that Amma was flying neat, straight, lines. Lines that would alert any observer that the flyer was not a bird, but instead a rational being, performing a search. "Spiron! Amma's flying too neatly!"

The Patrol First was quick to understand. "Fractus, can you speak to her?" There was a sudden lack of images, and then they resumed their flow in Shanna's mind, and she frantically switched her view back to Allad's. Amma was now swooping and circling like any one of the birds flying above the canopy.

Spiron dropped a hand on Shanna's shoulder and squeezed. "Good pick, Shanna," he said quietly.

"Let's hope there wasn't a Garsal watching her," she whispered back.

The time wore onwards as Amma circled and swooped, and Allad watched, and Shanna began to wonder at the other girl's physical endurance. She seemed to be tireless. As she looked through Amma's eyes, Shanna could see that she had cleverly managed to cover most of the search pattern. She'd begun by disguising it in a series of flourishing loops and swirls, every now and then wandering past the rim edge, so that if anyone was idly watching, her flight pattern was not confined to the bowl.

Allad continued his watch from above, maintaining his circling flight, but also managing to look as if he was meandering his way through the air. There hadn't been a hint of a sentinel between the outer ring and the inner fencing around the ship and the hive site, and Shanna had begun to feel hopeful about their chances of penetrating the compound once more. She had no qualms about their ability to hide themselves once they were inside, but the issues of escaping with Garsal captives in tow were much more complicated.

Amma made a dizzying turn and Shanna realised that she'd decided to return, and thankfully relaxed her concentration slightly, shifting her attention to Allad, who was still sweeping the horizon. He too made a turn, and dropped lower towards Amma, intent on joining her on her return trip. Shanna could 'feel' the thermal he'd seen, and glided down into it with him. He waggled in the air as he joined Amma, and they flew together towards the spire, making an oddly doubled vision of the spire inside Shanna's head. The images ceased and Shanna wriggled slightly as she relaxed from concentrating, using her own eyes to look towards the specks that were Amma and Allad winging straight towards them on the spire. Something didn't feel quite right, but she shrugged it off as fatigue from concentrating for so long. She wondered how tired Amma and Allad were, and also began to consider removing her own flight suit. It was cumbersome and hot when she was on the ground.

As she watched the two Scouts approach, her sense of unease began to grow, itching at the back of her neck. She shook her head, annoyed at herself for silly fancies, because the risky portion of the flight was now over, and resumed her watching.

She knew, at the same moment that her cats did. And the two flyers' cats did. A snarl rent the air as a red line lanced above the treeline towards Allad and Amma, and Shanna took two steps, and leaped off the spire, followed almost immediately by Spiron. Her two cats hissed and snarled as one of the flyers began to spiral awkwardly, and the other one dove towards its floundering flight. Shanna cursed herself as she looked frantically for thermals as she dropped. Why hadn't she realised? Why hadn't she listened to that nagging sense of danger? Two birds didn't join together side by side and fly in a straight line. Someone had been watching. And now she and Spiron were targets too. The gunner fired again from somewhere in the foliage below the crippled flyer. This time the shot went wide as the two flyers, now just below the bowl rim, flew in unpredictable patterns, one crippled, and the other one trying desperately to assist.

Shanna spotted the air current she needed, angled herself towards it, and dove towards the crippled flyer. She had no idea what she'd do when she got there, but she knew she needed to get there fast. As she came closer and closer, she could see that Amma's wing suit had been crisped completely on one side, smoke still drifting from the wing. She hoped frantically that her friend was uninjured. As she neared, she realised that Allad had managed to manoeuvre himself under the damaged side of the suit and level Amma out slightly, but that they were still spiralling lower and lower very quickly. She took a quick glimpse below her, and realised that they were on the inside of the ring of sentinels and inside the Garsal area of control.

She streamlined herself more tightly and increased her speed, shooting towards the wobbling pair. She heard Allad's voice faintly, "Turn around Shan! Go back Spiron!" His voice was tight with strain, and she ignored it, concentrating only on her trajectory and the air currents surrounding her. Dimly, behind her, she could hear Spiron, echoing Allad's cry. *Why?* She wondered, and held her line. Another red line lanced through the trees, now close below them, incinerating leaves as it flicked close to her left side, and leaving a sharp smell of burning and heat as she flew on.

She ducked under the undamaged side of Amma's wing suit and felt the strain immediately. "Fly higher, Shan!" came Allad's voice, desperately, urgently, and as she looked below, she realised just how close they were to the treetops. And the ring of sentinels. "And to the right!" She searched the thermals frantically, angling herself in what she could find, trying to push Amma's weight higher, and further to the right, hoping that they could spiral out of danger and then get past the line of sentinels. A flash of red on her right side pushed them leftwards, and she put all of her energy into balancing them as they slipped sideways and downwards, trying to stop the deadly plummet.

"Leave me!" was the whisper from Amma in her right ear. They ignored her, and now began to work together, arms and legs creaking with the strain. Deliberately, Shanna reached into the depths of herself as another red beam sizzled past Allad, and faded all three of them. The strain on her body increased fivefold. She had no energy patch stuck to her skin, providing that buffer of energy, just her own resources, so she gritted her teeth and held on.

"Merge," Allad ordered.

As they started to mesh Shanna could tell that they weren't going to make it over the rim – they were losing height too fast. Beside her she could feel Allad turn them back towards the hidden grove they'd found on their last trip.

"Allad, you need to stop us hitting anything!" Shanna said through the merge, as they lost more height.

"How?"

"If you can lift a rock, surely you can push us up if we approach the ground or a tree too fast?"

"I can try." His voice was tight with strain despite their meshing, and Shanna knew that the long flight, followed by the struggle to keep Amma aloft, must have depleted the big Scout's reserves. The treetops were flashing by beneath them now, and they were still dropping too quickly. She watched the air currents carefully, making what corrections she could, as Allad was doing on the other side, trying to ignore her own rasping breaths.

"Slow down in three, two, one, now!" They lifted into the wind and slowed their speed, but it was sluggish with the three of them in close contact, and they dropped too fast. Shanna felt Allad groan and then something pushed them sideways slightly as her boots hit the first tree, and then they were falling between two huge pungo trees. Somehow their rate of descent slowed, and Allad's breath became ragged. "Ready to land! Push up, three, two one, now!" They rocked slowly to the vertical, and then three pairs of feet hit the ground, hard.

Shanna felt as if her ankles were about to break, and she hastily pulled in her flight extensions, simultaneously trying to turn to her right and catch Amma. She was Below, inside the Garsal compound, and without her cats.

She blanked that thought out as she stumbled under Amma's weight and then eased the girl down, hastily making sure that there was nothing danger-ous on the ground. "Amma? Allad?" Her voice was quiet, suitable for Below. There was silence from both of her compatriots. "Allad?" she said, as she lowered Amma's silent body the last few centimetres to lie supine on the ground.

"I'm OK, Shan." Allad's voice didn't sound OK. It sounded exhausted, and uncharacteristically, he hadn't assisted her to lower Amma. Shanna glanced a look at him. He was lying crumpled on the ground, pale even in the dim light filtering through the canopy. "I'm not injured," his voice was a hoarse rasp, "just exhausted." She fumbled one of the energy patches out of her thigh pocket and slapped it wordlessly onto the back of his hand. As some of the colour began to flood back into his face, Shanna turned her at-tention to her friend.

Amma's wingsuit had been completely charred down the right hand side. The material was a melted mess from the wrist clip to the ankle clip. Amma appeared to be unconscious. She was breathing, but her face was very pale. Apprehensively, Shanna began to check her from head to toe, slowly easing the fasteners of the wing suit open, thankful for the two huge pungo trees they'd landed between. At least they had a small measure of safety, she thought.

Allad joined her, crawling over, limbs barely able to hold him, but his eyes urgent. "Is she alive?"

"Yes, but I don't know how badly she's hurt," replied Shanna quietly. "We need to remove her suit." The two of them began to ease Amma's wing suit off her, pausing as they surveyed the melted mess down the side. "What do you think, Allad?" Shanna's voice shook slightly.

"It needs to come off, but slowly, in case she's burned badly, and the suit is stuck ..." his voice trailed off. Shanna took a deep breath, and began to ease the suit off Amma's arm. It was still warm where the beam had melted the material, and she held her breath as she carefully began to roll the material away from Amma's forearm. The melted portion had stiffened as it cooled, and it was difficult to remove it slowly, but sweating, Shanna peeled it slowly back, while Allad steadied Amma's arm. Flakes of black sifted from the sleeve, and she could see redness beneath. As the suit finally began to come free of the arm, however, Shanna could see that while the skin was reddened it was not even blistered. Not for the first time, she blessed the skill of their Starlyne allies. The suit had melted, but also protected her friend as it did so.

It took time, but the suit was finally off, and it was clear that Amma had survived largely unscathed. *If,* Shanna thought, b*eing Below, trapped in a Garsal compound without your starcats is unscathed.* Why she was still unconscious was unclear. Shanna hoped it was just exhaustion, because the Garsal knew that they were somewhere close by, and they might need to move at short notice.

Allad had slowly regained some strength, with the assistance of the energy patch, but it was clear that of the three of them, Shanna was in the best shape. Not a promising thought, she realised, given the shape she was in. She felt a pang of longing for her cats, a longing for the security and safety that their presence meant, but more importantly, she longed for the closeness of their companionship and love. Faintly, she thought she felt a wash of blue/violet love flicker through her mind. At least Spiron wasn't trapped inside with them, or at least she hoped he wasn't. She really had no idea what had happened to the Patrol First. She wondered if Fractus could still hear her, and called experimentally to him, but there was only silence in response.

"Well, let's get you two safely stowed," she said, and then, forcing a quiver of apprehension down, "and then I'll go and see what's happening."

# Chapter 15

SHANNA crouched behind a rock, faded, as one of the climbing machines clanked its way past her position. Faintly at the edges of her mind, she could feel her cats. They both had an edge of anguish about them. She could feel where they were, just as she had when she flew, but this time, she could feel that they desperately wanted to be with her. Again, she called silently to Fractus, but there was no answer.

She wanted to make sure that her concealed friends were safe before climbing one of the taller trees and attempting to refine their position inside the Garsal lines. She had a vague idea of where they were, and she knew they'd been heading in generally the right direction when they'd crashed, but she wasn't sure, and her location sense wasn't as well developed as Verren's. Once again, she regretted the limited time they'd had to explore their abilities. With her cats by her side, she knew she would have been more accurate, but they weren't with her, and there was nothing she could do about it. Second best would have to do.

She carefully considered the tree she'd picked. She'd reasoned her way through a number of points. Firstly, they were inside the ring of sentinels, and it was likely that the mechanical devices had reduced the number of prowling carnivores significantly. That was good, but reduced didn't mean there would be none. Secondly, the fence around the ship area would have accounted for some more, but again it still didn't mean that there were none. Thirdly, she was fairly certain that no mechanical device would stop a group of sliders completely. That was something she hoped never to experience again. Without her cats' superior senses, she felt half blind, and almost powerless. Shanna was struck by how much she depended on her starcat partners when Below, but she resolutely went back and reminded herself of the fourth point. She was alive and she had friends who'd be trying to reach her.

She listened. The normal sounds of Below filtered through the vegetation around her. Birds sounded their bell-like tones, and there was the rustle of small creatures busying themselves about their daily tasks. Very faintly, she could hear the sounds of the climber fading into the distance.

She watched. There were no flights of startled birds, no shivering of vegetation that might signal a large predator or Garsal vehicle, and no sign of the mechanical sentinels. There were a number of nut bushes, which she carefully harvested, making sure to leave two-thirds of the nuts for the bushes. There was a small clump of plybrush just to her right, and she took a moment to make sure she could find her way back to this spot, should they need some.

Then she moved, soft footstep after soft footstep, carefully skirting a carnivorous vine, stepping around a barbed palm, and moving silently towards the large tree she'd targeted. It seemed to take forever to reach the safety of its trunk. Each time she moved, she had to memorise precisely where she'd come from so that she could be sure of finding the other two. Without her cats, she was reliant only on her own hard won skills.

Shanna took a moment to survey the area around the tree, and then swung herself silently up into its lower branches. It was a buttressed gum and was much larger even than the towering pungos they'd crashed between, but the number of its branches made it ideal for climbing. It would possibly serve as a hiding place should the small grove they'd camped in last time prove too difficult to reach. The buttressed part of its name came from the immense hollowed portion formed at its base as it grew taller and taller. It was big, and it was climbable, but it also meant that it would be home to many birds and animals. Buttressed gums formed their own mini ecosystems.

The memory of the fire moss uppermost in her mind, Shanna climbed carefully, making sure she'd sighted each handhold before she placed her hands. It would be very easy to place her hand on something deadly if she climbed too fast. As she climbed she listened, watched, and tried to 'feel' for wildlife around her. It was difficult, and after several minutes, she let her fade go, knowing that she didn't dare use any of the few patches she had in her pockets. She had too few of them as it was. As the strain of holding the fade left her, she extended her other senses, trying to 'feel' ahead.

Ah, there was a treemarmal, and over there, a hollow with a sugar climber tucked safely inside. She'd skirt that branch, because of the zapper bugs, but climb this one, because it had nothing more innocuous than a purple diver's nest. Slowly she climbed the tree, relying more and more on her extra senses to know where to place her hands to avoid the more dangerous of the creatures living there. Finally, she hoisted herself up on a branch that poked itself above the surrounding canopy, and for the first time, she could see the sky.

Carefully positioning herself on the branch, she pulled her map and compass from her thigh pocket. The familiar features of the bowl allowed her to determine her position accurately, and she was relieved to confirm they were where she thought they were, and not far at all from the small grove they'd found last time. They were well inside the ring of sentinels, only recently plotted on her map, but closer than she liked to the ship. She pushed herself to her feet, balancing on the branch, and took a look towards where she could 'feel' her cats. In the distance, she could just see the rock spire she'd launched from. They were much closer to the sentinel ring now – she looked at her map – they were probably at the previous night's campsite, given the bearing on her compass. She sighed heavily, sat herself down on the branch and carefully plotted a course to the grove from her present position. Knowing where she was, allowed her still developing sense of direction to place her companions on the map, and she pencilled in a small circle.

What to do next? Both Allad and Amma would need food and water as soon as possible. Her pockets contained some dried fruit, and the nuts she'd harvested. She had her belt knife, and her glowstone, and although her fire making kit was in her pack, if she needed to, she was quite capable of starting a fire without it. Not that that was likely with the Garsal searching so hard for the three of them. She hoped that the other two were still safe. Water was the first priority, and establishing whether the other site was still safe. If it was, they'd be fine for water, so she decided that she'd work her way there first. Then if all was well, guide Amma and Allad there. If Amma could walk that was, or was at least conscious.

All the issues came crashing down on her at that point, and she almost let out a sob. How was she going to make sure her companions were safe, when she wasn't even sure that she could keep herself safe? She'd almost let that out that sob, but almost was better than actually doing it, and although her breath was ragged, she grasped her courage with both hands and began to descend the tree. She carefully extended her senses as she descended, trying not to focus on her missing starcats. She could still 'feel' them there, still feel their longing, still feel their direction and their love, but they were out of reach, as far away as the moons were, for all practical intents and purposes.

***

"Zoash!" The Overlord's voice cracked through the command centre. He was angry. Somewhere humans were within the sentinel ring.

"Yes, Overlord?" His hatching sib's tones were careful.

"Push the searchers harder. At least one was damaged. It should be easy to find."

"We are recommencing the grid search, Overlord, and I have also dispatched several climbers to the known water sources. They will sit and wait. The invaders will require water."

"I need answers, Zoash." There was an unspoken threat in the Overlord's voice. "How is it that they have undetectable flyers? Flyers that do not even register on our scanners?"

"I have my best technicians working on it Overlord. They tell me that it will be some time until they have their preliminary findings."

The Overlord paced, furious. Those same technicians had still not unravelled the humans' ability to avoid visual or mechanical detection either. It was an anomaly. Garsal conquest had relied on two things – technological superiority and numbers.

"Push them harder Zoash."

"It is likely they are dead, Overlord. The fall should have killed them." Tones of conciliation overlaid the words.

"It is likely, you say." The words escaped the Overlord in a hiss, and the room quieted suddenly. "It was *un*likely that we would encounter an invisible enemy, or humans on this planet. It was *also un*likely that the Great Enemy would be here." The silence thickened like the air before a thunderstorm, and the Overlord realised that, in his anger, he'd revealed more than he'd intended to his underlings. No matter. They had defeated the Great Enemy once, so they would do it again. "And now they fly as well." He swung around and looked out over the stilled command centre. "And we will prevail against them all. I demand it." His faceted eyes grew hard, and then the silence was replaced with the sounds of industry.

"Zoash, I will notify the Matriarch of the developments. You will arrange the appropriate offerings." Without waiting for a reply he stalked from the room.

***

Shanna reached the others after another tension filled trek, relieved to find them undisturbed. As she slid silently between the two towering pungo trees, Allad cautiously lifted his head from under the screening branches. "Shanna?" His whisper was almost inaudible.

"I'm here." She scooted over to him, and began to remove the pile of leaves and twigs. "How's Amma?"

"Still unconscious, but nothing else seems amiss," he replied. "Do you know where we are?"

"Yes."

"How far are we?" A sudden crunching noise had both of them suddenly alert, and Shanna dropped horizontal and crawled on her belly to the nearest tree. She faded herself and then peeked out from behind the tree. Two weldens were grazing several metres away, and one had pulled a branch from a frondan tree and was pawing at it with one foot, seeking the juicy inner part of the limb.

Shanna relaxed the fade and moved back over to Allad. "Weldens." She took a breath. "We're a little way off, but it's a bit tricky and I don't know how we'll get there with Amma unconscious."

"Can you reach Fractus?" asked Allad.

"No, you?"

"I was hoping it was just me," he sighed quietly. "We should have been in range – I could still hear him when we were flying – so I hope nothing's happened on the outside."

"Perhaps they've had to move out of range. There are a lot of vehicles moving around and the aircraft have flown over several times. I can 'feel' my cats, though."

"You can?" Allad seemed slightly reassured. "Maybe it's only Fractus who's moved then." The two of them carefully uncovered Amma. She was still motionless, and Shanna kept a careful watch as Allad again went over her unconscious body. As he ran his hands through her hair, he stopped, and Shanna saw his hands move backwards and forwards, and then he peeled an eyelid back, and then the other. "Your glowstone, Shanna." He held his hand out, and Shanna hastily slipped the chain over her head and handed it over, and then went back to watching and listening for any signs of danger. It was very difficult to prevent herself from looking back to see what Allad was doing.

Another rustle sounded, and she faded again and made a quick silent circuit around Allad and Amma. The two pungo trees would keep most predators away, but it was never wise to be complacent Below and Shanna's human senses were no match for a starcat's. She relaxed deliberately, and allowed herself to 'feel' the surrounding creatures. The two weldens were still grazing, and there were several marmals moving surreptitiously from cover to cover. She expanded her senses again, feeling oddly constrained without her cats. The thought of the approaching night sent shivers of apprehension down her spine.

"Shanna," came Allad's soft voice, and Shanna withdrew her senses and moved the few steps to his side. "I hope she's only concussed, but I've found a large lump in Amma's hair."

"So what should we do?" asked Shanna. Allad sat back on his haunches and ran a hand through his hair. He closed his eyes briefly and then looked at Shanna with a frown creasing his forehead.

"I don't see that we have many options, Shanna. This spot won't be safe tonight without cats. If you can fade us all, I'll carry Amma, and we'll make for the grotto." Shanna felt her heart sink. She was already tired, and fading all three of them was likely to exhaust her completely.

"I'll need to use a patch, Allad."

"Do it. There's no point saving them if we die here tonight." It was the first time Allad had said the word 'die' in Shanna's hearing. Without another word, she pulled a long acting patch from her pocket, trying not to count the few remaining there, and slapped it onto her arm under her shirt sleeve.

"Try and mesh with me," Allad said, "and I'll try and augment your fade." Shanna laid a hand on his arm as he hoisted Amma carefully onto his shoulders.

She felt Allad's fade immediately, but this time meshing with Allad, without their cats, eluded her, so she mentally shrugged her shoulders, and carefully extended her bubble over all of them. Despite the patch, she could feel the strain on her body — as if she was still carrying her pack. She stifled the regret that she wasn't. The loss of her starcats tugged on her again, and there was a faint wash of violet and blue across her mind from afar, and the weight eased slightly. She pushed the wonder to the back of her mind, and with Allad's hand now on her shoulder, they began the long trek towards what meagre safety the little grotto might provide.

Fortune favoured the first half of their trek, and the only Garsal presence was a faint rumble far in the distance. As time wore on though, the strain of holding the fade began to slowly wear Shanna's endurance down. She was aware of the sun slowly lowering and the green tinged light of the canopy began to dim around them. With darkness came greater danger from native predators, and she mentally recalculated the distance and their estimated time to the grotto.

She took a moment to orient herself, then pushed on. Behind her, Allad's breath was becoming louder and more laboured under Amma's weight. She skirted a carnivorous plant, carefully guiding Allad around it with one hand, and then crouched to peer through an overhanging screen of leaves. Her hand went involuntarily to Allad's on her shoulder, and she took a step back as silently as she could.

"Tuskers." The scaly creatures weren't large, but they did travel in groups and each was equipped with sharp, blackened, tusks on their foreheads. Hurriedly, Shanna checked the wind, then relaxed. It was blowing from the tuskers towards the humans. They should be able to sneak around the excitable and aggressive creatures. Three steps later, the wind changed, and faintly through the leaves, Shanna saw several heads lift in sudden alarm. A snuffling snort echoed and then multiplied.

"Run, Shan. As quiet as you can, but fast – try and get us downwind!" Allad's voice was urgent in her ear, and Shanna needed no further prompting. Casting a hurried glance towards the tuskers, she leaped into motion. From the corner of her eye, she saw the first tusker throw itself through the screen of leaves.

Frantically navigating while trying to keep Allad or herself from running into anything dangerous, Shanna almost lost her fade. As she ran, she caught a glimpse of her left hand, and with an effort, pushed the bubble of fade back over them all. The tuskers could smell and hear them though, and the thunder of stumpy limbs crushing branches sounded loudly behind them. As she ran, her body cringed at the thought of those pointed tusks just behind her.

Again she calculated, estimating distance, direction and time, and came to an unavoidable conclusion. She jumped a small log, hoping that Allad would feel her body lift in time to avoid it, and heard his grunt of effort as he pushed himself up and over. She couldn't imagine how he was still able to run with Amma's heavy weight on his shoulder. Sweat began to trickle between her shoulder blades as she arced them around towards where she'd last seen the Garsal. Avoiding a barbed palm, she felt a slash on one leg, and realised that one of the tuskers had almost caught them. It must have been tracking by scent alone.

Something hot ran down the outside of her leg. Now the smell of blood would be added to their trail. She caught a glint of metal through the trees. A Garsal vehicle. She made her decision quickly.

"Garsal. When I signal, separate from me then drop behind. You'll have to try and fade Amma as well, Allad. I'll lead the tuskers in front of them."

"Ready." There was a grunt among the heaving breaths behind her, and she felt Allad's hand tighten momentarily, and then she was past the tree she'd marked in her mind. "Now!" She felt Allad's hand drop, 'felt' him go to ground behind a boulder, and deliberately relaxed the fade for a few seconds. Letting the tuskers see her she sprinted away, pulling the fade back over herself like a hooded cloak. The nearest tusker lunged with a shrieking snuffle, and she felt something strike her leg, hard, but she pushed through the pain and ran faster.

A flurry of confused legs thundered after her, and she led them, faded, in a straight line, bursting out of the trees right in front of the Garsal climber. For a few seconds nothing happened, but then it roared suddenly into life as the tuskers poured across its nose, startling them into a flurry of legs and heaving tusks. The leader charged towards the vehicle and the others followed. Shanna used the confusion to sprint downwind of the tusker herd along the side of the vehicle and then she was back into the concealing bush. Within moments she was shrouded in greenery, while behind her, she could hear the shrieking snuffles of the tuskers interspersed with sizzling strikes from the Garsal weapons. She took a quick look behind her, realised that she was free of the tuskers, and looked around to see if she could find Allad. The sound of her panting was loud in her ears, and she tried desperately to quieten it as she headed back through the trees. She was tired, tired and hot and sweaty and dirty and fearful. Fearful that some of the tuskers might have found her friends. That some of the others might still be following her, and afraid she might not find Allad and Amma, and end up alone, trapped behind the Garsal front lines.

There was a hiss, and she started slightly, and then her fear turned to relief as her eyes interpreted what they were seeing. Allad, Amma still unconscious on his shoulders, easing himself out from behind a tree. "Come on, Shan, we need to keep moving."

It wasn't until later, that she wondered how he'd even known she was there.

# Chapter 16

THE Matriarch sat statue-like on the dais in her reception chamber as the Overlord concluded his summary. The offering tray sat unregarded on its pedestal near the doorway, and Laretai stood silently at her side, their position on the slightly raised dais carefully planned to the last detail. The Matriarch was careful to let no hint of emotion colour her eyes, keeping her attention fixed on a point just above the Overlord's head.

"Our old Enemy is here, Matriarch. This is our chance to completely crush the Starlyne race."

The Matriarch lifted a manipulator arm as if in thought, and then, very deliberately, stood. "You are certain?" She paced forwards with stately deliberation. Two steps, no more. She wished to remain elevated.

"We vanquished their world long ago. This must be only a remnant. The scans are clear, Matriarch, but we suspect that they are few. We have detected no large habitations. My technicians estimate only a small population."

Keeping her expression neutral, the Matriarch allowed herself to feel a sense of scorn. His technicians estimated no such thing; in fact they were currently at a loss to estimate anything. Laretai's spy taps had been most illuminating. She turned and sat down again. "Is the hive secure? And what of the humans?" So far he had neglected to mention the flyers detected and downed. "Could they be allied?"

"It is possible, Matriarch." He made the concession grudgingly, the words dragged out one by one. "But we are secure. The sentinel ring has been extended, and even now, my aircraft raid the human settlements on the plateau." She noted the use of the possessive pronoun and tucked it away for further thought. "There is no evidence of an alliance, however." He was lying, she was sure.

"I am displeased." There was no qualifier in her phrase, and she saw the shock hit home. The Overlord would now be wondering what she was displeased about – the Starlyne presence, the human presence, the security of the hive and ship, or the raiding aircraft? Precisely as she and Laretai had planned. "You will keep me informed." She waved a manipulator arm, and departed through the exit behind the dais. She felt, rather than saw, the moment of stunned dismay. He would be standing there, caught in confusion. She heard the click of Laretai's feet as she descended the dais, followed by her musical tones as she ushered the Overlord out of the room and back into the main ship.

Her attendants approached, and she gestured. "Estei, Hirtoi – I would speak with you privately." The two young females approached and fell gracefully in behind the Matriarch as she proceeded to her private chambers. She motioned to a slave as the double doors opened. "Bring the new human to my chambers." The slave bowed her head and hurried off to do the Matriarch's bidding.

She sat and indicated for the new initiates to join her. A chamber slave brought drinks in elaborate vessels, and they sipped together. "Leave. Admit no-one but Laretai and the new slave." He bowed formally, face to the floor, and left. The Matriarch heard the door shut firmly behind him. "I would hear how you are progressing with our new slave." There was a small hesitation, and then Estei replied.

"Matriarch, the process is slow, as the slave is most distrustful. His name is Kaidan, and he is very young, just a child as the humans measure time."

"He has been treated most dreadfully by the Overlord, Matriarch," said Hirtoi. "Our best attempts at befriending him are rebuffed with suspicion."

The Matriarch sipped her drink as she contemplated. It was to be expected. It was early still, but it appeared that her time to implement the plan was becoming shorter every day. The door opened and Laretai entered. She acknowledged the two young females and sat herself down beside the Matriarch. "He is unbalanced, Matriarch, as planned, but I am concerned that his drive to conquer, and his desire to dominate, may overrule good sense and planning. We must proceed with caution, and yet, all haste." The door opened, and the new slave entered and prostrated himself.

"You are correct, Laretai," replied the Matriarch, and then turned her head and regarded the new slave. Now clean, she could see how young he really was. She shrugged his youth off, there were no other choices available to her, so he would have to do.

***

Kaidan entered the Matriarch's presence for only the second time since Zoash had handed him over to the two female Garsal. He was uncertain, unsure, and terrified. His treatment in the female enclave was much better – there were no beatings at least – but the female Garsal frightened him. They pried, asked him questions, and attempted to engage him in discussion about the human presence on Frontier, and he lived in a constant fog of fear that he would divulge something he shouldn't. He prostrated himself, and then had to force himself to keep still as a shock ran through him.

He was sure that the Matriarch had said the name Lacey had entrusted to him – Laretai. The weeks in the female enclave had provided him with the beginnings of an understanding of the Garsal language, but as yet, he could only decipher the occasional word as they conversed. He rolled the name over in his mind again. Yes, she *had* said the name. In a moment of panic, he wondered whether Lacey's secret had been discovered, and whether the slave she'd told him to contact had been discovered. For a moment all of his faint hopes died.

"Kaidan." The words came from the Matriarch herself, and Kaidan tucked his head down more tightly. The movement stretched some of the slowly healing scars on his back and they stung slightly. "Stand." Her pronunciation of his language was different, but understandable, and Kaidan pushed himself hesitantly to his feet. As trained, he left his eyes firmly on the floor. He found himself holding his breath, and tried to relax unobtrusively, and then found himself trembling instead. The tall Garsal female walked slowly around him, filmy robes trailing behind her. She said nothing, completed the full circle, and then beckoned. "Laretai." To Kaidan's shock, her aide stepped forwards and replied.

"Yes Matriarch?"

"He is now your property. You know what needs to be done."

"Yes Matriarch."

Kaidan almost staggered, and his trembling increased. Fear vied with astonishment. Surely Lacey hadn't known that Laretai was one of the Garsal? And if she had, why hadn't she told him? He struggled with the dichotomy. Was Lacey a human traitor? Was she the informant that he'd thought Edon was? He had no idea, and now he was set adrift once again, the personal property of a Garsal female. A female who 'knew what needed to be done.' Whatever that was. For a moment he almost panicked and ran, but where would he run to? In a daze of confusion, he heard Laretai call him by name to follow her.

***

Very quietly, Shanna pulled up her trouser leg. They were finally safe in the grotto with Amma propped on a soft pile of pungo leaves near the rocks on the far edge, and she and Allad were taking stock.

"How's your leg?" Allad asked, concerned. Her trouser leg was soaked in blood, and the leg had begun to throb and ache.

"It's a pretty big slice, Allad." Shanna propped her leg on a rock near the spring as they talked as quietly as possible. It was dusk, and the early sounds of night time had just begun. The grotto was small but secure, or, amended Shanna, as secure as you could get Below without starcats. It was ringed in pungo and bordered on one side by rocks. The small spring welling up in a rocky basin was fresh and cool, and as she carefully dripped the water on the congealed blood, the chill was very welcome. It cut through the throb and she sighed quietly in relief.

Allad fished through his pockets, carefully sorting through his limited possessions. "Do you have anything antiseptic, Shan?"

"No," she replied. Allad prised open a small tin and extracted several wads of gauze.

"This'll have to do then." He dabbed gently with a moistened one and began to loosen the caked blood. Shanna dribbled more water as the wound slowly appeared. It wasn't too deep, but it was long, and dirty. The last thing she needed was an infected wound to top off their already precarious situation. It was clear that Allad was exhausted after carrying Amma, and so was she. The night was looking very long with only the two of them to share the watches. The separation from her cats weighed heavily upon her, and she 'felt' instinctively for them again. They were still where she'd 'felt' them earlier, but the faint sense of anguish washing across her mind had grown slightly.

There was a sudden sound from Amma, and Shanna dropped her foot off the rock and hurried over to her. The other girl was stirring restlessly, her skin pale in the gathering dusk. Shanna was relieved to see her stir, but fearful that the sounds might encourage something nasty to visit, or bring the Garsal down upon them. "Amma?" she whispered with a hand on Amma's shoulder. "Amma?"

Amma moaned again, and Shanna hastily covered her mouth, feeling dreadful about doing it, and then looked more closely as the girl's eyes finally opened. She looked slightly panicked, and tried to raise herself, but fell backwards against the rock behind her with a groan, stifled again by Shanna's hand. "Sorry Amma," she whispered. Amma's eyes blinked rapidly, and then, with a feeling of huge relief, Shanna saw reason and recognition return, and she cautiously removed her hand. "How are you?"

Amma opened her mouth to reply, and then turned even more pale, and hastily turned her head to the side and vomited. Feeling helpless, Shanna left her hand on her friend's shoulder as she heaved, and then proffered her water bottle when the other girl slumped back against the rock behind her. "Thank you." Amma's voice was unsteady and she rinsed her mouth out several times before taking a sip. "Where are we?"

"In the grotto not far from the ship. How are you feeling?"

"Horrible, actually. Bad headache, nausea, and my right side feels hot."

"Allad hoped you were just concussed. You've got some mild burns down the right side – no blisters or anything, but it's pretty reddened. Could you eat anything?" Amma looked nauseated and shook her head.

"I'll just try and drink, I think. How long have I been out?"

"Most of the day. Just rest. Your water bottle's full, and Allad and I will keep watch." Amma closed her eyes tiredly and slumped back against the rock as Shanna scooted back to Allad. He'd taken the opportunity to circle quietly around the grotto.

"We'd better get this leg dressed before we lose the light, Shan." She propped her foot on the rock again as he pulled another piece of gauze from his tin. She hid a flinch as he loosened the last of the blood and began to dab the wound dry. Even in the dim light, Shanna could see small flecks of dirt were still embedded in the long gash. "We'll have to look for a soothall bush tomorrow, or anything else that might be useful as an antiseptic. I'm going to need better light to remove all of that grit." She nodded.

"Amma's still pretty ill, Allad. What if she doesn't improve?" They both paused as the warning cries of a flock of nightwings sounded on the breeze, and the sound of breaking vegetation came loudly through the trees. They both relaxed as the sounds lessened. Whatever the creature was, it was heading away from them.

"We'll jump that hurdle when we come to it, Shan." He put her foot back on the ground, and she winced slightly as her leg started to throb again. He hesitated. "Can you take the first watch?" It was an admission of exhaustion from Allad, normally so capable that Shanna had difficulty imagining him even faintly tired.

She felt her heart thud, but she nodded in the remaining light. "Yes, go and rest."

"Thank you."

As Allad moved to cushion himself on the ground near Amma, Shanna stood resolutely. Rubbing another handful of pungo leaves over her exposed skin and clothing she circled the grotto silently, desperately wishing her cats were with her. They weren't, so she delved deep into her waning resources and let herself 'feel' what was around them. Silently, exhausted and fearful, she began her watch.

***

Kaidan had fetched and carried for the female Garsal, Laretai. Her quarters were roomy, and filled with artworks, or at least, what Kaidan assumed were artworks. She had made no attempt to converse with him, or to dig deeply about Frontier, but he'd caught her watching him when she'd thought he was engaged in a task. Her faceted eyes were unreadable to him, and her body postures were very alien. Hours had passed, and numerous slaves and other Garsal had come and gone.

He rolled Lacey's last words to him around in his mind. "You will remember a name. That name is Laretai. When you have the opportunity, you will say my name. Nothing more, nothing less, and in no-one else's presence. You must say nothing about this to anyone else, and you must not be overheard. If you do, you'll most likely be responsible for more death and despair than you can possibly imagine."

His mind raced even more than it had when the Overlord had interrogated him. Had she meant for him to trust a Garsal? Or was she a spy for the Garsal who was delivering up a juicy morsel of information? He deposited the tray of food he'd collected for Laretai on a small table near her seat, abased himself and then stood by the door as he'd been trained to do. Across from him, another man stood. Kaidan snuck a look at him. He was much older, and stared fixedly at the floor. Apart from instructions, none of the humans in the female section of the ship had attempted any conversation with him. He felt even more isolated than he had in the slave hold. Slaves spent the nights locked in small bunk rooms unless they were on night duty, and there was no conversation beyond that necessary for essentials. He'd never met a group of people so cowed by their experiences that they even refused to communicate. The conditions he'd just left were materially worse, but there was at least some kind of human contact, even though it was fraught with the fear of informers.

He'd tried to talk to some of them, but after he'd been ignored several times he'd ceased his attempts. It was as if they'd had the humanity beaten out of them. Perhaps they had, he reflected – he'd certainly come close, and without Lacey's encouraging words and advice, he probably would have as well.

He snuck another look at Laretai, and then looked back down at the ground again, hoping she hadn't noticed his eyes move. She was looking at him again. His skin crawled. The goosebumps on his back actually hurt. His heart thumped and he tried to relax himself but couldn't help the way his eyes kept wandering back towards the female Garsal sitting so quietly in her chair. She was still looking at him. He pretended he hadn't looked and kept his eyes on his feet, but the thoughts he'd initiated wouldn't stop stampeding around his head.

She spoke. "Kaidan." He trembled, but forced his legs to move and dropped to his face in front of her. "The rest of you – leave." He remained, head down, as the sounds of departing slaves and Garsal echoed on the hard flooring. Finally, the door shut behind the last one. and all was silent except for the sound of tapping from Laretai. She was using the rectangular shaped piece of technology she carried with her everywhere. Kaidan waited, trembling again, with Lacey's words echoing around his mind. What had she meant? Had she really been his friend? They were alone. He was alone. This was his chance, but could he risk it? He didn't know – was it possible that a Garsal was part of a secret human underground? Or was Lacey part of the Garsal informant network?

Her words and her actions had preserved his sanity – he knew that. Her words had helped him to limit what he'd told the Overlord to things that were unlikely to damage his people. Her words had comforted him. The silence drew itself out, broken only by Laretai's tapping. What did she want of him? He owed Lacey his life and his sanity, so finally, he decided. Keeping his face on the floor, he took a trembling breath and then he spoke one word – "Lacey."

The tapping ceased.

# Chapter 17

IT HAD been a very long, very tiring, night. Shanna's eyes felt gritty and heavy, as the sunlight began to slowly slip its way through the canopy. She'd watched for as long as she could keep her eyes open, trying to give Allad as long a rest as possible. Finally, when the adrenaline that spiked through her body at every sound had no longer sufficed to keep her alert, she'd woken him apologetically. He'd been hard to wake, but uncomplaining once his eyes had finally opened. Shanna had sunk thankfully onto the ground, her eyes closing almost of their own volition. Sleep had been like falling into unconsciousness, and she'd had to force herself awake when Allad's shaking had penetrated the blackness in the early hours of the morning. For most of the final watch she'd had to try to change her position as often and as silently as possible to keep herself focused and alert.

The night had worn on slowly, but at least they'd survived it.

She woke Allad again, then lowered herself wearily to her knees beside Amma's recumbent form. "She's just sleeping," he said. "Can you keep watching while I forage?"

Shanna nodded and stretched herself as quietly as possible, and then took a few steps, limping slightly on her injured leg. It improved as she moved, so she nodded to Allad and then began to circle quietly around the grotto. The early light slanted through the trees, tinging their leaves to glowing green in all its shades. She rubbed her eyes with one hand as she ghosted from cover to cover, careful to pause each time and survey the area before she moved. A number of the smaller carnivores scuttled into the undergrowth just ahead, and a carnivorous plant closed itself around an unwary marmal. The marmal struggled briefly before the plant drew it inwards and engulfed it in its digestive cup. Her stomach rumbled, and she hoped Allad was finding something edible close by.

She felt slightly uneasy as she finished her circuit. She'd harvested a few nut bushes on the way around and had been fortunate enough to discover some of the tubers that were so tasty when baked in the coals of a fire. They weren't nearly as nice raw, but still, they were food, and she resigned herself to the thought of chewing the tough roots.

As she deposited the roots and nuts on a convenient rock, Amma sat up. She was still pale, and struggled to move, but finally managed to lever herself to her feet using the rocks at the rear of the grotto. Shanna waved a hand signal query to her, asking if she required help, but Amma shook her head and propped herself on a rock, drinking deeply from her water bottle. Shanna returned her attention to the surrounding bush, eyes and ears alert for any sound out of the ordinary. She still had an undefined sense of unease sitting in the back of her head, but she dismissed it, and concentrated on 'feeling' the surrounding area, pushing her senses outward. There was nothing large in the immediate vicinity, but she could 'feel' several marmals cowering in their burrows, a flock of bellers in a tree twenty metres to the east, and Allad. He felt like a column of strength at the periphery of her 'vision' and he was moving steadily towards the grotto. Nothing else of note was close by, so she relaxed slightly and began to mentally catalogue the plants in the grotto, looking for anything useful.

When Allad finally returned, the three of them took turns eating and watching. Shanna shooed a dozen inquisitive stinkrats away as she was shelling her share of the nuts, feeling reassured by their presence in such numbers — it meant that larger predators were unlikely to be nearby. The nuts were at least tasty, and she saved them until last, after washing down the tough tubers with mouthfuls of water and bites of the greens Allad had supplied. Slowly her stomach stopped complaining.

They took an inventory of the energy patches each of them carried on their person, and then Amma broke the bad news as the three of them crouched near the edge of the grotto, eyes outwards.

"There's another storm coming."

Shanna's heart sank. No cats, limited shelter, and the three of them stuck inside the ring of sentinels. Her feeling of unease suddenly made sense.

"How bad?" asked Allad.

"Bad. It'll be here within two days. It's an intense one, and quick moving as well, so it'll retain its strength for some time over land. Not as much rain as some, but enough."

Allad sat back on his heels, absently smearing a handful of pungo over himself. "I think we can make the rocks safe enough to shelter in, but it'll be very uncomfortable. At least we won't have to worry about the Garsal for a day or so, though." He frowned in thought. "Can either of you hear Fractus?" Both Amma and Shanna shook their heads. "Can you still 'feel' your cats, Shan?"

"Yes, I'm pretty certain they're at the last campsite, and they're not happy."

"I'm sure they're not," he replied. "But then, none of us are. The others should be fine — they can drop back to one of the new waystations if they need to, or shelter near one of the spires. I'd like to see if we can contact them somehow though, because I have another idea."

"You do?" asked Shanna, wondering what Allad might have in mind.

"Yes, although it's quite risky," he replied. "I think ..." he broke off as the beller flock erupted into the air with cries of alarm and the three of them made haste to conceal themselves. The mechanical sounds of one of the

Garsal vehicles came clearly through the morning air. Allad hand signalled silently, and they all faded. Shanna swept her eyes across the vegetation and extended her senses again. Without her cats she wasn't as adept, but she could clearly 'feel' the panic of the fleeing small mammals and reptiles as they crawled, slithered and scurried away from the alien vehicle. A glint through the trees showed the position of the climber, and again she held still, hoping that it would pass them by.

A few minutes later, they relaxed slightly, dropping their fades to Allad's whistled signal after the climber had passed, and then gathered together quietly in the shelter of a rock. Shanna noticed that Amma was again pale and wobbly, and the dark circles under her eyes seemed to have enlarged. She staggered slightly as she drew near. "Sit down, Amma," whispered Shanna. She pulled the last couple of nuts from her pocket and handed them to her friend. Amma looked momentarily nauseated, but she began to force them down, one by one, gagging slightly as she swallowed. Some of the colour began to return to her face.

"Can you travel Amma?" asked Allad. His face radiated concern.

"I think I'll have to use a patch," she replied. "Or you could leave me here." Allad shook his head.

"If you had Spider, I would, but without her? No." His voice was final. "You'll use a patch, and eat whatever we have left among us, and whatever we forage on the way. If we need to fade, Shanna will fade you." Shanna nodded, hoping she was hiding her own apprehension, as she was far from adequately rested. "Amma, we're going to need your weather sense badly for what I've planned, so you need to be ready and well rested."

"What have you planned?" asked Shanna. Allad deliberated for a few moments and then nodded decisively.

"If we can contact the others, I think we should stage a break in during the middle of the storm." Amma's eyes widened in shock, and Shanna felt a thrill of fear mixed with excitement push a surge of adrenaline through her body, then her eyes narrowed.

"But what if we can't contact the others?"

"Then we'll just have to try and break *out* during the storm, or enter the ship." All of the alternatives seemed equally impossible. "Without our cats we can survive for a time," said Allad soberly, "but we'll become more and more tired, and our ability to gather food is limited. We can rest up here for a day or two, but sooner or later the Garsal will come through here. They *know* we landed, and it's unlikely they'll stop looking for us. I wouldn't, in their place."

Shanna knew he was right, but she was troubled. If they were to invade the ship, they'd have to do it faded, and once they were inside they'd have to try and retrace their steps to the slave quarters, and then without cats try and get out again. The burden of hiding themselves, and anyone they took with them would fall to her. If they were to break out of the encircling ring of mechanical sentinels, one of them would have to disable the sentinels, and that meant her, and her skills were much cruder than Taya's. "But how?" she asked. "If there was only a high point to launch from, one of us could fly out."

"And risk being shot down?" said Amma. "They'll be on the lookout for that for sure."

"If we can communicate with the others, I'm going to suggest they try and break in at multiple points around the ring. They have Taya, Kalli and Karri. And it's likely that engulfing a sentinel in flame or electrical current might kill them also. I suspect dropping a large rock or tree on one might be effective too." Again, Shanna felt slightly ashamed of her own self focus. All the discussion about her own abilities had led her to neglect to consider that some of the others might have skills to contribute to the problems at hand. Allad had years of experience to draw on, and his thinking showed it. "First things first, though, lets move. Hand signals only, Shanna on point. Amma, you're in the middle. Use your patch now." He flicked a hand signal, and once again, Shanna glided to the forefront, engaged her extra vision, wished fleetingly for her cats, scanned the area quickly with all of her senses, then headed out.

***

The concussions rocked the old storm shelter where Cerren sat with Watchtower and Starfall's remaining councillors in the underground operations room. The acrid smell of smoke tinged the air faintly in the board-hung room, and they all winced as a loud detonation nearby made the roof tremble. "This is the second time in the last twelve days, Cerren," said Payne with a grimace.

"Do you think Dinian's archers will take out another craft?" asked Peron.

"Perhaps," Cerren replied, "But it appears that the Garsal have learned their lesson well, and are staying higher than our people can shoot their arrows. Still, Dinian's got them up there, and this time we had enough warning to position them before the attack. We just have to hope that their positions are still standing." The wait during the raid had been long and frustrating. The first raid had capitalised on the initial strike that had left so much destruction in its wake. Large parts of Watchtower were now in ruins, but fortunately the loss of life was much less, due in large part to the evacuation and dispersement plans put into place after Tamazine's death. Scout Headquarters had again escaped unscathed in the attack twelve days ago, but Cerren knew that it wouldn't escape damage if the raids kept coming.

"You've transferred all of the important equipment and supplies underground?" asked one of the older councillors from Starfall.

"Yes, the last load went down yesterday," Perron said, glancing towards the doorway. He was awaiting the initial reports of the ongoing raid, and a steady stream of messengers had been coming and going.

"Our people are well practiced in their evacuation drills," added Cerren. "I'm sure they're safely tucked away." He wanted to pace while he waited, but he restrained himself, knowing that he needed to appear calm despite his inner agitation. Too many of Starfall's councillors had been badly shaken after Tamazine's death. Some had been almost unable to function in the wake of the initial attack. Cerren had wondered at it, briefly, but after some reflection, he'd come to a few conclusions. Life in Starfall was comparatively easy compared to that experienced by the residents of both Watchtower and Northaven. Secure, centralised living had reduced the resilience levels of those unaccustomed to Frontier's wilder areas. Cerren made a mental note to bring up the issue of complacency one day when he had enough time. Once again, he blessed his own posting to Watchtower. As a Scout he'd spent years in the wilderness areas of the Plateau and working in the dangers of Below, but he'd not appreciated the impact that the lack of exposure to real danger had had made on his fellow councillors. That is, until Tamazine's machinations had exposed them.

He made a mental note to address the issue once the Garsal threat had been eradicated. Perhaps there should be some kind of prerequisite before elevation to the Council. Or at least a term of service in a small settlement. That had added advantages, he mused to himself. The prospective councillor would gain the needed perspective of life in more dangerous areas of the plateau, and begin to understand the isolation and fortitude of the small villages. While those more remote areas would benefit from their expertise and education.

Another concussion shook the storm shelter, disrupting Cerren's musings, and fine dust sifted from the ceiling.

"That felt close," said Peron. The hair on the back of Thunder's neck was standing on end, and the young cat hissed. He ceased abruptly as Socks hummed a caution to him, and his tidemarks began to flicker in embarrassment. The burning smell thickened briefly and then began to subside.

Cerren hoped against hope that the damage would be less this time. But he knew, from the persistent string of percussive blasts alone, that his hope was futile. Socks hummed reassuringly to him, and he rubbed her upturned head gently.

A starcat appeared at the door, paused briefly, and then went directly to Peron. He removed the tightly rolled message from its clip in the cat's harness. "Toman says that there are three aircraft again. They're concentrating on the market square, Scholar's precinct," he paused, wincing slightly, "and Scout Headquarters."

Cerren's heart sank, but he bowed his head in acknowledgment and forced himself not to leap to his feet and pace. "How bad?"

"Not sure yet," replied Peron, still scanning the note. "There it is." He read from the note. "*Early reports estimate significant damage to the western* end of Scout HQ. The eastern end appears unscathed at this point. The arena and tunnel entrance are secure." Cerren made himself nod as if he'd expected this. It wasn't a lie; to a certain extent he had expected it, but the reality of it was much more devastating. Peron read calmly on as another concussion rocked the ground, and the walls shivered. "The aircraft are concentrating on this area of town now, apparently," a wry grin twitched his lips, "and it appears they're hitting any building that looks official."

"That explains the pounding we're feeling here then," replied Payne. "I hope they get tired shortly and decide to pack it in and go home." He grinned at the others. "We have too many other things to do, rather than sitting here idly."

Cerren snorted. "Idly, you say?" Each time a note had come in, Payne had listed the points neatly on the blackboard across the end of the room and then noted any casualty or damage estimates on the map. His group of aides were efficiently collating damage reports and beginning the task of allocating rescue teams, just as they did during the great cyclonic storms. The team was well practiced, and Cerren knew that as soon as it was safe to do so, Payne would begin the monumental recovery task. More and more he'd come to admire the man – Payne continued to work, good humoured and rock steady, no matter the devastation around him.

"At least there are no signs of ground attacks," said another of the councillors. The woman was worrying the ends of her robe in her fingertips.

"Not yet," replied Cerren. "But I'm sure they'll come."

"But when?" asked the woman.

"Who knows?" he replied. "But they will come." A messenger entered the room at a run, and rushed straight to Peron.

"Direct hit on the Council building, Sir. Archers managed to damage an aircraft, but not badly. Master Dinian says he thinks the attack is tapering off." More messengers entered the room and hurried to Payne's aides and the noise level in the room rose as the operations room activities escalated.

Peron and Payne began to confer with two of the aides as more damage reports came in and were added to the board. While the majority of the population was now sequestered at the old storm shelters outside the town, there were still a number of areas of the town critical to the defence of the area. Healer's precinct and the militia barracks had extensive underground shelters from the early years, but underground shelters needed above ground access. More importantly, the town walls were still needed to keep dangerous denizens of the plateau away from the still inhabited areas.

Despite the dire nature of their predicament, Cerren found himself resenting the idea of having to rebuild so much of Watchtower when they finally triumphed. "Do we have any reports from the Starlyne communications network?" he asked.

"Nothing much yet," replied Peron, almost absently. He was flicking through a clip-boarded list. "Payne will send messengers as soon as he can. But no, no reports of aircraft anywhere but here so far." He beckoned for another messenger, handed her a note and sent her off at a run.

They were still using children, Cerren noted sadly. That was young Ella, one of Josen's if he remembered rightly. Instead of sitting tight in Hillview with her family, the youngster was running messages in a war zone. As were many of the others. Idly, he wondered if Anjo was recovered adequately to resume his duties as a messenger. Or if he could. He'd sent Semba to Healers Precinct. She was still traumatised, still struggling to form relationships, and he wondered if she'd ever recover enough to become a normal member of society. As the operations room began to hum with activity, Cerren wondered what might happen if they did manage to defeat the Garsal. What would they do next? It was certain that the Garsal would one day revisit Frontier, or Haven as the Starlynes preferred to call it. He shook his head. They were still in the middle of the first task – they had yet to defeat the Garsal. Anything else could be left until this was over, one way or the other.

"Cerren!" Payne beckoned, and the Master hurried over. "The aircraft have headed south again. I'm sending out the first damage teams. There'll be an escort of militia awaiting you at the entrance. They'll escort you to Scout Compound." Cerren nodded, flicked a hand signal to Peron across the room, who acknowledged it, then he and Socks left to see what was left of Scout Headquarters.

The whole western end of the building was a mass of scorched and tumbled stone. The squat sturdiness of the eastern end was largely untouched, but the main entrance had taken a direct hit, not once, but many times. The old wooden doors were shattered and smoking, and the Garsal weapons had scored deep, blackened, lines across the entire front of the building. In places, whole chunks of walls were missing, and the western stairway was completely gone. A team of firefighters dressed in Scout fatigues laboured away, smothering flames and hauling rubble away from the shattered end.

"Cerren!" Erilla's voice cut through the sounds and smells of devastation. "The eastern end is fine, but we'll need a new dining hall when this is over."

"No-one's hurt?" Socks butted his hand gently.

"No-one," she confirmed, pushing a grimy strand of hair back behind one ear. "The ground's a bit scorched in the arena, but the tunnel access is secure. Once we've extinguished this, we'll begin to camouflage it even more. Yendy thinks we can use some of the rubble to pretend that the arena's taken a direct hit too. We're hoping it might prevent any further attacks there, or at least minimise them." He nodded, relieved to hear that there were no Scout casualties but angry at the destruction he saw before him. There seemed to be so few ways to hit back at the Garsal. He hoped that the patrols Below would manage some kind of retaliation. On the plateau, it seemed as if they were simply trying to ride out the occupation. Once again Erilla had the right words. "We're doing what we can, Cerren. And Below, the others are doing what we can't."

Sadly, he nodded. "Well, let's get ourselves back together as best we can then. You have the new first years on clean up duty?"

"I do. They're coming along well, and Toman's pushing them as hard as she can. They'll be dispatched to a Starlyne habitat as soon as we're done here. She's sure they all have the spark, so we'll see what the Starlynes make of them. Are Northaven and Starfall secure?"

"At this stage, yes. They're mobilising as many Patrols and Militia as possible. They'll feed us what they can spare. I'm waiting on word from Below." Erilla nodded, and her eyes flicked to the horizon. Cerren followed her gaze. Characteristic clouds had formed.

"There's another storm on the way," she said. "Amma's brother confirmed it for us just as the attack began. A big one, apparently. He thinks it might brush us by this time, but it's likely to be intense and interfere with our people Below. We've sent warning via the Starlyne network."

"Then let's hope they'll be safe and secure. Let them know *we're* still secure via return message. And if they have any new information, I wish to know it immediately."

Erilla turned to go, but paused briefly and rested a hand on his arm. Socks hummed gently at her and flicked her tidemarks in pensive patterns. "We'll make it through, Cerren. Not all of us perhaps, but I do have faith in our people, and in our allies, and that's what needs to keep us going when times are darkest."

"And are they the darkest yet?" Cerren mused, eyes still on the smouldering building.

"Probably not," replied Erilla. "But we're not yet at the end of our resources either. This is dreadful, and so much of what we've worked for lies before us in ruins, but it is only stone and wood this time. Our wealth is in our people, not buildings or things, and our people are still standing."

Cerren nodded, catching Erilla's eyes, and then he and Socks began the trip back through his ruined home to the operations room, where he belonged, making plans and mustering resources. Frontier's wealth was in its people, and its people had only just begun to fight back.

# Chapter 18

SHANNA edged her head sideways around a rock and hand signalled back towards Amma and Allad. Their journey towards the sentinel ring had been fraught with difficulty. The Garsal seemed to be everywhere. The climbing vehicles were very nimble when using their 'legs' rather than their tracks, and it appeared that the Garsal had deployed many of them inside their secure zone. They'd had to pause, fade, and then back track multiple times, and had had several close calls with some of the dangerous wildlife trapped inside the ring with them. Fortunately for their safety, it was clear that the numbers of surviving predators were relatively few compared to a normal area Below. Yet Shanna couldn't help but feel sad every time she found a new corpse, partly because it wasn't only the predators she'd found dead. Relatively harmless plant eaters had been indiscriminately slaughtered, and their bodies left to rot where they'd fallen.

It was unthinking destruction on a scale she hadn't previously considered. Despite Frontier's dangerous denizens, the settlers had mostly developed a live and let live policy. They did destroy dangerous predators in well settled areas, but the Scouts avoided killing when possible, and no-one killed for the sake of it, and definitely not a herbivore unless it was going to become dinner. The number of corpses had attracted swarms of insects, and the carnivorous plants in the area were feasting. Several times they'd had to deviate around normally quiescent plant tendrils. Gorged with unexpected bounty, the carnivorous plants were more active than usual, and more hazardous.

The longer they'd travelled, the more Shanna's leg had begun to throb, until now it was an almost continuous heavy pulse thudding away uncomfortably below her knee. Her concern now was that her wound had become infected. With no time to stop and look she filed it away for later and tried to dismiss the worry.

Inside her head, Twister and Storm were closer. She'd been vaguely aware of them moving towards her as she and the other two slunk their way towards the perimeter.

The now familiar sounds of a Garsal climber came faintly on the breeze, and she hand signalled a warning. Shinnying her way up the nearest safe tree, she automatically extended her fade over Amma as she lifted herself into the lowest branches. It was difficult, but the constant practice seemed to be making it easier to expand her bubble more precisely around the two of them. She hoped that it would conserve her energy as well.

The surrounding bush grew silent as the vehicle drew closer. Shanna peered down through the leaves, carefully watching as it stalked its way towards them. Like nearly all of the vehicles they'd seen that day, it was moving on its 'legs' rather than its tracks. It looked like an ungainly spooner spider, and each time she saw one, Shanna's flesh crawled. The clanking of its mechanical joints was harsh, and grated against her ears, but although it came uncomfortably close, it continued past without stopping, leaving a trail of crushed and bruised vegetation in its wake. More and more frequently, they'd come across tracks left by the vehicles. Although agile, they were still heavy enough to leave the smaller trees in their path shattered.

Shanna lowered herself gently from the tree, dropped the fade and glided forwards again, hand signalling the all clear to the other two. Amma nodded tiredly. Despite the patch, she was struggling. Shanna slowed her pace, hastily checking the area in front of them with her extra senses. The constant use was honing that skill too, but she wondered how long she could keep it up. She pulled one of the spare tubers from her pocket and determinedly chewed on it as she scouted the path ahead, wincing as a piece of dirt she'd missed crunched between her teeth.

An hour later she saw the first sentinel post, just as her map had indicated. She could 'feel' Twister and Storm easily now. Their emotions were very clear. Washes of violet and blue were flitting across her mind almost continuously, but even at this close range, she was unable to hear Fractus. Their ability to communicate via the Starlyne network had become a small bastion of security, and its absence made her feel even more uneasy. Concealing herself behind a bank of low scrub, she signalled Allad and Amma forwards.

"Sentinel. I can 'feel' the boys easily, Allad." He nodded, and took a careful peek over the top of the scrub. Amma had carefully turned her back into the bank, and was watching their rear. With her cats so close by, yet so inaccessible, Shanna felt even more vulnerable.

"I can't see anyone. You said you see their tidemark colours in your mind?" asked Allad.

"And when I'm close, their emotions. It's a bit like 'feeling' your way through the scrub."

"Are you close enough to see *through* their eyes?" he asked.

"Never thought of trying it!" she whispered.

"Then try now." Allad rolled his eyes at her, and Shanna took a deep breath and then extended her senses. There was a huge sense of strain as she reached out towards the two starcats. It was like pushing her bubble of fade out further and further from her. Just when she thought she'd reached her limit, her vision bifurcated into two distinct images, and she nearly fell over. There was a wash of emotion from her cats so strong she nearly sobbed aloud in her relief at the contact, and then she had to struggle to orient herself before she threw up.

"I have them," she gasped out. "They're not far."

"See if you can get one of them to bring Spiron to where we can see him." She nearly said, *And how am I meant to do that? All I can do is see through their eyes* … but held her tongue, held onto the threads of vision, and then concentrated strongly on her need to see Spiron. It was the only thing she could think of doing. There was a blue sprinkle of amusement that pattered across her mind, and then the world swung about in one spot, and she could see Spiron following behind the starcat. In front, the blue tinged vision had let its emotion reduce slightly, and she 'knew' that Storm was guiding the Patrol First towards them.

Reluctantly she withdrew her vision, and then sagged tiredly where she was. "They were already bringing him." They all shrank back as a crackle of vegetation startled them, and then Amma spoke.

"It's all right, only a falling branch."

"Amma, you keep watching. Shanna, I'm going to need to know at what angle I can throw a rock with a written message over the sentinel so that it doesn't send its flyers out. Work it out for me." Shanna had no idea how they were going to throw a rock that far, but she simply nodded, pulled her map and pencil from her pocket and began to calculate on the back of her map. The maths was complex, and she had to try and guess a few of the figures, and dredge some of the others from memory. She had no doubts Kaidan could have done the calculations in his head, and had to pause to collect herself at the thought of her brother. Finally she had the final figure and tapped Allad's shoulder.

"It's only a guess though, Allad."

He nodded. "How far are they now?"

Shanna thought for a moment. "They're slowing down. I'd say they're right opposite us now."

"Good. Wait here." He slid out from the sheltering bank, and began to move as close as he dared to the mechanical device. The ground sloped slightly, and Shanna's anxious eyes watched the surrounding vegetation closely as the big Scout glided through the bush. At the top of the rise, her trained eyes caught a flash of colour. A violet ear tip sparkled briefly, and she knew it was Twister. It was quickly followed by a green one, and then two blue ones. All of their cats were there. Shanna wondered momentarily how the Patrol had kept Satin in line. A small flickering in the trees drew her attention, and then she saw Spiron's form faintly through the bushes. They all seemed further away than the moons, and her throat tightened.

Suddenly, Allad stepped into full view of the watching cats and Spiron. His hands flashed quickly in the signals she now knew so well. *Wait, message, throw, all safe, old camp.* And then he was back under cover, and moving towards Amma and Shanna.

"I'm going to boost the message with my gift," he whispered, pulling a folded notebook page from his pocket. "I need a rock." Shanna carefully turned several rocks with a stick before finding one the right size that didn't harbour something nasty on the other side, and handed it to Allad. He wrapped the rock in the note and then fastened it firmly using thin pieces of a tough vine. "Amma, check the air currents for me please, and then I'm going to see if I can get this over the barrier. Shanna, you're on watch. If there's the faintest sign of anything, let us know." He returned to his previous spot, stepped out into the open, and after a quick hand signal to Spiron, launched the rock into the air. Shanna desperately wanted to see whether it went where she'd calculated, but restrained herself, keeping her eyes on the surrounding vegetation, and her ears open.

For a long moment there was nothing except the normal sounds of the bush. And then "Yes!" hissed Amma. "It's gone up and over." More normal sounds, and the waiting drew out longer and longer as Shanna watched the surrounding trees and allowed herself to 'feel' the state of the animals and birds around them. All was quiet.

Finally. "He's on his way back." And then Allad was back with them again.

"It's done. Spiron agrees. We'll try and take out as many sentinels during the storm as possible. It'll be dangerous, but no more dangerous than staying in here without our cats, while the Garsal hunt us. It's imperative that neither of you falls into Garsal hands." With that statement, he pulled his map from his pocket again. "We'll be responsible for two sentinels – this one here," he tapped the map, "and that one." Amma and Shanna nodded. They were adjacent, and both were near rocky outcrops that might offer some shelter from the cyclone. "The others will target these ones." He indicated two on the opposite side of the bowl, also adjacent to each other, and then three others, spaced at intervals around the ring. "Whatever happens, we'll rendezvous at the grotto as soon as it's safe to move." He looked at them both seriously. "It'll mean exposing ourselves at the height of the storm, when it's most dangerous. Shanna, you noted a stand of plybrush?" She nodded. "Then we'll collect some on the way. The two of you will work together, and I'll handle the other one. We'll be at most risk from flying debris, but I'd like us to be tied on to something as well. Amma, we'll need frequent updates on the storm's arrival times. Can you manage that?"

Amma nodded, but Shanna could see that her friend's face was pale and set. "We've a fair way to go Allad," said Shanna, "so I assume we're not going back to the grotto tonight."

"We'd better not," said Amma. "Given how long it took us to get here, it's going to be a close run thing just to get to the sites and get set-up. Particularly if we've got to harvest plybrush on the way. I think I'll have to use another patch."

Shanna looked at her, concerned. "Are you OK?"

"Not really, but there's not much choice is there?"

Allad regarded Amma steadily for a moment or two. "No, there's not," he replied finally. "Do what you need to, Amma. Shanna." He gestured her in the direction of the plybrush stand.

She felt wretched as she took the first steps further away from Storm and Twister, but a few minutes later, she realised that they were pacing her, shadowing her path inside the ring from the outside. There was a sudden grunt from Allad, and she looked back towards him, but he waved her on. She wondered what had caused the Scout to make such an unaccustomed sound. Placing the worries at the back of her mind, she got on with the task of trying to get them where they needed to go – safely.

The storm began deceptively gently. Like so many of the great spiralling weather systems, the outer edges consisted of gradually rising winds and slowly increasing rain. As the first raindrops began to fall, Shanna peered out from the rock cubby she and Amma had wedged themselves into. Their plybrush tie downs were anchored securely around two of the taller spires, and the small rock hole was deep enough for both of them to sit inside out of the rain. Investigating its dark depths had been nerve wracking, though. Fortunately their two glowstones had provided enough illumination for Amma to determine that there was nothing deadly living inside it. Some time in the past, though, a family of stinkrats had clearly spent some time inhabiting it, and the girls had resigned themselves to adding stinkrat to their already odorous scents.

The rain intensified suddenly, and Shanna drew her head back into the smelly dryness of the cubby and leaned back against the wall. Secure in the knowledge that the vast majority of Frontier's dangerous predators would be taking shelter from the storm, she finally had enough time to attend to her leg. The throbbing had been escalating over the hours of storm preparation, and Shanna lifted her trouser leg with some trepidation. The wound was red and angry, and the edges were swollen, with small pustules beginning to form in places. "Nasty," said Amma. "It looks like you've got quite a lot of dirt in it still." She rummaged in her pockets, and then pulled a small leather case from the bottom of her thigh pocket. She extracted a pair of tweezers from it and then gestured for Shanna to prop her leg on her lap.

"Thanks. Allad cleaned it out while you were unconscious, but he said he couldn't get all of it. You don't have any antiseptic as well?" Amma shook her head and began to carefully pick bits of dirt from the wound. Shanna shuddered and tried to keep her leg still as the probing tweezers sent small shocks of pain shooting through her. She gritted her teeth as Amma worried at a particularly deep piece of debris.

"Here stick this out to catch some rain if you can." Amma pulled her water bottle out of its pouch, and Shanna put the neck of the bottle under a rivulet of water coursing down the rock face. The coolness momentarily distracted her from the niggling pain in her leg. A gust blew some of it inside, and the fine spray felt good on her exposed skin, cooling the heat of the infection slightly. As Amma finished with her leg, Shanna swapped Amma's full bottle for her own. The rain had begun to pour steadily and the wind gusts rose rapidly. It took no time at all to fill Shanna's bottle.

Amma leaned back on her side of the cubby with a heavy sigh.

"How's your head, Amma?" Shanna asked.

"Aching," sighed her friend. "It's better though. I might try and nap if you're right to watch?"

"Go ahead," said Shanna. She could feel her cats somewhere reasonably close by, and she was struggling to contain her emotion. She wanted to contact them again, look through their eyes, and feel their emotions. She could feel them hovering on the edge of her consciousness. Amma closed her eyes and her breathing slowed almost immediately. Shanna let herself 'feel' everything around her, and peered out through the now heavy rain. As the storm intensified, it became darker and darker. Finally, satisfied that everything dangerous in the vicinity was sheltering from the storm, Shanna allowed herself to reach out towards her cats.

She slid smoothly behind their eyes and was enveloped in love. It soothed her, pouring like a warm balm on her soul, and she just rested there for a few moments, receiving love and transmitting it herself. Finally, she allowed herself to look through both sets of eyes. There was no disorientation, because wherever they were, was dark. There was a sensation of warmth and security, and she had the impression of purrs. For a while, she just communed with her cats and then reluctantly withdrew, but this time, there was a persistent light contact, as if her cats had linked themselves to her in some fashion. She wondered at it briefly and then realised that her time with her cats had been much longer than she'd planned.

The wind was howling, and Amma was still asleep despite the noise and the flying rain. As Shanna leaned forwards to peer into the dimness of the storm, a large branch tumbled past the opening. She jerked back reflexively, and then huddled as deeply as possible into the pocket sized crevice. Amma had snuggled back into her corner while Shanna had been communing with her cats.

The hours wore on. After what seemed an age, Shanna woke Amma and attempted to sleep herself. Finally, among a maze of half formed bizarre dreams, Amma's voice intruded upon her. She shoved her eyelids open and looked blearily at her friend. "It's almost time, Shan. The eye is close." Shanna wriggled slightly, trying to unstiffen herself as much as possible in the cramped confines. The rain and wind had reached a peak of intensity she'd rarely seen. The water was pouring off the rock above them, curtaining the hollow with moisture, and rivulets had begun to seep into their rocky haven.

"I'm so stiff."

"Me too. But at least the headache's gone." Amma looked a lot better, Shanna thought. Her own leg was throbbing again, and her body felt as if it was about to twist itself into a huge knot. She attempted to stretch again, fairly unsuccessfully. In her mind, the link to her cats was still there. It was as if there was a tiny chain of love, linking the three of them together.

"How long do you reckon?"

"Not long at all. Here, have some nuts."

Shanna ate them as they sat, waiting. The wind howled to a crescendo of furious gusts, and then, suddenly, it was still. A faint thread of sunlight penetrated the gloom, and the eye was above them.

"Come on then," said Shanna. "Let's do it." She crawled painfully out of the niche into a world of water and debris. Branches and leaves were piled in drifts around the spires, and the water was falling in steady streams down the rocks. Shanna had to waste precious moments locating the plybrush ropes they'd fastened before the storm had begun. With fumbling fingers, she knotted one around her waist and then she and Amma fought their way through the debris, to place themselves as close as possible to the sentinel without setting it off. She'd half hoped it had been blown away during the storm, but it was still there, sitting malevolently at rest in a shaft of sunlight.

"Ready?"

"Yep."

Shanna closed her eyes and reached out as Taya had done. The sentinel was very complex. Normally, she operated by instinct when she stopped a machine, but as she ran Taya's technique through her mind, images of the sentinel's interior exploded into her mind, and she staggered, almost overwhelmed. Overwhelmed by what she was seeing, and overwhelmed because she had no idea what to do with it. For a moment she panicked, feeling as though the ground has just dropped out from beneath her, and then she felt her starcats steady her. Their longing to be with her, physically, was almost painful, but it was anchoring, a moment of reality among the madness of complex technology.

"Hurry up, Shan! I can see the eye wall approaching!" Amma's voice briefly interrupted her, disturbing the march of images, and then, with Storm and Twister's help, she slowed the flashing images, reached back into her memory, and dredged up what Taya had done. Ignoring Amma's pulling hands, and the renewed spatter of raindrops she hunted through the images. "Shan! We've run out of time! We have to move!"

And then she had it. The power source. She reached out firmly, 'yanked' as Taya had, and then the illuminated images vanished in a flash and she opened her eyes to a thin spiral of smoke oozing from the sentinel. The wind hit like a stampeding horgal, and she staggered under its onslaught. Rain blinded her, and she struggled to orient herself in the sudden dimness. Vaguely, she could feel Amma's pulling hands, and then they were staggering against the wind. She felt Amma's arm reach across her shoulders, turning her, and guiding her hands to the other girl's waist. She held on for dear life, and followed Amma blindly, realising that Amma was reeling them in using the plybrush ties. Leaves and small twigs spat themselves into her eyes, and Shanna shook her head, eyes stinging. She didn't dare lift a hand to clear her vision.

After an eternity of stumbling, buffeted by ever strengthening gusts, Shanna felt Amma drop down, and realised they were back at the tiny rock hole. She dropped to her hands and knees and crawled the last metre over the lip of the cave and into its protection. She was drenched, and suddenly completely drained. She couldn't imagine how she would have coped without Amma. She wondered how the others were, and whether they'd managed to take their sentinels out, and survive the storm. Brushing water and shredded leaves out of her eyes, she looked at Amma.

"Thank you." The other girl nodded, and she felt a fleeting brush of satisfaction from her cats.

# **Chapter 19**

THE alarm claxon sounded, disturbing the Overlord's moment of rest. He'd decided to rest during the peak of the storm, knowing that the humans would be as incapacitated by the cyclonic winds as the Garsal were. If he was fortunate, then perhaps they'd perish in the storm. Zoash had the plans for the after storm raids well in hand, and he couldn't imagine that any unsheltered being would survive the dangerous winds. He anticipated finding human corpses after the winds had died down and the torrential rain subsided.

He rose from his cocoon and tapped to open a line to the operations centre. "Report!"

"Sentinels down in multiple places, Overlord."

"Not in one section?"

"No, Overlord. They're down in six places. There are two places where adjacent sentinels have ceased to function, but the others are singletons."

"Did they all cease functioning at the same time?"

"No Overlord. But they did cease functioning within minutes of each other."

"The other sentinels are still online?"

"Yes, Overlord, everything else is functioning normally. No unusual alarms have been recorded."

"Was their telemetry sent as they failed?"

"We're analysing it now, but early data suggests several different causes. One stopped after an electrical spike, and another appears to have been crushed by something – one of the aerials provided an image of a falling tree before it lost power itself." The tech's voice hesitated.

"Go on."

"Data has just come in – two appear to have burned out power supplies, while another two sent sudden temperature spikes just before they stopped functioning. Another has burned out components on the motherboard – enough to stop anything but telemetry back to here, and the final one has lost its power supply and is operating on battery only. Again, enough power for basic telemetry, but nothing else."

The Overlord considered briefly, and then tapped the communicator again. "Turn-off the alarm. Inform me if any pattern is found. It's most likely a result of the storm – lightning strikes, wind damage, falling trees and debris." Nothing would be outside in weather like this. Even the great colony ship shuddered under the onslaught of the winds.

Unable to rest, however, the Overlord called Zoash to attend him, and then sat back, contemplating his plans for conquest of the plateau, and the elimination of the Great Enemy. The door chime sounded.

"Enter."

"Overlord?" His hatching sib's voice was curious.

"The sentinel ring is malfunctioning. It is possible it's a deliberate breach, but unlikely. You are certain there were only three flyers?"

"Yes, Overlord, I am certain." He tapped at the screen on the Overlord's desk, and an image appeared. He tapped again, and it enlarged rapidly. The haze of overhanging leaves resolved into three black flecks plummeting towards the canopy from a hazy sky. "This was extracted from the climber's images. I've had it enhanced as much as possible." A few more taps and the image became clearer again. The flecks became figures, basically human shaped, but oddly elongated at the limbs. They appeared enmeshed, and two were quite obviously supporting the other one. The images played one by one until the conjoined flyers struck the canopy and vanished. "We've been working on extrapolating the location more accurately, and believe we now have a better fix. We'll have searchers out there immediately the storm ends."

"Well done," replied the Overlord, but Zoash tapped the screen again, and a map overlaid it. Coloured corridors overlaid it in interweaving patterns. One area was highlighted with a winged icon. Several colours crisscrossed it.

"Unfortunately searchers have already been in that area with no success." He closed the screen and regarded the Overlord. "I believe it is unlikely that we'll locate them there. They've either perished, or moved elsewhere. They seem unafraid of this planet."

"And yet these three have no feline companions. Surely that would reduce their chance of survival. One was clearly injured."

Zoash said nothing, simply inclined his head.

"Your plans for the plateau are in order?"

"Repairs on a number of vehicles are in progress, but we should be ready to leave on schedule. Hoth's intelligence and the aerial mapping from the flyovers have provided many insights. I will have the preliminary target listing available within a few hours for your approval, Overlord."

"And that feline? The one killing our troopers?"

"There have been no fatalities for some days, Overlord. We know it was wounded. Perhaps it has perished." The Overlord flicked his manipulator arms in satisfaction.

"I will await your listings. Attend me two hours after you submit them."

"As you wish, Overlord." Zoash withdrew, and the Overlord sank into contemplative silence, feeling the ship shudder under the wind of the storm. For the first time, he was truly unsettled, but he brushed aside the feelings as improper for his position. The hive construction was well on schedule, the outer perimeter had all but eliminated the large marauding animals inside its boundaries, and once the damaged units were repaired, would do so again. He leaned forwards and tapped a command into his desk tablet. The engineers would need to study the problems associated with the great storms of this planet, and devise a way of storm proofing the sentinels.

***

"You are sure, Laretai?" The Matriarch paced the length of the room, filmy robes fluttering behind her. The sounds of the storm vibrated on the edge of her hearing, adding to her feelings of edginess.

"Yes, Matriarch. He said the name clearly, and on questioning, repeated it. She is apparently here, on this ship, in the general slave quarters." Laretai's voice trembled openly now.

"Does Kaidan know what the significance of this is?"

"No, he's completely unaware of the implications as far as I can tell. I believe that the humans on this planet have truly been isolated for several hundred years. Until our arrival, they had no idea of the real state of affairs in the galaxy." There was silence for some moments and the Matriarch continued her pacing. It helped her to think. The implications of finding Lacey here, on this ship, on this planet, at this time, had brought the reality of the precariousness of their situation crashing home. The stakes had always been high, but now they were even higher.

"What chance do we have of moving Lacey into this section of the ship?" asked the Matriarch.

"There are a few possibilities, but they all carry risks. Kaidan was a novelty, Lacey isn't. We cannot ask for her by name or risk raising the Overlord's suspicions. As far as I can tell, he has none at this time. It is as if everything has aligned for this brief time – perhaps the plan might find fruition at last!" It was a mark of Laretai's discomfiture that she sat without asking permission. The Matriarch joined her, moving with a grace and composure that belied the turmoil she was feeling.

"Then we will have to do the best we can with the tools at hand. You have kept Kaidan separated?"

"Yes, he's sequestered in solitary confinement in one of the holding rooms adjacent to my chambers. Only Estei and Hirtoi are permitted near him. They persist in their efforts to befriend him. Despite the situation I judged that the opportunity was worth the risk." Again Laretai's voice trembled.

"You judged correctly, as ever." The Matriarch made her voice as warm as possible. Her Senior had served long and faithfully, and her skills were without par. This was not the time for her to begin to doubt herself. Uncharacteristically, she extended a manipulator arm and rested it on Laretai's. The physical contact was unusual enough that Laretai started.

"Matriarch?"

"Laretai, we have worked together towards this goal for many years. We will prevail, no matter the complications. We will adapt, just as we have so many times before because there is no other choice."

"But Matriarch, how should we proceed, now that we know of Lacey?"

The Matriarch sat quietly for a moment, feeling the vibrations of the storm through the body of the ship and pondering.

"Laretai, we will proceed as we had planned. With one difference. You will spend two days observing Kaidan. Have him attend you as your personal slave during work-hours, but keep him isolated at night. Make sure he is who we think he is."

"And Lacey?" asked Laretai.

"We will watch, and wait, and if an opportunity presents itself, we will move. The leader of the human underground – here, at last, on our ship is something we'd never considered. I'm sure there's a story attached to it, but there is nothing else we can do at this time." She stood. "Leave me now, I would think on our plans for a while. Make sure you have your taps in place. We need every edge."

***

Kaidan stood as the door opened, keeping his eyes firmly on the floor. "You will attend Laretai." It was one of the two young Garsal females who'd tried to extract information from him. Hirtoi, he thought. He kept his eyes on the floor as he followed behind her. The days since he'd whispered Lacey's name had been confusing. He was no longer in the normal slave quarters in the female section of the ship, but in a small room adjacent to Laretai's quarters, and it was almost as if the Garsal females wanted to be *friends*. His mind refused to process the idea properly. The Garsal had come to his planet, killed people he knew, enslaved Anjo, enslaved and tortured *him!* He felt spun about, his foundations unstable. He'd prided himself on his ability to strategise, to solve complex problems, and he'd thought he'd managed to do so, despite his position on the Garsal ship. Somehow, he needed to help his people, but how?

His musings were cut short as they entered Laretai's quarters. "That will be all, Hirtoi." Kaidan stood at the door, uncertain.

"You will attend me today, as my personal slave. You will fetch and carry, and heed my every word, human."

"Yes Laretai." He kept his eyes downcast.

"But first, I have seen you flinching. Are your wounds still unhealed?" Kaidan couldn't believe what he was hearing. She was enquiring about his health? His mind reeled, and he struggled to form a coherent sentence.

"Um, no, I mean, yes, some of them are. Unhealed I mean." He looked at the floor and tried not to shuffle his feet.

"You will remove your shirt then." Her tones were unreadable, but he felt awkward, fearful of further hurt, and hopeful all at the same time. Slowly he removed the shirt and stood, eyes on the ground, facing her. "Turn your back towards me." He rotated so that his back was towards her. There was a moment of silence followed by a small tinkle, and he realised that she was ringing a bell. Quick Garsal footsteps sounded and there was a flurry of conversation in the harsh sounding Garsal language, followed by a presence behind him. An odd tickling sensation began near his nape, and with a goosebump filled shiver, he realised that a second Garsal was running her manipulator arms down his scars. He tried to prevent a flinch when she probed a particularly painful, partly healed spot, but was unable to stop the hiss of surprised pain that escaped his lips.

"Follow Estei. She will begin the process of repair, and then you will return to attend me." Kaidan's head whipped around involuntarily to see Laretai watching him steadily. He cursed his inability to read the alien body language, or understand more than a few words of their language. Why was she being so kind? *Perhaps it's a plot to get you to trust her so that you give away more secrets,* whispered his mind. *And perhaps it's not. Perhaps these female Garsal are different.* whispered another portion. "Go now," said Laretai's voice.

By the end of the day, Kaidan's back felt as if it might finally be healed. His shoulder, which had been persistently aching, had also been seen to. It appeared that the Starlyne people were not the only ones with healing skills. "Your scars will persist, but the infection is now gone, and they will close normally. The tendons of the shoulder joint will heal to normal length, so that your shoulder does not prevent you serving Laretai to your full capacity," the medical technician had said, her cool tones dispassionate. He had no doubt about *her* motives. She wished him repaired, much as another technician would have repaired a machine, so that he would serve all the better. There was no compassion behind her treatment that he could detect, just efficiency.

After a full day of fetching and carrying, for the first time in weeks without pain, Kaidan felt as if he might finally be able to sleep a full night. Hirtoi returned him to his solitary room, where a bowl of slave slop awaited him. As the door closed, and he lowered himself tiredly to his sleeping pallet, he paused, alerted by something he couldn't quite put his finger on. He stood up again, turned a full circle, inspecting every millimetre of the room. He felt as if he was being watched. Perhaps he was. There seemed no end to the Garsal technology. But what did it matter, he wondered to himself? There was nothing for them to see. He pulled the bowl of food over. It wasn't tasty, but it did seem to contain everything his body needed.

He put the first spoonful in his mouth, swallowed, and then hesitated again. Something was different. Not wrong, precisely, but different. Again he scanned the room, wondering if he'd missed something in his first circuit. As he spun in place, he paused. *There.* But it couldn't be. His mind refused to believe what he thought he'd seen. Once again his eyes returned to the spot. Nothing. Absently, he spooned another mouthful and swallowed, and found his eyes scanning restlessly. Finally, finishing the slop, he pushed the bowl through the slot in the bottom of the door and returned to his pallet.

He laid himself back onto it, marvelling at the lack of pain, and closed his eyes, exhausted. The lights would turn themselves out at a predetermined time, but for now, he didn't care. He dropped almost immediately into sleep, musing on the vagaries of hope.

Sometime later, he awoke. Awoke to the warmth of another body. A furry body. "Bootsy," he murmured, half caught in a dream of home. And then woke fully. "You're not Boots!" A faint blue glow woke from the tidemarks of the starcat beside him, and he was suddenly very much awake and not dreaming any more. His mind raced. *How could there be a starcat inside the Garsal ship?* And then he remembered the faint blue twinkle he'd seen when he'd been taken inside. He'd dismissed it, but there was no doubting that there was a starcat sleeping on his bed right now. But who? There was a very faint hum from the cat, and Kaidan realised that the starcat was angling its head towards him for a caress. He obliged, and the cat sighed slightly, and then purred very softly. It seemed as starved for company as he was.

None of the patterns matched any of his family's cats, but they did seem vaguely familiar. He racked his brain as he scratched the cat's cheek, almost brought to tears by the companionship. One by one, he ran the starcats of his acquaintance across his mind. None seemed to fit the tidemarks lying beside him, until a faint memory stirred. Boots and Satin. Their courtship. Kaidan delved deeper, and a memory, shocking in its sadness finally surfaced. A chocolate skinned man, laughing as he paid over his money to Patrol Ten's informal bookkeeper, accompanied by a blue toned starcat. But that man was dead! Kaidan had seen his name of the list of fallen, killed during the initial raid on the Garsal ship, if he remembered rightly. But if that was right, then this must be …"Dipper?" he whispered, and the cat's tidemarks flickered slightly in recognition. Kaidan wrapped his arms around the cat as far as they'd go and hugged him tight, tears pricking his eyes. Tears both for himself and for the cat who'd lost his companion. He must have remained in the area after his partner had perished. Kaidan began to run his hands over the starcat – surely he'd been thought dead too?

A long, hairless scar marred the soft coat all down one side. Now that Kaidan could feel it, he could see how it damaged the graceful tidemarks down the cat's side. It must have been painful for a very long time, but it seemed well healed, although the starcat was a mite thinner than the peak condition he was accustomed to in his home cats. But how was the cat remaining undetected inside the ship, he wondered? And why had he suddenly decided to make himself known to Kaidan? There were too many questions, but the obvious answer to the first question was that the cat must have remained faded, undetectable to even the Garsal technology.

For the first time in a long while, he found a slight hope – a hope that perhaps he might actually escape the ship with the help of Dipper. He knew he could fade if he was near a cat, but how long could he fade for? Would it be long enough to escape? Would Dipper choose to help him? Kaidan knew that in theory, a starcat whose partner had died was a law unto itself. Some did re-partner, or choose to stay with particular humans, while others appeared and disappeared, homeless by choice, particularly if they had no mate.

Kaidan decided that for this moment in time, he didn't care. Dipper would do as he pleased, and perhaps this was a sign that he wanted Kaidan's help, or to help Kaidan, but for the moment, the starcat smelled and felt of home. Dipper snuggled closer, and despite his misgivings, Kaidan quickly fell asleep again, lulled by warmth and familiarity, trusting that Dipper would wake them both before anyone found them.

***

"Matriarch, you must see this!"

Laretai whisked into the Matriarch's chamber unannounced, and hurried over to the desktop tablet. The Matriarch followed. A few flicks of Laretai's manipulator arms and images of the sleeping human boy appeared in front of her. He appeared to be wrapped around by one of the huge felines that had struck such fear into the Garsal. Both were fast asleep. The image had been captured by Laretai's surveillance equipment.

"How?" was the only word she managed to utter.

"Watch." Laretai tapped and the images blurred backwards. They watched Kaidan enter an empty room, eat, spin around a few times, shake his head, finish eating and lie down to sleep. The time stamps advanced an hour and the room darkened, and Laretai's equipment switched to dark vision. And then, all of a sudden, the cat appeared, wrapped itself around Kaidan's sleeping body, closed its eyes, and apparently went to sleep. Two hours later, the images showed Kaidan stirring, mumbling and then starting awake. He appeared to share a few words with the cat, snuggled back up to it and then the two of them went back to sleep. "It's still there, and they're both still asleep. Shall I call the guards?"

"No." The image of the girl that the Matriarch had pondered on for so long, reappeared in her mind. "This may be the solution to one of our dilemmas. So far no-one has been harmed by this beast?"

"Not for some time, Matriarch. It must be the beast left behind after the initial assault – the one that killed so many of the troopers and sentries after the humans left. One of my earlier taps shows Zoash commenting on the fact that none have died for quite some time. They have assumed that the beast is dead." Laretai sat back in her chair.

"Then it is likely that the beast has been roaming the ship for some time, undetected and harming no-one?" Laretai nodded. "And now it appears that it has found what it's been looking for. Is there any way of detecting it?"

Laretai tapped at the screen impatiently. "Not that I've been able to determine. The Overlord has his technicians working on the problem and I've been monitoring their progress, as well as thinking about it myself. It appears that the beasts can appear and disappear at will, along with their human companions."

"We must be doubly careful then, or it may be that Kaidan escapes before we are ready."

"And if he tries to escape tomorrow? How would we know?" There was consternation in every line of Laretai's posture.

In a moment of decision the Matriarch spoke. "You will take Estei and Hirtoi into your confidence. Estei is my chosen successor, and Hirtoi has the skill to be yours. They are close friends as well, much as you and I. Do I have your agreement?" Laretai was shocked, the Matriarch saw. Successors were chosen only in times of great danger, or when death approached, but as she watched, she saw her old friend accept the decision, turn it over in her mind, and reach agreement.

"They are well chosen, Matriarch. I will speak to them both immediately, and then I will send Estei to you. It would be well to begin their instruction immediately."

The Matriarch felt a stab of sadness as she caught and held Laretai's gaze. It seemed that moment by moment the stakes became higher.

"You must give Kaidan no opportunity to escape until the plan is at fruition point – or we win his trust. One of you must monitor the room day and night, and the door must not be opened unless he is visible to the naked eye. The beast will do as it wishes, I suspect, and I suspect that in daylight hours it will be invisible. Three of us will meet each day at this time, while the other watches."

"And if it harms one of us?" The Matriarch knew Laretai wasn't referring to Kaidan.

"Then it will be as it will be. I see no reason why it should start now if it hasn't already. How could we deal with an invisible, undetectable, killer?"

# Chapter 20

SHANNA started to full alertness, shivering with cold, drenched through by the rain. "They're coming, Amma!"

"Who's coming? The Garsal?" Amma struggled to a sitting position, alarm in every line of her body.

"Sorry, should have said 'The boys are coming!' Which probably means that Spider will be here soon!"

"Are you sure you broke that thing?" asked Amma worriedly.

"As sure as I can be. And they're sure too." She could barely talk for the wash of joy that threatened to overwhelm her. Blue and violet sparkled vividly in her mind, and despite the rain that persisted in blowing into their rocky haven, she felt her spirits buoy as Storm and Twister neared. She had only a few seconds warning before three wet, loving starcats attempted to press themselves into the crowded space. There was a flurry of purring, humming, and love, as the separate parts of the whole came together. Shanna felt herself tearing up as she hugged the two heads to her chest. Despite the discomfort, the cold and the wetness, they stayed like that until a voice penetrated through the loving fug.

"We're drowning out here, and it's likely that now the barrier's down in a few places there'll be some visitors. Let's get moving!" Arad's voice was quiet, but penetrating. Shanna struggled to her knees and had to push Storm gently out of the way in order to exit the cubby. Every muscle and joint creaked as she stood.

"We'd better remove the plybrush ropes before we leave, Arad, or the Garsal might realise that it was more than just the cyclone." Arad nodded and flicked a hand signal behind him, and Verren and Nelson appeared, laden with extra packs. They handed them off to Shanna and Amma, and as Shanna eased her wet arms through the straps, she felt an enormous relief flood through her. No longer alone, no longer trapped, back with her cats, and equipped for survival. It had been a harrowing few days. It took a few minutes to locate the two plybrush ropes through the still driving rain, and as Verren carefully hanked and attached them to the outside of Shanna's pack, he rested one hand briefly on her arm.

"Glad you're OK." There was a wealth of unspoken emotion in the short sentence.

"We are too," said Shanna, in case anyone else had heard, but she knew that Verren would know what she meant.

"Lead off Verren," directed Arad. Nosey positioned herself carefully in the middle of the group of starcats, and they moved off towards Allad's position, while Shanna automatically took the rear, directing her two cats to guard them on both sides.

It was hard, dangerous work trying to move in the remnants of the storm. Shanna realised that Arad must have decided to move in as soon as it looked like being physically possible. She had to lean into the wind just to stay upright, and flying twigs and leaves plastered them all with debris. *Extra camouflage*, Shanna thought wryly. Fortunately Frontier's native trees were well adapted to the weather. Although the occasional branch fell, few of the native trees had been uprooted by the wind's onslaught. As the winds began to slowly abate, their passage became faster, but more cautious. Now was the time that marauding predators began to move, and if they could move, so could the Garsal. As the winds began to drop, Shanna began to feel more and more unwell. Finally, she was moving in a haze of shivering, and realised that Twister had taken himself off the rear watch to hold her up. She felt too unwell to chastise him.

Sooner than she could have hoped, Shanna saw the familiar signs of the little grotto which had become their haven yet again. As she stumbled between the still flailing trees, Shanna saw that the grotto held Allad, Spiron and Barron and their three starcats. Satin was sitting almost on top of Allad, and Shanna almost giggled despite her exhaustion and illness, as she saw Allad's slightly pained expression. Despite the wet and the cold, it was a little like coming home.

Barron signalled that he and Hunter would take the watch, and vanished through the trees. His wet weather gear blended into the foliage almost seamlessly. "Verren, Arad, take Shanna and Amma and check them over," said Spiron, "Allad tells me that both have been injured. He jerked a thumb towards the rocks at the back of the grotto, and the four of them stepped into the relative dryness of their shelter. Shanna thankfully dropped her pack onto one of the rocks, and herself on another, and began to hunt out some drier clothing and her rain gear as fast as she was able. Her leg ached, and she had begun to shiver violently.

"Arad, can you warm us?" asked Verren.

The other Scout nodded, grinned, and flicked a finger at Nosey. Now a chubby teenager, she ambled over to her partner, blinked her long eyelashes, and climbed into his lap. Almost immediately, the pair began to emit a warmth that washed over Shanna like a hot fire. "Thank you, thank you, thank you!" sighed Amma. Arad smiled at her, and Nosey hummed in a smug manner, purring loudly.

Verren began to check Amma over, while Shanna pulled out a dry set of clothing, teeth chattering still and leg throbbing, along with her last clean pair of socks. Her rain gear went on one of the rocks, ready to put on, and she leaned back on her own one and began to pull her boots off. Her cats lay on either side, and she could feel the relief and the love radiating from them. As she removed her tattered trousers, she realised that the infection in her leg had worsened, despite Amma's best efforts with the tweezers. It was haloed in angry red, and gave an especially violent throb as she looked at it. Trying not to wince, or shiver too much, she pulled her dry trousers on carefully, and then changed her shirt. "Don't think I didn't notice that, Shan," came Verren's voice. "Roll your trouser leg up and leave your boots undone."

Verren's hands were very gentle as he examined the long gash. "It's pretty dirty, Shan. Amma said it was a tusker?"

"Yes. Allad picked out a bit of the grime, and Amma got a bit more, but that was all we could do." He felt her forehead and neck with the back of his hand.

"And you feel like you have a fever. Are you feeling well?" Shanna shrugged noncommittally, trying to suppress another violent shiver, and Storm hummed sceptically and twinkled his tidemarks at Verren, who smiled at her and rolled his eyes slightly.

"Apparently you're not."

Shanna shrugged helplessly, and made a face.

"Well, I'm going to have to clean this properly, I'm afraid. Despite the concussion, Amma's actually in better shape than you, so she can help." He pulled a variety of implements from his pack, propped Shanna's leg up on a convenient rock and began to moisten the ugly scab with a mixture of disinfectant and water. A few minutes later, Shanna was grateful the rock she was sitting on had a backrest of sorts. Despite Verren's gentleness, the wound was excruciatingly painful as he slowly cleaned away the accumulated filth. "I'm going to have to scrub," he warned her, and she gritted her teeth as he took up a clean swab and moistened it. Thirty seconds later she heard, "Catch her Amma!" And then she woke up, flat on her back, leg no longer throbbing, and finally warm. Her wet weather gear had been carefully spread over the top of her.

"How'd I get here?" she mumbled.

"You fainted," said Arad, who was the only one still with her. "Which was probably good, because then Verren *really* cleaned your wound while you were out to it." He grimaced slightly. "Glad it wasn't my leg. In the end he had to use some of the soothall salve. He said it was pretty infected under all the dirt. Here, drink this." He handed her a leafy cup and Shanna recognised the fruity smell of soothall berry tea.

"Really?" she asked.

"Really," replied Arad drily. "Verren said that without proper treatment, that wound would have incapacitated you in a couple of days, and probably killed you within a couple more. You're to drink that and do nothing but rest, and I'm to keep you warm."

"The others?" asked Shanna, drinking the tea. It was, as Verren had said in a time that now seemed so long ago, delicious.

"All here. And safe. Go back to sleep, Shan. It's almost dark." With warm cats on either side of her Shanna did as he said, more tired than she'd realised, finally secure in the knowledge that her friends were watching.

She woke to discover the whole Patrol assembled in the grotto. After the isolation and fear of the preceding days it seemed almost crowded. There was minimal noise, and the hint of ever circling starcats. Hers were still stretched out on either side of her. As she struggled to a sitting position, Storm opened one eyelid and blinked lazily, yawning and stretching his enormous length. Twister hummed sleepily on her other side and wriggled slightly closer.

Several small groups bent over maps, and as Shanna sat completely upright, Verren hurried over. "How are you feeling?" She pondered slightly and wriggled her leg and foot experimentally.

"Much better." And she was. The background throb had reduced to a murmur, and she had more energy coursing through her than she'd had for days. Perhaps she'd been more tired than she thought. Verren began peeling away the dressing on her leg, and she leaned forwards as he exposed the wound. The angry swelling had reduced, and the now clean wound had already begun to close.

"You've been very lucky, Shan. A couple more days and you'd have been really ill."

"So Arad told me."

He nodded. "You were lucky I still had some soothall, or you'd be at death's door by now." He paused, his eyes unable to meet hers, and for a moment she didn't know how to respond. When Cirrus hummed gently and nudged him with her head, he blinked and began to smooth on more of the soothall. His hands were very gentle and the murmur from her leg faded completely as he finished, and covered the wound with a fresh dressing. "We'll leave that one on for a few days and you'll be right as rain."

"Verren, what happened to Fractus?" The question that had been burning in her mind for several days finally had an outlet.

"I forgot, of course you wouldn't know. When you three fell out of the sky, the Garsal sent searchers all over the place. Fractus knew he'd be detectable, so he retreated to the closest way-station. Unfortunately that meant he couldn't relay for us, so now we're on our own again."

Relief washed over Shanna like a wave. She'd become very fond of the Starlyne, and as day after day had gone by, she'd worried that something had happened to him. "I was worried when we couldn't contact him."

Verren nodded. "We knew you would be, but there was no way to contact you – or so we thought – until Allad lobbed that written message over that barrier." He smiled. "Maybe one day we'll stop thinking of new ways to use our gifts."

"I hope not," Shanna said.

"There you go." Verren finished dressing her leg and pulled her trouser leg down. "Can you get up? We'll see how you go when you're vertical. Spiron has plans and we need your input." He helped her up, and she put her boots back on after checking to make sure nothing had taken up residence inside them. She wriggled her toes as the slight dampness chilled them a little and then, after a few tentative steps, realised that her leg was *much* better.

"Thanks. I hadn't realised how bad it was, Verren." She was disappointed to discover she didn't need to lean on his arm, but shrugged the thought away and placed her mind back where it belonged – on defeating the Garsal.

Several hours later, Spiron had divided them into groups again. In pairs and trios they began the arduous task of re-familiarising themselves with the area around the ship. It was extraordinarily difficult to avoid the roving Garsal vehicles. They seemed to be everywhere. In the aftermath of the storm, they seemed to have renewed their hunt for the downed flyers with increased vigour. Shanna wondered if they'd put the failure of their fence down to the humans. She hoped not.

It took time to plot their movements, as they seemed to be ever-changing, but finally a pattern was beginning to appear. Shanna's leg had performed better than she'd believed was possible, but she was still more tired than she wanted to be. Not really fatigued, more mildly drained, but the need to fade on and off all the time hadn't helped. With her cats by her side she'd been able to relieve the drain, and the enhanced link meant that she would have one in contact with her as soon as she was even contemplating fading. But with all of the urgency of their situation, Shanna hadn't had time to consider the changed nature of their togetherness.

As dusk began to darken the sky, they congregated once more in the grotto.

"It seems clear from this that the Garsal will sweep this area within the day," said Spiron, outlining the search pattern on the map, "so we'll need to move. Allad you have another base for us?"

The tall Scout nodded, and leaned forwards and tapped a spot on the other side of the bowl. "They've already been through here twice today, and each time they've passed this spot close by, but not passed through it. The trees grow very thickly just here – probably too close together for any of their vehicles to pass through, and they're still reluctant to venture outside of them." He smiled, and the grim amusement was echoed around the group. "We should relocate there tomorrow first thing, Spiron. There's water and a small rock shelf that would do in a storm if it had to. We'd get pretty wet and cramped, but it's at least sheltered on three sides, and from above."

"And Kalli, you saw an assembly of vehicles?"

"Yes Spiron. The numbers suggest that they may be about to attempt a full assault on the plateau."

There was silence, and Shanna could almost hear the gears ticking over in everyone's minds as they contemplated the last statement. Barron and Spiron exchanged a long look, and then Spiron raised an eyebrow at Allad. He nodded decisively.

"Then we act," said Spiron. "If they're going to send troops in force towards the plateau, we'll have the best chance we'll ever have to get inside the ship in numbers great enough to do substantial damage. It's also our best chance to rescue some of the slaves Semba said had access to valuable information." Kaidan's name remained unspoken, but it hung there in the air above them anyway.

Shanna took a deep breath and looked at her fellow cadets. Determination sat like a badge on each face. Almost instinctively they'd looked for and found each others' eyes, and she could almost feel their resolve.

There was a quiet hum from all of the cats surrounding them in the grotto, and Shanna turned to see all of the tidemarks cycling in a dancing chorus of agreement.

"Apparently they agree," Arad said. Nosey nudged him and bounced irrepressibly. Now a half grown starcat, she vacillated between grown up gravity and cub-like enthusiasm.

"Kalli, you and Sandar will break out tomorrow and take a message back to Fractus. You'll break the same sentinel you did on the way in, so hopefully the Garsal will think it's just a persistent malfunction. Once the message is delivered, you'll be our exit strategy, so bring as many of Patrols Four and Eight with you as possible." Both nodded. "Cadets, Allad, you'll be our primary strike team. You'll penetrate the ship, survey it, and break out any slaves that you're able." He paused for a moment consideringly. "Ragar, Allad is your second." There was a ripple of surprise around the group, but Shanna saw Allad nodding approvingly, and Barron's smile, and realised that he, Spiron and Barron must have already discussed this. Ragar looked startled for a moment, but then nodded, looking thoughtful.

There were a couple of raised eyebrows around the group, but no dissent. "Arad, again you and Nosey will hold the retreat safe against the Garsal. You'll be stationed just outside the inner fence line with Nelson." They nodded. "Myself, Barron, Karri and Perri will roam inside the fence line, and if we have the opportunity, will attempt to penetrate the hive. We'll make sure we hold the line to Arad. As we're able, we'll sabotage anything we can." There were more nods. "Verren, you'll navigate tomorrow. Take us to the other site as fast as possible, but plot your route around the known Garsal patrol routes. And everyone — I need an inventory of your patches. Anything you take with you will be taken on your person. Packs will be left at the new site, to be retrieved when you're able." More nods, and Shanna began to run her list of stuff through her mind, prioritising some items for transfer to her pockets and belt. "For now, it's dinner. Normal watch roster. Shanna, I need to speak to you."

The others dispersed, and Spiron beckoned Shanna over towards him. Both Allad and Barron joined them. There was no feeling of apprehension from her cats, but she wondered what he wanted. "Are you well, Shanna?" he asked.

"Almost, Spiron. Still a bit tired." Honesty was always the best policy with the Patrol First. He had an uncanny ability to know when a cadet was lying. He nodded. They were probably all 'a bit tired' if they were honest.

"You'll have a lot resting on your shoulders again, Shanna. Will you be able to concentrate on the mission, knowing that you might *not* rescue your brother?"

She gulped slightly and took her time answering. "I hope so, Spiron. I .. I can't promise *not* to think about him, but I will promise to do my best to remain focused." The three Scouts looked at each other without speaking. Allad gave a short nod, Barron looked at the ground and tapped his fingers on his belt a few times and then nodded as well, and then Spiron turned back to her.

"In that case, I have several instructions for you. Firstly. Ragar speaks with my voice."

"Yes Spiron." Shanna nodded gravely.

"Secondly. If there is a chance of rescue, Ragar will direct it, and his decision on the matter is final. If he chooses to send you in another direction, then you will go where he sends you." She took a breath and nodded.

"Thirdly. Your group of cadets and you yourself, are more important than rescuing captives. If a rescue attempt fails, your priority is to do everything in your power to extract firstly yourself, and secondly, your group. This is also something Ragar knows. He will prioritise your safety above everyone else's. Your gifts are too great to be lost to our people."

"But Spiron!"

He held up a hand. "There is to be no argument. Even if all of the rest of us fall, you must survive. Cerren's last message before Fractus left was imperative. If the worst comes, and our attempt fails, you, and any other surviving cadets and Scouts will rendezvous here." He handed her a grid reference. "Memorise it and then destroy it." His eyes caught and held hers and she found herself nodding despite her mind screaming at her that this was not something she should agree to, and then her mouth framed the appropriate words.

"I will try to do so."

Spiron raised an eyebrow, but she held his gaze steadily, refusing to back down.

"I told you, didn't I?" asked Allad, and Spiron nodded.

"That will do then. I have your word, that you will try?"

"You do Spiron. But I'm first and foremost a Scout." Shanna tried to keep the anger out of her voice, but it came out slightly defiantly anyway. The unspoken rule of the Scout Corps was 'No-one left behind.'

He sighed. "And yes, you are." He looked sternly at her again. "But sometimes we have to look beyond what we see with our eyes." His eyes were bleak, and she didn't understand, but she did her best, softening slightly.

"I've said that I'll try, and I will, Spiron. The boys and I will try to the best of our abilities." The Patrol First shared another long look with Barron and Allad, and then Satin hummed quietly at the other two cats, and they both hummed at their partners.

"In that case, go and eat, and then you've got the first watch." Shanna nodded and went to do as she'd been told, still feeling rebellious. Storm and Twister flickered their tidemarks and then she felt a wash of determination from them. About what she was unsure, but they were with her, and that was enough.

# Chapter 21

ON THE day after the cyclone, Kaidan awoke slowly. "Move over Bootsy," he mumbled, and then shot to a sitting position as he remembered the night's events. "Dipper!" he whispered. The starcat purred sleepily and then stretched. The room was still dim, and Kaidan listened carefully. None of the normal early morning noises were audible, so he relaxed slightly and turned around to look at the cat stretched out on his sleeping pallet. The great violet eyes were sad, but his tidemarks rippled in patterns of comfort, and Kaidan rubbed Dipper's blue toned cheeks gently. "I'm glad you're here." The cat purred again and then moved himself into a sitting position. "You'd better not let them know you're here," said Kaidan. Dipper's tidemarks flickered slightly, and Kaidan had the distinct impression that the cat was amused.

Dipper yawned lazily, and stretched again, as Kaidan looked around. The illumination in the room was brightening slowly, a sure sign that the day was about to begin. He concentrated briefly, as Shanna had taught him, and he managed to make his form flicker and fade briefly. Dipper leaned companionably on his leg and the fade steadied a bit. "I think I'll need to practice," said Kaidan. "It's been a long time since I've tried that." He was hungry too, and worried about one of the Garsal catching a glimpse of the starcat. The lights came on fully, and then footsteps sounded. A plate of food was pushed through the flap at the bottom of the door, and Kaidan hurried over and picked it up.

An almost inaudible hum sounded from behind him, and he turned to see a pair of violet eyes watching the plate avidly. "I suppose I'll have to share then," sighed Kaidan as his stomach rumbled audibly. Dipper purred as Kaidan divided the morning food into two portions. He ate one, quickly, and then put the plate on the floor for the starcat. His stomach rumbled quietly to itself, but the purr from Dipper made him push the emptiness to the back of his mind. Finally, he had a real chance to escape. And if he could escape the Garsal ship, and if Dipper decided to stay with him, he might actually be able to make his way through Below to the plateau. Although, surely somewhere there would be Scouts nearby. He couldn't imagine that they didn't have the Garsal under surveillance somehow. Perhaps Dipper could lead him to them.

Kaidan's mind whirled with plans and thoughts so fast he was almost dizzy. Perhaps he could escape the ship, make his way home and then help lead an expedition back to the ship. He dismissed that one as silly. They already knew where the ship was. Perhaps there were people outside the ship now, and all he had to do was get off it somehow and meet up with them to be safe. Perhaps he could free all of the slaves … Lacey! Perhaps he could free her somehow and take her off the ship. Or maybe not. He still didn't know what to make of the connection between the female Garsal and the old slave, and Laretai had not been forthcoming.

The warning chime sounded, and he hurriedly scooped up the plate, threw a warning glance at Dipper, who faded slowly before his eyes, and stood as he'd been taught, before the door. The lock clicked and he stepped out and placed the plate on the trolley. The blank faced slave pushed it onwards, and as she moved away, Kaidan could see that one of the young Garsal females was already there awaiting him. "Follow," she said.

He followed after her, and nearly tripped over as he realised that the tickle on his right leg was Dipper, pacing him, faded. His heart pounded as he looked around involuntarily, then returned his glance to the ground as a proper slave should. The female Garsal was walking faster than normal. Kaidan ran her features through his mind again and decided that it was Hirtoi he was following. They didn't have far to go. He was back in Laretai's quarters within a few minutes and he knew that Dipper had entered with him. The faded starcat was exploring the Garsal's quarters. With his eyes on the floor as he'd been trained, it was even harder than normal to catch the shimmer that a faded starcat occasionally made. But then Kaidan's heart nearly leaped out of his chest when Dipper let a faint blue tidemark flicker briefly. It was obviously deliberate, and after the third time, Kaidan surreptitiously flicked a 'fade' signal that his parents used, at the cat, hoping that he'd get the message and stop doing it.

"Kaidan, show me your back," commanded Laretai as she entered the room. Awkwardly, Kaidan disrobed and turned his back towards the Garsal female. He felt, rather than saw, her scrutiny. He stood there uncomfortably for some minutes, before she instructed him to reclothe himself and await her near the work station. The wooden table was surrounded by a half circle of screens, all showing images, or what he assumed to be writing in the Garsal language.

He waited there for at least an hour as as she worked at her devices, before she sent him to fetch food and drink from the service area in the next room. Whatever it was that Laretai had been doing at her work station she considered it important. Her many-faceted eyes peered at the screens intently, and several times she'd flicked back and forth through a myriad of images before settling on just one to study. As he'd deposited the tray on the desk, she'd closed an image hurriedly, but not before he'd seen his sister's face in it. It seemed to be a close up, and Shanna was staring directly towards the gadget that had captured the image. He hoped he'd managed to conceal his surprise as he returned to staring at the floor. Very carefully he altered his position, angling himself so that he had an oblique view of her screens.

For a few moments she ate in silence, all her attention on the screen in front of her. Occasionally she adjusted it with a few taps, or delicate motions, using the divided digits at the end of her manipulator arms. Then she pulled one of the screens on the far end closer and enlarged the image on it. It was Shanna again.

Kaidan was fascinated, despite his worry over Dipper. What was a picture of his sister doing on the Garsal ship? What had his sister been doing *on* the Garsal ship? The background meant it couldn't have been anything else. Had she been a part of the Scout mission that had destroyed their communications systems? He'd heard enough snippets of information during his message carrying to know that someone had. He realised that he'd been staring at the image and hurriedly returned his eyes to the floor, but he couldn't help sneaking peeks through his lashes. Laretai had sat herself back in her chair and was studying the image. A few taps, and Shanna dropped back into normal size, and Kaidan could see the whole image. Starcats and humans – Patrol Ten and the cadets struck a pang of homesickness through him so strong, that he nearly doubled over in pain. Only the fear of betraying his people further kept him from moving. He gritted his teeth and tried to prevent the moisture that suddenly welled up in his eyes from betraying him.

He was even more unnerved when Laretai spoke. "Kaidan. Tell me of the felines in these images." Finally able to look directly at the images, he was almost too choked with emotion to reply. His mind raced as he decided what to say. Being silent wasn't an option as his sessions with the Overlord had proved. His back tingled with remembered pain.

"They're called starcats," he replied.

"Where did they come from?" she asked.

"From here."

"Are they sentient?"

"Sentient?" It was a question he'd never considered.

"Yes, sentient. Able to reason, experiencing consciousness of themselves, intelligent, independent?" It was as if she was reeling off a learned definition. For a moment, Kaidan was completely adrift, not sure what to say. All of those terms did seem to apply to starcats, now that he thought about it. Then she went on. "Are they independent creatures in their own rights – creatures that you're allied with?" And then it crystallised. She wanted to know if they were yet another type of alien to subjugate.

"No, they're simply pets," he replied, hoping that Dipper wasn't going to feel insulted. He saw a faint flickering of blueness across the room, and hoped that Laretai hadn't noticed it.

"Do all of you have such pets?" she asked, and he was certain that he could detect curiosity in the alien tones.

"No, not all, but there are many of them." He hoped that the notion of many would give the Garsal pause.

She turned back to her screen, and enlarged the image containing his sister again. Her gold-streaked braids were untidy and wispy, and her bright green eyes were looking piercingly towards him. She was 'Shanna the Scout' in that picture, caught in a flurry of movement, flanked by her cats and surrounded by like-minded companions. Despite the obvious gravity of the situation the image showed, knowing that Scouts had penetrated the ship at some point made the prospect of rescue seem possible. "Tell me about these people. Who are they?"

Kaidan stammered. "Th … they're Scouts." He'd said more than he'd planned in those two words, and hastened on. "They explore." He hoped that would satisfy Laretai.

"Explore what? And where? And what would make them suitable to invade this ship?" The questions came thick and fast, so Kaidan changed tack and relied on the lies he'd told the Overlord.

"Just the planet. I don't know anything more – I'm only a school child." Laretai met the last sentence with silence. Then she pulled another picture up onto a different screen. It was Kaidan – wearing his unmarked Scout fatigues – the clothes he'd been wearing when he was captured.

"Perhaps our Overlord forgot what you were wearing when you were captured." She made a sweeping gesture and brought the two images together, side by side. "You appeared to be wearing the same clothing." She tapped the screen and enlarged the images. Kaidan began to improvise frantically.

"They have insignia – see!" He pointed to the shoulder badges on Shanna's shirt. "My clothes are just what everyone wears everyday." Laretai again said nothing, just tapped her screen again and another image appeared. It had been taken from the air. She enlarged it, beyond what Kaidan had thought would be possible, and the inhabitants of Watchtower appeared, clad in their normal, everyday clothing. Although many wore utilitarian trousers and shirts, few wore the fatigues of the Scout Corps. The evidence almost floored Kaidan, but he rallied slightly. "I'm a messenger when I'm not at school."

The silence from the Garsal female seemed even more pronounced. Kaidan felt his heart accelerate, and began to think frantically. He'd spun a believable web, or so he'd thought, under the duress of the Overlord's interrogation. Surely he could withstand a few questions. But this time, there was picture evidence. Evidence that perhaps he was a bit more than he'd seemed. He decided to go with the messenger story. It was what he'd told the Overlord, and the uniform could be explained away fairly easily. Or he could refuse to answer. The idea shot a thrill of fear through his body again and the newly healed skin on his back tingled, and his knees trembled. For the first time, he wasn't sure if he'd be able to hold up under more torture, then a warm feline form brushed gently against his leg and he took heart.

"I was a messenger for the Scouts. I ran messages from place to place. I didn't know what was in the messages." He kept his voice steady by letting his left hand brush against Dipper's soft fur. Laretai leaned back and tapped her work surface idly, fixing him with an inscrutable stare.

"So it seems. This is what you've told the Overlord. But there's the matter of Lacey." It was the first time in several days that he'd heard Laretai mention Lacey's name. "And those felines. We've encountered them a number of times now." She paused and tapped the desk several times more. "I would know more. There was one travelling with you when Trooper Hoth captured you. Tell me about it."

"He didn't belong to me," said Kaidan. "He belonged to the other messenger." Laretai's questions went on and on. He was exhausted by the time she sent him to get the midday meal. The whole time, Dipper had been next to him, giving him the courage to keep going, and to keep denying any more knowledge. The only bright spot had been the lack of violence. He wondered at it at the same time that he was suspicious of its lack, and more than once, worried that Laretai was lulling him into revealing more than he wanted to. In some ways it had been easier to withstand the pain of physical torture. He'd had to empty his mind of everything except the things he'd decided to tell, and then hang onto them until there was nothing else to do but shout them out.

As he presented Laretai with her meal, she indicated that he should sit and eat his own food nearby. It was the first time he'd been permitted to eat while on duty for the Garsal, and he sat awkwardly, trying to eat as neatly and quickly as possible. Thankful, but slightly guilty that he couldn't share, he shovelled the slop down, and then sat awaiting Laretai's next command. The silence wore on. She took each bite slowly, peering at him, and then the screens in front of her, in turn.

The meal seemed to wear on and on, and steadily Kaidan became more unnerved. Had it not been for the presence of the faded starcat beside him, he might have broken down under her stare. Finally, she finished, and motioned for him to remove her tray. He did so quickly, glad to remove himself from her presence, and glad to have a moment alone. Dipper stayed beside him the whole time, pacing invisibly next to him, just close enough to brush Kaidan's leg to remind him that he was still present.

The day wore on, and Laretai hammered him with question after question. Kaidan felt as if he'd been physically pummelled, and turned inside out by the time he returned to his solitary quarters. He lay back on his pallet with a sigh of exhaustion, still accompanied by the starcat. Dipper tucked himself around Kaidan and purred, slowly appearing in all his sleek blackness. "Dipper. What are we going to do?" Kaidan murmured, running a hand down the cat's flank. The starcat rolled and exposed his belly to his new friend. He seemed unperturbed by Kaidan's fear. Kaidan absently rubbed the exposed tummy, and Dipper's purring redoubled in volume. A warning clatter, and the evening slop arrived through the slot.

Once again, Kaidan divided it into two portions, thinking gratefully of the previous meal. Then, guiltily, he pushed the two portions back together, sighed, and placed the plate on the floor. He motioned to Dipper with his free hand, using the gesture his family used to signal food to their cats. The cat looked up at him, hummed gratefully, and devoured the food. If this went on, both of them were going to be very hungry, very soon. Somehow, he was going to have to convince Dipper to do some sneaky foraging. Or escape within the next few days.

He lay back again on the pallet and looked at the ceiling. Dipper curled himself around Kaidan again, washed his face in a leisurely fashion, and then lay back himself, purring. Kaidan ran his hands over the cat's fur and began to think.

***

The Matriarch looked up as Laretai entered. Her body posture indicated frustration and fatigue. She patted a chair next to her, poured a drink and waited until Laretai had taken her first sip. "How far did you manage to get with the boy today, Laretai?"

Laretai put her drink on the table with a thud. "Not far." Her tones were frustrated, annoyed and worried all at once. "He admitted to a small connection to the others – they're called Scouts apparently, and they explore – but as a messenger, nothing else." She tapped as she so often did when she was thinking or frustrated, on the table top.

"You will need to take a different approach, then. Perhaps a direct one."

"Do you think that is wise, Matriarch?"

"I don't think it's wise, but our time grows short. Tomorrow the climbers leave to assault the plateau." The Matriarch watched as Laretai absorbed the news. "Show me the boy's room."

Laretai pulled her portable tablet out and placed it on the small table. A few taps and the camera feeds showed Kaidan's form stretched out on his pallet, once again wrapped around by the huge feline. His eyes were closed, and his face appeared pale and drawn. "Was the feline with him today?" asked the Matriarch.

"I am unsure, but I think so," replied Laretai. "Once, I thought I saw a flicker of blue in a corner, and just when I thought I'd surprised him with the pictures of the invading humans, something stiffened his resolve. I will examine the surveillance feeds later with Hirtoi's help. She is monitoring this feed as we speak." She raised tired eyes to the Matriarch and spoke again. "You are right Matriarch. Our time grows short. I will be direct tomorrow." She picked her cup up again and took another sip.

"Estei has proved a fast learner. She will be a worthy successor," said the Matriarch, choosing her words carefully. "I have decided to undertake an inspection of the slave quarters tomorrow afternoon. The Overlord will have no choice but to allow it. You will come with me, leaving Hirtoi monitoring Kaidan." Laretai's head jerked up.

"Is this wise, Matriarch? What reason will you give the Overlord?"

"No, it is yet another thing that is not wise. I have decided that it will be the first inspection of each section of the ship." She leaned back resignedly in her chair. "It will be wearying, but necessary if we are to allay suspicion. At each inspection, we will request to review a number of slaves and workers. The slave inspection should allow you an opportunity to speak with Lacey."

"But Matriarch, what if the Overlord is suspicious?"

"It is the risk we must take." The Matriarch allowed herself to exhale heavily. It was a heavy risk, but there was nothing left but risk in every direction now.

***

"Zoash, are the preparations finalised?" The Overlord looked up from his evening meal as his hatching sib entered the room.

"Overlord, all is as you have commanded. The climbers are provisioned and crewed. They will leave at first light tomorrow morning."

"And the breaks in the sentinel ring?"

"All appear to be storm damage and are now repaired. There were several burned out components in common. It appears that at least four suffered the same component failure. Of the other two, one was crushed by a falling tree, and the other one appears to have burned itself out with a fire. Perhaps an overload from the others failing." He paced forwards, placed his tablet on the desk and pulled up a list of troop numbers and dispositions. "Here are the final plans for the plateau invasion. Once they reach the assembly point on the plateau, they'll call for air support and the attack will begin." The Overlord nodded in satisfaction. Not long, and the humans would be subjugated. "Are there further signs of the Great Enemy?"

Zoash's form stilled to absolute motionlessness and then spoke. His words seemed carefully chosen. "No Overlord, however, they are well known in legend as skilful deceivers. No sign does not mean that they are absent. Our intelligence is very limited. I have no doubt that they are somewhere on the plateau, perhaps lying in wait, secretly. They were known to have some devastating weaponry."

The Overlord heard the caution in his sib's voice, but he dismissed it. Finally the tide would turn on this planet. The humans would make a welcome addition to his slave pool. With them added to his labour force, the establishment of the hive would occur that much faster.

"Have the troops assemble outside with their climbers before departure. I will address them."

"Yes Overlord."

The Overlord waved a dismissal to his sib. His plans were now almost at fruition. He could sense victory at last.

# Chapter 22

SHANNA sent her cats towards the glowing fence. Once again they were poised, ready to penetrate the Garsal colony ship. She flicked a quick glance over her shoulder. There was a nod from Ragar, and she let her vision flow with her cats'. Accustomed now to seeing through Storm and Twister's eyes, there was no nausea or disorientation, just a smooth transition to a different view point. Shanna swallowed as their eyes showed rank upon rank of ominously silent metal climbers assembled outside the ship. There were many more of them than she'd expected.

Twister's viewpoint changed, and she realised he'd climbed a tree. She had a much better view from his new perspective, and the extent of the assembled force shook her to the core. She hand signalled to the others, and within moments, Spiron was by her side. "Spiron, the numbers of vehicles are even greater than we'd thought." She tried to keep her voice steady, but it still trembled slightly.

"How many?"

Shanna dropped back into Twister's eyes and counted as many as she could see.

"At least fifty. Probably more. I can only see what Twister can. Storm's on the ground. The front rank is at least ten vehicles wide. Twister can see back five ranks, but I think there are more behind."

The Patrol First nodded slowly and signalled for Fury to circle in. He tucked a note in the cat's harness and sent him off with a quick hand signal. "Wait here and watch, Shanna. I've sent an estimate to Kalli. She'll pass the message to Fractus, and he'll alert the plateau." He was gone so silently and so fast that it was almost as if he'd vanished.

Shanna settled in to watch, absently scanning the ground before she crouched behind a rock. Automatically her brain catalogued her surrounds. Barbed palm there, the strong scent of pungo just behind, frondan palm to the left, sneaker creepers in *that* hollow, the small patter of stinkrat feet .... She'd changed so much in such a short time. As she waited, she tried to avoid thinking about the possibility of encountering her brother on the ship, but the thought was constantly there, niggling away in the back of her brain. A tiny sound alerted her, and then Allad was by her side. "Any movement yet?"

"Nothing." She returned her vision to Storm and Twister. More and more, she was able to perceive their emotions and intentions, and they hers. Without any signals, Storm slunk along the fence, barely concealed in the vegetation. Shanna's view changed and she was able to see a tall Garsal, standing in front of the neat ranks, surrounded by an entourage. It appeared to be exhorting the assembled troopers. She could now see that there were several Garsal next to each vehicle, lined up in formation. The insectoid creature finished its speech with several emphatic gestures, and then barked a command, so loudly that faint echoes came on the breeze.

The sounds were repeated in force by the assembled creatures, and then repeated over and over again until the area echoed with the harsh alien tones. Unaccustomed to such noise Below, all the Scouts went to ground. Shanna crouched lower behind her rock. Storm and Twister froze to absolute stillness, and the vegetation seemed to be holding its breath. Faintly on the wind, the first roars sounded. Attracted by the sounds, every predator within the outer ring of sentinels would be headed in this direction. It probably wouldn't be many, but the storm must have brought a few through the gaps left by Patrol Ten's break in, and any large predator Below was a danger to someone on foot.

Momentarily distracted, Shanna lost the connection with her cats. As she re-established it, she could see that the alien creatures were entering their vehicles. Within moments, the Garsal had made themselves scarce, vanishing inside the metallic vehicles standing motionless in their lines. For a moment, all that could be heard was the sound of approaching predators, their snarls echoing through the trees. There was a soft whistle from behind, and Shanna recalled her cats and withdrew to the nearest large tree. With a few swift movements, she was up the tree with her cats perched on branches nearby.

Suddenly, a different sound split the air, and the ruby toned fence lines winked out. There was a snapping and crunching of vegetation, and then the mass of climbers moved as one. To Shanna's eyes, they were like a swarm of huge metal spooner spiders crawling malevolently across the landscape. The front rank breached the fence line, and as the first scaly predator reached the perimeter, turrets swivelled, and the creature went down under a spray of red beams. Shanna's heart almost stopped. The idea of those mechanical monsters bearing down on her family chilled her to her core.

She could feel her starcats' disquiet – their statue-like postures and simmering anger washed across her mind like a hot wind. As rank after rank of the climbers marched past, vegetation snapped and crunched beneath their tracks, and the wave of oncoming predators perished before them. The noise was indescribable. Shanna felt as if her planet was screaming and shuddering silently under the onslaught. They left a wide swathe of devastation in their wake, and as a group were moving much faster than the single vehicles they'd seen previously. Shanna was dazed as vehicle after vehicle roared past.

Another whistle sounded, and she was brought back abruptly to reality. The fence was down. There were still more vehicles marching through the gap. She dropped out of the tree, landing silently in the vegetation, and faded.

Reaching out with her senses, she extended her bubble of fade over her friends and felt her cats fade as well. She sent them out with a thought, and then began to move towards the fence line.

It was daunting moving towards the Garsal in broad daylight, but Spiron had decided to take advantage of the dropped fence. She 'felt' the others gather closely behind her, groped blindly behind her with one hand and felt Allad's close on it. She whistled quietly and they quickly began to move towards the boundary, their speed increasing rapidly. The anger in the grouped starcats was like a palpable throb now, and as the faded group began to run, she felt their anger fuel her determination to do everything she could to prevent the invaders from destroying her planet.

As they drew near the line of fence posts, Shanna realised that the final rank of climbers was just about to move through them. "Faster!" she hissed, and lengthened her stride, tugging on Allad's hand. She slipped past the posts, just as the last climbers rumbled through only metres away. Mindful of the danger, she ran onwards towards the ship, Storm and Twister ranging ahead, and the other cats circling. The lines of red sprang up again as the last climber passed, and then Shanna slowed down to a walk, crouching instinctively, despite knowing that she was invisible to Garsal eyes. She was sweating, and her leg ached faintly.

Allad's hand squeezed hers, and she stopped completely, keeping her eyes on the area near the ship. There was a whisper from Spiron. "Separate now."

"Hands," said Ragar. Shanna felt Allad draw her hand to one side, and then another hand found her shoulder. "Shanna, take us towards the entrance. The rest of you, prepare to take your own fades. On my count. Three, two, one, now." Shanna relaxed and felt the strain ease as she reduced her bubble to herself. She felt the hand on her shoulder tap briefly, and then she led them off towards the ship entrance.

***

"You have done well, Zoash," said the Overlord as the last of the climber assault group vanished through the vegetation, their rumble slowly dying away. His hatching sib bowed his head in modesty, as he and the Overlord walked back to the ship, surrounded by their escort.

"Hoth leads," said Zoash. "I judged him to be worthy of the task."

"And you were correct," said the Overlord. "Again you have chosen well. Our gene pool is most worthy of continuation. The Matriarch will no doubt be in agreement after our victory on the plateau. Do you have an estimated time of arrival on the plateau?"

"The climbers are nimble, Overlord. Now that the route is established, the time is less each journey, but massed as they are, they will move swiftly, protected by their numbers. Two days, no more. We will lose some climbers to the beasts, but not enough to affect the attack. I have directed them to travel night and day. There will be no warning for the humans on the plateau."

They paused by the ship entrance, as the guard saluted with his weapon and keyed the entry code. The Overlord looked around as the doorway opened, and turned once more to purvey his growing empire. The hive entrance had been well tested during the storm. The sturdy stonework was built directly into the hillside and ensured that the decorative archway had weathered the wind and rain untouched. Despite the laser fencing ringing the area, and the need for the sentinels, he knew that his domain would grow steadily until he could take his rightful place as a ruler of many, with multiple offspring. For a time, the lack of communications equipment was forgotten, and the memory of the Great Enemy receded into the dream of triumphant accomplishment.

For several moments, the Overlord stood and looked. The freshness of the vegetation surrounding the ship site, well watered since the cyclone, disguised the scorched ground around the colony ship. He savoured the thought of the mineral wealth of this planet – his planet. Untapped riches awaited his exploitation, and the rare, glowing gems would provide an exotic export sure to extract wealth from the upper echelons of Garsal society. The fresh human population was strong, and there were interesting opportunities for exploitation once they were captured and enslaved. Each day his researchers discovered more from the samples they'd taken from the captured child and the body of the deceased adult.

"Zoash, the Matriarch wishes to inspect the ship today. You will provide suitable offerings, and arrange the itinerary. Laretai has sent a list of venues she wishes to observe. We will finish at the hive once again. Ensure that the finishing touches are well under way in the female quarters." He turned slowly, allowing himself a moment of pleasure as he surveyed the activity inside the fence line. Then the breeze changed, and the stench from dead and blackened denizens sliced into his daydreams of victory, and his mood darkened. "I will have hourly progress reports delivered from Hoth, Zoash. See to it."

"Yes Overlord." His hatching sib's voice was inscrutable, and the Overlord stalked through the doorway without another backwards glance.

***

Hoth bent over the detailed maps constructed from the data collected from the aircraft flyovers and his own journeys. With the added safety of numbers, and the knowledge he'd gained from his first trip to the plateau, he'd plotted a fast path to the base of the plateau. The track through the vegetation was now well established, but the aggressive predators of the planet were still a major source of danger to his force. He'd agreed with Zoash's directive to keep the ranks of climbers moving, even during the night hours. There were plenty of troopers to take shifts at the controls, and there would be time for a rest period near the base of the plateau before the assault began.

He traced the path they would take with one manipulator arm, and then beckoned to one of his troopers. "Transmit this location to all of the vehicles. We will use it as our rendezvous point." He turned back to the map. The three major settlements were marked on the map. He tapped a control, and the closest settlement expanded in as much detail as the technicians had been able to provide. Aerial images, combined with data from his own explorations, provided information about the fortifications and probable locations of the other human habitations. Small, satellite settlements ringed the larger one. The climber lurched slightly, and then shook, as the turret cannon fired. Hoth cursed quietly, and took a firmer grip on the image table. The beasts of this planet were overly ready to attack anything that moved.

He turned back to studying the maps. The town was surrounded by a substantial stone wall. Easily large enough to prevent the most aggressive of predators from gaining access, it would still be simple to breach, if enough climbers combined to blast its stonework. The buildings inside the town were all strongly constructed. His mind appreciated the reasoning. The storms on this planet were like nothing he'd ever experienced. It wasn't surprising that the residents had built so strongly. He zoomed the map outwards again, studying the outlying villages and settlements. The big question was whether to assault the major town first, or pick off the settlements one by one, and then go for the town. He clacked his palps irritably, and closed the program down.

The Overlord would be pleased with a quick victory. He was unlikely to be pleased with a slower, but safer, program of settlement assault. Against his better judgement, he decided that the force would assault the town, subdue it, and then take on the smaller villages one by one. His force was large, and it had the advantage of technological superiority.

There was always the Great Enemy, though, in all its unpredictability. The idea played on his mind briefly. There was still no explanation as to why the initial four crawlers had vanished during their assault on the humans. It was an unanswered question that niggled in the back of Hoth's mind, but his hope of offspring was high, and for the moment, he dismissed it.

***

The runner burst into Cerren's office, now relocated to the plateau tunnel complex. He looked up tiredly, as the young man placed the message on his desk and came to attention. Socks hummed a query at Cerren and he pushed himself forwards slowly and picked up the paper. As the words penetrated his brain, tiredness vanished in a spurt of adrenaline. "Fetch Peron, Yendy, Erilla, Payne, Shari and the two most senior councillors from the operations centre. Now!"

The messenger vanished at a run, and Cerren allowed the import of the words to sink in. Socks flickered her blue tidemarks at him, and then paced across the floor to lay her head in his lap. He allowed the warmth of her love to assist him to think at a more measured pace.

Running feet sounded outside his office, then one after another those he'd requested filed in. Payne arrived last, his limping gait still handicapping his normal fluid stride.

"It's about to start," said Cerren, rising to greet them. "I have word from the network Below. They've sent a force of climber vehicles towards us."

"How many?" asked Payne.

"Preliminary figures suggest upwards of fifty," said Cerren. He handed Payne the note. "And Spiron has decided to make his move under the cover of their own troop movements."

"He has?" asked Erilla.

"He has," replied Cerren, "and I concur with his decision. Those climbers are fast. And they know where we are. There was nothing that the Scouts Below could have done to prevent that many vehicles from going anywhere they wanted to. Our best hope remains in that small group of people penetrating the ship, and wreaking whatever havoc they're able. Our job is to protect as many of us as possible." He sighed tiredly.

"We'd best begin the evacuation then," said Peron. "Will we mount any kind of defence here?"

"We'll defend the smaller places," said Cerren. "The old storm shelters are more easily defended, and several of the smaller villages. Erilla, do you have the plans?"

Erilla nodded, held up one finger, and put her head outside the door. Cerren heard a few words followed by more running feet. "The plans will be here within moments." She moved to the map tacked to Cerren's wall. "Our priorities are these: Hillview, Storm Shelters 15, 23, and 48, and Buttress." She tapped each spot on the map. They held the starcat breeders, three storm shelters full of Watchtower's cleverest technicians, and a farming community set in a rock-walled valley. Unlike most of the other farming centres, nearly all of its citizens had remained where they were. Its natural defences were formidable, and it would be difficult for any invading force to assault, despite the agility demonstrated by the climbers. It was now the primary source of fresh produce for those sequestered in the old storm shelters around the southern plateau.

"The children will be dispatched to our Starlyne allies immediately," said Yendy. "I'll have messages sent as soon as we're finished here. Do you mean to allow them into Watchtower without any attempt at defence?"

Cerren shook his head. "No. We'll mount a token defence. Just enough to convince them that we're here in force, and then retreat into the plateau tunnels and the nearest Starlyne habitation. Our allies will aid us as they're able."

He looked sadly at the assembled group, emotion choking him briefly, before he was able to go on. "They have a number of volunteers who will join us once we've sent word." There was silence in the office for several moments.

"You mean that they'll sacrifice themselves," said Payne bluntly. It was more of a statement than a question.

"Yes." Cerren kept his answer short. "They'll stop as many of the climbers as they can, and then return to their loved ones to die. If they can." He shook his head.

"They lack our numbers, but they share our love of this planet, and they value the freedom to live as they choose as much as any human being. They might have manipulated us genetically, and hidden themselves from us when they could have helped us, yet now, at the time of greatest need, they would sacrifice themselves." Erilla's eyes were moist.

"They truly believe that together we will be the salvation of the Galaxy," said Shari. She headed the militia. Her forces would soon join the Starlynes in the physical battle against the Garsal. Her body, clothed in its militia drabs, was strongly built, and her slanted eyes hinted at resources yet untapped. "I've spent many hours with Speaker, preparing for this very moment. The vast majority of the Starlyne people are in agreement with Keeper's vision." And then her face broke into a smile and the tension eased slightly. "He wouldn't elaborate on exactly how that might happen, however. Just left me with the impression of absolute faith." She shook her head. "It was all a bit mystical for me."

"That aside," said Cerren, "the practicalities await us." He tapped the map. "Shari, you've integrated the Scouts I've assigned you with your units?"

"Yes. I've placed most of them with the archery units under Dinian, and they've also set as many traps around Watchtower as possible." She shook her head slightly. "The archers are our best chance of breaching the vehicles, but there are only so many of them. How much of a fight do you want us to put up?"

Cerren's heart quivered, but he kept his voice firm as he replied. "It must look real, Shari." The woman nodded, but Cerren knew precisely what she was thinking. What everyone was thinking. Real meant casualties. Real meant fighting to the death in some places. Real meant losing people – people who could not be spared, and people who had families and loved ones. Erilla had told him that sometimes there weren't any good choices, and that he just had to make the best of the choices available to him. This was one of those times. "Your people know this?"

"They will," she promised. "And we will try our best to make it look real, while minimising our casualties. We have a few surprises awaiting the Garsal." Her face was grim, and Cerren had the impression she wanted to say more. He looked at her, raising one eyebrow, but she shook her head.

"Peron, you and Erilla will command the Scout Corps. Peron, you're Shari's liaison. Erilla, you'll make the final decisions on the Scout depositions.

Yendy, you'll evacuate and remain with the Starlynes in the Buttress habitation. Speaker will join us in the command centre here, so all communications will be relayed through him. As previously agreed, he'll coordinate our allies. I believe they also have some surprises prepared for the invaders."

For a moment Cerren paused. He took the time to look at the group assembled before him. Peron, tall, broad shouldered, and accompanied by Thunder, was like a bastion of strength. Erilla, dark complexioned, lithe and green eyed, shadowed everywhere by Nimbus. Yendy, shortest of all of them, yet full of compassion, and with his organisational skills second to none. Payne, tall and dark, still limping, but unbowed. Shari, in her uniform, straight backed and competent, and last of all, the young man from Tamazine's group of aides, accompanied by his young starcat, now a promising councillor, learning from Payne. Griss was his name. He'd stood silently, listening, not saying anything. He returned Cerren's gaze evenly.

"I'll be your aide, Cerren. You can't spare a Scout for the job, and my current role is redundant until this 'emergency' – he flicked an amused eyebrow at the use of Tamazine's flippant term – is over. I am efficient, and Payne has made sure that I know all the planning in depth."

"Thank you," replied Cerren. "In that case, we'll get to work. I need reports as regularly as you're able. Griss, go and meet Speaker, he'll come to the tunnel entrance. I need the communication network up and running as fast as possible." He took one more look around at the group,

"And thank you. Thank you all." There was a flurry of silent, dignified nods, and one by one, they departed, and Cerren sat down again in his chair. Socks leaned herself across his legs. "And, lady cat, what do you think? Will we prevail?" Blue washed across his mind briefly, startling him, and he was left slightly disoriented. She purred.

# Chapter 23

HOLDING her breath, Shanna sent her cats out and around the group of Garsal clustered at the entrance to the ship. She couldn't believe their luck in finding the ship open to them. She just hoped that the door would remain that way long enough for them to slip past. Concentrating hard, she let her vision dissolve into three layers. One for her own eyes, and one each for her cats. Storm slipped past the guard and into the ship. Through his eyes Shanna could see that the secondary door was open. Shanna took a quick look around with her own eyes, kept part of her mind on Storm, and with a peep from her silent whistle set Twister on guard near the entrance.

She tapped the hand on her shoulder, waited a few seconds, and then moved forwards as silently as she was able. Her heart pounded as she threaded her way through the Garsal formation in front of the door. Their neatly spaced ranks allowed her to weave her way around them. Her mind's eye imagined the line following her. If she angled herself too sharply, someone would brush against one of the Garsal and the consequences could be catastrophic. She tried to keep her breathing soft and silent, but she kept finding herself holding it, and was then forced to allow it to ooze quietly between her teeth.

For some reason, the group of Garsal stayed where they were. Shanna decided not to wonder why, but kept moving until she was inside, in the dimness of the Garsal ship. As before, she moved to one side of the doorway as she entered and led the others to the far end of the entry chamber. Storm moved further into the ship, and Shanna peered through his eyes as he glided down the corridor. Garsal hurried everywhere. It looked like an unthreadable maze. Another peep and she called him back.

She kept her group motionless in the vestibule for what seemed like hours. Finally, the group outside the entrance moved inside and as both doors closed behind them Shanna felt for the hands in the line of cadets and Allad behind her, and tapped on Taya's hand. There was a brief squeeze from the other girl, and then, several moments later, a coded 'all safe' tap. Shanna let the fade go.

"There's too many of them moving around inside at the moment. I'm not sure we'll be able to sneak our way through." She kept her voice quiet, barely whispering.

"I was afraid of that," Ragar replied. "Three options. Firstly, we split up and reconnoitre in pairs. Secondly, we wait here until the activity level reduces. Thirdly, we do both — split up now, reconnoitre, and rendezvous here this evening. Then we pool our information and decide what to do based on that. Comments?" There was a brief silence.

"Option three," Allad said. "It's the best option. How will we re-enter the room though?"

"Taya can open the doors. Shanna can too?" He looked a query at her, and she nodded.

"Just let me link with Taya when she opens this one and I'll make sure."

"We divide into pairs and one group of three. Taya will pair with Verren to make sure she gets back here. I want you two to stay on this level. Once you've completed a search of this level I want you to station yourself here, outside the door, taking note of how often the Garsal go in and out. We'll need a good exit strategy this time, so you'll be planning it. Shanna, you're with me – we've got the bottom of the ship. Amma, Zandany, Allad, you're to work your way down from the top.. Three groups, only one without a door opener. Allad, you'll send Satin ahead to alert Taya and Verren when you're returning." There were nods.

"We'll need to get moving, Ragar," said Taya. "I don't think it's wise to leave the monitoring device nonfunctional for too long." Ragar nodded and went on.

"You have six hours. I want routes memorised, no hurrying, no rushing. Take your time. We need information before we attempt anything else. OK, everyone ready?"

Everyone nodded.

"Then fade."

Even as the command was issued and the last one faded, the inner door opened and a troop of Garsal marched through accompanied by several human slaves. Instinctively, Shanna flattened herself onto the inner wall. She felt Ragar's hand on her shoulder, and heard a flurry of Garsal communication. Two of them detached from the group, and hurried over to one side of the room, and prodded a panel. As they did, she 'felt' Taya rummage around inside the gadget's machinery and then the two stepped backwards. Despite their alien forms, she could tell that they were puzzled.

She was so intent on watching them that Ragar had to tap her on the shoulder twice before she reacted. Fumbling her whistle into her mouth she darted through the door. Both cats moved with her. Storm took the front again, while she 'felt' Sparks take the rear. Twister roamed on their right flank. Nervously, she made her way around the hurrying Garsal figures, heading directly for the mobile room she remembered from the last visit. It was hard to dodge the moving groups. Even though she was accustomed to working her way through dangerous vegetation and dodging predators, this was an even more alien environment. Finally, in response to Ragar's hand pressure, she slowed their progress, and began to take more than cursory notice of what they were passing.

Memory returned. *There* was the ramp which had finally led them back to this portion of the ship. *There* the scorch marks burned into the wall from Ragar's fireballs, and the unmistakable scars left in the smooth walls from the Garsal weapons. Although there were no bodies scattered around the doorway, memories of the desperate dash they'd made down the corridor were still vivid. Obedient to Ragar's commands, she committed the corridor to memory, while simultaneously guiding the two of them around the obstacles. Grateful that this time she wasn't having to fade multiple others, she concentrated on the task at hand, although each time a new group approached, she couldn't help scanning it in case her brother was present.

Finally they reached the mobile room. The end of the corridor was a busy place, so they had to stand back out of the way, watching, as groups constantly hurried in and out of the ever opening doors. Finally, after an age of watching, she felt Ragar pull her backwards and she followed him slowly to the ramp down into the ship. She'd come to the same conclusion. They would have to retrace their steps to the bottom of the ship on foot. At this time of day, three huge cats and two humans would be easily detected by feel inside the crowded little room.

The descending ramps were almost empty. It was as if they were redundant. Shanna relaxed slightly as they moved away from the jostling alien crowd, and as they moved ever downward carefully counting the levels, Shanna thought about the logic of it. If you had a room that automatically took you up as many levels as you wished in a straight line, it would be an efficient use of time to use it. Then why install ramps? She supposed that it was possible for a malfunction to occur, and if it did they'd need an alternate route. A time saving device then, but not necessarily a space saving one. Two systems instead of one.

Level after level they descended, passed only occasionally by the Garsal inhabitants. Several times human slaves trotted past, unaccompanied, but all wearing the bright orange ankle bands she'd seen on Anjo and Semba. Each time, she felt reflexively in her pocket for the carefully packaged vial of flotter mist. Each time, she and Ragar allowed them to pass by, and each time, she felt her cats' anger mount higher and higher. The human slaves looked undernourished and cowed, and all carried bruises. Their clothing was mixed, some in rags, while others were clean and in some kind of livery.

Several hours of slow, careful descent passed. Then, just when Shanna thought that they would have to turn around and go back up, she heard the soft murmur of voices coming through the wall nearest to her. She tightened her hand on Ragar's arm and felt his squeeze in return. Alone in the ramp-well, he stopped and whispered into her ear. "Send the boys out. Tell me what you see." She flattened herself carefully against the wall at the end of the bend, and sent her cats forwards. Twister went at a run, Storm more slowly, and almost reluctantly she submerged herself in their vision. There was no nausea.

Both pairs of eyes looked down a row of tiered cells. Bars fronted most of them, and a miserable collection of mainly human forms sat listlessly within them. Many were empty. Shanna remembered the slaves they'd seen moving up and down the ramps. They were probably in the midst of their work day. Storm was full of slowly bubbling anger, and Twister was like a simmering cauldron. One bit of extra heat and he'd boil over. Shanna found herself deliberately trying to cool him down, fearful that if he bubbled over he'd do something unwise.

"All clear, Ragar. Row after row of slave quarters. Not a lot occupied right now." Her whispered voice seemed loud in her ears.

"We'll go in then, and make a head count of the cells, check the access and see what the locking mechanisms are like. Ready?" She nodded and faded and led the way in, carefully keeping watch through her cats' eyes until she rounded the corner. She could 'feel' the anger emanating from Sparks as well. Using her own eyes, it was still plain that the slave hold was a place of pain and suffering. Huddled forms sat in some cells. In others, empty of their occupants, old marks on the walls were a testament to fear and dread. Sounds of the unhinged floated down through the stacked cages, and in several cells at one end, blood stained restraints hung limply, their emptiness not a promise of hope, but a threat of punishment.

The guilt she'd felt at having to leave people here last time, had woken Shanna at night on more than one occasion. Now every step she took through the prison felt like a declaration of war renewed against the Garsal. Her eyes hunted unceasingly for her brother, hopeful, yet fearful, of finding him there amongst the pain and misery.

Her cats sparked to maximum alertness, their colours shivering to brightness in her mind, and she halted mid step, pulling Ragar with her behind one of the central pillars. At the other end of the hold, the doors of the mobile room slid open.

A troop of Garsal soldiers marched out, followed by a group of Garsal clothed in multihued filmy cloth. The foremost one was elaborately dressed, and escorted by a tall Garsal wearing an embellished weapon harness. Unlike that of the soldiers, this Garsal's harness bore insignia made from precious metal studded with gems. His air was of absolute command, and complete control, while at the same time, he was oddly deferential to the brightly clothed Garsal. His demeanour puzzled Shanna; command and deference made an odd mix. She shelved the oddity, and concentrated on making sure she was out of the way and well faded. She was beginning to tire slightly, but she was reluctant to use any of her carefully hoarded patches until she absolutely needed to. She could feel Ragar beside her, mind alert and watchful, and she could feel the heat poised within him, should he need it.

Slowly, the group approached. They moved in the manner of an inspection, and Shanna was puzzled. A suspicion began to form in her mind about the rainbow hued group. There were at least a dozen of them. Her first impression was that two were of higher status than the others. The other ten deferred to them, listening attentively, and at least two appeared to be making notations on some kind of tablet. Behind them, Shanna could see glimpses of the same livery she'd noticed on the human slaves they'd passed on the ramp. She sent Storm and Twister out to either side of the group with her silent whistle, and then looked through their eyes. Each time, it was easier.

***

The Matriarch paced slowly through the slave quarters. At this time of day, many of the slave pens were empty. She dawdled as long as possible, hoping to delay the end of the inspection until the slaves were back in their pens. Laretai's spy taps had indicated that Lacey's cell was at the far end. She hoped to coincide the end of her inspection with the return of the slaves to their quarters. "How many slaves has this planet consumed, Overlord?" She stopped moving, forcing the Overlord to stand still to answer.

"We have lost some, Matriarch. As you will be aware from my reports, although this planet has substantial resources, it has many dangerous animals and plants. Our losses have slowed as we've extended our control within the sentinel perimeter." She waited him out, slightly amused at his bumbling attempt to avoid answering the question directly. Finally he spoke again. "Although initial losses have seemed heavy, it is likely that the situation will be remedied very shortly." She continued to stand still. Beside her, she felt Laretai's approval, and at her back, she could feel the attention young Estei gave to the conversation.

*Good,* the Matriarch thought. *She will need every skill she can learn to ensure the success of the plan.* She knew it was a death thought, but she was resigned to the idea of her own demise should the plan require it. She continued to wait. Finally the words she'd waited for came.

"We have lost almost fifty per cent of our original slave quota, Matriarch." The words came one by one, as if they were being spat out through a grinder, in pieces. It was petty, and beneath her, but she allowed herself to feel a small satisfaction as he admitted the disquieting numbers. She played the moments out one by one, before turning her head, beckoning to Estei and then stepping slowly forwards with her chosen successor by her side. Laretai dropped back as she'd been instructed and began to watch the Overlord and his hatching sib.

Behind them, the lift doors opened with a quiet hiss. The sounds of many feet echoed through the slave hold, and the Matriarch stepped out with more confidence. The escort closed around them more tightly, but the Matriarch neither slowed nor speeded up. Estei paced next to her, completely composed, her posture regal and assured.

A group of slaves hurried past, their heads bowed, faces hidden, eyes carefully on the floor. Most were filthy from labouring in the hive. The Matriarch restrained herself from craning her neck to search each face. Again, Laretai's spy taps had proved their worth. The Matriarch ran the human's features through her mind yet again. It was unnecessary with Laretai accompanying them, yet she wished to be certain she could recognise the human woman if necessary.

"How much of the slave hold do you wish to inspect, Matriarch? We have further development inside the hive for your approval." The Overlord's obsequious tones grated on the Matriarch's ears.

"I have neglected this inspection for too long, Overlord. Although I yearn to see the hive progress, I would be remiss in my duties should I avoid a thorough examination of the slave quarters at this time. I would be pleased to inspect the hive tomorrow, however. Laretai will confirm this with Zoash on our return." She walked onwards, and was pleased to hear the lift doors open and close once more. Slaves began streaming past, orange tracker bracelets flashing beneath their rags and livery. Once again, the Matriarch blessed the foresight that had the slaves serving the female Garsal housed inside their enclave. The sounds of clanging cell doors began to echo down the hold, as more and more slaves were incarcerated within their tiny boxes. The sounds of feet treading the gridded walkways above rang sharply above the sounds of human sadness. There were few slaves from the other races on the ship, nearly all were human.

She paced steadily onward, slowing as she approached the general area of Lacey's cell. Once again she paused as the lift doors hissed open again. "How many of the non-humans have survived, Overlord?" He didn't prevaricate this time.

"Very few, Matriarch. Their physiology is less capable of adapting to this planet. We have restricted the few survivors to the ship and hive environs." She stepped off again as another group went past, and then stopped again.

"I will inspect this row more closely."

"Are you … yes of course, Matriarch."

She took several steps towards the end of the hold, and then turned to her left to study the humans in the closest cells. A sturdy woman, rather better fed than most, kept her eyes firmly on the floor. "Your name?"

"Edon." The name was familiar. *Ah, the Overlord's informer.* She'd reported on Kaidan every night on his return to his cell. The Matriarch stepped closer to the bars, curious to see what kind of human being sold her own race for extra food. She was no different to the others that the Matriarch could see. Her small human eyes remained on the floor, but her body showed the effects of extra food and drink. Her clothes were not ragged, like most of the others on this level.

"Look at me." The woman raised her eyes. They were a muddy brown, and looked as if they'd seen horrors. They had, of course. In the depths of the night, the Matriarch had sometimes wondered how she might have fared had she been the one enslaved. It had been a revealing train of thought, and afterwards she always rose the next morning more firmly committed to her part in furthering the plan. She took several steps to her left. That cell was empty. Had she missed Lacey? No. She almost flicked her manipulator arms irritably, but stilled the impulse as it formed. That was the cell in which Kaidan had been kept. Lacey's was the next one.

For a moment, the Matriarch feared she hadn't taken enough time, and that this cell was empty too. But then the pile of rags in one corner moved, and an old woman got slowly to her feet, unfolding one limb at a time. The Matriarch studied the woman whose name had provoked this inspection. Grey hair grew in spirals from her scalp, and dark blue eyes met the Matriarch's faceted ones so briefly that she almost felt that she had imagined the contact. She looked at the woman again. Her eyes were properly on the floor, as if they'd never been anywhere else.

"Your name?"

"Lacey." And there it was. She was the one. How one of the leaders of the human underground had ended up here, she couldn't imagine. The Matriarch looked at her for some moments, searching for the proper phrase.

"Your planet of origin? I would understand your indebtedness." There, she'd included the correct code word.

"I was from Diandro. One of the inner worlds." The coded response was included in the woman's reply.

"You have a large debt, then." The woman placed her eyes back on the floor, and the Matriarch moved on. She spent similar amounts of time with another four slaves, carefully speaking to each for varying amounts of time. They were a spineless lot, she thought as she finished the inspection. But would she have been any different had their places been reversed? She was in a pensive mood when she returned to her quarters. Later, as if by afterthought, she had Laretai send a message to the Overlord, requesting two more slaves – Edon and Lacey. She hoped that her request would be written off as a vagary of her position.

***

Shanna and Ragar left the slave hold as fast as they could once the official party had left. The strain of remaining undetected had been extreme, as the slave hold had filled with returning humans and Garsal, all trying to skirt the inspection party. Faded, they'd still had to avoid any physical contact with either human or Garsal. Their cats had had no difficulty, with their fast reflexes and silent feet, but the humans had needed to work harder. Shanna had had to give up the attempt to look through Storm and Twister's eyes in order to concentrate on her own safety. She'd had only a glimpse of the human slaves, but she was confident that Kaidan had not been among their number – if he had been, Storm or Twister would have found him. She wondered where he was, but in the back of her mind, there was a sad recognition that perhaps he wasn't even alive.

For some time, they'd had to stay silently in one place, tucked behind the pillar that was both their salvation and their prison. On either side, prisoner after prisoner had filed past, accompanied by their Garsal guards. The stream had been so constant that Shanna and Ragar had had no opportunity to leave.

When they finally began to ascend, they moved as fast as possible, knowing it was likely that they would be the last to return to the meeting point. Shanna was frustrated and fearful all at once. They were confident that they could return to the slave hold at will, yet the intelligence they'd hoped to gain was scratchy at best. It was clear that they would have to return to locate the named slaves – but how could they leave the others behind in that hellish hold? And the numbers of slaves inside the ship exceeded even her most nightmarish estimates.

Sending Twister ahead, Shanna rounded another bend in the ramp, and was pushed backwards by Storm. The sound of marching footsteps came clearly down from above. It sounded like a whole troop of Garsal was on the way. She looked around. There was nowhere to go.

# Chapter 24

"RAGAR!" Shanna whispered, "Storm's pushing me back, we need to get out of the way!" She looked around frantically. This section of the ramp, although not particularly narrow, offered no hiding place that she could see. The tramp of marching Garsal became ever louder as they backtracked down the previous incline and then around its bend. Shanna stuck her whistle back into her mouth, and whistled for Storm to precede them, while Twister took the rearguard.

"Down one more level, and then we'll exit through the door there. Let's hope it's unlocked." Shanna nodded, even though she knew he couldn't see her, and followed Ragar. She could 'feel' Sparks pacing by his side, and realised that the starcat was helping him hold his fade, something she could do for herself with little effort. But then, she was still struggling to light a fire, let alone throw a fireball without her cats' help. They were moving as fast as possible, and it was difficult to keep her hand on Ragar's shoulder, but she didn't want to risk losing contact with him.

Despite their speed, the thud of marching feet became louder and louder, and Storm, behind her, was urging her to move faster. Ragar rounded another bend, and Shanna could see the door he'd mentioned. Like many of the Garsal doors, it had a pad next to it.

"Do what the slaves did, Ragar!" Shanna hoped that this door would respond as others had, to pressure on the pad. There was a hiss and a click, and then the door opened, and Shanna signalled Storm through first. She and Ragar barely paused before following him, and then Shanna heard the hiss as the door closed behind them. She looked around, only then aware of how dim the room was. And then she realised that the room was enormous, lit only by a few overhead lights. Their reddish tones lent an eerie air to the cavernous space. She squinted, finally able to make out in the far shadows, dark ranks of squatting crawlers, the vehicles that had been so difficult to stop all those months ago. At the far end were larger shapes, each with a familiar silhouette. The aircraft. There seemed to be many more than three, however, and a dark chill struck her to the core and she stopped moving. The sound of marching feet reached a crescendo and died away as Ragar pulled her to one side of the doorway and allowed himself to become visible in the dim lighting.

"I don't think there's anyone in here," he whispered. "And I can't see any of those devices that Taya said were monitoring us." His voice sounded tired, and as Shanna dropped her own fade, she looked at him in concern.

"Are you all right?"

"Yes, just not used to fading for so long." The dim light made it hard to see well, and Shanna decided to take his comment at face value.

"Should you use a patch?"

"I will if I need to," he replied. "But we need to meet back with the others as soon as we can, so we'd better get moving again."

"But Ragar – this must be the vehicle storage!"

"I'm sure it is, but we have a rendezvous to make, and then we'll decide what to do." Shanna was about to object again, but he raised a hand. "We stick to the plan. This just gives us more options."

Sighing, she nodded. "We'll count the levels on the way up?"

"Yes. Now, can you and the boys keep us safe if I keep Sparks beside me? I need to conserve my patches for as long as possible."

"Yes, we'll be fine. Do you want me to fade you too?"

"Not at this stage. I suspect we'll be relying on you a lot, later." Shanna nodded in the dark. Her memory replayed the images from the slave hold. There must have been several hundred of them there. She imagined trying to fade them all, trying to escort them all through Below, and shook her head. There must be another way. But how could they leave any of them? Then she remembered Semba – if she'd had any choice, would she have wanted to be rescued? She wondered how many of the slaves were too cowed to choose to leave their captivity.

For a few moments, she and Ragar listened at the door, and then, when there was complete silence, they faded, opened the door and slipped through it. As they made their way up through the levels, Shanna counted, fixing the numbers of ramps and doors to the vehicle storage in her mind.

***

A bell rang out from Hillview. Anjo looked up from the fence line camouflage he'd been repairing and called Ember. The two of them jogged up the hill towards the house. He scanned the hillside as he ran, trying his best to penetrate the screen of vegetation now transplanted to hide the house. Screens made of Frontier's creepers shadowed the windows, and the door had been painted to match the surrounding stone. The large metal doors into the cat cavern had also seen the attentions of the painters, and were now mottled grey, green and brown, and hung with netting festooned with fast growing plants. Anjo had recognised them as some of the arboreals Kaidan had pointed out so long ago.

As always, the thought of Kaidan pained him. Each night, as he slept in Kaidan's bed, lying in Kaidan's room, he felt the same pain, tinged with guilt, that he hadn't been able to save him. Ember hummed consolingly at him. The young starcat had liked Kaidan, and Anjo knew that the starcat missed him too. *But not as much as his parents do.* Anjo's mind niggled the words at him. He was still in awe of Janna and Adlan's ability to take the man who had failed to save their son into their family. In some ways he understood it. He was the reason their children were no longer with them, but their children had both fought to save him and protect him. They were honouring their children's courage.

As he reached the top of the rise, he began to puff, and his leg began to throb gently. Despite the miracle of the Starlyne people's medical care, it was still sensitive, and he was still out of condition. Kaidan would have made some kind of comment, like "You really need to toughen up a bit, now you're one of us!" or "Didn't they ever teach you to run on that pretty planet of yours?" He dismissed the memories sadly, but under their sting, ignored his own discomfort and jogged on. No matter what, he would do his part in keeping Kaidan's family safe. There was a complicated twinkle of tidemarks from Ember, and he nearly stopped running. He was sure that the cat was agreeing with him. Although he'd become accustomed to the cats' ability to understand verbal commands and even short conversation, he hadn't said anything out loud. He shook his head. The bell was ringing in the urgent sequence.

He could see Janna at the door, waving urgently, and from all over the property, he could see figures approaching at a run. There were starcats everywhere. Partially trained youngsters and fully trained adults hurtled towards the habitation. As Anjo slowed to a halt near Janna, he saw three of the breeding females lined up with their cubs at the entrance to the cavern. Despite the gravity of the situation, several of the cubs were bouncing and jostling, and a red toned female had resorted to standing on the tail of one of the more boisterous kittens. Each of the breeders had taught their cats to respond to the bell, as well as their voices or whistles. It had been a simple thing to do with so many experienced trainers.

"Messenger from Watchtower!" Janna said. "Marked urgent, top priority." More people arrived and assembled on the rise until everyone was accounted for. "From the Senior Councillor – Master Cerren," Janna said when the last one had come to a halt. The silence was absolute. "Message from Below, via the Starlyne link. Ground force on the way. Multiple climber vehicles." Her voice shook slightly, and Anjo knew that she was remembering what he'd told her about the vehicle that had taken Kaidan.

"Initiate Plan Delta Four." She stopped and looked around. "There will be a militia unit joining us within an hour or two. As you know, we are a priority asset in Delta Four. There will only be a token defence of Watchtower mounted. Children will be evacuated immediately to the nearest Starlyne habitation. Time is short, so parents, ready your children. As planned, Bellato will take them." She gestured to a large man, standing to one side, flanked by several starcats. The breeding females will accompany them, also as planned."

Janna looked around at the group. "Any questions?"

"Are there any requests from Watchtower?" asked Josen.

"None at this time, just the watching brief as per the plan. The rotation is listed inside on the board." Janna and Adlan had turned one of their walls into a large message board. Rosters and duty rotations were pinned to it, along with a list of current plan numbers and codes. "We may end up with a Starlyne liaison if there is someone to spare," she said. "Which will help if we receive some casualties who can't make it to the nearest Starlyne habitation. Anything else?" There were shaken heads all around. "Then let's get to it," said Janna. "I need Anjo and Josen. Josen, I'll be in the house after you've sorted out your children. Anjo, follow me." Anjo nodded, he had specific duties to perform, and then he and Ember, along with all the adults and trained starcats, would settle in to defend Hillview. His stomach did a back flip. Once again, he would come face to face with the Garsal invaders.

***

Kaidan lay back on his pallet, still incredulous. Dipper was once again curled around him, warm blackness cradling his human friend. Again, Kaidan had shared his meals, and once again, his stomach was rumbling. His last meeting with Laretai had shocked him to the core. She'd called him to her quarters, removed everyone else, imparted the incredible information, and then had him locked up again. Now, six hours later, he still didn't know what to believe.

"Do you think she was telling the truth, Dipper?" The cat purred softly and tucked himself more comfortably around Kaidan. "That's no help, cat." He rubbed the cat's cheek gently, and rolled onto his stomach. Dipper stared deeply into Kaidan's eyes as his purring rumbled through Kaidan's body. Kaidan was becoming reliant on the starcat, his presence a buffer against the impersonal coolness of the Garsal females, and the fear evoked by the males.

Dipper's head jerked up, and Kaidan leaped to his feet, just as a rattle sounded at the door. Instead of the evening meal he'd expected, Hirtoi was at the door. Panicked, he looked behind him – Dipper had vanished. His stomach rumbled, and he had a guilty thought about the possibility of eating another meal in the presence of Laretai. Then he wouldn't have to share. He dismissed the thought. If he could, he'd pocket anything solid for Dipper.

"Follow." The female Garsal's voice was as curt as ever, and Kaidan moved quickly to drop in behind her, eyes on the floor. He was surprised as she took a different route than the one to Laretai's quarters. He'd become accustomed to it, and the sudden turn to the left took him by surprise, jerking his mind from Laretai's revelations. Several minutes later, he was standing in the Matriarch's presence. Hurriedly, he fastened his eyes to the floor. He knew that Dipper was close by, but he hoped the cat was keeping himself well hidden. He didn't dare scan around the room for fear of giving the cat away.

The Matriarch sat in a throne-like chair. By her side, Estei stood, but her presence seemed to have taken on an air of regality that Kaidan had never previously noticed. Laretai sat at the Matriarch's right hand, and Hirtoi took her place nearby, standing as Estei was. Each wore the colourful, filmy robes affected by the female Garsal. The Matriarch nodded to Laretai, and she leaned forwards and tapped one of her ever-present tablets. Despite his determination not to, Kaidan looked up to see what she was doing. On the wall in front of him, was once again the figure of his sister, this time enlarged to fill the whole wall. The impact was staggering, and while he was still recovering from the shock of seeing Shanna depicted wall sized, the Matriarch's voice sounded.

"Bring her in." Estei hurried from the room, while Kaidan's eyes stayed fixed on the image of his sister and her cats. His mind did backflips – they were bringing in Shanna?

"Kaidan." Kaidan's eyes snapped from the image as his name sounded and he hurriedly fixed them to the floor. "Look at me." Surprised, he lifted his eyes to the Matriarch. Her alien eyes were inscrutable, although her posture was different. He was musing on that when she spoke again. "We have a proposal for you, but first," she gestured and Estei walked back into the room, prodding Edon before her. Kaidan almost collapsed with relief that his sister was still safe. But why was Edon here? The woman fell flat on her face. "As a gesture of good faith, we will give you this slave."

Kaidan's eyes nearly fell out of his head, and he stammered. "Y…you'll *what?*" The last word came out as a squeak. His mind whirled with all of the permutations of Laretai's information, and the fact that the Matriarch, and also the two younger Garsal females knew of it, left him speechless.

"She is an informer." The Matriarch's voice was flat. "She deserves no mercy."

Edon looked up at the words, "I didn't mean to. You don't know what they're like!" Her voice shook and trembled, and he had the impression of tears in her eyes. Reflexively, he drew back, horrified, not knowing what to do, or who to believe. He'd guessed she was an informer, and Lacey had confirmed it, so he'd fed her small pieces of information as Lacey had suggested, assuming that anything he'd said would end up at the Overlord's ears. He looked aghast at the four female Garsal in front of him, confused and fearful.

Had the Matriarch really meant what he'd thought she'd meant? He was so confused, so exhausted with the ordeal of trying to keep everything straight in his head, and the revelations from Laretai had astounded him so much that he began to tremble. It was hard to make sense of anything. Then there was a brush of warm fur on his thigh, and his emotions steadied. Everything was upside down, but Dipper's touch helped him make one sure decision. The others could wait.

"Why did you do it, Edon?" he asked.

"Because there was nothing else I could do. You don't know the Garsal like I do." Her dark eyes pleaded with him.

"You think I don't know them, Edon? After seeing me dragged back into that cell day after day, beaten and bloodied?" There was silence from the woman. "You don't think I know them, after being interrogated daily by the Overlord himself? After seeing and hearing the rest of the slaves? After being 'trained,'" his voice was scornful, "to serve them?" He shook his head in disgust, and the other woman broke into helpless sobs. "I *do* know them. I know them as I'm sure you've known them — masters of despair and destruction."

Kaidan lifted his head defiantly and locked his eyes on the Matriarch. "Destroyers of worlds. *That* is what *I* know of them." He looked back down at Edon. "And I know one other thing. I know me. And despite what they've offered me. I will not mistreat you further, no matter what these *Garsal*," he spat the word, "offer me." He lifted his head again and stared directly at the four Garsal in front of him, eyeing them one by one, and then leaving his head lifted.

Dipper was at his side. He knew he could fade in a few moments if he needed to, and have at least a tiny chance of making it out of the ship alive, but they were all still. The Matriarch lifted a manipulator arm in a tiny gesture, and Estei rang a small bell. Four slaves hurried into the room and removed Edon bodily as she continued to sob.

A few seconds later, another slave entered. Clean, and dressed in the livery of the female Garsal, Kaidan almost didn't recognise her. And then she spoke. "Thank you Kaidan. You have passed the final test." She nodded familiarly at Laretai. "He will do. He is the one to take the message. He is a product of his people, and his actions have told us what we need to know. It was a risk bringing me here, but it's a risk that has paid off. He is the one. The plan can proceed."

"Lacey?" Kaidan couldn't keep the incredulous tone out of his voice. "You mean it's true? What Laretai told me this morning?" The old woman moved forwards and took one of Kaidan's hands in her rough one.

"It's true. And we need you to take the message to your people."

Kaidan looked around the room, feeling panicked. "But how? How can I take the message? How can I escape? How can I survive Below?"

Laretai tapped her tablet again, and the image changed. Kaidan gasped. It was his room, and the image showed both him, and Dipper. "We believe that this creature might be of assistance?"

Kaidan felt Dipper's body quiver, and he realised that the cat next to his leg was on a knife edge, poised to attack if he felt threatened, or perhaps if Kaidan was threatened. He carefully placed a hand on the starcat's head, making the movement very obvious.

Lacey froze. "It's here? In this room?" She looked at Kaidan's hand, apparently poised in mid air. "In front of me?" Her normally confident voice was unsettled.

"Dipper is here, by my side." Kaidan let the import of that statement sink in. "He is not *my* starcat. He will listen to me, after a fashion, but his partner was killed by Garsal, and he may not always obey my commands. Unless he chooses a new partner, he is a law unto himself. I would suggest that you all remain exactly where you are, as he is uncertain of your motives towards me."

There was a small reflexive drawing back, stilled very quickly by all of the Garsal. Lacey remained exactly where she was. "Are we secure, Laretai?" she asked.

"We are."

"Are you able to command him to visibility?" Lacey's voice was calmer now.

"I can try." Kaidan left one hand on Dipper's head and then flicked his hand in the signal that his parents used to lift a fade, hoping that Challon had used the same one. There was a flicker of blue, and slowly, protestingly, Dipper's form wavered into view. This time, the four Garsal were unable to prevent themselves leaning backwards, away from the starcat. Kaidan had the impression of indrawn breath. Lacey held herself to absolute stillness.

"Dipper," Kaidan said, "Rest." The cat turned his head and looked at Kaidan, and then slowly sat down, and then finally lowered himself to the floor. Lacey looked at Kaidan.

"Is it safe for me to move?"

Feeling weirdly as if the tables had suddenly turned, and with a renewed sense of regaining his own direction, Kaidan nodded. It seemed that for the first time since his incarceration on the Garsal ship, he might have the upper hand. "I need to know everything. I need to know the truth of what you've told me. All of you." He included Lacey in that statement. "And then I need to know what you want. Only then will I decide if we will take your message."

***

Finally, after a much more cautious ascent, Shanna and Ragar reached the ground level portion of the ship. The corridor was much quieter now. Her mind was full of the things they'd seen, and she wondered what the others might have to add to their intelligence. Storm brushed her hand with his head as he moved past her when he and Twister switched paces, and then, all of a sudden, he halted, and she stepped on his paw. Storm growled as Shanna staggered, almost falling, saved only by Ragar's hand on her shoulder. Fortunately there were no Garsal in the hallway at that point. "What's up?" Ragar hissed.

"No idea," she whispered back. "Storm just stopped, and I trod on him."

There was a moment of confusion, and then Storm moved onwards, and as he did, a wash of blue ran over Shanna's mind. It had a kind of controlled excitement contained in it that Shanna was at a loss to interpret. She tapped Ragar's hand on her shoulder as they moved, indicating that they would need to talk at some point.

Finally, they were back at the vestibule, standing outside the closed door. Carefully looking around, Shanna placed her hand on the pad. It opened immediately – apparently it wasn't locked from this side, and she sent Storm through first. A blue ear tip flickered and she and Ragar ducked through the doorway. The door closed behind them. Shanna placed a hand on Storm's harness and let him lead her to one side. There was a quick flicker of starcat tidemarks, and then the others appeared, and Shanna gratefully let the fade drop.

"Ragar," Allad said. "I think there's another starcat on the ship."

# Chapter 25

"HOW do you know there's another cat?" asked Ragar.

"Satin," said Allad quietly. "We worked our way upwards using the ramps, and about halfway up, she refused to go any further, and once she'd stopped, they all stopped."

"But that could have been anything," replied Shanna.

"Pull your glowstone out, Shan," said Allad. He extended his palm as Shanna fumbled with the chain around her neck. As the stone came out from under her shirt, she could clearly see black hairs on Allad's palm, flecked in places with the characteristic colours of a blue tidemarked starcat.

"Perhaps we left those last time?" suggested Ragar.

"We weren't anywhere near there last time," said Allad.

"Then … Dipper?" asked Shanna quietly. It was the only thing that made sense. "And why is he on the ship?"

"That's what we thought," replied Allad. "As to why, well who knows, when it's a bereaved starcat …." Tears pricked Shanna's eyes as she thought of the desolation she'd seen in the eyes of a cat whose partner had died. "Perhaps he's seeking revenge."

"We can't stay here," said Ragar. "Shanna and I found the vehicle storage area. It was deserted an hour ago, so we'll relocate there. It'll give us a breathing space to talk and plan more securely. We have a lot of information."

"As do we," said Amma quietly.

"And us as well," replied Taya.

"We need to move then," Ragar said, "or they'll send another repair crew for the monitor. Ready?" There were nods, and the group faded. Shanna was relieved to only have to fade herself again.

"The monitor is up in three, two, one." Taya's voice was quiet, and then the door slid open, and Shanna sent Twister through it and followed immediately after them.

Feeling Verren's hand on her shoulder, she tapped the all clear, felt warmed briefly by his proximity, banished the thought firmly, and led the group as quickly as she dared towards the ramp system.

After a nerve wracking descent, they congregated inside the vast hold. Once again it appeared deserted, but as a precaution, Ragar had half the cats search through the echoing space, then sent Allad in one direction and Shanna in the other to find a small, safe space where they could talk undisturbed. It took quite a while, but finally Allad located what was most likely a disused storage area.

The empty room was dark, with only a few scattered crates in one grubby corner. The rest of the ship had been pristinely spotless, and Shanna found it strangely reassuring to discover that even the invaders had messy storerooms. The door had been open when Allad had come upon it, but after a quick glance at Taya, Ragar had pressed the appropriate button and closed them in. A few moments of silence later, and Taya spoke. "There's nothing in here monitoring us but some kind of passive detector, over there – on the roof. I think it might be to detect fire?" She sounded fairly confident, and Shanna marvelled once again at the girl's talent, she simply didn't have anything like Taya's instincts for anything mechanical or electrical.

"Glowstones please." Shanna pulled hers out once again, and looked around at her friends. All of them looked tired, and there were tense expressions on all of the faces. Eight starcats ringed them, although Shanna noticed that Satin had carefully placed herself next to the door, and was very obviously keeping watch. She flicked a finger and sent Storm to join Allad's cat. It felt bizarre to be hiding in a room of an alien ship, and not under a canopy of green leaves. She wondered how the others were getting on, and even more, what was happening on the plateau.

"We'll each summarise the important points, and then we'll plan. If we can, I'd like us to all to have an hour or two's rest before we have to move again," Ragar said, and Shanna turned her attention back to the present.

"We stayed on the entry level," said Taya, "From what we could tell, there are four troop barracks fairly close to the entrance. It probably explains why it was so difficult for us to exit last time. There are about twenty troopers in each barracks. There was a switch over of sentries not long before we returned to the meeting point. The rest of the level appears administrative." Ragar nodded thoughtfully and then looked at Allad, Amma and Zandany.

"Allad?"

"Apart from the issue of the starcat – and I agree it's likely to be Dipper – on that same level was an access point with a sentry. There was a whole section of the ship behind that access point that was inaccessible from anywhere else."

"What do you think was behind it? And did you check any other levels?"

"Yes we did," replied Zandany. "There were at least four full levels above and below that point, and we were unable to find any access except for that door." Shanna frowned slightly.

"That's odd."

"That's what we thought," said Allad. "Any ideas?"

Ragar shook his head, and Verren looked thoughtful.

"More weapons?" he asked.

"Why would they guard that point and not this one then?" asked Amma. "That's what we thought originally, but it doesn't seem logical. Not unless they're guarding it from themselves."

"There was a strange arrangement on the outside too," said Zandany. "Like a hatch or something. No idea what that was about."

"It's a puzzle," said Ragar. "And the question is, should we investigate further while we're inside? Is it a priority?"

"What did you and Shanna find?" Allad asked. Ragar looked grave, and then he and Shanna took turns relating their experience in the slave hold.

"What's your best estimate of numbers?" asked Allad finally.

"Too many," said Ragar. "What do you reckon Shanna?"

"There were more than a hundred, probably more than two hundred actually," said Shanna. "And they were only the ones we could see. I really don't know how many more there were." She sighed and answered the unspoken question. "We didn't see Kaidan." There was silence after she'd spoken for a moment or two and then she screwed up her courage and spoke again, trying to keep her voice steady. It came out slightly higher pitched than she'd wished. "It doesn't mean he's dead. Perhaps he's somewhere else." She cleared her throat as quietly as she could and looked down. Twister nudged her gently with his head. "And I forgot – Storm stopped suddenly, not far from the entrance. Maybe he smelled Dipper!"

There was a flurry of quiet discussion, and Shanna was glad to fade into the background for a moment. The loss of her brother was a constant ache, and as she confronted the possibility of his death, she struggled to control her emotions once again. Spiron's words echoed in her mind though, and with an effort, she deliberately shut the emotion down, swallowed, and began to participate in the discussion. The warmth of Twister's weight on her leg helped to steady her, and she could feel Storm's calming blue flicker inside her mind. Then Verren touched her hand and she was nearly undone again. Although it was only the briefest of touches, she knew he was telling her how much he understood.

"Shanna, how tired are you?" The question took her by surprise, and she had to think quickly for a moment.

"Not bad, Ragar, nothing more than normal fatigue really. I haven't had to fade anyone else much, so I'm good."

"How many do you think you can fade? And for how long?" Shanna felt slightly panicked. Surely Ragar didn't mean to try and get *all* the slaves out?

"I don't really know. It would probably depend on how long." He nodded. "We need to take as many of the slaves Semba identified as possible – their information is vital – but I'd like to rescue more if we're able."

"This area holds a lot of possibilities," said Taya. "I could damage most of the machinery here."

"But what about the sealed part of the ship?" asked Zandany. "I think we need to find out what's in there."

Ragar frowned again. "There's a lot to consider, but we all need to rest before we do anything else. And I think we need to wait another couple of hours before we do whatever it is that we're going to do." He quirked an eyebrow wryly at the group. "It seemed very simple before we entered – penetrate the ship, rescue some slaves, leave. Now it's not. We need time to think and consider. Shanna, I want you and the boys to do another circuit of this area, and then I want you to get some rest. Taya, rest now. I suspect you'll be very busy once we get moving. Zan, you're on first watch. Verren, second. Allad, you, Amma and I need to talk!"

Shanna nodded, called her cats, put her glowstone back inside the neck of her shirt, and then carefully pressed the button to open the door and sent Twister through the widening gap. She followed a moment later with Storm. It was dark after the illumination provided by the glowstones. She took a few moments to allow her eyes to adjust. The darkness and quiet were welcome after the emotion charged discussion, but it took a lot of willpower for Shanna to stop her thoughts drifting back towards Kaidan.

As she slunk around the perimeter of the vast room, she marvelled at the sheer numbers of vehicles sitting in their silent rows. There was room for many more, and she assumed the vacant slots had been left by the climbers, now on their way to the plateau. At the speed they were moving, they must be nearly there by now. She shuddered slightly, horrified by the thought of her parents under attack by the alien invaders. Once again, she was distracted, and once again she had to redirect her attention. Fortunately her starcats hadn't been diverted. Twister paced ahead. She could feel him easily now, just as she could feel Storm gliding silently behind her. Their presence in her mind was now a constant, a presence that seemed to becoming steadily stronger, which was why she realised that there was a door opening at the same time her cats did.

She faded automatically, looking behind her to make sure that there was no sign of light from the abandoned storeroom, and then slunk closer. Two Garsal walked into the room, talking in their harsh sounding language. Both carried tablets, and as they entered, one turned, and then all the lights in the room turned on. Despite their reddish cast, Shanna was nearly blinded, and she screwed her eyes up against the sudden light. Blinking, she managed to squint against the sudden glare to see the two Garsal begin a slow inspection of one of the vehicles. She signalled her cats with her whistle, and they continued their patrol around the room.

She decided to get closer and see what they were doing. Calling Storm in, she concealed herself behind another vehicle, dropped her fade, attached a note to the cat's harness and sent him back to the others. Then she faded again and sent Twister ahead while she moved closer and closer to the two Garsal. They were working their way slowly around the crawler, and as Shanna moved closer, she could see that part of the vehicle was disassembled, and one of them was searching through the exposed parts. There was an exclamation, and then it held up something small, but shiny, and both creatures stood up again. There was a discussion over whatever it was, then the smaller one pulled a metal object from a toolkit, fiddled with the machinery, placed the outer covering back on and climbed into the cab.

There was a roar from the machine and it shuddered into life, and then Shanna realised that the other Garsal had moved over to the far wall. It tapped a large box set to one side of that wall, causing part of the wall to move outwards before sliding to one side, revealing an upward sloping tunnel. With a feeling of exasperation for her own slowness, Shanna realised that *of course* this section of the ship was below ground. They'd entered at ground level, and had gone down multiple levels, so the doors, which were apparently part of the outer hull, opened on a well constructed tunnel that led to the surface. She wondered what was at the other end.

Resisting the temptation to follow the tunnel, she scooted closer to the Garsal at the wall, wondering what it had done to operate the doors. She felt Storm draw closer, and dropped her vision into his eyes, sending him across to the tunnel entrance. She assumed that the vehicle was about to move out on a test run. Perhaps she could send Storm up and back in the time it would take the vehicle to go out to the surface. She added Twister's eyes to her mind, and tucked herself carefully into a niche close to the Garsal at the control box, and watched. The vehicle, one of the huge crawlers, was beginning to lumber forwards from its spot in the line. She decided to take the risk and sent Storm at a blurring run up the tunnel.

For a moment she was disoriented, and then her vision steadied. Smooth walls passed by at starcat speed, and then Storm was at the egress. Another huge door had been set into the end of the tunnel, and was now open. Shanna could see the light from three moons throwing confusing shadows across the clearing. Storm went through the doorway so fast she was almost breathless, passive observer though she was. He circled the clearing, pausing just long enough for Shanna to realise that the tunnel exited just near the hive entrance. The doors had been cleverly camouflaged inside the mound that sheltered the hive. It was only luck that had revealed them at all.

She recalled Storm as the crawler exited the hold through the tunnel, fearful that he'd be stranded outside, and the cat, feeling her urgency, blurred faster and faster. He was only just in time. Through Twister's eyes, Shanna saw the Garsal's top set of limbs dance across the panel in front of it, and the door in the ship's hull began to close. She could see through Storm's eyes the lighted gap beginning to narrow, and her heart thudded with the pace of his run before he threw himself through the narrowing space, just before the doors shut.

Shanna felt as if she'd run every step with her starcat, and as he arrived by her side again, she was unable to stop herself from hugging his warm body to her own. Vaguely, through Twister's eyes, she saw the Garsal technician slide the panel closed and move towards the entry point. As it left, the lights went out, and Shanna and her cats were alone in the dark again. She made for the storeroom immediately.

Once inside, she reported almost breathlessly. "We've got a second exit option!"

Ragar smiled. "Good news, Shan. Did you attempt to see if you could operate the controls?" Shanna's face fell, in her hurry to get back and report, she hadn't even considered trying.

"No, I didn't. I should have, though."

"Or maybe not," replied Taya. "You might have set an alarm off if you had. I'll go out with Shanna now and have a look. We won't open the door, but we'll have a look and establish if we can use the controls, or whether one of us will have to break into the machinery to use it." Once again, Shanna was struck by the calm confidence that Taya displayed in her skills. It was a far cry from the animosity that had so coloured most of their time together in their first year as cadets.

"Allad, go with them and keep them safe. I'm assuming you'll link?"

"I think so," said Taya. "Shanna's strong, but I'm the one with the finesse." She smiled apologetically at Shanna, "So I'll have a look, and show Shan what to do if she needs to do it by herself."

Ten minutes later, Shanna, once again immersed in the flickering flow of images inside Taya's mind, marvelled at the skill with which the other girl seemed to instinctively understand how something was put together. "Here, this is the spot, Shan. If you push *here*, while holding *there*, I think both doors will open. *But,* you'll need to shove *this* first. If you don't a whole lot of alarms will go off." Shanna nodded, glad of Taya's expertise. She was sure she could have opened the door by breaking the mechanisms, but actually using them was much less likely to draw attention to them if they needed to exit that way. Through the link with Taya, she could feel Spinner's pride in his partner, and the subtle boost that the starcat provided. It was fascinating, and she would have liked to explore it more thoroughly, but they were inside an enemy starship, and all she had time to do was accept the fact that it happened, and appreciate it.

More and more she was amazed at the way their starcats enhanced their partners' skills. "We're done, Allad," said Taya, and the three of them made their way back to the storeroom.

Shanna tucked herself up in a corner of it with Storm and Twister. The floor was hard, but her cats were warm, and she could feel their love like a small piece of sunlight tucked away in her mind. Taya lay beside her, idly playing with Spinner's ears, and Amma and Verren were on Taya's other side, both rubbing their cats' heads. Shanna leaned her head on Storm's flank, and Twister laid his head on her middle. He was quite heavy, but he was warm and full of familiar comfort. She closed her eyes in the darkness and tried to compose herself to sleep. She was certain that the next few days would push her right to her limits of endurance. Even if she couldn't sleep, she needed to rest her body, so she concentrated on relaxing each bit of herself, and slowing her breathing. There was an amused hum from Storm and another from Twister, and their tidemarks flickered so quickly Shanna couldn't interpret their patterns, and then she was asleep.

"Shan!" The whisper was urgent in her ear. "Shan! Get up!"

"What?"

"You've been asleep for two hours!" It was Amma's voice in her ear, and Shanna yawned and sat up, surprised she'd been able to sleep. She felt very rested.

"Oh good."

"Lucky you!" whispered Amma back, as she pulled out her glowstone.

"That's very bright." She squinted against the brilliance.

"Come on. We're eating, and then we'll be on our way."

Shanna pushed Twister's head off her middle, and stretched as she sat up. Storm blinked his eyes at her, and yawned himself, showing a large amount of pink tongue and a lot of sharp teeth. Shanna's stomach rumbled. She patted her pockets, and removed a slab of jerked meat, breaking off a couple of bits to share with her cats. It was slightly squashed in its leaf casing, but still edible. Twister ate his bit, looked sadly at Shanna and flickered his tidemarks ever so slowly, that she gave in and broke off a larger bit for them both. "Sooks." She smiled at both of them fondly and ran a hand over each head before joining the others.

As she stood with them, she sipped from one of her water bottles, carefully hefting the others to see how much water she had. There was plenty, so she made sure she drank well as she listened to Ragar, and then let her cats lap from her hand, one at a time.

"We need to do three things, I think," he said. "It's not quite what we'd planned, but we're inside now, and we have a good chance to pull all three of them off. Firstly, we'll divide into two groups. Allad, Shanna, Verren and Amma will explore the hidden area of the ship. We need to know what's in there. You'll do everything in your power to gain access, explore it, and then return here. Taya, Zandany and I will be sabotaging as many vehicles as possible while you do that. We're less able to fade by ourselves, and our gifts lie more in that direction. In addition, I want Shanna as well rested as possible, so that when we leave the ship, she'll be able to hide as many people as possible." He looked at them all very seriously. "Finally, we'll return to the slave hold together, and break out as many of the slaves Semba had named as possible, but I also want to offer the chance to leave to as many as Shanna thinks she can hide." He set his mouth in a firm line. "This might be the only chance we have to rescue them." Shanna saw Allad grimace slightly, but her mind replayed the sounds of despair, and she nodded slowly. "We'll exit through the tunnel here. It's larger, less defended, and gives us the best chance of taking them by surprise. Questions?" There were none. "In that case, if it all goes wrong, you have two tasks. Cause as much damage as possible, and then get yourselves out of the ship and to the first shelter. Shanna and Allad have alternate coordinates if necessary."

It was a sobering thought. This was a supremely important mission, but its chances of success relied on them using their talents as they'd never used them before. A small chill of fear worked its way up Shanna's spine. There was a wash of comfort from her cats, and she looked down, surprised. Both were looking at her with love and confidence in every line of their sleek bodies. The thought of losing either of them, in the chaos that was sure to follow, was horrifying. Her hands drew the huge heads to her hips, treasuring the softness of their fur, and then she steeled herself for what was ahead and nodded at Ragar.

# Chapter 26

ANJO helped heave the final barricade into place and then slowly straightened up. Night had fallen, and his back felt as if he'd spent years in a bent position. The pace of the preparations had been relentless.

"That's the last one," said Adlan with a sigh. In the faint light shed by the three full moons, Anjo could see the man looking out over his home lands. He'd probably never thought that they might become a battleground. It was very peaceful so late at night. Faintly, Anjo could hear the sounds of others finishing their tasks, and he could smell the delicate spicy scent of massed starcats when he concentrated. The smell which now meant 'home' to him.

"Do you think they'll find us, Adlan?" asked Anjo.

"Maybe not straight away," replied the man, "but if the worst comes to the worst, we'll be finding them." He sighed. "And we'll know if it comes to that, thanks to the Starlyne network." There was silence between the two of them for a moment, not uncomfortable, just faintly sad. A delicate looking female Starlyne had arrived during their flurry of preparations. She wasn't small, but her way of moving put Anjo in mind of a dancer. She had given her name as Dreamer, a name that seemed to fit her air of other worldliness. On her arrival, she'd calmly informed them that she was their communication link, and final defence, then asked what she could do, and where they would like her to set up her equipment. Apparently she'd brought a small infirmary with her.

"Why do you think they do it?" asked Anjo.

Adlan shook his head slowly, and reached out a hand to rub Boots' ears. "The Starlynes? I don't know. And I don't know if I could myself, even knowing that my sacrifice would save them, for complete strangers. They are a people different to us in many ways, different, but in the end, still the same, still human, or perhaps even more human than we ourselves are."

For a moment the statement baffled Anjo, but then he nodded thoughtfully. Somewhere, in an old text, he'd read words that had followed mankind across the galaxy. 'Greater love has no man, than he lay down his life for a friend.' They seemed to fit what Adlan had said.

"Time to get back to the house, hopefully there's food waiting."

It was a practical statement, and Anjo's stomach rumbled as they walked back up the hill together. Anjo could see Boots' and Ember's tidemarks glowing steadily against the darkness, and as they walked he admired how their marks stood out against the gloom. He marvelled at the way his life had changed in such a short time. Alone and hopeless he'd arrived on this world. Alone and hopeless he'd been sent out with an exploratory team, and then it had all changed. Hopelessness had been replaced by hope, solitary fear had been replaced with friends, a new family, and most of all, the love and companionship of a starcat. Once again his thoughts turned to his lost friends and family. They were gone, but now he had new reasons to fight, and new reasons to love.

Whatever the next few days might hold, Anjo had more hope now than he'd had a year ago. No matter how dark and dire those days might become, once again he was with people he loved. He would do everything he could to see Kaidan's family remain safe. Ember's tidemarks flickered in the darkness, and once again, Anjo knew that the starcat was in complete agreement.

***

"Commander."

"Yes," replied Hoth as the climber lurched slowly to a halt.

"We are within striking distance of the plateau."

Hoth climbed out of his sleeping cocoon, flicking the last stiffness from his limbs.

"Good. Show me where we are." The operator highlighted a spot on the map spread across the screen. "Losses?" Hoth demanded.

"We lost eight to the beasts, Commander, and another three are too damaged to make the climb."

"Transfer their personnel to other vehicles, and signal the group forwards. We will take *this* route to the top of the plateau." He highlighted the waypoints with a tap. "We will advance towards the main town at dawn."

"Yes Commander."

"Call me when we crest the top."

"Yes, Commander."

Hoth tucked himself back in the cocoon, carefully setting the controls to adjust for the changes in attitude required once the climber began its ascent. A veteran of many battles, he was able to sleep almost immediately, secure in the knowledge that his skills wouldn't be needed until the morning.

***

Kaidan sat back in the chair next to Lacey, his mind buzzing from the information so recently shared. At the Matriarch's request, Hirtoi had hurried from the room and returned with food for all of them, including Dipper. The cat was now couched by his chair, lazily washing himself. His tidemarks glowed brightly with the comfort of a full belly, and he'd relaxed from full alert, to a watching wariness. The old woman next to him, watched as he ate the final piece of food on his plate. He had no idea what it was, and didn't really want to know, but it was tastier and more filling than anything he'd eaten for weeks. He sighed with contentment and rubbed Dipper's head absently as he pushed the plate away.

Beside him, Lacey watched the starcat warily. "Are you sure it's safe?" she asked once again. For the woman she was, she was strangely hesitant to trust his word about the starcat.

"Of course he is," replied Kaidan, and then qualified the statement. "At the moment. If anyone tries to attack me it might be different." He was fairly certain Dipper would do his best to protect him. He certainly hoped he would. As despite the basic self defence training he'd had, he wasn't sure he'd be able to protect himself should the female Garsal decide to attack him, and he'd never used his skills anywhere except the practice mat.

Lacey shook her head, took another slightly apprehensive look at the cat, who chose that moment to extend the claws of one of his back paws so that he could clean them. Kaidan tried to put himself in her place. She'd never seen a cat that large before, and when he imagined not having grown up with them, perhaps he could understand a little of what she was feeling. Dipper's claws were very long, and came to needle points. He also had a full head of sharp teeth, and had been wandering around the ship, invisible to any eyes for some days. He could have attacked without warning at any time, in fact *had* been attacking without warning for some time while he'd been outside the ship. "He's quite relaxed right now," he said, stretching the truth slightly, but he was worried that if he didn't manage to calm them all down, he'd never get the answers he so desperately wanted. "You promised me answers after we'd eaten, so I think I'd like them now."

***

Once again, Shanna and her cats were sneaking through the Garsal ship. This time, she was following Allad. Faded, they were moving as silently as possible up the ramps, away from the vehicle storage room. Behind them the lights were still dimmed, and the vehicle that had left had still not returned. Ragar had hoped that meant they'd have uninterrupted time to damage as many vehicles as possible before the ship started to wake up again. No matter how much she hoped, Shanna knew that it was unlikely that their planned activities would be complete before dawn. It had to be well past midnight already.

Ramp after ramp they moved upwards, until finally Allad signalled they were on the right level. Shanna wondered what they were going to find. With only one point of entry, it must be something that the Garsal treasured. Allad paused, and she felt him tap her hand. She tapped back, and passed the message on. The door slid open, and she sent Storm through it at a run, following with Twister, immediately moving to the left of the doorway. As Allad had said, they were in a large room. One with only the familiar doors of the moving room to her right, and the guarded access point directly ahead, but at least twenty-five metres away. It was puzzling. Why have such a large room?

The Garsal sentry was still there, and Shanna could see it leaning forwards, peering at the open doorway. To its eyes, there would be nothing visible, just a door that had opened all by itself, and then shut again. She concentrated hard, and was able to 'feel' where her companions were. Allad to the right of the doorway, Verren next to her, and Amma further over to Allad's right, almost at the mobile room.

The sentry had resumed its original posture, apparently unworried at the mysterious self-opening door. Shanna moved forwards as planned, slowly stalking the unsuspecting sentry. Amma stayed by the mobile room's doors, guarding them, and Verren and Cirrus watched the door they'd entered by. She could feel Allad by her side as planned, and Shanna placed one hand on Twister and concentrated, trying to seek out the mechanical monitors. Taya had said they'd be quite easy to sense. *Ah, there was one, and two more. She looked around the room and located them, concentrated again, and there was another.*

Carefully, now beginning to sweat with the effort, she began to alter them one by one as Taya had described. She was sure the other girl could have done it in the blink of an eye, but she found it much more difficult. Breaking something was easy, disrupting the flow of information and making it show what you wanted was much more difficult. The images of the machines' internal construction flickered through her mind slowly, and it took her quite some time to make sure that she had the right bit to adjust. She pressed and prodded as Taya had described, and when she'd finally done the job, she was shaking with fatigue.

She pulled a fast acting patch from her pocket and fumbled it onto her wrist, feeling the jolt of energy with relief. She moved slightly sideways to where she could feel Allad, and tapped his shoulder. He gripped her hand and tapped three times in reply, and she counted off the seconds. Three, two, one, and then the sentry was flung to the ground, struggled briefly, and then moved no more. Allad blinked into sight as Shanna relaxed her fade. Storm and Satin appeared, standing over the sentry, satisfaction flickering from their tidemarks.

Shanna and Allad hurried forwards, and hastily dragged the corpse over to the door. The body was heavier than Shanna had expected, and she tried not to think about having killed yet another living thing, and this time an unsuspecting one. As Verren opened the door, they faded. Shanna extended her bubble over the body and then they carried it quickly down two levels and shoved it into a small covered recessed area they'd found on the way up. Shanna closed the hatch on the body and then both of them jogged quickly back to Amma and Verren. Both were still visible to the eye, so Shanna relaxed her fade and began to examine the mechanism near the door.

"Hurry Shan," whispered Allad, "We have no way of knowing how soon the sentry was to be relieved." She nodded, slightly irritated, as she placed a hand on each of her cats and attempted to visualise the mechanism as Taya had. It was similar to the one near the vehicle tunnel, but seemed to have several more layers of what Shanna assumed was either locks or security.

"It's very complex, Allad. I may have to break it, and I'm worried it'll set off an alarm."

"Just do it. We'll deal with an alarm if it goes off." She grimaced, and then *shoved* as hard as she could where she thought she needed to. Again she was sweating, and her heart rate accelerated. There were no loud claxons, no flashing lights, but there was a loud click, and a tray extruded itself from the wall to her left. She nearly fainted with shock, but dismissed it as an oddity, signalled to the others, faded herself, positioned her cats and then used one hand to slide the door to one side.

Once again, the lighting was dim, and as Shanna scooted through the door, she felt her cats become suddenly alert. Complicated sensations outlined in blue and violet washed through her mind, and she had the oddest feeling that they were satisfied. *But with what?* she wondered.

***

"This way Kaidan," said Laretai. Kaidan followed as fast as he was able, Dipper by his side. The cat had stayed with him throughout the entire evening, and as far as Kaidan could tell, was content to ignore the female Garsal as long as Kaidan had remained calm. His head was still buzzing with too many thoughts, but he knew one thing. Somehow, he needed to get a message to the Scout Corps, and Dipper was his key to doing it.

"Put these on," Laretai said, pausing next to a small room and indicating a small pile of clothes.

With an exclamation, Kaidan picked up his old clothes. They'd been mended and cleaned, and felt of home. The mottled shirt and pants were designed to blend into Frontier's vegetation and would make quite a difference to his escape attempt. His boots were there too, cleaned and with fresh laces, but still scuffed on the toes where he'd kicked rocks on his travels with Anjo. With no concern for modesty, he shed his slave clothing and donned his old clothes. He shrugged comfortably into the shirt and began to do the buttons up. He looked up to find Laretai watching him intently. He blushed.

"Once you're dressed, I will take you to an exit several levels down. It's an escape hatch, for use in space should the ship be breached. It will take me several minutes to override the controls, so once you're in the airlock you will need to be patient."

"How will I get past the perimeter?" asked Kaidan.

"I will drop part of the fence line – it will look like a malfunction. After that it will be up to you. There are sentinels set around the perimeter, but we are certain that there are others like you within that second perimeter. At least three fell from the sky several days ago, and I believe more may have breached the sentinels during the storm. The Overlord believes they malfunctioned. I do not." Kaidan gulped. The idea of being alone, Below, both terrified and exhilarated him. All too clearly he remembered the pains his sister had taken to keep his small group of archers safe, all those months ago. Thinking about the archers made him wish even more for his bow. He hoped desperately that Dipper would choose to stay with him once they left the ship.

"And if I don't find them?"

"Two days from now I will be here again, awaiting you. We can at least keep you safe until another opportunity presents itself." Kaidan nodded. *Fell out of the sky? How could that be?* Mentally he shook his head, and then finished doing up his boot laces.

***

Shanna moved silently through the large room on the other side of the door. Unlike most of the rest of the ship, this area was decorated. Carvings and stone sculptures had been carefully placed to draw the eye in and soften the otherwise regimented lines of the spaceship walls. Complex tapestries adorned the walls here and there, and there was a harmony of colour and beauty that Shanna hadn't imagined could be part of the Garsal heritage. Once again there was no-one around. She located the others, 'feeling' their locations and chanced a whisper. "What do you think this is all about?"

"I have no idea," replied Allad quietly. "We'll explore as fast as possible, and then return to the others." Satin's voice hummed urgently at him, and he went on, surprised. "I think she believes that the other cat has been in here." Shanna sent her cats ahead through the room, and followed them through yet another door. Once again, the area beyond the entry was not as she had expected. The decorations continued, tasteful artworks, sculptures and colours, so different to the rest of the ship. The illumination was dim, but along the length of the corridor, lighted entries suggested that in this section of the ship at least, not all were asleep or off duty.

There was an urgency to Storm and Twister that Shanna hadn't felt before, and she could feel Satin almost straining to run ahead. "The cats ..." whispered Shanna to Allad.

"We follow." His voice was soft but certain, and Shanna let her cats draw her forwards. Silently, they ghosted past the first of the light streaming doorways, and Shanna stopped dead on the other side and then nearly fell over as

Allad cannoned into her from behind. She steadied herself with a hand to his arm.

"Allad – females?" She'd caught glimpses of slightly smaller Garsal forms, clothed in filmy, colourful robes, working away in some kind of technical centre.

"I would guess so. But why so hidden? Why locked away?" She felt his body quiver through her hand on his arm, and guessed he was shaking his head. "No matter. We explore as far as we can, confirm what we think, and then get back to the others as fast as possible. Lead on."

Twister nudged Shanna urgently, and she moved off, following him as fast as she was able, trusting that Allad would let the others know what was happening. She could feel her cats accelerating with every step, and she peeped a 'slow down' with her silent whistle. Running headlong at this point might well lead to discovery. Blue and violet dragged at her senses, but she resisted the impulse to hurtle after her cats, and felt them slow slightly, protesting.

***

Kaidan finished with his boots, and then stood and turned to Laretai. "I'm ready."

"You have the information memorised?"

"I do."

"Then follow me." She turned away from him briefly, in a swish of filmy robes, and then flickered her manipulator arms across her tablet and punched the button near the doorway. It hissed open and he followed her through, flicking a hand signal to Dipper. The starcat responded immediately and they began to descend a series of ramps. Kaidan signalled frantically for the starcat to fade, and somewhat reluctantly, he did.

Very shortly, Laretai opened yet another door, took Kaidan through a long straight corridor that seemed to go on forever and then paused in front of a row of doors. She accessed her tablet again and the nearest one slid open. "Once through the door, you must wait patiently until the outer one opens. When it does, exit immediately and go directly towards the laser fence. You must not be seen. Do whatever you need to remain concealed. No matter what happens, no matter what you hear, you must wait, hidden, until the fence drops."

"I will," replied Kaidan, and then feeling awkward, said, "And thank you. I will do my best to get the message through, but Below is very dangerous, and I'm untrained."

"Find your fellows," said Laretai. "We are certain they are close by, despite the Overlord's overconfidence." There was the sound of distant footsteps. "Go now." She pushed him through the doorway and began tapping at the tablet urgently. The door slid shut behind Kaidan and Dipper and he dropped his hand to the cat's coat as he stared around the small empty chamber he found himself in. A row of some kind of protective suits hung to his right, and his ears popped suddenly. The starcat flickered into visibility again, and looked up at Kaidan.

"We're on our own now, Dipper. Please stay with me." For a moment Kaidan was almost overcome by the fear of Below alone, but then Dipper flickered his tidemarks and hummed reassuringly, and the fear receded. At least he would be free of the Overlord. He stood there in silence, hand on the starcat, and then the wall in front of him slid outwards, and the sounds and smells of Below blew in. With tears of relief pricking at the backs of his eyes, he signalled Dipper, placed a hand on the starcat's back, and willed himself to fade. They exited the room together, dropping softly the thirty centimetres from the ship to the ground. Kaidan scanned rapidly, trying to detect any dangerous vegetation, and then they moved forwards together, towards the ruby lines of the fence line.

***

Twenty minutes later, the Matriarch looked up to see Laretai stride through into her quarters. "It is done?"

"Yes, Matriarch. He's out of the ship, and so is the feline. It will take me some time to drop the fence, but hopefully he'll remain concealed for long enough." The Matriarch nodded slowly, feeling suddenly aged. The plan was finally active. The message had been sent, and the pieces were in place. She watched her Senior at work, manipulator arms tapping at the screens in front of her.

"So, now we wait," she said. "Once we are sure that he is out of the compound, we will alert the others. They must know and be ready to act. It is unfortunate that so much relies on just one human child though."

Laretai stopped tapping and looked at her. "He appears resourceful and he has the feline. Lacey is confident."

"You place that much faith in one human, Laretai?"

"I do. Lacey has ever been a keen judge of character. It has been many years since I first encountered her — it was when I was under the instruction of my predecessor. She initiated me into our company, and introduced me to our liaison with the underground — Lacey. She was my first human friend. I have often wondered what happened to her. For her to turn up now, here, at this time? There must be some meaning behind it." The Matriarch gestured her agreement.

"Everything seems to have aligned, Laretai, but the Overlord has many troopers, and even now they will be approaching and attacking the plateau settlements. That attack might undo everything." The Matriarch felt uncharacteristically uncertain. Everything was in place, but at the same time, everything hung in the balance. She ducked her head irritably. "It is done. And in this place, at this time, we have done everything within our power to ensure that the plan succeeds. And if it fails or succeeds, it might still be that no-one will ever know. The loss of the communications equipment was a double edged weapon." The Matriarch watched as Laretai resumed her deft work with the systems. Her Senior tapped away for some minutes, and then stopped once again and looked at her.

"Perhaps. But if we do succeed, we will have all the time we require to begin the greater portion of our work." She turned back to her tasks, and the Matriarch leaned back in her seat and watched – pondering.

***

Shanna passed yet another doorway, drawn forwards by Storm and Twister. Entry after entry had led into rooms full of the smaller, decoratively clothed Garsal. In some they slept, cocooned in podlike beds, while in others they worked away on unknowable tasks. Nowhere was any weaponry seen, or anything other than accommodation, or work stations in this portion of the ship. Storm and Twister's urgency continued unabated, until they stood outside the doorway of a tiny, cell-like room. They'd threaded their way through a maze of corridors until Shanna, despite her developing sense of location, was slightly lost. Rows of identical doors lined each side of the corridor, each one locked and containing only a small hatch at the bottom.

The two cats reached the doorway and then Shanna felt a crushing sense of disappointment emanate from them. Wondering, she dropped to her knees and lifted the flap to peer through the hatch into the room, hoping she wouldn't alert the inhabitant, should there be one. It was still brightly lit, despite the late hour, and all she could see was a pallet on the floor and a few fittings. Both starcats snuffled at her, and she leaned back to allow them to stick their noses through the hatch. Again, disappointment lanced through her, followed in quick succession by two large heads butting at her hands.

"They're trying to tell me something, Allad," she whispered.

She felt Allad's hand on her shoulder. "It's Kaidan," he said.

The shock turned her knees to water as her mind scrambled to put the pieces together. "Then where is he?" she asked in an agonised whisper.

"I don't know," Allad replied, "but let's find him."

And then the same alarm that they'd heard the last time they'd been inside the ship, went off with a clamour of sound, and Shanna felt her hopes die.

# Chapter 27

KAIDAN hid concealed himself carefully behind a convenient tree near the fence line. The familiar smell of pungo settled his nervousness slightly as he settled into wait. Dipper perched himself comfortably next to him, and Kaidan ran his hand down the starcat's coat again, allowing himself to relax his fade with a sigh of relief. He hadn't realised how difficult it was to maintain, and wished he'd practiced the technique more often. But there'd been so many other things to distract him over the months since his sister had taught him how. His stomach rumbled, and he cursed himself for not bringing some kind of food. What kind of messenger was he? He didn't even have a water bottle. It was a measure of how little the Garsal knew about surviving in the wilderness, and how distracted he'd been by the information he was carrying, that he hadn't considered it until now.

He explored his pockets, checking them one by one to see what might be inside them. As expected, they were empty, bereft of his pocket knife, his compass, maps and spare bowstrings. He sighed resolutely, and decided to look around for anything he could eat or drink, or might be helpful as soon as there was enough light. He was half tempted to sneak around while it was still dark, but there was a hint of early morning on the horizon, so Kaidan settled back to wait for dawn. The danger of detection would increase, but he could fade, and he needed to be close to the fence to be ready for when Laretai dropped it.

And then Dipper came alert, nose sniffing and ears twitching, tail held straight out behind him, his coat flickering in a myriad of complex tidemarks.

***

The climbers crested the edge of the plateau, levering themselves up onto its heights in a shower of displaced vegetation. Rocks tumbled behind them, crunching down the side of the plateau, where scars now marred its green sides. Hoth sat strapped into his command seat, its suspension allowing him to ride the jerky passage easily. The horizon was lightening slowly as his climber settled itself at the head of the formation. He checked his maps again. The major town was close by. Travelling at top speed, they would be ready to attack just as the sun rose.

"Give the command to assemble as planned," he barked. "Alert the ship of our position, and provide them with this time frame." He tapped his screen with one manipulator arm, sending the information to his underling. A few moments later, the climbers spread out into formation, and on his signal, they clanked forwards. He checked their positions once more and then sat back, satisfied. The humans would have no idea what was about to descend upon them. In the back of his mind, the presence of the Great Enemy tickled at his mind, but in all his searching, he'd still only seen one. Perhaps their numbers were very small. A remnant perhaps. All the same, the thought continued to niggle at him.

***

"Cerren!" The words penetrated Master Cerren's brain foggily, and he dragged himself slowly out of the exhausted sleep he'd fallen into. "Cerren! They're here. We have an hour, no more!" Erilla's voice finally jerked him into full wakefulness, and he sat up, scrambling to put his brain back together.

"Everything is ready?"

"Yes," she said simply, although her green eyes said considerably more. This was her home, and she was about to allow it to be sacrificed, and although they had planned to minimise casualties, Cerren knew it would be impossible for them to come out completely unscathed. That lives would be lost in the defence of Watchtower. He just hoped that the Garsal would believe they'd really conquered the town, and be satisfied to fortify themselves within it, until whatever miracle the Starlynes believed in so fervently, occurred. He knew his people were resilient, clever and tough, but … he shook his head, tossed off that train of thought and pulled his boots on. Socks ambled over to him, blue tidemarks twinkling through her grey fur, confidence in every line of her body.

"You're still confident, aren't you lady cat?" he murmured to her, and she hummed deep in her throat and angled her head so that he could scratch her favourite spots.

"Nimbus is the same," sighed Erilla. "They're smart, and they know when things are difficult, but they don't seem particularly edgy about this threat at all. Determined, yes, and angry at times, but not at all fearful."

"It's a puzzle," said Cerren, finishing tying up his boots and standing. He took the water bottles Erilla handed him, slung them from his hips, added the knife sheaths and his cased bow and checked his emergency ration pack and first-aid kit, straightened his shirt, and then looked at her. "Well, to battle then." He paused for a few seconds, and then hugged her roughly. "Stay safe, my friend. I'll see you on the other side."

"And you," she replied, green eyes glinting with emotion. She and Nimbus turned and left Cerren's room, straight backed and competent as ever. Socks bumped him consolingly with her head and then they walked out together. Peron awaited him outside, Thunder standing soberly by his side.

Socks gave Thunder a stern look, and the young starcat hummed briefly at her, and then she winked her tidemarks deliberately at him, and he ducked his head.

"We're ready?" asked Cerren.

"Everything is in place. Yendy has sent word from Buttress. The children and elderly are safe, and everyone else is in position."

"So, we wait, then."

"We do." He gripped Cerren's hand in his large one, and then turned to leave with a firm nod. Cerren placed a hand on his shoulder and stopped him.

"Take care, Peron." He searched his friend's eyes, and found only determination there.

"I will do my best, old friend. Make sure you do the same." He returned the shoulder pressure, called Thunder, and then they were gone too.

"So, Socks. It is time then." The starcat came to his side, and the two of them headed towards the command centre near the arena. As he entered, he could see his staff arrayed, waiting. Payne and Griss came towards him.

"We estimate half an hour Cerren. The Starlyne relay is working well, and the militia are in position."

"In that case, let me have the reports in sections, while we still have time." He settled into his chair and let his mind begin collating the information.

***

Anjo was already tired. Preparations had lasted well into the night and he'd had little sleep. Once he'd finally found a moment to lie down, he'd found several extra people already snoring in Kaidan's room. They had left the bed for him, but it had been quite awkward to pick his way through the sleeping bodies to get to it. Ember had simply bounced from one spot to another, agilely and silently. Finally, he was able to lower himself thankfully to the horizontal, and then he'd lain awake worrying about the conflict to come.

Now, as the tired light of early morning echoed his weariness, he sat in the kitchen area, carefully listening to the militia sergeant outline the defence plan.

"Anjo, I would speak with you," said a voice. He looked around, puzzled, as he'd tucked himself into a corner. The voice came again. "Anjo, I would speak with you." The voice was quite insistent, and then he realised it wasn't audible to his ears – it was the voice of the Starlyne, Dreamer, speaking directly into his mind. "I am within the cavern." He stood quietly, excused himself, and with Ember worked his way through the crowd in the kitchen and slipped into the breeding cavern.

It was full of starcats. Every breeder at Hillview had a few, ready trained starcats with them, and like every starcat he'd seen, they were attracted to the Starlynes like insects around a nectar bearing flower. Dreamer had set her infirmary up towards the back of the cavern, and had coiled herself neatly near it. What seemed to be every starcat in Hillside, was rubbing itself up against her. Her hands were busy tickling the multitude of heads, as their tidemarks flickered in a rainbow of exuberant colour. Ember joined the throng as Anjo waded through it, gently moving heads and bodies out of his way. Part of his mind still couldn't believe that he was fearless in the presence of so many fierce feline predators. Dangerous though an angry starcat could be, Anjo now knew that they would never willingly harm a human being.

"Dreamer?"

"Anjo." She looked at him with her huge eyes, unblinkingly examining him, and he felt stripped to the core, and vulnerable. "Will you be able to do what needs to be done?"

"What needs to be done, Dreamer?" he asked, puzzled.

"You will know when the time comes," she said. "There is much riding on it." Her eyes seemed to be dissecting his soul as he stood there in front of her, not knowing how to respond. Finally, she relaxed. "And you will do well."

"Do well with what?"

"With whatever comes your way," she replied. He'd had a number of conversations with Starlynes. Most of them he'd enjoyed, but every now and then he had one like this, so ambiguous that he left uncomfortable and taken aback. Ember hummed at him. The starcat seemed completely at ease. He wondered what Kaidan would say when he related the conversation to him, then with a pang of suppressed anguish remembered the loss anew, the pain biting deep into his heart.

"When the time comes, you must put that aside, and do what you must." Her eyes were deeply compassionate, and Anjo swallowed slightly, trying to ease the tightness in his throat.

"Whatever it is that you're trying to tell me, I don't understand Dreamer."

"It is enough," she replied. "You will do well." She uncoiled herself. "You will be on the front line here, should the Garsal come?"

"I will be, Dreamer." She bowed her head.

"In that case, go with my wishes of strength, and the fortitude to do as you must." She ran her hands over Ember's smooth coat, and the starcat flickered his tidemarks so fast that Anjo had no chance of reading them. Then Ember was back by his side, and he could hear Janna calling his name.

"I must go," he said.

"You must," she replied, and turned back to the starcats around her. Their numbers had dwindled, as their partners had recalled them one by one, but the last few were still smooching themselves luxuriously along her long length, and he could feel her enjoyment of their companionship.

"Well, goodbye then." Still confused, he left the cavern, and went to take up the weapons that Janna had provided, and then join her behind one of the barricades on the slope. A few minutes later, he saw the long form of the Starlyne join Adlan at the next one. She coiled herself neatly and turned her attention to a listening watch.

Less than an hour later, the noise of massed climbers came on the breeze. Memories of the last time he'd heard that sound chilled Anjo to the bone. In his mind's eye, he saw the beauty of Delicata trampled into a quagmire of death and blood and steeled himself for what was to come. There was a flicker of movement further down the hill, and a uniformed Scout appeared with a starcat. She was old, and with a shock, Anjo recognised Cally and Ghost. Despite her limp, Cally moved rapidly from cover to cover, and then she was conferring with Adlan and the militia sergeant. A soft whistle brought Janna scrambling from their barricade to join them.

A few moments later she was back, signalling the alert. "They're on the road. They'll either pass us by, and continue on to Watchtower, or realise we're here and attempt to pick us off on the way. Anjo, go and ready the trap crew. Do nothing unless you hear the signal arrow. If they pass us by, we'll ignore them. Cerren reminds us that the longer we're hidden, the less they know about us and our capabilities." Anjo nodded, and then he and Ember were off, using every technique drummed into him by Cally and Kaidan. As he moved, he sent Ember to alert his trap crew, and then the four of them were together at the bottom of the hill, concealed among a clump of trees.

"Up the tree and watch for the signal arrow, Jareth." Josen's eldest was up the tree in a flash, while his newly partnered starcat kept guard below. The clanking and grinding from the climbers echoed loudly through the trees, slowly mounting to a deafening roar. Anjo looked around, making sure that the other two were ready, and then picked up his own cord in a gloved hand. The young woman, Beren, next to him, nodded and poised herself with her firemaking kit. She was fast and efficient, and if the signal came, she'd light the oil soaked torch stuck in the ground in an instant, and then the three of them would light their cords.

The ground began to shake and shudder, and the mechanical sounds escalated into a thunderous cacophony. Flocks of birds erupted from the trees as they approached, and a small herd of wandering horgals galloped past, snorting in terror. Ember's ears flattened, and Anjo could feel him growling deep in his body, where his flank pressed against Anjo's leg. He chanced a quick glance up at Jareth, but the young man was motionless, his body tensed for action.

A family of marmals scurried past, panicked, and then the first rank swung into view. Eight wide, they felled trees as they came, red beams carving a path of smoking destruction on either side of the roadway. Anjo looked left, trying to discern if the hard work of camouflaging the turn-off into Hillview had been sufficient to disguise it. To his offworld eyes it looked like the vegetation was an unbroken line of trees and shrubs, but he knew the hastily disguised entrance was clearly visible to the sharp eyes of the Scout Corps. He hoped fervently that the Garsal were even less observant than he was.

The thunder of the climber advance reached a crescendo of crunching destruction, and the front rank appeared over the rise in the roadway. Anjo held his breath as they clambered down the road using a combination of tracks and limbs to manoeuvre themselves around the obstacles on either side of the roadway. He flinched as one of the red beams sliced into the vegetation a bare metre in front of him. He looked hastily at Beren, still poised with her firemaking kit, and checked the cord lines that stretched from their location to the firetraps constructed across the road. The plan had been to avoid using them unless the Garsal turned directly towards Hillview. Now though, there was a chance that one of the beams might accidentally ignite the trap even if the Garsal passed them by.

"Anjo! What happens if they go up from those?" whispered Beren.

Anjo shrugged helplessly. "If that happens, we'll just have to hope they think it's a road trap and nothing to do with a nearby habitation."

She nodded, and turned back to her task, but Anjo could see that her hands were shaking. Up in the tree, Jareth was still motionless, and next to Beren, Drest crouched, hands steady on her cord. The red beams came thick and fast now, and the first rank of climbers was only a few metres up the road. Anjo braced himself against the tree trunk, and kept his eyes flickering through the bush as Kaidan had taught him, breath coming short and fast. Glints of black, gleaming metal caught the slowly rising sun and then the first rank was directly in front of them, and the ground shook under Anjo's knees.

A small tree toppled, and its topmost branches came to rest not far from Jareth's legs. Anjo didn't dare move, and somehow, up in his tree, Jareth had remained rock steady. The second rank thundered by, and then the third, and then the first firetrap erupted in a fountain of flame, and black smoke began to rise, just ahead of the first rank of climbers. Anjo cursed as Beren and Drest looked with panicked expressions at him. He scribbled furiously on a small piece of paper, tucked it into Ember's harness and sent the cat blurring towards Adlan. "Hold! Don't do anything yet," he said, thinking furiously as the ranks of Garsal climbers came to a grinding halt. The sudden silence was almost painful, and it was as if the whole world was holding its breath.

Ember returned, and Anjo fumbled the note from his harness. "Just wait. Do nothing unless the signal arrow goes up." Jareth's head appeared briefly, to show that he'd heard, and then went back to watching. Anjo couldn't imagine how he was able to keep his concentration so firmly on Hillview, when his own eyes were drawn continuously towards the metal body of the climber standing in front of him. Slowly, the flames from the first firetrap died down, and then one climber jerked into action and stalked forwards, retracting its tracks into the base of its body.

***

"Scan the surrounds!" commanded Hoth. The climber he'd sent forwards relayed a torrent of data to his vehicle, and Hoth surveyed the summations as his tech interpreted the raw information. The screen in front of him flickered, and then the data settled into neat columns, superimposed on the topographical map. He leaned forwards and studied it, tapping the screen to enlarge some of the detail. He leaned back, thinking. There were no signs of life nearby, and the screens were a morass of merging and distorting blobs, something that seemed to be common on this planet. Something prickled at the back of his mind, though. "Pull up the overflight images of this region." Within a few seconds, they were layered over the topographical information. There were several different versions, taken over several flights, and he tapped through them thoughtfully, and then checked the map again. "Find me the earliest flight scans." The tech hastened to do his bidding, and then the earliest scans dropped into place on the screen.

For a few moments he pondered, tapping the screen thoughtfully, and then sent a command to the front rank, and then another to the rear. The front rank advanced to the now dying flames, and stepped over them, and then continued on down the road. Hoth watched his display carefully, monitoring the feed. "Move on." His own climber lurched forwards as the massed ranks moved again, bent on annihilating the town ahead.

***

Anjo let his breath out in a long sigh, as the ranks of climbers resumed their thunderous advance and began to move off down the road. The first rank disappeared around the far bend. The four of them held their positions, and Anjo felt himself relax, tension slowly draining from his limbs. He shared a look of relief with Drest and Beren, still poised over her equipment. Jareth's head reappeared. "Looks like we got away with it."

"It does," replied Anjo, quietly. The fate of Watchtower played on his mind, though. In a very short time, Watchtower's defenders would be facing the firepower of those same massed climbers, and in Watchtower were people he now counted as friends. The last rank of climbers drew level with their position and Anjo watched them stalk past, feeling relief mixed with heartache war within him.

"We'll move back to the house as soon as they're down the road a bit," said Anjo. He shifted position slightly to ease a small cramp in his leg and rubbed Ember's head. The cat was still on edge, all his attention on the last eight climbers clanking down the road. His tidemarks flickered and flowed and he was still grumbling deep within his throat.

There was a sudden increase in sound, and then four of the final rank separated off from the rest, and spread out down the road. There was a slight pause while Anjo struggled to understand what was happening, and then all four picked up speed and began to clamber rapidly towards Hillview. "Beren, now!" he shouted, as realisation struck him. The girl grabbed for her firemaking kit and with trembling hands tried to strike a spark. It took her three tries as the climbers strode forwards, narrowing the distance in rushing steps. "Hurry!" Finally, a flurry of sparks poured onto the oil soaked torch and it blazed into life. Beren and Drest shoved the ends of their cords into the flames and they sputtered into life, and two trails of fire whooshed off into the bush. A few seconds later, two firetraps flared into life. One engulfed the climber nearest to Watchtower. The spray of flames licked hungrily at the climber's body. The other just missed the third climber, but continued to send sprays of flame into the air.

Anjo threw himself sideways as the closest climber lurched directly towards them. Ember hissed and spat, snarling as he flung himself at one of the jointed legs. "Ember!" Anjo landed heavily, rolling, and came up against a rock. His mind flung itself from the fear that he'd neglected to check the ground for something deadly, to force his body through a frantic roll away from the climber's rear limb. It slammed into the ground next to his head and he jerked backwards. Anjo found himself pinned against the rock and scrabbled frantically to flatten himself into the smallest space possible. Then the leg lifted again and the climber stalked on towards Hillview, red beams spearing from its turret to strike randomly at the hillside.

He struggled to his feet and groped around for his cord, heedless of the possibility of sticking his hands into something dangerous. Finally, he found it, and crawled over to thrust it into the flames. The fire scooted down the cord and then the final trap sent its flames flying sky high, forming a barrier in front of the climbers. The lead climber spun its turret, cutting a swathe of destruction across the hill, and causing two of the barriers to erupt into flames. Anjo leaped to his feet, "Ember!" The starcat appeared by his side as if by magic. "Drest, Beren, Jareth, fall back!" Beren and Jareth spun and ran in the appropriate direction, but Anjo couldn't see Drest.

He looked frantically around, and then spotted her still form, slumped against a tree trunk. He scrambled over to her, and grabbed her arm, trying to pull her towards safety. For a moment, he tugged at her, not understanding, and then he realised that her face was blue, and there was a spreading stain on the tree trunk behind her. His trembling hands sought the pulse in her neck, but there was nothing, and with a sob, he left her body where it was, and took himself back to the camouflaged barricade. Three of the climbers were moving steadily up the hill, sweeping their weapons back and forth, but the fourth was motionless, a smoking ruin.

"It's lit, Anjo!" Beren's voice was tight, but she held another cord firmly. Jareth was crouched with her, eyes fastened to the stalking vehicles.

"Hold, hold, ready, and … now!" All three of them touched their cords simultaneously, and another three trails of fire leaped away from their position. Without waiting to see what would happen, Anjo led the other two to their next position.

"Where's Drest?" Jareth's voice was unsteady.

"Gone." He kept his voice flat, as he had so many times on Delicata. There was a muffled sob from Beren, and a strangled sound from Jareth.

"Time for that later," said Anjo, "We have a job to do."

One of them took a sobbing breath, but they both kept running, and then they were at the next barricade. Anjo risked a look upwards just in time to see one of the climbers hurdle the line of flames. Another was stranded in the new fountain of fire from their last trap. Half-a-dozen Garsal boiled out of it, abandoning the vehicle as it smoked and burned. From higher up the hill, the militia had begun to launch ragged volleys of the explosive arrowheads with the new formula the Starlynes had tweaked slightly, so that the liquid inside could cling to the shiny metal skins of the climbers, but it wasn't enough. The Garsal's weapons had burned through a number of the barricades as if they weren't there and the defenders' lines were now too fragmented; their arrow strikes weren't concentrated enough to give the Garsal vehicles pause.

Where the arrows struck, the liquid burned furiously, dripping flames into the vegetation and starting small spot fires. "Garsal to the right," said Anjo. He didn't mention the devastation he'd seen up the hill. Time for that later. For now, there were other, more important things. "There are two climbers left, but we'll leave them to the others. They're beyond this line of traps. Jareth, are you ready?" The young man nodded and pulled a whistle from around his neck. "On my signal then." He chanced another look, raised his hand, waited, and then dropped it. Jareth signalled, and then the three of them charged, accompanied by Ember and Jareth's cat. As he ran, Anjo pulled his knife, wishing that the settlers of Frontier had developed the projectile weapons he'd been accustomed to during his days as a guerrilla fighter. He signalled with one hand and Ember sped ahead, joining half-a-dozen of Josen's starcats as they blurred down the hill towards the Garsal.

Anjo's breath came faster and faster as he ran. Red beams of light lanced towards the three of them, and Anjo leaped sideways as the grass beneath his feet erupted into flames. Faintly, he could hear the crunching sound of the two remaining climbers advancing towards the house at the top of the hill, but his attention remained on the six Garsal ahead. They were taking full advantage of an abandoned barricade to fire at Anjo and his two companions. There was a stifled gasp from Jareth, and a grunt from Beren, and he saw her throw herself forwards, under one of the burning beams, roll and then run onwards. There was a blur of fur and teeth, and all six of the Garsal went down under the rush of starcats. Their snarling was clearly audible, but the insectoid invaders were no match for seven furious cats, and none rose from the brief melee.

Anjo kept running, though, as the starcats turned, and signalled furiously to Jareth. He heard him slow as he fumbled the whistle into his mouth. Anjo

                    *Leonie Rogers*

called again, too out of breath to whistle Ember, and the cat returned to him, uninjured, but his normally sleek fur was bristling, and spotted with the milky Garsal blood. Anjo moved forwards to the group of dead Garsal, searching among the bodies for an undamaged weapon. He found one, and fumbled with its weight for a few moments, dredging through his brain to remember how to operate it. It was slightly different from the ones he'd salvaged and learned to use on Delicata. Finally, his hands found the triggers, designed for a six limbed entity, and fired his first shot up the hill towards the nearest climber.

It missed, off target by a long way, and he muttered under his breath before sighting again and pulling the triggers. Closer. The defenders at the top of the hill launched a barrage of flaming bladders at the two remaining climbers, and as they struck, they exploded. Another climber was engulfed in flame, and Garsal troopers spilled from its body. A group of militia poured out from their hiding place, accompanied by two Scouts and their cats. "Send them, Jareth!" The group of starcats with Anjo, Jareth and Beren blurred into action, reinforcing the humans, and the three young people raced to help.

Another sizzle of red flew from the Garsal troopers pouring destructive redness in all directions. At the top of the hill, the top turret of the remaining climber swivelled constantly, and the auxiliary weapons spat death as well. Anjo could hear cries of pain and rage, and pushed himself faster. This was his home, and this was his family, no matter how little time he'd known them.

His old injury began to ache with every step, but he was fuelled by anger now as he saw the destruction meted out by the Garsal. He roared with rage as the troopers cut down several of the militia and then he heard a scream of pain from a starcat. "Ember!" But somehow he knew it wasn't his starcat. As he ran he saw new friends fall under the beams of destruction and ran harder. Dimly, he saw the group of Garsal taken down by the starcats and humans together, and changed his trajectory towards the remaining climber. What he was going to do when he got there, he didn't know. Ember was suddenly by his side, and he slowed slightly, and took a good look at the tableau before him.

The climber was beyond the firetraps, and had missed the concealed pits dug in the hillside, and now it stood almost at the crest of the rise in front of Hillview. He could see a group of militia rearming the bladder catapults, frantically pulling the explosive arrowheads out of their quivers and aiming them towards the climber. Anjo's breath came shorter and shorter, and then he was under the climber. It was stationary, swivelling its turret to keep the defenders in front of it at bay. He took aim with the Garsal weapon, hit the triggers, and missed the spot he was aiming for. His sweaty hands slipped on the smooth finish, and he rubbed one hastily on his trousers, and then the other, trying not to listen to the sounds of pain from in front of him.

Again he took aim, took a deep breath, and held it, and then fired. The beam flew true, and struck the sensitive spot on the climber body. Its legs sagged, and then it straightened and he pulled the triggers again, and the foremost limb froze in place. He shot again, and again, but still the turret spun. Finally all of the legs stopped moving, and Anjo moved from beneath the machine, searching for any kind of vulnerable spot at the front of the machine. Finally one of the catapults struck it full on, and it began to burn furiously.

At that moment, Anjo realised that he was back at Janna's barricade, nearly at the front door of Hillview, and looked to see her crouched with Sabre, almost at his feet. A final red beam lanced from the smoking turret, and then it exploded, sending pieces of metal flying through the air towards them. Without thought, he launched himself sideways, in front of Janna and her starcat. His last thought was that he owed Kaidan and Shanna everything, and then it all went very black.

# Chapter 28

THE alarms sent the Matriarch to her feet. "Are we discovered, Laretai?"

Her Senior's manipulator arms flew across her screens. "No Matriarch. I haven't even dropped the fence yet. All I've been doing is setting it up so that it looks like a genuine equipment failure." Her tone was puzzled.

"Kaidan?"

"There is no sign of him in the system, or on any of the screens. I have a watch program on alert for him — it would have alerted us if his image or name was detected anywhere in the system." Her manipulator arms moved faster. "Ah! The sentry outside our quarters has vanished." She tapped furiously. "No, not just vanished, his body has been discovered two levels down." She turned towards the Matriarch, apprehension colouring her voice.

"The humans!" The Matriarch was certain. "Not only are they within the sentinel ring, they have penetrated the ship. In fact, it is likely that they are within the female section of the ship. Fetch Lacey immediately!"

"But the fence, Matriarch? Kaidan will be waiting, hidden."

"His message will mean nothing if the humans decide to kill us, Laretai, and I have no doubt that they would be both justified, and very effective in doing so. We need Lacey. She may be able to assist." The Senior bustled from the room, urgency in every line of her body, and returned with Lacey within moments. The old woman was tousled from sleep, rubbing her eyes and yawning. The Matriarch was reminded of how fragile their hopes were, hanging as they were on an old woman and a boy. "Lacey, I believe that the free humans have penetrated the ship and perhaps even these secure quarters."

The old woman frowned. "Are you certain?"

"Our sentry is dead, and his body discovered two levels down. There will be troopers in these hallways within seconds, and despite the lack of images, I am certain that there will be more of those felines with the humans.

"We must wait then. And I must wait with you. But I must seem no more than a slave unless absolutely necessary, and if the humans arrive before the Overlord, I will do my best to explain."

"That was my thought also," said the Matriarch, inclining her head. "It may be that Kaidan will meet up with some of them as we planned, but it also may be that we encounter them before he does. And if the plan demands our sacrifice, then so be it. Estei is as prepared as time has allowed, and she is well supported by Hirtoi. I have sealed the files indicating her succession, should I fall." The alarm klaxons continued, deafeningly, and the first sounds of rapidly moving footsteps sounded outside the room.

"The Overlord has directed a level by level search, beginning at the entry level of our quarters, Matriarch. We must expect it and behave accordingly."

"Laretai, alert Estei and Hirtoi, and the rest of the seniors. No matter what happens, we must maintain a semblance of normality. Send three of the seniors to delay the Overlord at the door. We must allow the situation to play itself out, but the least we can do is to prevent a full scale invasion of our privacy. There are things better left unseen in these quarters."

"Hirtoi mirrors my activity, Matriarch. She has set a watch routine on the Overlord's personal tablet."

"Is that wise?"

"Hirtoi will surpass all of my skills given time, Matriarch, and in the writing of such code, she already has no peer." The Matriarch nodded, thinking furiously.

"Our preparations are complete then, and what will be, will be. We will wait, and act as the occasion warrants."

***

The alarms had sent Shanna and her companions into an urgent huddle. "What do you think's alerted them?" asked Verren.

"It could have been the missing guard, or something Taya, Ragar and Zandany did," replied Allad quietly. "Or something completely unrelated. Nevertheless, we know what's up here now, so our priority is to rejoin the others. Verren, take us back as fast as possible. Shanna send one of your cats ahead with Cirrus, and then take the rear."

Faded, Shanna began to follow the others, stepping quietly at Amma's heels. Storm ranged behind them, and she could feel his concern slowly escalate as they came closer and closer to the access point. When they'd entered, the area had been deserted, and few Garsal had been abroad in the hallways.

Now, Shanna and the others were forced to flatten themselves repeatedly against the walls as filmy robed females moved past in groups, hurrying in all directions. As they closed on the access point, Shanna could see more and more activity up ahead. She almost ran into Amma as they approached the doorway into the reception area. Some kind of altercation appeared to be taking place, and Shanna could hear loud, harsh sounding syllables, reverberating in the large room. She checked behind, made sure Storm was watching the rear, 'felt' for Twister ahead with Verren, and settled her back against the wall to concentrate.

***

"Zoash!" The Overlord stormed into the command centre, manipulator arms still attaching his rank badges.

"Overlord, we have found a body."

"Where? And whom?" He was displeased to be wakened so early by the screaming alarms.

"The honour sentry was found in a storage unit two floors from his post. He was dead." Zoash paused. "There were claw marks on his body."

The Overlord stiffened. "Could it be the renegade cat that has been attacking our troopers within the compound?"

Zoash flicked his manipulator arms uncomfortably. "It is possible, Overlord. However, the medical technicians are of the opinion that the body exhibits signs of more than one assailant, and there is no reason to believe that the feline would deliberately conceal the body."

The Overlord felt an unexpected chill course through his body. "How is it possible they are inside the ship?" he asked, barking the question, voice harsh. He beckoned peremptorily to his hatching sib to follow, and stalked from the room. "And they are as far as the female quarters?" His hopes of offspring shook and quivered. The Matriarch would crush them with a word if her precious enclave suffered an attack of any kind. He increased his pace. The alarm klaxons rang ceaselessly.

"We were unable to discover how they penetrated last time, Overlord, or escaped. Once again, they have surpassed our security technology." Zoash's voice was reluctant.

"You are certain that there were only three flyers? And no felines?"

"We are, Overlord, but in retrospect, the perimeter failures during the storm may have had a more sinister meaning." Zoash's voice became quieter with every word and the Overlord halted, and then ground out each word separately, voice thundering the syllables.

"In retrospect. You told me that our technicians were working on the problems, and that the perimeter failures were all explainable. Until now. And now, they suddenly become breaches by a hostile force?"

"Overlord," they were the most obsequious tones the Overlord had ever heard from his sib, "it is often easy to see things in hindsight, as more facts become available." The Overlord resumed walking, tapped the elevator keypad, entered with Zoash on his heels, and turned to face him as the elevator began to descend.

"*Your* job is to look ahead, not behind. This should have been one of the scenarios placed before me. We will discuss this later. In more detail." He turned away from his sib, noting the sudden blanching of colour on his carapace. As Overlord, he had many powers, and without a recommendation from him, Zoash would be denied offspring. No doubt he had had plans for his progeny to rise and conquer. A small wave of satisfaction wafted through the Overlord's mind, but was buried quickly by a torrent of unease. For months, just one feline had preyed on his troops outside the ship and hive. Over those months, the death toll had become truly impressive. Just one. The words rolled around inside his mind, causing more discomfort than he'd believed possible.

Perhaps it was 'just one' inside the ship. 'Just one' was a dreadful thought. More than one suggested death, terror and disaster. The doors opened, and he strode out into the midst of an argument. Filmy robed seniors stood firmly in the doorway, preventing his troops from accessing the female section.

"Troopers, stand down," Zoash ordered

At least his sib was still good for something the Overlord thought irritably as he strode forwards. "Why are you denying us entry? Your security is breached."

The oldest Senior stood motionless, tidily and precisely clothed, despite the early morning hour. "Overlord, our quarters seem perfectly secure. There is no disturbance within."

"Your sentry is dead, and his body concealed two levels down."

She brushed the comment aside with a disdained wave on her mid section limbs. "Your male feuds have nothing to do with us. The never ending jockeying for position you indulge in is no business of ours." The Overlord scrambled for a reply, uncharacteristically nonplussed.

"My apologies, Senior, but there was no feuding involved." He inclined his head to her. "The sentry appears to have been mauled by one of the dangerous felines that infest this planet."

Her demeanour changed to one he was hard pressed to decipher, and he saw her calmness slip so slightly he was unsure that it had. "But there is no sign of any such feline within our quarters, Overlord. I am certain that there is nothing amiss."

"It appears that they are able to remain undetected by our security systems, Senior." It pained him to admit it, but it was unavoidably true. "We are rectifying the matter as we speak." He disguised his uncertainty with vocal confidence. "Nevertheless, it is essential that for a short time we have a security presence within the enclave. It will be brief, but we must ensure your safety. Will you conduct me to the Matriarch?"

"I will send a message, and we will commence our own search immediately, Overlord." She turned to one of her underlings, giving him no time to insist on immediate entrance. The Overlord had the feeling she was deliberately delaying, but the niceties of protocol required to enter the female enclave had millennia of tradition behind them, and he was forced to patience, despite the urgency of the matter. With visible evidence of an incursion by the felines he would have been able to insist, but with no evidence to back up his claims, he was forced to stand idly, awaiting the Matriarch's graces. As he watched, one of the younger females departed rapidly, her robes floating behind her gracefully. Taking his message, he supposed.

"Silence that klaxon!" he demanded. He might not be able to force his way into the female quarters, but he could take his anger and discomfort out on the obvious scapegoat. "And send troopers to all critical locations." Zoash bowed his head without speaking and stepped away to do his bidding.

***

Shanna flattened herself more firmly against the wall as another of the female Garsal moved past. This one moved decisively, bent on some errand. She stretched her ears, still trying to overhear an understandable word from ahead. The altercation seemed to have ceased, but the way was still blocked. She wondered what was happening. She couldn't imagine what was preventing the immediate arrival of the Garsal troopers. A hand touched her shoulder and tapped it. She interpreted the instructions carefully.

*Be Alert. Move soon.*

She tensed herself, poised herself on the balls of her feet, mentally located her starcats again, and inched slightly closer to Amma. And then back again. She didn't want to impede her friend's movement. Gently, she extended her senses, trying to pierce the metal bulkhead in the same way she was able to see what was ahead when she was working her way through dense vegetation. She marvelled that she'd come to feel that such sensing was 'normal' in such a short time.

The bulkheads seemed denser, more difficult to penetrate using her 'extra' vision, but slowly, the blankness resolved into fuzzy outlines, and then more succinct images. She counted, and then placed her hand on Amma's shoulder and tapped.

*Ten Garsal, two groups, spaced out.*

She used the same coded tap she'd have used for dangerous predators, reasoning that they'd all understand what she meant. She felt Amma's surprise, and then her acceptance in her body posture, and a moment later her friend tapped back.

*Soon. Doorway. Two steps. Patrol.*

Shanna translated in her mind. Move shortly, make for the doorway, then the other doorway and head for the rendezvous with the other three. Amma's shoulder muscles tightened, and Shanna felt her lean forwards slightly. She fumbled her silent whistle from her shirt neck to her mouth and signalled her cats to be ready, and then she felt Amma move forwards. She dropped her hand from her friend's shoulder, trusting to her senses to 'feel' where they all were, and then took her first few steps.

Silently, every muscle tense, and every breath taken as gently as possible, Shanna began to weave her way through the Garsal clustered near the doorway. It was wide enough that the female Garsal standing just on the other side was spaced just far enough away for a human form to slip through – if that human was careful. Shanna signalled Twister through, knowing that the faded starcat would leave nothing more than a faint disturbance in the air.

She saw the Garsal's filmy robes lift briefly in the wind of his passing, and almost sighed in relief, catching the sigh on the inhale and slowly allowing her breath to ease past her lips. She 'felt' Cirrus duck through after him, once again leaving nothing but a tiny eddy in the air. Her extended senses 'felt' Verren approach the doorway, and then 'felt' him slide through, pause, and then move between the two groups of Garsal to stand near the doorway to the ramps. Satin, Allad, Spider, Amma, and then it was her turn.

Shanna wove her way past the final Garsal form, hesitated slightly, and then ducked through, carefully keeping her body in contact with the cold metal of the door frame. Her heart nearly stopped when the tickle of the Garsal female's robes slapped her hand.

The female had turned suddenly, causing her robes to swirl as she did so, and the outermost layer had struck Shanna's hand. She froze, convinced that the creatures would notice the interruption of the smooth swing of the fabric, and then forced herself to move. She slipped past the Garsal, feeling the large faceted eyes stare right through her; smelling the slightly pungent odour she'd come to associate with them ever since the removal of the corpse from the flying machine.

A few more steps, and then she felt Storm slide through as well, not even stirring the floating material. She realised that once again she was holding her breath, and joined the others at the far door. None of the Garsal appeared to have noticed anything. For a moment she wondered what they were waiting for, then realised. If the door suddenly opened and shut by itself, the Garsal would know that someone was there. Yet every second they delayed, standing in the room with ten Garsal, meant that it was more and more likely that one of them would walk into one of the hidden Scouts. Shanna tried to keep her breathing even and silent, but this type of stationary skulking was even more difficult than hiding from a staureg with just a frondan tree and a rock for cover. In fact, hiding from a staureg seemed child's play compared to standing faded in a room full of Garsal.

Time seemed endless as they stood there, waiting. Shanna had time to wonder what was happening with the other three, to wonder what precisely had alerted the Garsal, and wonder how her family and friends were faring on the plateau. She ruthlessly crushed the thought that any of them might be dead, or wounded, or captured by the Garsal. Then her mind flitted to thoughts of Kaidan and she had to struggle to convince herself that she wasn't abandoning him by leaving this portion of the ship.

Finally, the Garsal female spoke again, and the ten Garsal came suddenly to attention. She stepped aside, and they all entered, filing through the door, each bowing its head to the robed one in what seemed like a respectful fashion. She stepped through after them, and then the door closed, and finally, they were alone.

"Let's go," came Allad's whisper. "This might be our best chance." The door opened, Shanna whistled Storm through, and then they were back on the ramps, moving as fast as they dared.

***

"Matriarch, the Overlord is without," said Laretai. The Matriarch flicked a quick glance around the room. Lacey stood behind her chair, eyes on the floor, the very model of a cowed slave. Laretai stood at the doorway, and Estei and Hirtoi sat in position on either side of her.

"Allow him entry." She pulled herself taller as the doors opened. "Overlord, what news have you?"

"Matriarch, it appears that at least one of the felines has entered the ship." She noticed that his wording reflected what he wanted her to believe, not the reality.

"And how is this known, Overlord?" She heightened the disapproval in her voice, and watched the impact strike him.

"We have found a body, Matriarch. Your honour guard, in fact. There is evidence of claws and teeth."

"My Senior tells me that the body was concealed two levels down – hardly the work of a feline!" She allowed the syllables to crack out, each one scoring a strike on the Overlord's ego, and she felt Laretai stiffen behind her. She knew the danger she was courting though, just as she knew how to needle the pompous male, arrogant in his overconfidence like so many of his type. "Has it not occurred to you that it may be a deception, engineered to divert suspicion from a feud?" The agreed upon approach was very plausible to any who knew the male Garsal mind. "There have been precedents." She watched the barb strike home. The Overlord's line was well known for its use of such subterfuge, and there had actually been a scandal not that long before the colony ship lifted.

"I assure you Matriarch, it is no deception," said the Overlord, and she nearly pitied him. For once, he was earnest in his desire to please, but his motivation was still defined by his desire for offspring.

"We will wait and see," she replied disdainfully. "Sit with us if you wish. Perhaps you can update us on the invasion of the plateau, since you have seen fit to disturb us at this ridiculous hour." She settled back into her chair, deliberately arranging her robes for maximum effect. He was torn, she could see. Torn between trying to locate the felines he was so obviously fearful of, and of demonstrating his tactical prowess. She gave him no quarter.

Finally the Overlord signalled regret. "I must return to the command centre, Matriarch. I will leave Zoash here, directing the search. He will provide you with as much information as you request." He waved a manipulator arm at his hatching sib, and the Matriarch flicked him a glance.

*One to watch,* Laretai had said. They had been words of caution.

"Of course, Overlord," she said graciously. "Your personal warnings are appreciated." She stood, and he had no choice but to take his leave. She could see his displeasure though, it flickered through every step he took.

***

The tension filled descent of the ramps ended outside the vehicle storage area. The door stood wide open, and there was a flurry of Garsal activity inside. The harsh alien syllables seemed to be becoming louder by the second. "Send Storm in with this." Allad's whispered instructions were followed by a note tucked into Shanna's hand. She nodded, despite knowing he couldn't see it, and bent to tuck the note into her starcat's harness. She rubbed his head briefly, and sent him on his way. "Stay together unless a large group comes past," said Allad, "we'll be wanting to move directly to the slave quarters once the others join us. How's the fatigue levels?"

Shanna thought for a moment. She was mildly weary, less than she'd expected actually, and then flicked her fingers over the patches stored in her thigh pocket for easy access. She checked the one still on her wrist. Almost depleted. She'd burned through it at a fairly high rate. "Good at the moment," she whispered, "and I've still got a fair few patches, but I'm burning through them fast." The others whispered similar comments. At least fading was her primary talent. She suspected that the last couple of hours had been harder on her friends than herself. She rubbed Twister's neck as he pressed against her leg and stood quietly, faded, waiting.

She felt no alarm from Storm, just a sense of waiting, so she relaxed slightly, sent Twister patrolling up and down the nearby ramp, and pulled a few slices of dried fruit from another pocket. She handed them around by the simple expedient of 'feeling' where her friends were, locating their hands and pressing a slice into their hands. She was unable to resist leaving her hand in Verren's slightly longer than she should have, but finally gave it a squeeze and then let it go.

She 'felt' Storm approaching, and tapped the others to alert them, and Ragar circled them in, sending the starcats to sit as sentries at either end of the ramp. "Report."

"We managed to immobilise or damage about half the vehicles before that alarm went off," whispered Ragar. "What did you do?"

"Not sure it was us, but we think they discovered the body of the sentry. The female quarters were behind the door. I'd guess they're held in higher regard, or at least guarded carefully – or maybe even both." replied Allad.

Ragar nodded. "Back to the basic plan then – down to the slave quarters, break out as many as possible, and get them out, and whatever we can, we'll break on the way out." His voice was determined, and Shanna felt her resolve stiffen. So far, despite extensive searching, they'd remained undetected. Perhaps they had a real chance of escaping from the ship with the slaves. She felt more hopeful than she had for some time. She'd never really realised how effective being invisible to the naked eye would be, even if they were moving in a group.

She checked herself for fatigue, decided she'd need a new patch shortly, and stepped off. She felt as though she'd been running up and down ramps for hours. But then again, she had. She hoped desperately that her family was still safe from the invaders, and then put the thought firmly out of her mind. Now was not the time for distractions.

# Chapter 29

CERREN winced as the sound of percussive weapons fire reverberated through the command centre. Socks growled deep in her body as the building shook. "Reports!" he snapped as two messengers hurtled through the doorway.

"They've breached the wall, Master Cerren — the main gate's gone and a section of the wall about fifty metres long." The messenger took gasping breaths as she bent forwards, hands on her knees, red faced and sweaty.

"Shari sends a message," said the other one, a tall young man with one bloodstained arm slung by his side. "We took ten out with the fire traps outside the wall, but they've concentrated their fire to destroy another section of the wall and swarmed through and are now advancing rapidly. Our frontal positions are overwhelmed. Dinian's archers have taken four more, but their positions are compromised. They will regroup as planned, if they're able." As he spoke, a starcat blurred through the door. It was Nimbus. He pulled up in a slide in front of Cerren, who took the note from his harness while the cat waited expectantly.

Cerren's mind raced as he read. 'They're moving faster than our worst estimates. We'll buy as much time as possible. I expect our position to be overrun within minutes. We'll attempt to fall back to the tertiary position. Alert our allies.'

The building shook again. "Losses?" he asked, dreading the answer.

"Militia losses are high. Shari estimates fifty per cent." The answer was a blow that shook Cerren to the core.

"Your Scouts are faring better, thanks to their ability to fade. Erilla estimates twenty-five per cent." Cerren deliberately took a breath and released it again. Still too many.

"Tell Erilla — message acknowledged. And tell Shari that our allies will act."

By his side, he felt Speaker's firm agreement. There was a wash of regret and sadness, but his Starlyne friend damped it almost immediately, and Cerren could feel the determination increase as he spoke to his fellows.

"It is time, friends. Do as you are able."

Cerren felt almost privileged to be included in Speaker's message, privileged and desolate at the same time. The human casualties were high, but so were their numbers. Each Starlyne death would mean the loss of an intellect that had lived centuries. He felt the quick brush of four vast minds touching his own, feeling the love that motivated them, and the hope, and the farewells they broadcast.

Cerren crouched, watched as his hands affixed the purple flagging to Nimbus' harness, and sent the starcat on his way. "Thank you," he whispered, knowing that all of them heard. For one second he wished that he could communicate with his own people in the same manner, and then he was glad he was unable to. So many had already perished, that he couldn't imagine dealing with all of the sadness, destruction and fear that the Starlynes must be hearing and feeling.

He turned to Griss. "Bring the schedule forward. We need to start phase four of the staged withdrawal." The young man nodded and vanished.

The roof shook again, and Cerren, Socks by his side, ascended the short path upwards to the exit tunnel. He knew it was unwise, but he needed to see the final retreat from Watchtower with his own eyes. He knew that he would need the memory to spur him onwards later. Already, the injured were beginning to stream past him, those able to move under their own steam limping or staggering towards safety, others carried on litters by grime-streaked medics, while others were supported by non-combatants as they hurried down the tunnel.

The day was absurdly beautiful, Cerren thought, as he emerged into bright sunlight. It should have been cloudy, grey and dim to mirror the destruction, but instead it was one of those glorious days that commonly occurred shortly after one of the great cyclonic storms had passed.

It was almost too brilliant. He and Socks climbed the tiers of the arena to the observation post constructed to look out over Watchtower. The observers were noting flagged signals from the town, and messengers ran up and down the tiers.

The town. Cerren's eyes saw what the messages hadn't said. Smoke rose everywhere from piles of rubble and debris. The noise was hideous. Concussive shock waves rattled the sturdy structure he stood on, and red beams burned their way through house and business alike. He could see streams of people running from the marauding invaders all over Watchtower. Some were orderly, keeping strictly to the plan, but in other places, where the concentration of fire was heaviest, planning had obviously been overtaken by death, and the orderly retreat had become a panicked dash. The stench of death filled his nostrils, filling them with the odour of defeat, but he hung on, watching with eyes that burned with unshed sorrow.

"Cerren, my people move into position now," came Speaker's voice. An aircraft screamed overhead, and part of the old storm shelter crumbled before Cerren's eyes. "Dancer will concentrate on the aircraft, while the other three will bring down as many of the climbers as they are able. Give us another five minutes. I have spoken to Erilla and Shari directly. You will all know when they begin." Cerren nodded, knowing that the Starlyne was unable to see him.

"You have my grateful thanks." And he knew that they all heard him.

Another aircraft passed overhead and its beam slammed into the side of the arena. Great gouts of smoke poured from the stone, and part of the wall nearby exploded into flying shards. Cerren grabbed for the railing, hanging on grimly as the observation post rocked, and then steadied. His eyes searched frantically for his people as they poured out of Watchtower in disciplined streams to vanish into the surrounding vegetation, or made their way towards the arena from their posts all across the town.

Socks was tense with anger, and he could feel her fur bristle under his hands. The climbers looked like huge, four legged insects as they strode through the rubble. One erupted into flames as he watched, and the exiting Garsal were swarmed by starcats and Scouts as they emerged from its belly hatch.

A tight satisfaction surged through him as the insectoid invaders perished under the attack. Another rain of fragments followed the screaming whoosh of another aircraft, and then Cerren saw a group of archers appear on one of the flat roofed houses part-way down Watchtower's rise. They took steady aim at the oncoming aircraft, arms extended as they drew their bows to full draw. He saw the man beside them open his mouth to call something, arm raised, and then their building vanished into a pile of stone dust as three climbers concentrated their fire on it.

Cerren's rage rose, and his anguish, and then the shock wave rolled across Watchtower. One of the aircraft plummeted, spinning out of control through the air, falling towards the arena like the parody of a swatted insect. Cerren had little time to watch a dozen climbers freeze into statues, before he grabbed the nearest observer by the arm and leaped away from the observation post, landing three tiers down and rolling painfully to the ground. Socks landed lightly beside him, and urged him up. The woman he'd saved staggered to her feet clutching one arm, and limped away from the burning, dented wreckage of the craft and the crazily tilted tiers.

An opening appeared in the craft's shattered side and a Garsal crawled out, dazedly clutching its weapon and firing indiscriminately around. Cerren threw himself sideways and Socks snarled. Unthinkingly, he followed her towards the creature, pulling his heavy knife from his belt. She faded as she moved, and he followed suit, thanking Shanna mentally, as one of the beams from its weapons burned a hot path beside his head. All of a sudden, he 'knew' where Socks was.

Caught in the wonder of the discovery, he nearly lost an arm to another random shot. The hot pain on his left forearm jerked him back into concentration, and he moved forwards smoothly, coordinating his attack with that of his starcat. The trooper never had a chance. It died under the onslaught of knife, teeth and claws in seconds, and Cerren felt a righteous satisfaction as he stepped back and scraped his knife on the black carapace. He let the fade go.

Socks growled again, and hissed at the corpse, and Cerren ran his hand down her coat, smoothing the raised hackles as he lifted his eyes to the arena. The aircraft lay embedded in the sand, and the observation post had vanished. Half the tiering was gone, and the stream of humans had slowed to a trickle. Limp bodies lay, or hung, where the observation platform had been, and Cerren took a considering look. He grabbed the arm of a passing Scout.

"Report!"

"Two patrols hold the rear, Cerren. Erilla is with one, and Peron the other. Shari has most of her people in full retreat." He shook his head. "There were so many of them."

"Tell Griss to move to phase five, and that I'll be in shortly." The Scout nodded and ran towards the tunnel, accompanied by his starcat, as Cerren jogged towards the remaining tiering. He clambered up it and crouched at its rim, surveying as much of Watchtower as possible. The Starlyne sacrifice had made a dent in the Garsal advance, but he could see that it hadn't stopped it, just slowed it down long enough for the human combatants to escape. The grim tale was spread out before his eyes. The Garsal assault vehicles were strong — strong and fast. And there were too many of them. They were hard to stop and once too many of them congregated in one spot, virtually unstoppable.

He'd learned from this confrontation, but he was sure that the Garsal had too. On the ground, the Garsal troops were outmatched by their human counterparts; almost easily outmatched if his experience was anything to go by, but within their vehicles they were safe and superior. A flagged signal went up on the final line of retreat. He heard panting behind him, and Griss appeared.

"Master Cerren, you *must* come inside. We can't lose you!" As if to punctuate the young man's words, another aircraft screamed overhead, and burned its way towards a line of scurrying humans. Belatedly, Cerren realised that it was likely to be his Scout Patrols, and watched helplessly as they scattered, human and feline figures alike.

Falling pieces of masonry plummeted onto several figures, and they lay still and unmoving. Others darted out of concealment as the aircraft passed, and paused briefly by each form. Two were left where they lay, but one was picked up by two others and carried at a staggering run towards the arena. Cerren's heart was in his mouth as two of the climbers began to move towards the scurrying figures. Griss tugged at Cerren's arm again. "Master Cerren! Please! Move!" He shook the man's hand off.

"Not yet!"

"Cerren! They're coming!" Griss turned Cerren forcibly to the left, and then tugged frantically again. Another three climbers were clambering their way towards the arena building, working their way up and over the battered remains of Scout HQ. Cerren looked quickly in both directions, and then began to leap down the tiers towards the arena floor. He flicked a hand signal to Socks, and she shot off, blurring into top speed. Cerren leaped down the last level, landing lightly on the sandy ground of the arena.

"I'll meet you in the command centre, Griss!" The young man dropped onto the sand beside him and ran off, his young starcat by his side. Once he was satisfied that Griss would be safe, Cerren ran for the arena entrance, intent on the Patrol he'd seen from above. Socks would already be there. He'd felt the starcat's relief as she'd blurred into action. Paired with her fierce joy at her part in the death of the invader, it was an exhilarating mix of adrenaline and pent up energy finally released. As he passed the arena entrance, he faded himself and ran down the road.

The earth shook as the climbers crunched into view. Beams of deadly light scored deep marks into the buildings on either side of the road and more masonry fell. Ahead, he could see the first figures run into view. "Fade if you can!" He called, thundering the words out as loudly as possible. Several of the figures wavered into hazy approximations but the others remained visible to his eyes. One fell to a scorching beam as the others pumped their arms and ran, zigzagging unpredictably down the road, veering from side to side and leaping debris. Several of the climbers launched projectiles that scythed down the open roadway. "Drop!" Screamed Cerren, as he did, hoping that Socks was safe.

He could hear snarling and hissing even above the clanking monstrosities that stalked his Scouts. There was a flash of blue from one of the piles of rubble ahead. His eyes followed it and watched it leap from the elevated position to cling to the base of the climber beneath its body, resolving into a snarling grey starcat. A paw probed at the metal monster, and the belly hatch opened. The cat vanished inside the machine and then the climber ground to a halt, its turret spinning. It stumbled and rocked, and then the belly hatch opened and there was a flicker of blue faintly visible before the machine spun sideways and lurched into the side of a building. Glass and mortar sprayed over the roadway and then the faint blue flicker was on the ground. "Socks?" It vanished, and Cerren realised that the first running Scouts were nearby. He urged them on with his voice, still scanning for his starcat. Nothing.

They ran past, and then he could see the other two, burdened with their fallen comrade. He ran towards them as another of the monstrosities staggered. He glanced upwards to see that same blue flicker and then it, too, was lurching and swaying, burning wildly at the other side of the road with its weapons. By chance, it struck one of the oncoming climbers a glancing blow on the forelimb, and it stumbled, toppling forwards and burying its turret into the ground.

Cerren lunged forwards as one of the burdened Scouts staggered, and slid his shoulder under the injured man's arm. "I'll take him. Run!" The Scout nodded through a mask of blood and grime and jogged forwards, his starcat ranging ahead. Behind them, Cerren could hear the sounds of crunching steps, and he knew that more of the climbers were coming. The arena gate came into sight, and he and the Scout on the other side dragged the injured man between them towards it. The smell of burning escalated as one of the red beams swept past his right side, and Cerren threw them deliberately left. "Faster!" he grunted, although he was already moving as fast as he could. The beam swept back towards them, and he jerked them right, then left again, and then straight ahead.

The wounded Scout murmured something, but Cerren ignored it, focusing on the sounds behind and the beckoning access ahead. The sandy floor of the arena dragged at his feet. "Socks!" And then his starcat circled them once, showing herself briefly, before dropping behind again, and Cerren knew that she would be sudden death to any Garsal pursuing on foot. "Socks, follow!" It was something he'd practiced with her. And he knew that she would cut the timing fine, but be on his heels as they went through the doorway.

More dragging sand. He stumbled on a section slagged to glass by the Garsal's beam, feeling the heat strike up through his boots, and then the doorway was there and they were through. He dropped the injured Scout to the floor and turned to see his starcat slip through the closing door. Reinforced by Starlyne craftmanship, it closed with a heavy thud.

"Cerren, move!" It was Griss again. "We need to get deeper. Come on!" Mindlessly he looked to see where the injured Scout and his companion were, and saw them already vanishing down the tunnel. One on a litter, and the other limping behind. Gasping, with sweat stinging his eyes, he gave in to Griss' urging and he and Socks followed the figures through the next reinforced doorway. It too slammed behind them.

"Fire the charges now!" Shari's voice cut through the air like a knife, and there was a dull rumble, and Cerren knew that the access point was now buried deeply behind a layer of structured damage. Griss urged him deeper into the tunnels and he followed, slowly wiping the sweat from his face.

"Cerren." There was another hesitant tug at his arm, and he turned, irritated, intending to speak sharply to Griss, but it was Erilla, her soot streaked face solemn.

"Erilla! You're all right!"

"*I* am." She pulled at his arm again, and steered him towards the litter. There, lying on it, was Peron, face pale, cradling the still form of Thunder lying across him on the stretcher. Peron was breathing with difficulty, his giant frame shrunk with pain, and Cerren felt as if he'd been struck heavily in the gut.

"Peron!" The man's eyes flickered slightly, and they both opened. One pupil was pinpoint in the light, but the other eye stared blackly blown. Peron muttered something, and Cerren leaned closer to his friend, straining his ears to hear what he was saying. "Peron my friend ..." Cerren's eyes burned hotly, and his throat was suddenly too tight for clear speech. He fumbled for his friend's hand where it laid limply across Thunder's body. The young cat was clearly dead, but Peron's other arm was wrapped around it with all the force that was left in his broken body. He mumbled again, and Cerren leaned closer, trying to pick the words slurring from his friend's mouth.

"Saved us … Thunder did … And now the monsters have killed him …."

Cerren placed his other hand on the young starcat's lifeless form with respect. The still warm fur had concealed the huge gash in his flank as they'd run. "That he did, Peron," said Erilla. "He warned us so that we had time to leave before we were overrun." Peron's head stirred restlessly, and Cerren looked around wildly for a Starlyne medic. Surely the creatures could do something for his friend. Erilla placed a hand on his.

"The Starlyne came, but there is nothing for them to do here." Her green eyes were bright, glistening with wetness as she met Cerren's eyes, and he turned back to Peron. Peron's good eye searched for and held Cerren's as he laboured to draw each breath.

"Keep to the plan, Cerren. Preserve … our … people." His eyes held Cerren's and Cerren nodded, unable to speak, suddenly feeling every single one of his years. "Keep … faith. Listen … Erilla." And then suddenly, with one last smile, the last breath sighed from Peron's lips, his form shook slightly, and then, just like that, he was gone.

Cerren rested his head on the body of his friend, felt Socks slide her head gently under his free hand, and allowed the tears to fall freely, just for a moment – then raising his tear streaked face to Erilla's he gave a slight nod.

"We will Peron. We will." Socks nudged him gently, and he looked around. Dust sifted down as a faint concussion vibrated the rocky tunnel, and then he took a shaky breath. "And so our misery truly begins. We have work to do." Erilla nodded slowly, brushed one hand through Peron's hair, rested another gently on Thunder, and squared her shoulders.

"We do."

# Chapter 30

SHANNA led the way down ramp after ramp. Despite the silencing of the alarm klaxon, the ship was still a hive of activity. Troops of Garsal soldiers were searching each level methodically. Doors hissed open at unexpected moments, and there was the constant echo of hurrying footsteps. Both Storm and Twister ranged ahead of the group as they descended, while Allad and Verren took the rear, sheltering Zandany and Taya who still needed to keep in contact with their cats to remain reliably faded. In the back of Shanna's mind, a small worry gnawed away. They would need everyone's skills in order to exit the ship and wreak as much havoc as possible. Unfortunately her friends were most likely fatiguing, just as she did when she was forced to use a more difficult skill for extended periods.

She dropped a hand to her thigh pocket and counted her patches again. There should be enough left, and she had more in her pack — if she ever saw it again. She stopped that line of thought by counting the levels mentally again. There should be just one ramp left now, so she halted, slowing her steps so that the others would have some warning. At least for this moment, there were no Garsal evident on the upward or downward ramps.

"We're there," she whispered.

"Taya, ready?" Ragar asked. "Security stuff down first, then the cell doors."

"Yes, ready."

"Shan — you'll hold the door."

"Yes."

There was silence, and then Ragar spoke again. "We'll try for the names we have first, and then we'll take as many as we can. Tell us when you think your bubble's too big."

"Allad, Zan, Verren, Amma — you'll take down any guards."

"Yes." Allad hesitated slightly, "Ragar, we can't take them all. Even if we get them out, we won't be able to keep them safe Below. You'll have to make some hard choices."

There was an uneasy silence, and then Ragar went on, his voice rough.

"I know Allad. The ones we have names for first, and then we'll take as many as we can keep safe." He cleared his throat. "I'll begin with the first open cells. Tay, if you can, find the door locks and lock them. Except this one. We'll need it to exit. When we break out, Allad is rear guard, Verren, you're behind Zan and me, with Taya and Amma on the sides. Shan, you're in the middle. We can't lose you. There's to be no hesitation, no guilt, no slowness, just straight through everything, no matter what. And if we can, we link." There was a flicker of faint tidemarks despite the faded state of the starcats, and Shanna could feel Storm and Twister's determination. "Ready?" asked Ragar. "Let's do it."

Shanna listened carefully at the doorway. All seemed quiet, so she hesitantly touched the pad beside it and it slid open. As before, the soft sounds of sadness misted outwards in a miasma of pain. Shanna glided through the door, automatically ghosting to one side, leaving Storm outside, while Twister paced by her side. Her senses extended automatically, and she felt her fellows glide through the opening. As the group split up, each moving to their designated tasks, Shanna surveyed the slave hold, looking, *really* looking.

She could see three Garsal inside the area, but there seemed to be no more. Hopefully the alarm had diverted them to other tasks. She 'felt' Allad and Taya move towards the Garsal stationed in the centre of the room, seated among a nest of lighted screens, while Verren and Zandany separated to either end of the hold. She could 'feel' their cats as well, stalking silently on deadly paws towards their prey. It was war, and she hardened her mind to the acts they were about to perpetrate, and concentrated rather on the higher task – the freedom of at least some of the slaves, so long incarcerated. She felt a wash of comfort from her cats as she tried to ignore the fact that they'd be leaving some behind.

She *felt* the moment that the three Garsal died. Felt it in her bones and her mind, but closed it off behind a barrier formed of the slaves' pain and her anguish at her brother's loss, and then readied herself. She found herself reaching out towards Taya as the girl closed her eyes and concentrated, briefly linking with her with an ease she'd not managed before. She 'felt' the moment that Taya disabled the seeing eyes and hearing ears scattered all over the slave hold, 'felt' the moment that she overrode the locking system and opened the cage doors. And then Shanna was running forwards, dropping her own fade and slapping one of her own patches onto Taya's arm. She blurred into view as she fell, and Shanna barely reached her in time to catch her.

"Tay!" She shook her friend's arm, and the dark haired girl blinked several times, and then straightened her legs.

"Give me a moment," she panted. The colour began to return to her face, and Shanna looked into her eyes, troubled. "It was the fade – that and so many things to stop at once." Shanna nodded slowly, but leaned back slightly reassured as Taya straightened, and Spinner rubbed past her leg.

"Wait here and rest, Tay." Taya nodded back, and leaned back against the metal of the workstation, and ran a hand across her face. A wave of panicked sound brushed her ears and Shanna turned hurriedly back to the door. She hadn't thought to consider what might happen if the Garsal all suddenly collapsed, and a pile of human beings appeared out of nowhere. Not to mention the starcats.

"Listen!" called Allad, his voice booming so loudly that Shanna started. She hoped that the Garsal couldn't hear it through the walls or the locked doors. "Listen!" he called again as a babble of sound rose again. The sound lowered slightly. "We're here to get some of you out." The sound ceased so abruptly it was as if someone had thrown a blanket over it, and Shanna felt that she could have heard a leaf fall to the ground.

"How?" asked a voice scornfully. "And where would we go?" There was a murmur of agreement, and a slow rising of voices again.

"Did you see us come in?" asked Allad. The silence was suddenly thick. "We can keep you hidden, and we can take you off this ship to safety. I have names – Tarren, Prodan, Alli, Sorn."

"Kaidan!" said another voice. "He said there were others." The babble of sound rose again, and with a thrill of hope, Shanna heard her brother's name resounding from the walls.

"What do you know of Kaidan?" she couldn't help shouting the words into the noise.

"He said there were humans here. Free humans," said one voice.

"He said they were fighting the Garsal," said another.

"And he's gone," said a third, "gone to the Matriarch. And none of her slaves ever come back. And why only some of us? And how do you know our names?" The third voice was almost mocking, and Shanna felt her heart lurch, and her hopes plummet. Zandany took the steps up to the second level at a run, Punch by his side, as Allad and Verren began to pull the cage doors open on the ground level.

"Semba gave us your names. She believes you may have information that will help us defeat the Garsal. Come with us," said Ragar.

"Help?" said the third voice, full of scorn. "How do you think we all ended up here? Some of us have already fought, and look where that got us! Life as a slave!" It was a male voice, angry, yet frightened at the same time.

By Shanna's side, Storm's tidemarks flickered in concerned patterns. None of the slaves had responded to the list of names, and so far none had moved from their cells. The scornful voice sounded again.

"I am Sorn. And what about these?" An older man, beaten and worn, bearded face scruffy and marked with old scars moved from his ground level cell. He pointed to his vivid orange tracking bracelets. "There can never be any chance of freedom while I'm wearing these."

"We know," Allad said. He stepped forwards, towering over the man, who shrank back, suddenly afraid. Allad shook his head. "Let me show you. It won't hurt." He pulled a vial from his pocket and removed the cap. "Give me your leg." It took him only seconds to coat the skin around the bracelet, and then another few with a second vial to burn through the bracelet. He tossed it aside, and then held out his hand for the man's other leg. The bearded man shrank back.

"No! They'll kill me, or torture me slowly as an example now that it's off. Leave it on!"

"Not if you're with *us*, they won't." Shanna hoped fervently that the statement would prove true. So very few of the prisoners had emerged from their cells. She could hear Verren, Zandany and Amma, all urging them to take that first step, and Ragar was calling the other three names repeatedly, but so many of them were dreadfully cowed. She cleared her throat.

"I'm Kaidan's sister." There was sudden silence.

***

Zoash left the Matriarch's presence with no warning, at a run. She looked up, startled, as she was jerked from her reverie. The Overlord's hatching sib's presence had been an irritant, but she was concerned at what might have taken him away with no explanation.

"Matriarch, the slave hold has gone offline!"

"Have you dropped the inner fence yet?"

"Almost, but the Overlord will be alert and ready for anything as soon as he's informed."

"Then do it now. Wait the designated time, and then put it up again. We are committed." she was tired, so very tired, and she could hear the concern in her Senior's voice.

"Are you absolutely certain, Matriarch?"

"Yes, Laretai. We must give Kaidan his chance, and this might be our only moment." She watched as Laretai turned slowly back to her tablet, saw her swipe the tablet with her manipulator arms, once, twice, and then turn back towards her.

"It is done. It will reset after the agreed time."

***

The Overlord froze as the command tech's voice rang out. "The slave hold is offline, Overlord!"

"How?"

"Everything just went down, Overlord, no warning, no hint, just gone. All the cameras, all the listening bugs – and the doors have locked down."

"Get the sentries on the com."

"No answer, Overlord. And no signal." The Overlord began to pace furiously.

"Where is the nearest contingent of troopers?" The tech bent over his screen flickering his manipulator arms rapidly.

"Three sections up, Overlord."

"Send them there immediately. And get me Zoash!"

"On his way, Overlord."

What now? he wondered. Is it the humans again? And if so, what are they up to this time?

"I need a schematic of the slave hold."

"Yes Overlord."

"Are all the controls gone? All the links to the security system?"

"It's as if they were never there, Overlord. We are completely blind." The screen in front of the Overlord blinked once and he leaned forwards to study the image. The schematic showed what he didn't want to see. A secure, almost impregnable fortress within his ship, carefully planned as such so that no slave could break out once it was locked down. No-one had considered that *they* might need to break *in*.

Zoash clattered into the command centre. "The slave hold Overlord!"

"Yes, the slave hold, Zoash." The Overlord looked carefully at the image again, allowing his eyes to search it section by section. "This." He tapped the screen. "There's a manual override. Send a section to set it off, and then I will join you once we break in." He leaned back again, once again supremely confident. "We have them now. As many specimens as our scientists could wish for. Take them alive. All of them — and their felines. Once we discover their secrets, we will have our edge. Things work to my plan once again." The Overlord watched as his hatching sib left the command centre. A disaster had been narrowly averted, and with one successful move, he would be firmly in control and in possession of the potential to extend his rule. A rule that would extend not only over this planet, but also across this portion of the galaxy. And then once the communications system was fixed ....

***

It was taking too long, Shanna thought. Even identifying herself as Kaidan's sister hadn't moved many, and they had still only identified two of the slaves they needed. They were too cowed by their captivity, and once convinced to creep out of their cells, there was another delay as each set of bracelets had to be removed. Surely the Garsal knew they were here by now. Surely they'd be at her doorway any moment.

The group standing with her was pitifully small and, despite having taken that first step of deciding to leave, hopelessly scared. Already she'd twice demonstrated her ability to conceal them, partly to explore just how much she could extend her bubble, and partly to reassure the anxious slaves. At the rate they were joining her, she'd only have to conceal a group twice as big as their own numbers, which so far, wasn't too much of a stretch at all. She'd changed her energy patch in preparation, and once again she extended her bubble, testing how far she could push it, and then easing it over her fellow Scouts, spread out over the hold.

"Shan, you're making them nervous when I disappear." Amma's voice floated down from the upper level where she'd joined Zandany.

"Sorry!" She hadn't thought of that. Instead, she tried to encourage Sorn, who had eventually decided to escape, to touch Storm, hoping to reduce the fear that the big cats seemed to induce in them all. He took an involuntary step backwards as Storm stepped forwards, gently twinkling his blue tide-marks. Shanna noticed that he'd put his cub-like face on, pairing it with the huge round pupils, which she'd always thought of as his 'kitten-eyes' – surely Sorn couldn't resist that! Storm reached his head out, and crouched slightly, making himself appear slightly smaller, and although Sorn screwed up his face, he reached out hesitantly.

Storm held himself absolutely still as Sorn tentatively touched the top of his head. "He's soft!"

"Yes he is, and he likes to be scratched," said Shanna.

"R-really?" Sorn stammered. He moved his hand back and forth slowly, and then leaped back as Storm purred loudly. All the starcats came suddenly alert, and Sorn froze.

"What is it? Storm? Twister?" There was a brush of violet and blue swirling in uncertain patterns across her mind, and then a sudden sense of urgency.

"Noises!" called Amma. "I can hear noises up here."

"What kind of noises?" asked Ragar. "There's nothing here."

"It's a kind of clank, and there's a hissing ..." she broke off and Shanna heard running feet. "Something's flowing out of holes in the wall!" There was a coughing sound, followed by a heavy thud, and a howl of rage, that suddenly diminished into a descending spiral, as if the starcat had suddenly wound down like a clock.

"Gas!" Zandany's shout was horrified. "It's some kind of gas!" Clouds of white began to puff from all over the slave hold, and the slaves began to shriek and wail.

"I told you!" Sorn shouted. "No-one escapes the Garsal!"

"Run!" yelled Zandany. "I've got Amma, and I'll try and get down ..." There was another thud, and Shanna felt fear rise in her throat. She looked around frantically. Gas clouds were everywhere, and everywhere people where succumbing it to its effects, toppling sideways, or crumpling to their knees. Satin blurred towards Shanna, heading for the door. The slaves with Shanna scattered in fear before the starcat.

"Send your cats!" Allad's voice rose over the sounds of chaos. For a moment, Shanna's mind groped for his meaning, and then she knew. She hand signalled her cats, hit the door button, faded, and leaped through followed by a flurry of starcats, knowing without a doubt that she was leaving her friends to succumb to the gas.

***

Already on edge, the Matriarch flinched as Laretai emitted a strangled sound. "What?" she demanded.

"The Overlord has used the manual override on the slave hold quell gas."

"Do you have any sensor information yet?"

"Not yet, Matriarch." Laretai's manipulator arms blurred as they flickered across the tablet. "Hirtoi?"

"Nothing, Senior. I will keep trying." Laretai's protege was tapping as fast as her mentor was.

"Estei?"

"Yes Matriarch?"

"Inform Lacey." She sat back, waiting, as the moments drew themselves out one by one. Nothing disturbed the silence in the room except for the tapping of two pairs of manipulator arms and the sound of hurried footsteps as Estei swept out.

Momentarily distracted, the Matriarch nodded in approval; Estei held herself with dignity and just the right touch of majesty. She lapsed back into contemplation, allowing her racing thoughts to slowly assemble themselves into neat ranks of planning. It was a matriarchal thing, that ability, taught and fostered in those whose minds were suitable. Her own consciousness was now a reflexive thing after so many years of practice.

Today had been trying, and was now about to become more so. Plans within plans cycled through her mind, gradually settling into ordered columns as if she had all the time in the world. Of course, she didn't, and her resources were already stretched, but there was always the plan, now set in unavoidable motion, underpinning all of her moves.

Finally, after the minutes had crawled past slowly for what seemed like aeons, Laretai spoke. "They're back online, Matriarch, give me a moment more. Hirtoi, make sure you have the tracking program ready." Hirtoi's arms flew rapidly, and then she spoke.

"It is poised and waiting. I have the feelers ready."

"Matriarch. The screen."

The Matriarch looked up at the screen on her desk, and an image flickered into view. "There are only the limited feeds from the mobile units as yet, but the sensors are coming back online one by one. There is audio."

The handheld feeds were jerky, but the Matriarch could see the chaos in the slave hold. "Overlord! The cell door locks are broken." A voice shouted from the monitor, and Estei, returning, hurried over to the controls and turned the feed down slightly. The screen feed split into four, and the Matriarch flicked her eyes from one to another. There were slave garbed bodies on the floor. Some appeared to be missing the orange tracker bracelets, but most were still within their open cells. All were unconscious. She counted five, no six, bodies, garbed as Kaidan had been. And with a shock, she saw two of the huge felines stretched out near two of the native humans. They were on one of the upper levels where the gas had been released. Troopers were turning the prone natives over, rolling them roughly onto their backs and dragging them to litters positioned to one side of the hold. They were tied down, and the two felines were dragged into barred cages. One of the humans stirred weakly as he was rolled onto the stretcher, and with a shock, the Matriarch recognised one of the humans from the previous intrusion. "It is the same group?"

"It appears so, Matriarch. But this time, the Overlord has them. I've intercepted a message – he's sending them to high security for analysis and then interrogation." She tapped. "On your personal tablet now."

The Matriarch studied the images on the screen. Six unconscious humans. Two female, and four male, as far as she could tell. One appeared older than the others. Two felines. That made her wonder. It wasn't what Kaidan had told them. There should have been at least four more. A small chill wandered over her carapace.

The audio screeched and the pictures wobbled, and she looked away for a moment as a small thought struck her. "The fence is back up?"

"Yes Matriarch. It went unnoticed in the confusion. It may be that at least one thing has gone as we planned today."

The Matriarch sat back in her chair, idly toying with the tablet. Streams of messages flowed across it, and she pondered them all as the plans formed and modified themselves in her mind.

# Chapter 31

SHANNA flipped her silent whistle into her mouth, hoping and praying that all of the cats would listen to her. She whistled the recall, urgently and repeatedly, and then, still faded, left the landing at a sprint. The sounds of running Garsal feet sounded ominously close as she hunted frantically for somewhere, anywhere for them all to hide. She extended her senses as she ran, trying to tally the cats she had with her. She could sense Storm, Twister, Cirrus, Satin, Spinner, and Sparks, but there was no sign of either Punch or Spider. No-one else had made it out of the hold, and now she was alone, and possibly hunted.

Shanna's eyes darted frantically ahead as she ran, hoping that the sounds of her passage would be concealed by the clatter of the arriving Garsal. There was no time to think, and when her eyes saw the ladder affixed to the far wall near the next bend, she didn't hesitate. She hit the wall at a run, leaping the first few rungs shaped smaller than she'd expected for alien feet, scrabbled for a moment, then pulled with her arms and finally gained purchase with her feet. She cast a quick look behind her, and then pushed frantically at the hatchway above her. It held fast under her assault, but then cooler reason prevailed, and she looked for a button to press. There was always a button.

Finally locating it, she pressed, and the hatchway slid sideways into the cavity. Without hesitation, she hoisted herself into the roof void, calling the cats after her, trusting to their agility to see them up the ladder.

It was crowded in the darkness of the roof space, and once the last starcat was up with her, Shanna fumbled around looking for a way to close the hatch. Finally, she located another switch directly above the other one and pressed it. The hatch slid shut, sealing them into stuffy darkness. It was warm with all the starcat bodies around her, but Shanna didn't care, because for the moment they were safe. As she gasped for breath, she tried to still her mind to some semblance of rational thought.

She pulled her glowstone from the neck of her shirt, and allowed its light to illuminate the darkness and then relaxed her fade. Around her, multihued tidemarks flickered into view, swirling with suppressed tones of anger and anguish. "It's all right, we'll get them back." She didn't really know why she was vocalising the words, but they certainly made *her* feel better. She reached out, touching each huge head briefly. Satin's tidemarks were almost incandescent. The green toned cat was simmering with barely contained rage, and given her independent bent, Shanna eyed her with some trepidation.

"Satin," she whispered. "We'll get him back." Satin's eyes narrowed, and her tidemarks flowed and flicked in agitation, and Shanna wriggled closer to her, and placed her hand on the starcat's head. Green lashed her mind, but was swiftly buffered by blue and violet, as Shanna quivered under the onslaught of Satin's emotions. "We *will* get him back. We'll get *all* of them back."

She looked around, holding her glowstone high to see where they were. They seemed to be in some kind of access area. Piping trailed away into the darkness in either direction, and cabling ran in neat rows, fastened above her head with brackets. She wondered how far the void extended. With one hand on Twister, and the other still on Satin, Shanna closed her eyes and concentrated on trying to extend her senses. She strained, attempting to fix her 'now' in relation to 'where' she'd been, wishing she could place herself as easily as Verren would have.

She suppressed a pang of loss as she thought of him. *He wasn't lost,* she told herself furiously, none of them were. They were just separated. *Separated and at the mercy of the alien invaders, helpless and captured, while she was alone,* her mind said, and then the rational part spoke up. *And are you actually alone? Sitting here surrounded by six starcats? Are you really helpless? Really?* That part of her made her sit up, take a deep breath, and think, really think, about her situation. Yes, she was the only free Scout inside the ship, but she was accompanied by six starcats. Six masters of concealment. Six strong, capable, cunning, and deadly predators, who were currently seething with a mixture of rage and loss.

And outside the ship were the rest of the Scouts, and nearby were more, along with several Starlynes. She wasn't really alone. Just the only free human inside the ship – a human surrounded by allies. There was a multihued wash of amusement across her mind that momentarily obscured the rage. She lowered the glowstone and looked at them. They were still angry – she could see that in the speed of their tidemark flickers, the raised fur on the backs of their necks and the claws that kept sliding in and out of their sheaths. But their anger was now contained and purposeful. Satin hummed. It was a low, threatening hum, but Shanna knew that the threat was not directed at her but the Garsal.

"So," she whispered, "Are you ready?" There was a soft basso chorus of hums and complicated tidemark pattern shifts, and then six pairs of eyes looked at her. "I take it that's a yes?" She shifted slightly. "Well, first things first then. Let's find the others, and then figure out what to do." She extended her senses again, this time, augmented not by two, but by six starcats, thought for a moment, and then made a decision. "We'll stay up here for a bit, going this way," she pointed, "because if there was one hatch, there's likely to be more. We'll see." Crouching, she began to move carefully within the space, back towards where she'd last seen her friends.

***

The Overlord watched the camera feed dispassionately. The two captured felines stared malevolently from their cages in the secure room. One of the troopers had been careless as he'd manhandled the cages into place, assuming that the felines would remain unconscious for longer than they had. They were cunning. The red marked beast had moved with an uncanny speed, to embed its claws in the trooper's arm, and had then casually torn it from him. He was now in the infirmary. The beast's deep purple eyes stared up at the camera as if it knew he was watching it. The stare was unblinking.

He turned his attention to the other one. Blue toned instead of red, it had sat itself up and joined its fellow staring directly at the camera lens. Their combined glares unsettled him.

"Zoash, the prisoners." The feed switched immediately. Six human forms were scattered behind the bars of the holding cell. He'd deliberately left them together. All had now begun to stir, and one appeared to be sitting up. "Audio on." He watched as the headache struck, enjoying their pain in a perverse way. It would make them easier to subdue, which he would, just as he'd subdued the boy, and so many before him.

"Overlord, when will you interrogate them?"

"Soon, Zoash, soon. They need to realise just how helpless they are first."

"Will you isolate them?"

"I think not. Humans are weak. They hate the idea of one of their fellows in pain, or in danger of injury. These ones will talk faster if we make some examples, I think." He watched and listened as one of them wriggled in her restraints, manoeuvring herself around to check on her companions. Perhaps he'd start with her. Or maybe the largest male. It was always one of his favourite moments with a group of prisoners – choosing to hurt the one that broke the others. Perhaps he'd toy with them one by one, watching to see whose pain elicited the greatest responses.

"Another hour, Zoash. Alert the interrogation staff, and inform the Matriarch that the emergency is now over. Send me the reports from Hoth – and the images. I think they might prove useful."

***

"Matriarch, the Overlord sends word that the humans have been captured and that the emergency is over," said Hirtoi. She turned her face towards the Matriarch. Her expression was proper, but the Matriarch could see the question in her eyes.

"So he says," she replied. "Laretai, Hirtoi, I would watch the prisoners." The young female bent immediately to her task, while Laretai paused and turned back to her.

"You think otherwise?"

"Pull the images from the communications room assault, Laretai."

The images flickered into view side by side. There they were – humans and felines together – *starcats* she corrected herself, barely concealing a shudder at the trickle of fear that ran through her. She counted the visible forms and matched them with the human numbers. "The felines outnumber the humans by one, do they not?"

"Yes, Matriarch."

"And these are the same humans? You have matched faces?"

"They are certainly *some* of the same ones. This one," a highlight illuminated several figures "this one," a female, "and these." Two males, one a towering older male with the facial hair which had always disturbed the Matriarch. It seemed so odd. "The injured one was the deceased one. Not then, but later," she hastened to add. "And there were others outside as well – that seems obvious in retrospect." The Matriarch turned her attention to the other screen.

"The young one – she isn't with the captives?"

"No, Matriarch. The Overlord believes he has all of them."

"So, three of these have already been within our ship. And in your opinion, it is likely that these two may well have been close by?"

"Yes Matriarch, perhaps one of these 'Patrols' that Kaidan has spoken of?"

"Lacey?" The old woman stepped out of her role as slave and back into her role of co-conspirator.

"Give me a moment." She bent forwards and watched the screen intently, listening with her whole body. "There is something ..." She broke off and stood, hands on her hips, frowning. "They are able to vanish at will, yet so far, none have. Of course, restrained as they are, there is no point. No point at all." Her brow furrowed in thought as she watched and listened again. "I would say that they are planning. The words they speak are limited. Some are names, but not all. And there are too many names for the number of humans. Your summation is correct Matriarch. The Overlord may think he has them all. I do not. Perhaps he has all of the humans, but he certainly doesn't have all the felines." She turned her head towards the Matriarch. "They are not cowed or overly fearful. Much like our young friend. Their resources are not yet expended, so we must wait, and watch, and intervene only if we absolutely must."

"Are you certain?" asked the Matriarch.

Lacey snorted. "There are no images to back my words, just supposition, but from what we know of these people, I am certain that there is more to them than what we see. Trust me on this. I know my own kind well, and we have worked for too long and way too hard to come to this point to throw it all away."

***

A hot sweaty crawl later, and Shanna and the six starcats had come to what seemed like a dead end. She held her glowstone up again, sipping absently from her water bottle and looking for a way out. Her direction sense suggested that she was close to the slave hold. A blank, featureless wall stood in their way. She panned the glowstone around as she wiped the sticky sweat and an errant piece of hair out of her eyes with a grime covered hand. "We passed hatches at intervals on the way here, so it seems logical that there's another one here somewhere."

Six starcat faces watched as she swung the stone on its chain as she swivelled around, looking. After a fruitless search, they began to retrace their steps, Shanna swinging the glowstone from side to side, searching for a hatchway. Finally, a square shape came into view, cut into the floor of the duct, and she paused next to it. "Ready to fade?" She slid her whistle into her mouth, located the push button, tucked the glowstone away under her shirt, and faded herself. Six glowing sets of tidemarks slowly followed suit. She took a moment to compose herself and locate all of the cats by 'feel,' and then with one ear pressed against the floor, depressed the button.

The hatch opened, and the light streaming into the void nearly blinded her. She felt a whisper of air as a starcat dropped silently through the hatch, and then, squinting, she lowered her head down and peered out. Nothing. They appeared to be somewhere back in the ramp-well. She sent two more cats down after Storm, and then dropped through the hatch and paused on the ladder rungs. The other three leaped through, and pressing the button, she closed the hatch before descending.

Joining the starcats, she thought for a moment, 'felt' where she was, and then signalled the search and find sequence with her whistle. Placing a hand on Twister, she sent Storm and Satin ahead, requested Spinner and Cirrus to take the rear, and had Sparks range from flank to flank.

Without words, she and the cats were linked, linked in purpose and the intensity of their desire to find the missing pieces of themselves. As they ghosted forwards, Shanna knew the instant that Satin picked up Allad's scent. It was time to leave the ramp-well and follow the Garsal through the ship. She checked her patch and took a sip from her water bottle, swishing the water around in her suddenly dry mouth. Then she and her cats slid through the doorway and into the main part of the ship.

***

"Matriarch, he has begun." Lacey's voice held a tiny quiver, and the Matriarch turned her attention to the screen.

It would be difficult to watch, but she would do so. She would do it so that she knew what the cost would be. What the cost had already been for so many.

She shuddered as the interrogator flicked the lash at the first of the human captives. She forced herself to watch as the girl's legs quivered, but held firm in the face of the pain, and watched as the Overlord began to pace again, click, click, click. It was his preferred method. Build the anticipation to an unbearable level, heighten the captive's fear to a level impossible to resist and then inflict pain in an unpredictable, spiralling pattern. She held her manipulator arms to absolute stillness, lest her own distress increase Lacey's even more. The plan now depended on the unknown – the probability that the Overlord was wrong about the numbers of humans and felines, and upon Kaidan.

***

Carefully concealed behind a convenient tree near the fence line Kaidan settled in to wait. He had been scratching behind Dipper's ears when the starcat had come alert, nose sniffing and ears twitching, tail held straight out behind him, his coat flickering in a myriad of complex tidemarks.

Kaidan had held himself immobile as Dipper had flickered his tidemarks. The starcat had made no immediate move to run, or hide, or fade. But then he'd hummed quietly, and nudged Kaidan. He faded slowly – very slowly – and pressed himself against the boy's leg. Then hummed again impatiently.

Finally, realising what the starcat wanted he faded, and placing a hand on Dipper's neck followed where the starcat led. They moved from cover to cover, skirting the pockets of Garsal activity, and finally, as the morning had become early afternoon, stumbled to a halt far from the fence line.

"What are you doing, Dipper?" Kaidan whispered. "Laretai's going to drop the fence and we won't be there!" He was trembling with the strain of holding the fade, and scared of missing his chance to leave the compound. The healed scars on his back twinged with remembered pain.

The cat ignored him and led him a few steps further into a concealed niche, and then hummed again as he allowed himself to become slowly visible. There was another hum, and then another human and starcat pair flickered into view.

"Dipper?" The whispered exclamation came from Barron, Hunter by his side.

Kaidan gaped, lost his fade and blurted out. "Barron?"

"*Kaidan?*" Barron's voice was incredulous. "What are *you* doing out here? And with Dipper?"

***

"Report from Hillview, Master Cerren." Griss's tone was urgent, and Cerren roused himself. The grief of Peron's loss was raw, and he'd found his mind focusing on it too often. Socks hummed and rested her warmth against his leg. She wasn't unscathed herself. Scorched whiskers showed just how close she'd come to the Garsal beams. But her example had set off a series of chain reactions within Cerren's mind, and his tacticians were working on some revised plans.

"Tell me." He braced himself.

"They were attacked, but managed to defeat the climbers and foot troops. However, they feel that their position has been compromised. Somehow, the Garsal knew they were there, despite the camouflage. They will move out as soon as the wounded are stabilised." Cerren nodded slowly, jotted a notation on the paper in front of him.

"How many casualties?" He carefully avoided the word 'dead.' Casualties allowed him to distance himself slightly and keep him functioning. Griss turned his face slightly, looking at the wall behind Cerren, rather than at Cerren himself, and swallowed, making his Adam's apple bob.

"There are eight wounded, three seriously, and ten …" he cleared his throat, "um, deceased." It was as if he forced the word out. Poor Griss had had to deliver too many reports that ended the same way, and he looked tired and pale in the dim lighting.

"Who?"

"The seriously wounded include Anjo and Josen, and the other is a young militia woman, less seriously includes Janna and Adlan and young Jareth. The others are militia, but all will recover." He cleared his throat again. "The dead include Drest," Cerren closed his eyes. That news he'd have to break personally, "the militia commander, and one whole squad. I have the names here." Griss bent and placed a piece of paper in front of him. The young man had taken to personally naming the dead that Cerren knew, breaking the news in a human voice, rather than listing them on a sheet of paper. Cerren knew it was his own way of trying to soften the blow. It was very hard on him, but Cerren appreciated it, despite the pain it brought them both.

"And starcats?"

"Most are fine. We lost one and several are badly injured, but all of the youngsters and breeding females are safe."

"Thank you Griss. Go and rest and eat. We're going to be busy tomorrow."

He turned to the paper and began to add the names to the master list. When he had finished he stood slowly. He had an old Scout to speak to, to break the news of her granddaughter's death in person. He glanced at the list and memorised the notation next to her name and then trod heavily off to do his duty, Socks as ever, by his side.

# Chapter 32

THERE was a sense of urgency driving Shanna and the six starcats now, driving them faster and faster through the ship. It was a hive of activity, and although the starcats evaded the hurrying aliens with ease, Shanna had to work harder and harder to stay concealed and silent. It would have been much easier outside in the dangers of Below. She peeped a 'slowly' command at the cats, but Satin's green tones screamed across her mind in sudden crescendos of pain so strong that Shanna nearly exclaimed out loud.

*What?* her mind exclaimed. What was driving Satin to such urgency? Her imagination supplied the answer faster than she could suppress it, and she spurred herself to greater efforts. Her mind thought furiously. Would the two missing starcats be with their human partners, or kept separately? If the Garsal had any sense at all they'd be keeping Punch and Spider sedated, or caged, and nowhere near their humans. She looked around the hallway they were moving down, and with no Garsal close by, signalled the recall. She could 'feel' Satin's reluctance, but she insisted, and then all of the starcats were grouped around her.

Crouching, she whispered. "Punch and Spider. Now." Satin's green tones simmered, just brushing the tips of Shanna's thoughts, but the cool blueness of Storm restrained her, and Shanna marvelled at the depth of the newfound communication. A small part of her mind wondered if starcats had always communicated amongst themselves in that fashion. There were no words, but the colours and emotions told her everything she needed to know. There was a slight hesitation from Allad's cat and then she acquiesced, and they were off again. The urgency was still there, but Shanna knew that the starcat was too clever not to understand that eight cats were an even greater threat than six. And then she wondered how she knew. She put it away for later.

Several moments later, Storm and Satin slowed. Three Garsal guards were spaced along a row of doorways. None were shut, and faintly, Shanna could hear the rumble of a starcat snarl coming from somewhere beyond the first couple. She hesitated briefly, and then acted. Pulling her knife, she sent two starcats towards each Garsal guard. Silent and deadly, and at last able to act on their rage, the troopers never stood a chance against their ferocious assailants. A few seconds later, three unmoving forms lay on the floor. Shanna looked around, and then peered through the first doorway. Nothing, except another long hallway, pocked with openings. The snarl of the starcat suddenly escalated, and she jerked into action, moving before the rational part of her mind had had even a moment to form a coherent thought.

Darting through the far doorway, Shanna found herself face to face with an armed trooper. She ran full tilt into him, knocking him backwards, and staggering a bit herself. He stumbled with an exclamation and raised his weapon, pointing it randomly and pulling its trigger. She lunged sideways and low, swiping with her knife, as Storm and Twister leaped from either side. His weapon fired, scoring a smoking line into the ceiling, and then he was lifeless on the floor, milky fluid leaking from her knife score, and her cats' claws and teeth.

Another Garsal corpse lay crumpled in front of a barred cage where Punch and Spider hissed and snarled at the body through the bars. As Shanna caught her breath Satin slowly flickered into view in front of it. It was only one of a long line of cages containing native fauna. A long probe lay next to the alien form, still sparking and crackling blue at the tip. Shanna dropped her fade, flicked a hand signal at Satin and Sparks, and hastened forwards, stepping warily over the corpse and the probe, and trying to discern how to unfasten the cage. It had no visible fastenings that she could see, and the door seemed to slot directly into the side. "Storm!" her starcat hurried to her side, and she laid a hand on him, closed her eyes and concentrated, trying to 'see' as Taya would have. Rather than the sliced images she'd seen while helping Taya, she had a 'sensation' of a lock to one side. She placed her hand on the cage and concentrated harder – and there it was. She broke whatever it was, and then heaved the door open.

Punch leaped out with a snarl, followed by Spider. They worried at the fallen Garsal body, rage evident in every line of their sleek bodies. As Spider turned, Shanna stifled a gasp. There were scorch marks down one flank. Not deep, but painful and fresh. Looking more closely, Shanna could see where the Punch's red tidemarks had hidden several. "Punch, Spider!" She pulled a cat kit from one pocket, and hurriedly smeared antiseptic cream on their wounds while the others guarded the door, trying to convey her dismay and sympathy to them as she worked. Spider turned her head, and nosed Shanna gratefully as the final scorch mark was treated.

"Ready?" Shanna asked, heedless of the monitors she was sure were placed within the room. There was an answering chorus of hums and snarls, so she faded and then spoke again. "Let's find the others." She almost bared her own teeth.

***

"Matriarch!" Hirtoi's voice was startlingly loud. "The caged felines have been freed – by the girl in the image! And I count another six felines."

"Screen!"

The images appeared, replacing those that had kept them so painfully occupied, crystal clear in both image and sound. The green eyed girl from the communications centre raid was crouched, tending to one of the starcats. Her eyes were narrowed, and her jaw set, and there was determination in every line of her stance. She was surrounded by the huge felines. Angry felines if the Matriarch was any judge of posture. The glowing marks on their bodies shone and rippled in complex patterns, and there was a cacophony of sound echoing through the speakers.

"Does the Overlord know?"

"I have intercepted the feed, Matriarch."

"Well done, Hirtoi," said Laretai, "You have acted correctly."

"It is very well done," replied the Matriarch. "And now, we wait and watch. Prepare my retinue, and alert the seniors."

***

Kaidan ran, trying desperately to keep up with Barron. The older Scout moved faster than Kaidan had thought possible. Every now and then he stuck out a hand and casually steered Kaidan around an obstacle. Even faded, he seemed to know where Kaidan was.

Dipper paced him easily and he knew that Barron had sent Hunter ahead to alert Spiron.

"Not much farther, Kaidan," Barron said, "but this news can't wait. And once Spiron knows, we can send a starcat on with a message."

Kaidan's breath was coming in gasps. His captivity had de-conditioned him more than he'd realised, and the strain of holding the fade seemed to increase with every step. Barron caught him again as he stumbled and he staggered onwards.

***

Shanna and the cats crept closer to the heavily guarded room. Its central location, on this level of the ship, had been difficult to access, even with eight starcats around her. She wondered why the alarm hadn't sounded. Surely the Garsal monitors had revealed their actions as they'd rescued Punch and Spider? No matter. She concentrated on the matter at hand.

She sent Storm ahead, knowing that his steadiness would stand her in good stead, and then dropped her vision into his eyes. Shock slammed her mind through the images. Zandany's bloodied form was drooping from a metal post in the centre of the room. She could feel even Storm's steadiness begin to stagger. She took a deep breath and tried to convey 'be strong' and 'wait and watch' through her link with him, but it was hard, so hard. His body was quivering, and his eyes blinked rapidly, but he must have understood, because he turned his head slowly, panning around the room. Apart from the four guards at the doorway, two on either side, half-a-dozen Garsal stood around the room, holding their weapons. They were alert and on edge.

Three others stood near Zandany. One held a long, supple lash. As Storm watched, he struck with it again, and Shanna was hard put to stop her own body jerking in reflexive, shared pain. She felt Punch's red tinged tones quiver in her mind, and his anger had begun to simmer higher and higher. Thankfully Storm managed to retain his control, despite the aggravation, and continued to move around the room, silently providing Shanna with a good view. Behind a barred gate, her other friends lay. Each bore the marks of Garsal attention in restraints and bruises, bloodstained shirts and rent clothing. All watched unmoving, as one of the other Garsal barked a question, and then struck Zandany's face with his mid limb. The thud was audible even outside the room, where Shanna was crouched in the antechamber.

Guilt struck again, and for a moment, Shanna was almost overcome. *This* was what she'd left her friends to, while she stayed safe. And then reason reasserted itself. She was here now to rescue them. If she'd stayed, six starcats would have remained at large, and perhaps they'd have been able to rescue their human friends, but — and then there was a wash of violet denial across her mind from Twister. He knew what she was thinking, and he knew that in some skills, human beings were more capable than starcats. The violet disappeared, but Shanna knew what he meant — she needed to plan and then they would act.

She sent Twister to join his brother, looking around at her own position. Four guards to take down silently, even before she entered the interrogation room. Once in the room, she and eight cats had to take down another nine, without alerting the rest of the ship that something was wrong. Her eyes narrowed. There had to be a way. It was certain that there would be monitors in there, even if there hadn't been any in the cage room. She called Spinner to her side. He was familiar with Taya's abilities, and she hoped he'd be amenable to augmenting her own.

With a hand on his head, she extended her senses. It was hard work, but with the starcat's help, she was able to ascertain the locations of four monitors. He seemed to know what she wanted, and gave unstintingly of his strength, despite the undercurrent of anguish she could clearly sense running through him. She could take them out, or, she could sneak into the room with the starcats, position them, and somehow send a message to Taya. The other girl's skills far exceeded hers. But how? She dropped her vision into Twister and Storm's again. Steeling herself, she sought Twister's eyes and looked through them at her friends, trying to ignore the sounds of distress that kept disrupting her concentration.

Their hands were all restrained in bands that looked a lot like the orange tracker bracelets. She studied them through Twister's eyes, and was struck by a thought that nearly floored her. Anjo had said that they were locked by some kind of device, and hadn't both she and Taya already unlocked doors, broken sentinels and damaged monitors? Why hadn't they thought about the possibility earlier? If she could just get close enough, and give it a try, or probably more simply, alert Taya to the possibility – her skills were much more polished than Shanna's.

She spent another few moments thinking, and then decided. She flipped her whistle into her mouth, signalled all of the cats, and slunk forwards. Once again, she could feel their anger. One by one, they slipped past the guards and into the room. She left Sparks and Cirrus guarding the entryway, and then signalled soundlessly again, positioning the other six starcats. She slunk closer to the central Garsal herself, trying to get as close to the three of them and Zandany as possible, without betraying her own position.

*****

Kaidan gasped and puffed, bent forward with his hands propped on his thighs as Barron outlined his information to Spiron. The Patrol First's face was a study of astonishment, which changed rapidly to determination as they conversed, tucked away behind a large tree, not far from the ship entrance.

"You're right Barron, this changes many things," Spiron said when Barron had finished updating him. He scribbled rapidly in his notebook, tore the page out, and tucked it into the message slot on Fury's harness. "Karri, Fury! Fast!" Fury blurred into action faster than Kaidan had ever seen a starcat move. He faded as he ran, and then there was no sign anywhere that a starcat had passed. "And now for you, Kaidan. Are you well? Your sister's inside the ship. They're trying to break the slaves out and look for you along the way. Is there any chance you can get the rest of us inside?"

Kaidan frowned. "Perhaps." He was thinking as fast as possible. "If we wait two days, then Laretai will be expecting me." But Spiron was shaking his head as Kaidan whispered the information.

"Too long. We don't have two days, Kaidan. We have to act immediately. Let's hope that the others I've called can get here in time." He looked up at Barron. "We'll need to get in somehow. Call in Perri and send a message to Arad, Nelson and Sandar. We'll need at least two of them." He deliberated for a moment. "We'll leave Arad and Nosey stationed on the retreat and take whoever else is in the vicinity. I've told Perri to join him once she's sent Spangles to the others. It'll be at least three or four hours until the reinforcements arrive." He looked around, just as Fury materialised next to him.

Kaidan wondered again just how fast a starcat could move when it wanted to, or perhaps Karri had been closer than he'd thought. There seemed to be more and more he didn't know about them, despite living with them his entire life. Then he squared his shoulders and looked at the Patrol First. "Well, if you can get me back inside," he tried to keep his voice from quivering, "and once I know where I am, I can probably take you where you need to go."

"Good. Let's move. Bring Dipper."

***

Shanna held her breath, as the lash slapped down onto Zandany once more.

"Answer!" The harsh sound of her own language coming from the alien form was like a smack in the face to Shanna. She signalled quietly to Spinner with her whistle, and then watched carefully to catch the red glint he allowed to shine momentarily, as he positioned himself near the barred front of his partner's prison. She saw Amma start briefly, and then surreptitiously sneak her bound hands towards Taya.

Satisfied that that part of her plan had succeeded, Shanna slid slightly closer to the three Garsal tormenting Zandany. She moved slowly, conscious of the shimmer that occasionally betrayed a faded starcat to an observer, and then poised herself and began to extend her senses once more. Her heart thudded loudly as she tensed the muscles in her legs, and she felt a surge of anticipation flare through all eight cats, heightening her own readiness. She sought for, and found Spinner, positioned as she'd asked, made sure she knew precisely where all of her friends and their feline companions were, and then took one last deep breath, and as she let it out allowed one word to escape her lips. "Now!"

There was a snarling, howling cacophony of sound. She concentrated hard, 'felt' the restraints on Zandany's arms and broke the locking mechanism, and then threw her bubble over them all. It was hard. She was forced to duck and weave as seven of the eight starcats threw themselves at the Garsal guards and the fight began in earnest. "Unlock the bands, Taya!" She shouted the words as loudly as possible over the noise. "Guard him, Punch!" Zandany's form was huddled on the ground. She needn't have told the starcat what to do, she realised; there was little chance that Punch would do anything else.

Then she threw herself forwards and rolled under the blast of one of Garsal weapons, leaping to her feet to slam into the tallest of the three Garsal figures that had surrounded Zandany. Behind her, she could hear the three starcats snarling and hissing as they struck at the six Garsal guards spaced around the room. Sparks and Cirrus held off the four at the entrance. She could hear a babble of sound behind her as she grappled with the smoothly carapaced figure, then a Garsal body flew past her through the air and bounced off the far wall with a crunching snap. Good, Allad was using his gift.

Shanna rolled with the Garsal, blessing the training that Peron had so painstakingly provided. Its six limbs were problematic, but at least it couldn't see her. She'd grabbed the top two, and was using her legs to manoeuvre her weight and keep the alien creature from pinning her down. She wanted to capture it, not kill it. They still had to get out of the ship. Her sweaty hands slipped on the creature's limbs, and the centre set seemed to have locked around her waist, cutting into her flesh, but she gritted her teeth and tightened her grip again. The Garsal heaved under her, and then they rolled again, and she was pinned on her back. She didn't dare let go of him, but the sweat on her hands was making her grip slippery.

She locked her legs around the creature's 'waist', feeling the odd narrowness of its body there, and twisted again, trying to throw her weight far enough to one side to loosen the mid limbs from her own waist. They bit cruelly into her flesh. She changed tactics, and rocked forwards, momentarily relaxing her arms to bring her head towards the insectoid face. She butted at it with her forehead, and then flung herself backwards, trying to crush the mid limbs with her back. Stars exploded in her brain, and she shook her head, trying not to loosen her grip, and then realised that she'd lost the fade during the struggle. She tried frantically to regain it, but the Garsal had taken full advantage of her lapse, and was now struggling against her grip in earnest and she couldn't maintain enough concentration to fade more than herself.

The background sound of snarls and impacts spurred her on, and she changed her leg position slightly, and this time she managed to roll the Garsal over again. Panting, she jerked backwards against the imprisoning mid limbs, and felt one quiver and then begin to slide. She jerked again, and pushed downwards with her right arm, forcing the creature's topmost limb to buckle. She caught a glancing blow from one of the lowermost limbs that raked its way down her previously injured leg, sending a shock of pain rocketing through it. For a moment her leg felt numb, unable to move, and then as the Garsal bucked and heaved underneath her, she forced it to move, throwing her weight forwards again to bear down on the top limb.

Sweat dripped into her eyes, and she shook her head and it splattered in drops across her foe's carapace and head. The faceted eyes were difficult to read, but Shanna thought she read disgust in them.

Smoke began to burn in her lungs as a fireball wobbled past. Whoever had generated it wasn't fully in control of their gifts. Finally, the Garsal's 'arm' was forced backwards across its own throat, and Shanna increased the pressure. It fought frantically, throwing its weight from side to side, mimicking her prior tactic, as Shanna concentrated on remaining where she was, forcing it to exhaust itself in futile thrashing while the rest of the battle raged around them. Sweat trickled into her eyes again, burning, and her vision wobbled slightly.

Finally, just as Shanna wasn't sure she could hold the Garsal still any longer, a voice sounded in her ear. "It's OK Shan, you can let go now. We've got him." It was Ragar's voice, and once she'd finally processed the words, Shanna let go and rolled tiredly off to one side, blinking to clear the sweat away. She pushed a tired hand up and rubbed her face, and then felt the dull throb of her leg settle into a steady rhythm of pain.

"Did we win?" she asked, tiredly, still panting.

"For now, said Ragar, "but the reinforcements will be here soon, I'm sure. And we've lost two of them. They escaped in the confusion. The one you caught should be useful, though." His voice was hard. "Come on, up you get." He held out a hand, and Shanna used it to pull herself up. Her leg ached, and she limped slightly as she looked around.

Garsal corpses sprawled in ungainly poses around the room. Another prisoner was restrained by Amma and Spider. The starcat was prowling around the alien, each step a threat of violence, and Shanna could see the anger on her friend's face. Verren was crouched over Zandany, who was still prone on the floor, pulling the tatters of his uniform shirt apart to look at his back. He hadn't fared particularly well himself. His face and arms bore bruises, and there was blood staining his shirt in a splotches down the front, and what looked like burn marks on his shirt sleeves. Her heart dictated that she should rush over to him, but her mind reminded her that she had her small first-aid kit in her pocket.

She took the first few limping steps, and then her stride smoothed out as the stiffness eased. Storm hurried over to her as she walked, and she could see that Twister was crouched with Sparks and Cirrus, guarding the door. The wash of cool blue across her mind was soothing as she bent and offered the kit to Verren. "Thanks, Shan, do you have … thank heavens, you do." He pulled the small tub of soothall berry cream from the kit, and began to dab it carefully onto Zandany's wounds. The slashes were deep, and Shanna heard Zandany almost sob with relief as it began to take effect.

She cast her eyes around the room. All of them were battered, some more than others, and all of the cats bore the marks of their fight in scorched fur, cuts, and anger.

"How long, Verren?" asked Ragar.

"A couple more minutes," replied Verren, "and then he'll need a bit of help."

Ragar nodded. "Allad, can you and Satin check the corridor? Taya's going to see if she can fit the restraints to these." He motioned to the two captured Garsal. "Then we'll see if we can link and move. This one's called Zoash, and it appears he's of some importance. I'm hoping he'll be our safe passage out of the ship."

# Chapter 33

RUNNING feet sounded the alarm, and Cerren jerked awake, struggling to orientate himself. Socks nosed his hand as he struggled to a sitting position on the pallet he'd collapsed onto only a few hours before. "Cerren! Urgent news!" Erilla's voice struck his eardrums like an assault, and he pushed himself tiredly to his feet, trying to straighten his clothing. He could feel the wisps of his remaining hair floating around his head as he pulled his shirt straight and tried to shove his feet into their boots at the same time. Her green eyes were flashing with urgency.

"Have the Garsal found us?" he asked, as a surge of adrenaline hit, and shoved him fully awake.

"No! We've word from Below – you won't believe it!"

"Patrol Ten? And the second years? Have they succeeded?" He felt his hopes soar.

"No, not them," she replied. "It's almost unbelievable!"

"*What's* unbelievable?" he replied, frustrated, "You haven't told me what the urgent news *is*. So, if the Garsal aren't attacking, and you haven't heard from Patrol Ten, what is it? Tell me, Erilla!" He was nearly shouting.

And then she told him, and an incredulous smile spread over his face.

***

Kaidan hovered at Spiron's elbow, watching the entrance to the ship. Something was going on. Garsal soldiers were hurrying in and out and several of the patrolling climbers had assembled near it. Faded and concealed behind a large pungo tree, he still felt vulnerable, still felt as if he couldn't possibly have volunteered to go back inside the ship. Still felt as if it might have been the stupidest thing he'd ever done.

"What's happening?" he whispered.

"No sound." The words were barely audible, but Kaidan felt as if he'd been dealt a stern reprimand. There was a faint rustle, the barely seen flicker of a blue tidemark, and then he felt a quick pressure on his shoulder and they were moving back to a more concealed spot.

Once behind a grouping of rocks, Spiron spoke. "Drop the fade." More forms than Kaidan had thought possible flickered into view. Apparently every Scout nearby had arrived inside the compound.

"Arad's dug a hole under the fence," said Farron, "and Jeris waits by another nearby. There's another ten who can't fade close by, although most of us need our cats. We can have all of us through on your signal. Fractus and Radiant are also poised to act."

"Send a message to make sure that they don't sacrifice themselves," said Spiron. "It's *imperative* that they don't. Something's going on. I'd planned to go inside, track them down and let them know, but that might be out of the question now." He paused for a moment, and Kaidan watched on as he exchanged several glances with Barron, and then nodded.

"We'll spread out, half circle around the entrance, concealed, and we'll act on whatever happens. We've already left a few surprises around the hive, so if we need a distraction, we'll provide one. Otherwise we wait, and look for an opportunity. Farron, you're prime contact with Fractus and Radiant. Make sure you keep them up to date at all times." She nodded. "Kaidan, stick with Barron. Do exactly as he says. There's no point sending you out until we're all out, and there's no-one to spare to babysit you."

For a moment, Kaidan was indignant, but then reality asserted itself. He knew how unprepared he was to deal with the perils of Below, particularly when there was no guarantee that Dipper would help. He looked down at the cat lying at his feet. For the moment it seemed that he was content to stay. Whether that would continue remained to be seen. He dropped his hand onto the soft coat, happy in the knowledge that they were both out of the ship and likely to stay so. "But Lacey, the others …"

"What will be will be, Kaidan. You've done your best, and now it's up to us and the others already inside." Spiron turned his attention to the others, nodded at Farron, and with a few hand signals, dispersed the group. They faded silently through the bush to their assigned locations.

"Come." Barron beckoned with one hand, and Kaidan steeled himself and faded, feeling the drain as he followed him to their new position, Dipper padding at his side.

Once settled in position, Kaidan found himself directly opposite the entrance. The activity around it suddenly intensified as two more climbers clanked into position and paused facing the ship.

***

Shanna felt tension in every line of her body. Once again at the front of the Patrol, but this time linked with the others, she was still visible. Visible to every Garsal they'd passed in the corridors of the ship. She felt vulnerable despite being able to 'feel' each of her friends supporting her and poised to act on the slightest provocation. In the midst of the group stumbled the two captive Garsal. One was very cowed, almost bewildered, while the other, the one she'd wrestled to a standstill, stalked along, as if seething with anger. He probably was, she reflected.

Ragar had decided, and Allad had concurred, that their very visibility was essential to their exit. If they were faded, how would the Garsal know that they still held two of them captive? Perhaps they might have managed to make their way out of the ship faded. Shanna was fairly certain that she could have held the fade over all of them while they were linked, but they were too slow, and Zandany was too injured to move fast.

Still, it didn't feel right to her. After all of the hours of sneaking and hiding, followed by the fighting, it seemed wrong to just be walking out with their mission still unaccomplished. Behind her, she could feel Allad's readiness to 'push' anything out of the way. Even now, he seemed to be looking around every corner before they arrived at it. As they moved, Taya, hand now on Spinner, was casually breaking each monitor they passed. It seemed effortless in the link. Verren's sense guided them unerringly, and even within the ship, Amma's knowledge of where the air currents were enhanced Verren's skills. Beside her Ragar and Zandany felt like glowing balls of energy, held in readiness, although in his injured state, Zandany's flame felt slightly banked. Shanna herself held her ability to fade and shield her friends from sight, poised on the brink.

With her starcats ranging ahead, snarling at the armed troopers that ducked around corners and retreated ahead of them, and the rest of them circled by the others, they made quite a stir among the alien invaders. Before they'd left the battle zone, Taya had reactivated one of the monitors, and Ragar had made their position quite clear. They would have safe exit from the ship, and then they'd release Zoash and the other captive.

Shanna didn't trust the Garsal however, and held herself poised. The unity without the fade continued to feel slightly bizarre, and she felt as if she was somehow on one side of the others, not truly one, despite all evidence to the contrary.

There was a quiet hum from Storm, and she looked at him, surprised, but the blue washed soothingly through her mind, and she relaxed a little, allowing her vision to drop into both his and Twister's eyes. So far the terms of their exit from the ship seemed to be holding.

***

The Overlord seethed. How could Zoash have allowed himself to be trapped as he had been? Now he was forced to allow the humans and their hideous felines safe passage inside the ship. He'd been tempted to ignore his hatching sib's presence, but if he allowed the public death of a sib, he'd lose the alliance of all.

Despite the machinations and scheming ambitions of his people, hatching sibs were those most trusted and most treasured, once primacy had been established, and most definitely during military operations. To sacrifice one publicly for personal gain would leave him an Overlord no more. If Zoash had died as a result of hidden machinations, free of obvious links to the Overlord, the other Garsal would have applauded in private, and his stature would have risen. But a public sacrifice for personal gain was anathema.

"Inform the Matriarch!" he snapped. "And alert Hoth on the plateau. Have him track down a group of humans. Preferably with offspring. Or without. Any will do." He watched the progress of the humans. They were battered, but they were accompanied by no less than eight of the savage felines, their teeth bared as they strolled along his corridors. No matter. His word was good only for the interior of the ship – he'd made sure that his response to the demands had been carefully worded. The climbers were positioned, and sharpshooter troops had been stationed at vantage points around the exit. He would have his revenge, and he would have his specimens, and the humans upon this planet would know once and for all who was their absolute ruler. "Come. We will await them outside, and then they will die."

***

The Matriarch drew a long breath, watching Laretai's spy taps. "It is time. Assemble all. Lacey, attend me."

"Yes Matriarch."

Her voice was resolute, reflecting none of her inner turmoil. This was the moment when the plan would come to fruition, or die. And none her sister initiates, far away on their conquered worlds would know anything of her thoughts, struggles and decisions, or even the outcomes of this moment.

"Laretai. You have done as I wished?"

"Yes Matriarch. The files are sealed and poised. As soon as the communications array is replaced and operational, they will send. Hirtoi has duplicates concealed within her own personal, high security files. They will go, whether or not we live."

"You have done well, all of you." The Matriarch cast her gaze around the chamber. "Estei, Hirtoi, you will watch and wait. If we fall, then you are our chosen successors. You have watched and learned, and you will further the plan if we cannot." She felt unaccustomed emotion fill her voice and her mind, and bowed her head briefly at the two young females. They returned her gesture solemnly, and left their heads bowed, manipulator arms spread in respect. "Laretai, Lacey, it is time."

She swept from the room, Laretai, as always, one pace behind and to one side, Lacey in the place of a servant, and the assembled seniors fell in behind her, marching in formal lockstep.

***

The Overlord stalked angrily through the exit of the ship and then turned to check the troop arrangements. Five climbers sat angled around the area, covering it with their weapons. "Where are the others?" he demanded.

"It appears that the humans have sabotaged many of our mechanicals, Overlord," replied the aide at his side. The Overlord spun, furious.

"They've what?"

"Most of the reserve climbers and crawlers are unable to be moved, Overlord," the underling cowered, and then went on, "the technicians are working on the problem, but it is unclear how they've been immobilised."

"Is this *all* that we have?" The Overlord allowed his anger at Zoash's capture to colour his voice, and the underling cringed away from him.

"The technicians are working as fast as possible, Overlord," he replied, voice quivering slightly, "but it is proving difficult. I am in constant communication with them."

The Overlord turned away from the inefficient minion, furious at the damage the humans had wrought in their time undetected inside his ship. Even now, despite all the visual evidence to the contrary, his scanners were still failing to pick them up. With an uncharacteristic tingle of fear, he wondered whether there were others still inside the ship. No, it was impossible – if there were others, they would have joined their fellows, exiting the ship under escort. But a small tinge of paranoia remained.

He stomped into position on a small rise behind the climbers. It was high enough to oversee everything, and high enough to signal to his hatching sib. Zoash would know what to do when the time came.

***

The now familiar corridor loomed ahead, leading to the exit. "Almost there, Ragar," called Shanna. She'd had to clear her throat and force the words out, unaccustomed to speaking while inside the Garsal ship while linked. Ragar had insisted on vocal communications though, for most things – vocal so that the spies would hear and believe.

"Hold firm, then," replied Ragar. "You all know what to do when the time comes."

There was a murmur of assent from the others, and Shanna took a deeper breath, looked ahead, and then checked her last patch. There would be enough left, she hoped.

He stomach did a small flip flop, and she steeled herself as they tramped closer and closer to the exit. Late afternoon light shone through the open portal, and she felt her mouth go dry as they reached it. She paused, allowed her eyes time to adjust from the dim interior of the ship, took one more breath, checked the link, 'felt' where everybody was, then readied herself to step through, into the unknown.

***

Kaidan looked down onto the Overlord's rise. The sight of the black figure terrified him and his back itched. There'd been a moment when he'd almost run, as the creature had emerged from the ship, but Dipper had leaned his warm length onto Kaidan's thigh and steadied him. "That's the Overlord, Barron," he whispered. Barron nodded, scribbled quickly, and then tucked a note into Hunter's harness and sent him off at a run.

They seemed to be waiting for something or someone. After his long, painful familiarity with the Overlord, he could see the anger in his posture, see it in the way he moved, and in the way he dismissed his underling.

"He's angry."

Barron threw a quizzical glance at him, and then nodded. Kaidan returned his attention to the scene in front of him. Two starcats ghosted from the ship's entrance, one blue toned, and the other violet. Their tidemarks rippled in familiar patterns and positions. They were followed by a familiar figure — Shanna! Close on her heels came the rest of the cadets, and Allad, and then all eight starcats began a complex circling pattern. Two black figures stumbled at the centre of the group, one beside Verren, and the other with Amma.

"It's Zoash! The Overlord's hatching sib," whispered Kaidan. "The tall one. No idea who the other one is, though." The other Garsal captive looked dazed, almost unaware of his situation.

"What's a hatching sib?" asked Barron. "Is this why there's a welcoming committee?"

Kaidan explained the little of what he knew about Garsal 'family' as Laretai had described it to him, and then Barron was scribbling furiously once again.

"You are outside, as you wished," the Overlord said, his voice carrying clearly in the windless air. "Release Zoash."

"We will release Zoash when we have our safe conduct from this place guaranteed." It was Ragar's voice, not Allad's, which surprised Kaidan. He couldn't keep his eyes off his sister. She looked as if she was coiled, ready to spring. Her eyes moved ceaselessly, taking in the placement of troops. Every now and then, Kaidan noticed that one of her cats would pause, look deliberately at a fixed point, and then re-join the others in their moving, weaving pattern. It was so brief that if he hadn't been concentrating on it he wouldn't have noticed. None of the other cats were behaving in the same way.

"I think they've planned something, Barron," whispered Kaidan. Faintly, he could hear Ragar and the Overlord, fencing delicately with their words. He ignored the sounds, and concentrated harder on his sister.

"What do you mean?" asked Barron quietly. "Who's planned something?"

"All of them," said Kaidan. "The Garsal have something planned, I'm sure. The Overlord wouldn't want to lose face in this way, but I'm talking about the others — Shanna and the others — there's something ..." He frowned. And then all hell broke loose.

***

The Overlord continued the sham of negotiation, waiting for just the right moment, drawing the humans along. He could see Zoash. The crumbling cretin of a trooper was of no account, but his hatching sib was watchful and waiting. His posture spoke volumes. He'd allowed one of his mid limbs to drop into a signal posture.

The Overlord sprayed a derisive sentence at the small grouping, and then barked one word loudly into the air. The sniper beams struck. Two of the humans took direct hits.

***

Shanna flicked her vision into its multiple modes as she exited the ship, hand signalling all of the starcats. They moved immediately into their maze-like circling pattern as they'd planned. She held her fade on the brink, poised for the moment, but concentrating on the link as well. It was hard. Very hard.

Faintly, she could hear Ragar, negotiating with the Overlord, and she wondered how he was managing to maintain his focus on the discussion while continuing to be a poised ball of flame to her senses. Twister and Storm had located a number of weapon bearing Garsal 'concealed' around the ship. They were only 'concealed' to themselves — certainly not to a starcat's superior senses. Still nervous of Frontier's vegetation, they'd used only the most rudimentary of cover. Through the link, she showed the locations to the others. She felt Taya begin to focus on the weaponry, just as Zoash broke away from Verren, and then the Garsal began to fire.

She slammed up her bubble, faster than she ever had, and leaped fully into the link. She could feel pain screaming its way into her mind. Worse, she could feel whose pain it was. Both Allad and Verren had taken hits. She heard a whine begin to escalate from one of the nearby climbers, just as the starcats leaped into action.

Several of the red beams cut off, and then she was frantically trying to make sure no-one dropped out of the link, trying desperately to make sure that Verren and Allad were still with them. Strong violet washed through her mind, and she steadied, steadied while shepherding the group concealed in her bubble. The Garsal she dismissed. Zoash and the unnamed trooper were on their own. Her one task was to protect her friends and see them safely out of this compound.

Faintly, she thought she could hear someone shouting. She pushed the thought away, 'felt' where everyone was and kept moving. Behind her, Amma supported Verren, and Taya Allad, while Zandany let loose with a flurry of rolling fire balls. His injuries were draining him quickly, but she pulled them all to a run, dodging to the left, knowing that the fireballs were like a trail leading directly to them. Ragar followed Zandany's barrage with one of his own, and Shanna frowned slightly. Somehow, Allad had nudged them away from the group with his talent despite his injuries. She kept them moving though, feeling the unity rise within her of its own volition. Shielded, her starcats' eyes extensions of her own vision, she wove instinctively among the beams of light now slashing from the climbers.

All five of them were mobile and clanking, carefully staying out of each other's lines of fire, while very obviously tracking the lines of fireballs streaming from Zandany and Ragar towards the ground troopers.

She dodged them right, feeling the pain in Verren's stumble, the ache in Allad's legs, but drove them harder, and they responded, and then Taya broke the sniping weapons with her mind. Shanna felt her exhaustion, even through the link, but she could feel the other girl now turning her attention to the machines arrayed around them.

Thick smoke billowed as the scorched earth broke and stank under the Garsal fire, slagged to molten rock just in front of them. Shanna slid to an abrupt halt, looking frantically around from inside the fade. Instead of firing directly at them, the climbers were attempting to encase them in a ring of molten rock and earth.

# Chapter 34

THE climbers burned their way mercilessly around them. Shanna's mind screamed, despite the link, almost gibbering at the thought of having come so far just to be thwarted at the last moment. Then came the calm. Two-toned colours washed across her mind, becoming one with her, for just long enough that she knew how much she was loved. Her heart rate slowed, her breathing steadied, and then she knew, and finally she knew how.

She located them all. All of her cadet group, now her friends, and Allad, friend and mentor. Their cats formed a multihued pool of calmness within them, circling, protecting, fiercely loyal. But so was she, and now, she knew why and *how*.

She melded them into one. One group with many parts. One body with hands, feet, eyes, claws, and hearts. There was a joyous harmony about it all. The burning red beams scorched the air around them but this time they had no effect. Shanna looked within herself and turned her bubble into not just a clever screen of camouflage, but a bubble of true protection. She'd wondered. Her gift had seemed the easiest one for others to learn, so she'd wondered why the Starlynes had thought that she was so unique, and now she knew. Her gift was so much more than just fading.

The first beam struck her bubble and it absorbed the energy and then grounded it in rumbling vibrations that struck through the soles of her boots. She felt the others marvel, tossed it off as unnecessary, and then flicked her mind outwards. As she'd hoped, around the Garsal compound crouched many Scouts. The rest of Patrol Ten stood like beacons in her mind, so she gathered them into the link. Even Kaidan was there, to her stunned surprise. She quickly filed that thought away with a surge of joy, and then she found the lesser lights of Patrol Four. Some of the oldsters stood with them, burning with delicate colours and patterns. Their starcats welcomed her with joy, and then, faintly, coming closer, she found the blazing beacons of Fractus and Radiant.

"So, Shanna," came Fractus' words, "What we hoped for is now realised. You have found your true skill, and your calling."

She felt herself blush, even as yet another of the Garsal beams grounded itself on her bubble. She stood straighter, keeping the link strong, joining them all together as one.

"I'm not sure about my 'true skill and calling,' Fractus, but I think I can keep us all alive. At least until I'm too exhausted to keep going."

"Look further within," came the Starlyne voice. "Look and learn, and call." His voice receded, but his beacon did not. Shanna opened her eyes, and looked around at the destruction and devastation.

The climbers still burned their way through the ground. Crossing that would be impossible for some time, and it seemed that making her bubble impervious to Garsal firepower had made it visible. A steady stream of red struck it, vibrating it almost constantly. The Overlord, perched on his hillock, was gesticulating furiously towards it, obviously exhorting his climbers to concentrate their fire. More and more troopers poured from the ship, running to encircle the small group of humans and starcats. They were completely surrounded.

Shanna paused again, 'feeling' for her companions through the link. Allad's pain was knifelike, and she knew that his leg was barely holding him, and that he was hanging on to the link by force of will alone. Satin's emerald green strengthened him just as her cats strengthened her. Verren's pain burned like fire across her back and her heart, yet he was offering more – more of himself through the link. Taya stood steady, full of determination, and fully accepting of all of them now. Her fierce determination to protect the only family she had left was clear. Zandany, ever dependable, still aching and exhausted from the Overlord's torture, stood ready, ready to support and fight for however long it would take for them to escape. His mind simply knew that they would. It buoyed her more than she believed possible. Amma, her first real friend in the Scouts, stood tall with her, not envious, not jealous, just proud and ready, her understanding laid invitingly in front of Shanna. Ragar stood firmly at the centre of them all, the link that they all respected, full of burning determination. This time, however, he had taken a step to one side, clearly drawing Shanna in to stand in his place, and now, she did.

She took the step, gathered them up all together, and then reached out once again.

On her silent cue, fireballs poured in continuous streams from Ragar and Zandany, slamming into the crawlers and gathered troopers. Despite his pain, Allad offered waves of pure force, and she took them and used them, and the encircling troopers were mowed down in their ranks.

Chaos reigned, and Shanna and her friends stood in the midst of a glowing ball of fire and destruction. The Garsal were nothing compared to the force she wielded. And then, on the edges of her mind, something tickled, and then she felt Verren convulse with horror.

She followed his mind. Sliders! Masses of sliders, drawn by the cacophony of sound, and light, and heat. The concussive shock waves must have drawn every swarm within hearing towards the Garsal compound.

She recoiled briefly, and then stopped. Not knowing how she did it, but knowing that Verren was helping, she reached out, and redirected the swarms. They obeyed, merging into one heaving, slithering, loathsome mass.

There was a momentary flicker of thought between them all, and then with one concussive heave, Taya broke every sentinel and struck every laser fence-post, and all of the climbers ground to a halt. Shanna felt Taya's part of the link weaken, and reached out to steady her.

The sliders sat on the periphery of her mind, their insatiable hunger over-whelming almost every other thought, but somehow she fought clear of them and maintained her control, drawing them ever closer. She 'felt' her fellow Scouts, concealed around the perimeter, freeze to absolute motionlessness. She saw the sudden flare of light and warmth from Nosey and Arad ward the sliders away from them and their immediate surrounds, and she marvelled at it. She felt Barron cover her brother's body with his own and fade, but she diverted the sliders easily around them all, bringing them closer and closer to the Garsal.

She saw the first sliders slither into view, 'felt' and saw the horror erupt from the insectoid invaders, and saw one Garsal overbalance and fall scream-ing into the swarm. He didn't emerge. Then she held them poised.

Maintaining the link, she strode forwards to the edge of the hot ground, drawing her friends after her, until they all stood in front of the Overlord, standing stunned on his hill. The ship entrance lay open and disregarded. She stood at the edge of her bubble and spoke.

"We are poised to destroy you all. I have but to speak the word, and none will survive." She could feel the horror of the sliders shivering through all of her friends, but she walled it out and waited. Waited to see what the Overlord would do, and what he might say that would stay her hand.

"You threaten us with reptiles?" he replied, scorn in every word. He held up one of his manipulator arms, and another squad of troopers ran from the ship, once again surrounding them completely. Her bubble lay cool and bare-ly visible over them all.

"I threaten you with sliders," said Shanna. "Sliders to invade, and con-sume, and destroy you, down to every last tiny portion, and then to breed and consume again." She almost couldn't believe the words she was saying. She was threatening the invaders with the worst nightmare of her people. She allowed images of the sliders to flow through her mind – images she'd seen as a child and a student, and now relayed through Fractus and Radiant to all the waiting minds.

She saw the Overlord stagger, heard a murmur of sound run through the Garsal ranks, and then held up one hand. "And in case you disbelieve me." She beckoned with one hand, and the slider mass moved forwards one metre, and then stopped as she motioned again. Faintly, she could feel the revulsion running through her from her friends, but she continued, hoping she wouldn't have to make the threat a reality. An underling rushed up to the Overlord, speaking rapidly in the Garsal tongue and gesturing desperately towards the ship.

"Do you need a demonstration?" Shanna asked, despite the disquiet in her own stomach.

And then she was distracted as a group of filmy robed Garsal marched out into the clearing from inside the ship. It appeared to be a formal retinue, headed by an elaborately dressed and decorated female Garsal. She strode imperiously towards the Overlord and then paused and turned towards Shanna and her friends.

"I said …"

"A demonstration will be unnecessary." The Matriarch's voice wove the human vowels oddly, but strangely musically. "We will surrender to you immediately." There was a stunned silence, and then the Overlord, now attended by his hatching sib, spoke.

"You overstep yourself, Matriarch."

"No, Overlord, you overstep. My word is law, and binding, and you will do as instructed."

"The Garsal never surrender." The Overlord's voice lashed out. "We come, we hold, we breed."

"In this case," replied the Matriarch, "We have come, and with some grace, we may hold this small corner of this world, but to breed? You will *never* breed." Her voice was flat and final, and Shanna could see that she was holding the Overlord's eyes through force of will alone. "I have spoken, in front of witnesses. You will *not* breed. There will be *no* approval given."

Shanna held the sliders with one portion of her mind, the bubble with another, and the link with a third. She listened, astounded, as the Matriarch continued.

"And we will make alliance, both with the humans, and with their Starlyne allies." The Overlord stood shocked to silence.

For a moment Shanna stood stunned. The link wobbled slightly and she hastily firmed it, drawing strength from Storm and Twister, even as a wizened human female figure stood forwards from inside the Matriarch's retinue to face Shanna.

"The Matriarch speaks truly. I am Lacey. And on behalf of the Federation Underground I have allied with the Matriarch. It is an alliance long in the making, and many have died to preserve its secret – both Garsal and Federation."

Shanna's jaw dropped. "There are free humans? Apart from us?"

"There are some. Not many. And not only humans – others from the Federation still hide from the marauders, and we have spent years negotiating this peace with the female Garsal."

Joyousness flooded into Shanna's mind. Joy and almost impossible hope. It shouted from the mind of Fractus and almost caused her to lose control of the sliders, still poised to invade. She felt him accelerate and knew that both he and Radiant were almost there in person.

Wonder and hope flowed from the minds of her friends, overlaid with smugness from eight starcats. In fact, it seemed to be more than eight now, and then Shanna realised that there were echoes ringing in her mind from impossibly far away.

"Radiant relays." The thought was fleeting, but recognisably that of Fractus. "Keeper's dream comes to fruition here, and now. Can you do it, Shanna? Can you draw us all in?"

"But how?" she was dazed and almost disbelieving.

"Look within. Dismiss the sliders, and then expand."

She looked up at the Matriarch, looked carefully at her retinue. Saw the old woman nodding. One by one she felt for her friends and felt only hope, so she looked within, drew on Verren, and then turned the sliders around and sent them scurrying, far away from the clearing. Faintly in the distance, she could hear the sounds of some of Below's predators, so she sent them in that direction despite her revulsion. Even sliders deserved to feed occasionally, and the approval of her actions flowed from her friends into her mind.

Then she closed her eyes, and looked deeper. She sought within herself for the things she needed and found them in the love of her family, the care of her friends, and the wish of a Starlyne known only briefly. Hesitantly, she drew on the memory of Keeper's passing. Drew on his wish of a future without fear, without destruction, without invasion or slavery, and drew on the image of remembered love.

She felt first Storm, and then Twister, ignite their tidemarks in a glow of celebration and join her, and then a myriad of starcats joined her link, headed by Satin's fierce emerald glow. Fractus and Radiant handed her a rope of glowing Starlynes, all joined in series, and then through them she expanded herself throughout her own people. Some joined joyously, while others were swept up, resisting. Finally, she poised herself, and reached out to Lacey standing in the Matriarch's retinue. She was old and tired, but tired with the tiredness of final fulfilment. Through her, she reached for the first time towards her enemy.

The link wobbled. Wobbled as the reality of Garsal slavery struck. Wobbled as she felt the pain of her friends. Wobbled even more as she felt the echoes of her brother's pain and the pain of thousands of slaves and then even more by the memories of the Starlyne escape. For a moment she was tempted to recall the sliders and take her vengeance for their pain. She warred within herself with the desire to wreak havoc on the Garsal, just as they had destroyed hundreds of worlds in so many places over countless years. Then, just as she was thinking on the sliders, she felt Verren's wordless communication. The sliders still had a place on Frontier. They were still part of her home. They were an integral part of the cycle of life on her world, despite the horror they generated in her own kind. And in his presence, she was reminded of their newfound love for each other.

How were the Garsal any different? Here stood the Matriarch, surrendering to her unconditionally in defiance of the Overlord. It was a puzzle that she didn't understand so she reached out and drew in the Matriarch. She was ancient. She had planned, schemed, and hoped for many years. Supported by Laretai, and a hidden group of female Garsal, known as the 'Initiates', she and many others, had laboured over their plan for countless years.

Their plan to cease the senseless conquering and enter into peace had finally coincided with the discovery of their once 'Great Enemy' and a collection of free humans, living in isolation on a unique world. Many years previously, a dying Starlyne's wish had gained traction among the invading Garsal, striking a chord with the then Matriarch. For untold generations a small group of females had nurtured it, striving to bring it to fruition. And now, finally, on a lost world, stranded with no communication, the plan was about to succeed. The Matriarch was embraced and welcomed, and her fellow Initiates followed her into the link, and Shanna marvelled at the depth and the length of hope they'd held.

Then she held her breath, and extended the link once more – holding it out towards the male Garsal. Some rushed into the fold. Some ran from it. Far away on the plateau, Shanna felt the conqueror of Watchtower crumble and join the communion, stumbling away from his command post while some of his stunned underlings rejected it. Faintly, she felt the discord that might ensue once she was done.

Finally, she gritted her teeth and sent the link towards the Overlord's mind. He snarled, and then shouted, demanding that the guns recommence firing, berating the troopers around him as they stood uncertain, and then wrestled a weapon from the unresisting arms of one of the motionless figures.

He raised it and sighted on the Matriarch. "We come, we hold, we breed!" he shouted over and over in his own language, now understood from inside the link, while she stood straight and not cowed by his ranting.

Shanna 'felt' the moment that Taya reached out and casually broke the firing mechanism. The gun overheated, and the Overlord flung it away with a shout.

"Restrain him," said the Matriarch sadly. "He is too far gone in anger to understand the gift." Shanna held the link for a few moments longer, revelling in the joy of union with so many, feeling the unspoken welcome from the Starlyne people, the astonishment from her own, and then tentative, hesitant inclusion from the Garsal. It would be a long process, but it held hope. If accommodation could be reached on one world, then perhaps there was hope for many more.

She let the link go just as her patch ran out, and she staggered, completely exhausted once again. She hoped that the moment of unity would hold in the aftermath, and that she wasn't about to leave her friends defenceless.

# Chapter 35

IT WAS Remembrance Day. Instead of sitting with her immediate family, Shanna sat to one side of the hall, below the dais, with her fellow cadets and their starcats. The months since that day at the ship when the Garsal had surrendered had proved … tumultuous. She looked around the old storm shelter. The stone walls were cracked and battered, yet they still stood in defiance of all that the Garsal had thrown at them. The stone steps bore deep burn marks and the carvings around the entrance were scored and pitted.

The building was packed with 'people.' People who were humans, Star-lynes, and a smattering of Garsal seated to one side. Shanna was still struggling with the presence of the invaders at the ceremony.

Amma nudged her. "Look over there, Shan!"

Shanna followed her pointing finger. The old woman, Lacey, was seated among the Garsal, chatting amiably to the robed figure next to her. Not far away, she could see her brother, Anjo and her parents in a row next to Laretai. Verren's hand was warm in her own, and she felt herself blush as her mother directed a raised eyebrow back at her.

Her parents were still coming to grips with her holding hands with Verren. And Kaidan was enjoying every moment of teasing he could wring out of the situation, in the most infuriating fashion.

"Kaidan said Lacey would be here, and he's going to catch up with her later."

"Sssssshhhh," said Ragar, "Payne's starting. " Shanna diverted her attention to the dais where Payne stood, and then as the lights dimmed they all rose to stand in the familiar darkness that heralded the beginning of the Re-membrance Ceremony.

"Just over three hundred years ago, our forefathers began the task of learning to survive on Frontier." There was silence for several moments, then Payne went on. "Where did they come from?"

"From the Federation of Races." The massed voices spoke in unison, Shanna and her friends with them.

"Where were they going?"

"To a new home, of hope."

"What happened to the dream?"

"It was changed by a trial of fire."

Payne lit the first candle, and the glow spread gently across the front of the hall.

"This is the Candle of Remembrance for the dead." He paused again as the crowd bowed their heads and then added a phrase. "And this year we remember not only the human dead of the past, but the dead of our Starlyne friends, and the recent dead of all races, lost in the struggle for peace." The room stirred as the yearly ritual parted from the time honoured responses. "From this day onwards we will remember and honour them all. We honour their lives and sacrifices." Feet shuffled, and then the response began, slightly raggedly, but led by Erilla's clear tones.

"We honour them."

Payne lit the second candle. "This is the Candle of Endurance. We remember the courage that all of our peoples showed, here on a world full of fear, and now we truly stand together to survive."

Payne lit the third candle. "This is the Candle of Sanctuary. This candle symbolises not only that our human forefathers completed the first town wall, but the safety that this planet afforded the Starlyne people as they founded the community they named 'Haven.'" Shanna linked her arms with Amma on her right, and Verren on her left as around the hall everyone followed suit. Even the Garsal were included, and Shanna couldn't stop herself leaning forwards to see who linked arms with them.

She was slightly startled to see her brother step forwards and link his arm with Laretai's. Beside him Anjo, leaning on a crutch, had his arm firmly locked with Kaidan's on one side and Adlan's on the other. Her mother was pressed close to her husband but her right arm was linked with that of Dreamer. Between them all they formed the first part of the chain linking the three species now locked into the peace accord. She was impressed with Kaidan's bravery – not only for the physical contact with the erstwhile invaders, but by the public nature of his willingness to associate publicly with them. Her little brother had done a lot of growing over the past year.

Two of the youngest students walked forwards, accompanied by a Starlyne youngling. The children laid their pieces of rough stone to lay at the base of the candle, the youngling set a carved stone figurine alongside the stones, then the three of them stepped back and filed off to one side.

Payne lit the fourth candle. "This is the Candle of Promise."

"We remember the pledge of all of our forefathers to the precepts and rules of life on Frontier." This time the addition of one word was hardly noticeable, but then two of the senior students walked forwards accompanied by another Starlyne youngling. All carried heavy books which they laid at the base of the candle before they filed off to the other side.

Payne lit the fifth candle, and it was as if the entire hall of people ceased breathing. The silence was enormous in its intensity. "This is the Candle of Hope, and today we know that we *will* regain the stars. These are the new words." He cleared his throat as he was joined by Master Cerren and Speaker for the Law. Then there was a whisper of astonishment that rolled over the assembly as the Matriarch stepped forwards to join them. They spoke the words together.

"We look towards the future when we venture out into the stars. We pledge peace to the warring, freedom to the enslaved, hope to the downtrodden, and the offer of community to all who would join with us." Master Cerren stepped forwards and looked out over the crowd, Socks by his side.

"Please join with us." Solemnly and a little raggedly to begin with, the massed voices spoke the phrases. Shanna felt her heart lift and tears prick her eyes as she spoke the measured sentences. How they would achieve it all she had no idea, but here, on one tiny planet, a long way from anywhere, the seeds of peace were being sown.

Master Cerren raised one hand and the whole room followed suit.

"This we so pledge. We will continue to work here, making this world a home for humans, Starlyne and Garsal, and all members of races who choose to work towards peace. We agree never to forget those who came before us, those who have lost their lives for our freedom, wherever they may be. We will keep a prayerful silence." He bowed his head and everyone followed suit. A few moments later as he raised his head, the hall was lit by a multihued glow as every starcat and Starlyne present illuminated their tidemarks in an explosion of colour. There was a moment of hushed awe, and then they all sat, and a buzz of conversation rose.

***

Shanna sat on a small rise just outside Watchtower, looking up at the stars. The cool night air was crystal clear. Storm lay on one side of her, and Twister on the other. She looked down, and as ever, sorrowed at the scars marring their sleek sides. They'd have them forever. She snorted slightly – so would she. The scar on her leg wasn't disabling, but it wasn't pretty, and she'd discovered that when a cyclone struck, her leg tended to ache for the duration. She ran a hand over Storm's coat, and rested the other one on Twister's head. Both hummed reassuringly at her. They'd come out largely unscathed, unlike so many others.

The loss of Master Peron had cut her deeply. The huge master had been her mentor for over a year, and she missed him and his reassuring bulk and wisdom. Even now as she watched the stars, the number of dead almost overwhelmed her, and tears welled in her eyes and her throat tightened. They'd paid a high price for their peace.

The Starlynes had been able to assist most of her friends with their injuries, but both Zandany and Verren would be permanently scarred. The burn on Verren's back had seared through muscle and nicked a number of ribs. The muscle damage was repairing slowly, thanks to the Starlynes, but it was a slow and painful process, and nothing but exercise could restore his lost strength.

Finally, Shanna had come home. Home to Hillview, where a battle had destroyed much of the land. A home without fences, and a home where her parents had nearly died. She choked back a small sob, remembering their pale faces when she'd first seen them – still tired and traumatised and just into recovery. They'd been brought back from the brink of death by Starlyne technology. But even that wouldn't have sufficed but for Anjo's near sacrifice.

Anjo. She mused on the man from another world. One of many now. Sadly, neither he nor Ember had escaped unscathed and both would be a very long time recovering fully, but he'd come home to Hillview too and was now part of her family. She was still getting used to that idea, but her own brother regarded him as an older sibling, and she owed him more than she could ever repay.

Allad was also resident at Hillview, courtesy of Boots and Satin. He'd almost completely recovered from his injuries, but it would take more months for the muscles in his leg to become strong enough for field duty. His burns had left deep scarring, despite the best efforts of their Starlyne friends. In the meantime Satin and Boots were inseparable. And if Shanna was any judge, his field duties would have to wait a little longer than he'd planned because she was certain that Satin and Boots hadn't waited for permission to bring the pitter-patter of little starcat paws into the world.

She looked skyward again, pondering on the oddity of three races now relatively at peace on one world. One a race thought extinct, one a race largely enslaved, and one the conquering enslaving, marauding predators who'd destroyed most of the galaxy. There were a few others of course, but in very small numbers compared to the other three.

For the rest of the galaxy there was now hope. Hope that once more peace might come, and the enslaved races freed. Of course they didn't know that yet. Shanna was still bemused at her own part in the peace. Sometimes she struggled to believe that it had all happened, but then she'd see the flash of the filmy robes of the Garsal females vanishing down a hallway, and everything would come crashing back. Some nights she had nightmares.

"Shan?" Verren's quiet voice intruded on her musings.

"Verren." She patted the ground beside her as Cirrus joined Storm and Twister.

"You all right?"

"I think so. There's just so much to get used to." She sighed.

"I know what you mean. One minute we're at war, and the next, you've negotiated peace." He rested a hand on Cirrus, and looked upwards. She rolled her eyes at him.

"Can you imagine going out there?" He pointed towards the sky.

"I can barely imagine that we're safe," she replied and threaded her arm around his waist, scooting closer so that they were tucked together. It was new, this easy openness – new, but wonderful.

"So where to from here?" wondered Verren. "And if you had to, could you do that again?" Shanna knew what he meant – that transcendent moment when they'd all been linked together.

"I have no idea. When I think about it, I just get feelings of smug satisfaction from the boys." As she spoke, blue and violet tickled the edges of her mind, and her two cats hummed with amusement. "See?"

"Yep. Cirrus is the same." He sighed. "Starcats – will we ever gain the upper hand?"

Three sets of tidemarks flickered and brightened, and all three of them looked at their partners, violet eyes wide and innocent. Storm rolled over and presented his belly, cub-like, for a scratch. Shanna pulled a face at him, but obliged, allowing her free hand to find all of Storm's favourite itchy spots. He relaxed, purring thunderously.

"Master Cerren says that the discussions with Lacey and the Matriarch are progressing as well as can be expected. Speaker for the Law is now heading up the Starlyne delegation, and the planning is continuing. Apparently the lack of communication equipment is both a blessing and a curse." She grinned wryly. "A blessing that it gave us enough time to get to this point, but a curse in that we're now unable to contact the Underground."

Verren tucked his arm around her more tightly, and Shanna leaned into him, to recoil at his grunt of pain. "Sorry."

"That's OK. One day I'm going to hug you without fear of pain, interruption, or mud." His tone was determined, and Shanna laughed. The three starcats flicked their ears, and then Shanna heard the sound of footsteps and voices coming closer.

Sparks bounced into view, followed by Punch, Spider and Spinner.

"There you are!" said Amma. She sat down next to Shanna and then the other three were there with them. Their seven starcats lay around them, tidemarks flickering in tones of contentment and peace. All were marked in one way or another by their adventures. Cirrus and Punch still bore marks of the prod that had tormented them. Spinner's tail tip was missing, and Spider had a large patch of white fur where a burn had healed on her flank.

Once again all six of them were together, and Shanna looked around at her friends, content in the security that their presence always brought her. They were more than just friends now. The things they'd shared had taken them well beyond the bounds of ordinary friendship. Of them all, Taya had changed the most. With all of her close family dead, she'd had to make the biggest readjustments of them all.

"So what do you think we'll be doing next?" Zandany asked as he rubbed Punch's belly.

"Who knows?" replied Verren.

"When was the last time we did anything normal, do you think?" asked Amma. She lay down on her back and looked up at the stars.

"Never?" Shanna said.

"Well, there was that time way back in the beginning when we first start-ed," Ragar pointed out. "You remember – Shanna was really short, Taya was grumpy all the time, and the rest of us were just constantly exhausted." They laughed. It seemed so long ago now.

"I think I've grown," Shanna said.

"Maybe a bit," Amma admitted. "But I'm still taller."

"And I'm definitely not grumpy all the time now," Taya said and glared at Ragar. Spinner flickered his tidemarks at her and then she smiled ruefully. "Just some of the time." Amma gave her a friendly punch on the arm.

"Maybe we'll just go back into normal classes now," said Verren. "We've still a way to go before we're qualified."

"Do you reckon we will?" asked Shanna. The thought of completing her training was suddenly all that she wanted. "You know, I'd really like to." There were murmurs of agreement from the others.

Footsteps sounded, and Master Cerren and Socks appeared walking up the rise.

"In that case I have both good and bad news." He joined them on the ground and Socks touched noses with Sparks in greeting. "The good news is you're going to be resuming your training tomorrow. The bad news is you'll be teaching as well as training." He held up one hand to forestall questions and went on. "It will be some years until we're ready to go to the stars, but in that time we have a lot to do. More than anything we need others who can do what you can do."

"So, no rest for the wicked?" asked Ragar.

There was a smile in Cerrren's voice as he replied. "No, no rest. But at least a little respite. Erilla will head up the Scout Corps now that …." His voice broke slightly, and Shanna realised that she wasn't the only one griev-ing. "Now that Peron's gone." There was another moment of shared silence and then he went on. "Cally has been recalled permanently, and Toman, and many of the oldsters will rejoin patrols to fill the gaps left by the fighting. More than ever we need our Scouts, and more than ever we need all of you. The training schedule will stay accelerated, and we'll be doubling our intakes – as long as we find enough people with the spark."

"Master Cerren, it will take some time for our population to recover," Ragar said.

"It will, Ragar, but at least we have that time now." The three moons had all crested the horizon, and they were grouped in a staggered formation that shed brilliant whiteness across the landscape. For some moments they drowned out the starlight. It was a good reminder, Shanna thought. The stars were closer, but there was still much to do before her people would be ready to venture out among them.

"And there's the issue of establishing a lasting peace, settling the Garsal safely and securely, and integrating three societies, not to mention the other four races of people on the ship. There are few of them, sadly. They did not adapt well to this world in the early days. Then there's the question of the Garsal, like The ex-Overlord, who are not part of our new society. The Council has more on its plate than you probably realise."

Shanna nodded. "And when we finally get out there," she gestured at the stars, "What will we really find? Will they be Anjos or Sembas? Will they welcome us, or see only our differences?" She swept a hand around the group. Seven of them sitting there, bracketed by eight starcats, their muted tidemarks glowing in the moonlight.

"Well, we won't know if we don't try," Verren said.

They looked at each other, and once more they linked. Shanna drew them all in, and this time she drew Master Cerren in too. Socks brought the depth of a sparkling lake filled with the reflections of stars, as she slipped into rapport with them, and Shanna heard Cerren's indrawn breath as he joined them. He felt different to her friends. Different, but good. He matched Socks' depths with what seemed like a bottomless well of experience and wisdom. She felt his sadness for his friend, and she allowed him to feel theirs as well, and then she let him feel their determination, and their commitment.

His emotions sparked with hope and wonder, and Shanna smiled. There was no need to say more.

# List of Characters

**Scout Cadets**
Shanna – Storm and Twister
Amma – Spider
Ragar – Sparks
Zandany – Punch
Taya – Spinner
Verren – Cirrus

**Patrol 10**
Spiron (Team Leader) – Fury
Barron (Team Second) – Hunter
Allad – Satin
Nelson – Glutton
Karri
Kalli – Flyer
Sandar – Gryphon
Arad – Breeze/Nosey
Challon – Dipper
Perri – Spangles

**Patrol 4**
Farron (Team Leader) – Mist

**Other Scouts**
Feeny – Gem
Damar
Toman (senior Scout Master – retired) – Ghost
Cally – (Senior Scout/starcat trainer – retired) Mirror
Cam – Splash
Manda – (retired – Tempest)
Romon (Senior Scout – retired)

**Masters**
Master Cerren (Teacher/Council) – Socks
Master Peron (Scout) – Thunder
Master Lonish (Scout) – Samson
Master Yendy (Scout)
Master Vandon (Scout)
Master Kenwell (Scout)

Master Erilla (Council) – Nimbus
Master Dinian (Archery)

**Archers**
Kaidan (Student, Shanna's brother)
Camid
Gwen
Horden
Tasha

**Others**
Adlan (Shanna and Kaidan's father) – Boots and Moshi
Janna (Shanna and Kaidan's mother) – Sabre
Anjo (Garsal slave) – Ember
Semba (Garsal slave)
Hodan (Horgal wagoneer)
Josen (Starcat Breeder) – Anvil
Payne (Watchtower's senior councillor)
Tamazine (Skyfall senior councillor – The Senior Councillor of Frontier)
Griss (Formerly aide to Tamazine, now assisting Cerren)
Shari (Leader of the militia)
Jareth (Student, Josen's son)
Balto (Student, Yendy's son)
Hadder (Student, Erilla's son)
Ella (Student, Josen's daughter)
Drest (Student, Old Scout's granddaughter)
Beren (Student)
Lacey (Kaidan's mentor on the Garsal ship, leader of the human underground.)
Edon (Informer)

**Garsal**
The Overlord
Zoash (The Overlord's Hatching sib)
Hoth (Senior trooper)
The Architect
Hath (Hatching sib to Hoth)
The Matriarch
Laretai (First Senior to the Matriarch)
Estei (Initiate female)
Hirtoi (Initiate female)

**Starlynes**
Keeper of the Knowledge
Fractus
Radiant
Teacher
Speaker for Law (liaison with the council)
Promise of Hope (Fractus' mate)
Dreamer (Fractus' daughter)

Thank you for reading FRONTIER DEFIANT. We hope you enjoyed it.

If you would like to be kept informed of further releases by Leonie Rogers, or other new books from Hague Publishing, why not subscribe to our newsletter at:

**www.HaguePublishing.com/subscribe.php**

And if you loved the book and have a moment to spare we would really appreciate a short review. Your help in spreading the word is gratefully received.

# About The Author

ORIGINALLY from Western Australia, Leonie now lives in NSW in the Upper Hunter. She is the author of Frontier Incursion, Frontier Resistance, and Frontier Defiant (YA Speculative Fiction) published by Hague Publishing, and also works part time as a physiotherapist. She dabbles in poetry, and has had a short story published in Antipodean SF, and another in the Novascapes 2 anthology.

She has a past life as a volunteer firefighter and SES member, and once trekked almost six hundred kilometres with eight camels and several other human beings. She is married with two adult children, one dog and two cats, one of whom frequently handicaps her ability to use a laptop computer.

# Hague

# Publishing

www.HaguePublishing.com

PO Box 451 Bassendean
Western Australia 6934

www.ingramcontent.com/pod-product-compliance
Lightning Source LLC
Chambersburg PA
CBHW061020120726
47910CB00006B/2031